THE EYE OF EURYDICE

RYAN M. TALBOT

Fine print follows. Warning: It may bore you into a coma.

"Psychopathy Red" by Slayer is © 2009 AR LLC, used without permission.
(The author is an avid Slayer fan and will remove any reference from future
editions upon request.)

"Dead is the New Alive" by Emilie Autumn is © 2006 Traitor Records, used
without permission. (The author will remove any reference from future editions
upon request)

First Printing/September 2011
ISBN 9781453680445

Please do not allow pirates to steal my book. Seriously. I'm poor and a man's gotta
eat. I totally understand if said pirates have cannons and sabers and whatnot, but
please, at least *try* to kill them.

The author does not intend for anyone to kill anyone else.

Pirates aren't people.

The author has been forced to hire a new lawyer.

Please don't kill anyone.

Follow the author on twitter: @Emissary616

FOR SHEENA,
I LOVE YOU ALWAYS.

PART I:
THE EYE OF EURYDICE

CHAPTER 1

It was a quiet November night. A breeze blew through the apple orchards carrying with it the sweet smell of rotting apples, a taste of winter's chill. My rifle rested comfortably against my shoulder, the high power scope showed me a family of four eating dinner. I traced the profile of a beautiful young woman with the barrel of my gun. The crosshairs rested at the base of her milk white neck as she spoke animatedly to someone across the table. Her name was Annessa Francione. From my perch in an ancient oak tree four hundred meters from the house, I grinned and settled my cheek against the stock.

Save your judgments. She was the daughter of the prominent mafia captain inside, and she was getting ready to roll over on Daddy to avoid doing a twelve-year hitch for possessing enough coke to intoxicate the better part of the Bronx. Only, I couldn't let that happen.

They thought they were safe this far from Manhattan. I suppose they were, for the most part. They hadn't really counted on me. That's part of my charm, I guess. Most people, most Normals, don't expect people like me showing up to throw a wrench into their neat little world.

My name is Jason Beckett, and I'm a hitman for the Devil. I know what you're thinking; I sacrifice cats and strangle babies, right? Wrong. Cats work for the Devil, and if you don't believe that, you've never owned one. As for the other part, neither of the major players, that'd be Yahweh and the Devil, really want dead babies. They don't go to Perdition or Heaven, they simply cease to exist. Cruel? Kind of, but then again, so were the Inquisition, cancer and AIDS.

In case you've been sleeping under a rock for the last two thousand years, there's a war going on. The Devil and Yahweh, or as some call him God, are engaged in a battle for the souls of mankind. That's where I come in. My job, technically speaking, is to maintain relations between the Devil and the rest of the universe. The more practical application is something of a book–balancing act. If someone owes a debt and it looks like they might renege, I pay them a visit. If some Normal decides they suddenly want to get too active in the War, I pay them a visit. The balance is tricky. If either side gets too far ahead, another full–scale war may break out and trust me, you don't want any of that. So, I just grease the right gears; I push the right buttons and the rickety machine of life keeps chugging along.

Of course, it isn't all that simple. There are other parties that want to join the festivities. Aside from Heaven and Perdition, there are the Broken Temples, the Coinbound, the Fae, the Umbrals and so many more. The comfortable little world you live in is nothing like the real world. Part of my job is making sure it stays that way. Why? One night near a ravenous werewolf, and you'd never leave church again. We can have that, now can we?

Tonight, though, I wasn't here for any of that. No, this job was a lot simpler. I shrugged my shoulder into the stock and rolled my neck to ease out the kinks as I watched the leaves between my perch and the house. I let out a slow breath stopping it mid–way. The crosshairs in my scope moved in time to my heartbeat. With a thought, I stopped my heart, steadying my rifle. I let my eyes relax, and my mind faded into the background. All that mattered was the shot. My finger closed on the trigger.

That was when I sensed him. It was like the shock of cold water on my flesh. My finger jerked away from the trigger, and I nearly fell out of the tree. Another Emissary was here. I swore under my breath. A black Mercedes with tinted windows slowly pulled into the massive horseshoe driveway at the front of the palatial house. As the passenger side door opened, I made myself very small.

As soon as I saw the creature that stepped out of the Mercedes, everything about him made me recoil. There are powers in this world, and then there are Powers. Something ancient had laid claim to this man, if you could call him that anymore. Very carefully, I allowed my eyes to see beyond the fog of the Aether. Beneath the expensive Armani suit, goatee and slicked back hair, something writhed. It was like a mass of maggots wearing human skin. His Aetheric presence was oppressive and thick with hate. I retched and clenched at the tree. Something was very wrong here. I needed to go. I felt his presence expand as if he were seeking for other Aetherics. My heart leapt into my throat. I didn't know who this guy was, but I was feeling outgunned and needed to get away fast.

His presence rippled through the Aether like a black fog, its tendrils seeking and grasping at any signs of life. I looked frantically for a place to hide. I was stuck. Knowing my Master's thoughts on retreat, I played my ace in the hole. I rested my face against the bark of the tree and whispered an invocation to Hekate, the Witch Goddess.

At once, the bark of the tree shuddered, its rough surface wrapped around me like the embrace of a lover. I sighed, both in gratitude and apprehension. Even sorcerers like me don't make a practice of asking favors of Hekate. I rested against the skin of the tree. Just beyond the cradling warmth of its branches, I could feel the dark and twisted energy of the creature. The tree, on the other hand, was not content to merely let this *thing* pass by. The ancient Tree glowed with energy all its own. The black fog recoiled from the pure essence of the Tree. It was then that I understood. *Umbral.*

You already know all about Umbrals, though you

aren't aware of it. Theirs is the story that never changes. You know the one, "In the beginning, there was Darkness..." That Darkness, the one with the big capital letter in it, THAT Darkness is the Umbrals. They're what existed before existence, roiling and tearing at one another in a violent orgy of destruction. As the Umbral's mindseeking receded, the oak slowly released me. I crouched in the branches until he went inside. The moment the door closed, I dropped from the tree and raced back through the woods towards my waiting car.

I knelt at the side of the road and picked up a handful of dirt, whispered the car's name and tossed the dirt where I left her to end the spell that kept her hidden. The air shimmered for a second and she appeared, my beautiful Abbadonna. My car's a remarkable machine. She looks and feels like a BMW 650i and performs like a fighter jet. I like my car, but it's what inhabits her that makes her so seductive. You see, Abbadonna's the name of the Fallen Angel that possesses her.

"Hello, Beautiful," I whispered. The trunk lid lifted, and I placed my rifle in its fitted hard case and shut the trunk. The door opened as I came around the driver side. I got in and started the car.

"What troubles you, Emissary?" Abbadonna's question drifted through my mind.

"Umbral," I whispered.

I felt her shudder of revulsion as I pulled slowly onto the road, using the car's night vision rather than the lights or magic. No reason to get stupid now. I pulled my phone from my pocket and pounded Cassidy's number into the keypad. I gunned the engine as Cassidy's voice mail answered.

"Cassidy, it's Beckett. Call me. Now!" I hung up. I had to get to a crossroad and fast. My phone belted out the opening strains of Slayer's "Psychopathy Red" as I neared the outskirts of Little Haven, New York, the closest town to the Francione mansion. I yanked it out of my pocket and answered it.

"What's got you so eager to hear my voice, Little

Brother?" The faint trace of Cassidy's brogue came through in his mirth.

"I just ran into my very first Umbral." I said. "Aren't you proud?"

"Where are you right now, Jason?" His voice became tight and tense; he never used my first name.

"I'm outside some hick town called Little Haven, upstate." I pulled the car over at the crossroads outside of town.

"I'll be there in the morning, Little Brother. If you can help it, wait for me." He hung up.

If I could help it, I'd be far out of town by the time Cassidy got here, but I had a feeling I was going to be told something altogether different. I waited a minute after turning off the car to see if there was any traffic at this time of night. When I was sure that the road would remain empty, I stepped out to contact my Master.

Crossroads are handy since they're a passive threshold to the Veilside. The world is full of fun little resonances that let you cheat a bit and the Devil knows them all. I knelt in the center of the road, closed my eyes and let my mind reach out beyond my flesh. As I spoke the Prayer of Communion, I felt the skin over my heart ignite and the burn spread over my chest and arms, down my back and over my legs. They say that the two extremes of sensation, pleasure and pain, can bring one in tune with the universe. It isn't as simple as it sounds. First, you have to be willing to be subjected to that level of sensation. Second, you have to remain lucid and sane throughout for the magic to work. Trust me, you couldn't do it.

The ground around me shuddered, and the air shimmered like a heat mirage. I opened my eyes as the pain spread to them, tearing the fabric of reality and allowing me to see beyond the Veil. The vistas of Perdition opened before me. From my view from the skies above, Perdition was breathtakingly beautiful. I always think it's funny how most people view *Hell*. It was made by angels after all.

My master's palace lay just beyond the confluence of the River Styx and the River Lethe, perched on the precipice of a great cliff overlooking the frozen lake of Cocytus. Six crystal towers of adamant crowned the immense obsidian walls and surrounded the great central spire called the Tower of Grief. Atop that central spire, my master stood, his black wings folded against his back, his burnished silver armor glowing amid the perpetual twilight of Pandaemonium. His eyes fixed on me, great blue eyes burning like electric sapphires, arresting my breathing and stealing away my thoughts.

"What news, my son?" His voice seemed to come from all directions at once, in all octaves and was both kind and threatening.

"Master, I didn't kill the Francione girl yet," I began. Things were always a bit more formal with my Master. It pays to be a little less flippant when dealing with the Devil.

"Of this I am aware, child."

"My Lord, something strange happened." I took a breath. "An Umbral showed up at the mansion; he was actively mindseeking, as if he knew that I was there."

"Tell me of this Umbral. Did you look upon him with your Sight; was there anything of him that struck you? More importantly, did he see you?" My master's voice betrayed no emotion, yet suddenly I was afraid.

"No, my Lord, his arrival was a surprise. I only had time to hide. I had to invoke the refuge of Hekate in order to avoid him." I slumped a little. If there's one thing that all gods hate, it's their subjects praying to another god. As much as my ego dislikes hearing it, there are some things beyond even my sorcery.

"You are growing lax, my Emissary. " It was a statement of fact, not an accusation. "You are not quite immortal."

"What was I supposed to do, Master? I'm not equipped to go toe to toe with an Umbral," I asked.

"You did well to hide." He grew thoughtful. "You have informed my brother of this?"

Shit. I should know better by now. He always knows everything I do. I was going to punch Cassidy when I saw him again.

"I did, my Lord. I contacted his...Emissary." I knew somewhere Cassidy was howling. He hated that title.

"That was wise. We are too extended here to be of use in that battle. Let Satariel fight his chosen war against the Umbrals. I have my own battles to fight." His face hardened, and he looked at me. "Should I be concerned with your continued loyalty to my brother?"

My chest tightened and the fire seemed to burn even hotter, if that were possible.

"No, Master. I serve you." I bowed my head. "I spoke the words, I took my vow."

The flames cooled and I raised my face again.

"Is that the extent of your loyalty, my son?" His voice was nearly a whisper.

"I serve, Master." My jaw clenched.

"Tell me more about this Umbral."

"I felt sick. It was like...bathing in garbage and vomit and shit all at once." I nearly gagged as I remembered the Aetheric presence of the Umbral. "It was like a mass of maggots wearing human flesh, if that makes any sense." I didn't really have any other way to describe it.

"A Cathdronai, one of Arikael's brood, which means that Beleth is involved." Satan grew thoughtful. "Umbrals lie outside the mandate of Heaven. They lie outside the Accords and the Edicts of Banishment. You may target them using the entirety of your gifts without Heavenly repercussion."

"Are you saying you want me to go after the Umbral?" I really, really hoped not.

"I am saying, my wayward assassin, that you owe me a soul." His eyes burned with anger. "You will kill the Francione child and destroy any obstacle in your path, including the Cathdronai, if necessary."

He waved his hand and I felt myself thrown back to my own body. I collapsed and threw up. Veilshock sucks. The human body really, really hates giving up its soul, hence the whole dying thing. Aetheric creatures, witches, vampires, werewolves and such, are equipped to deal with it, but Lifesiders, that is, us normal animals, humans, are only meant to cross the Veil once. It takes a few minutes to get over the shock of crossing over. Which was fine because I really didn't want to think about what was coming and thankfully wicked dry heaves are a damned fine distraction.

Great, just fucking great. How the hell was I going to kill Annessa Francione in a house full of bodyguards, mafiosos and one great big nasty fucking Umbral? Cassidy needed to hurry up. If there was one thing that would come in handy in a situation like this, it was a big, scary, Umbral hunting, Irish werewolf. And of all of that, I think the Irish matters most. The Irish are too stupid to be afraid of anything. I'm only half–Irish. I think the other half must be coward. I spit, dusted off my pants, and headed back to Abbadonna.

CHAPTER 2

    To say that Little Haven is a small town would be a terrible understatement. According to the sign, the town had about a thousand residents. I think they included the dead ones when they did the census. I got a room in a rundown hotel across from the single largest building in the town, Wal–Mart, of course. I checked my phone every few minutes; Cassidy really needed to hurry. I yanked my cigarettes out of my jacket pocket and lit one. If the Umbral didn't get me, the small town charm would.

    Looking out the window at the moon, I wondered what favor I would need to return to Hekate for her intervention. It was almost impossible to guess. As one of the most ancient beings in the Multiverse, her whims were strange, to say the least. Once, I'd been tasked with engineering a tryst between two powerful Aetherics. Another time, it had been blessing a random child on the street in Hekate's name. My favorite, though, had been dancing with a young lady in the moonlight, naked. If only they could all be like that. I sighed and checked my watch, Cassidy needed to hurry up.

    It was just after three a.m. when he showed up. I never told him where I was staying. I didn't need to. Cassidy has a remarkable gift for finding things. Granted, being over a thousand years old means he's got some experience. It also means he's very, very dangerous. You don't survive fighting Umbrals, Fallen, Angels and Aetherics for a millennium if you're stupid or inept.

He didn't knock. I heard him whisper, felt an Aetheric push, and the door just opened. He stayed outside the door, his lambent yellow eyes looking expectantly at me. I lifted my left hand and the sorcerous wards I placed around the door glowed brilliantly and collapsed. He nodded and stepped in. His weather–beaten duster floated around him like a cloak in the wind. Cassidy looks every inch like some sort of deranged drifter. His blonde hair falls over his shoulders like a mane, and he's got least a three day growth of beard at all times. He exudes a feral essence, like a strange sort of aura.

"What have you gotten yourself into this time, Little Brother?" He asked, grinning He's called me "Little Brother" since I met him six years ago. He claims that since he works for the older twin and I work for the younger twin, I'm like his little brother. There's another reason, but I won't go into that now. Incidentally, Satan asserts that he is the older of the twins and Satariel is the younger, hence the Firstborn claims and all of that. For his part, Satariel says nothing about it or anything else now that I think about it.

Kind of funny how they leave that out of the history books, isn't it? Two angels alike in aspect and demeanor and both contested the Most High, though Satariel did it for love of Man and my master for love of himself. Come to think of it, maybe Cassidy's on to something. I damn sure don't do this for love of anyone, while Cassidy helps old ladies cross the street.

"I'm not sure, man. But whatever it is, I don't like it." I threw up my hands and told him what my Master ordered me to do.

"He's right about the Edicts, but as far as the Accords go, I'm not sure," he said. "The articles are very clear regarding the use of force in a contested territory. If you're careless, you'll bring the wrath of Heaven down in a very real sense."

"What do you mean?" This was a cause for concern.

I have no protection against Angelic attack, since I'm technically still bound to the Mandate of Heaven. In essence, I have diplomatic immunity only so long as I'm engaged in emissarial duties. Most of the humans that I kill are unaligned or are already claimed for Perdition, so I'm untouchable. However, should I kill a person or Aetheric who's angelically aligned without cause, I can be called to account for it. I'm allowed to defend myself, but general murder is off the table.

"According to my information, there are links between Vincenze Francione and the Higher Church." Cassidy shrugged.

The Higher Church is a euphemism for those that worship with true faith. That distinguishes them from the run of the mill everyday churchgoer, as it implies that they truly believe and don't just go to church because they feel obligated. I suppose if my side had a Higher Church, it would be Vegas.

"Francione isn't my target, man. I'm after his daughter. But if you're right, I wonder if it even matters."

"What'd the Old Man say?" He grinned at me as if he knew the answer.

"He said to kill her and that my friendship with you may have detrimental effects on my life, you asshole." I couldn't help grinning back. "At least as long as you're Satariel's Emissary, that is."

Cassidy's grin disappeared. I laughed. "So, are you going to help me kill this bitch or not?"

* * *

We slipped back onto the property through the woods. Cassidy led, we kept low and both of us were alert for any sign that the Umbral was aware of us. We stopped about two hundred yards away from the house and sat quietly watching for signs of movement. The massive three–story mansion stared at us like a predator in wait. The columns supporting the front of the immense structure glowed white against the shadows that seemed to drift across the entryway as clouds rolled in without warning. The woods and the property were preternaturally still. The black Mercedes was gone from the driveway. It was as if Nature herself was holding her breath, waiting for a sound to cover her deep exhalation. I looked at Cassidy, his pale face and hair dappled by shadow. His wolf's eyes glowed in the darkness.

"Something isn't right here," I whispered.

"No, nothing is right here." He peered into the darkness. I barely felt the aetheric push of his magic.

I let my eyes relax and looked beyond the Veil at the probing edge of his magic as it reached tentatively toward the house. We both dropped prone when the scream rang out. I yanked my Beretta from its holster in the small of my back and waited. Cassidy didn't hesitate. He leapt off the ground and before his feet even touched down again, he'd already shifted. He raced across the intervening space, a huge, black wolf with glowing red eyes.

"Shit." I jumped up to follow after him. I kept low, my eyes scanning for any signs of a hidden enemy. I heard the crash of several hundred pounds of angry werewolf hitting the bay window at the back of the house and broke into a sprint. It wasn't quite the bravery you might expect. After all, if there's a werewolf in front of you, who the hell's going to shoot *you* first?

By the time I reached the house, Cassidy was already crouched, in his human form, in the center of the solarium with glass shattered all around him. He sniffed the air and turned to me, his green tattered duster flared out around him like a madman's cloak.

"It's gone." He sounded disappointed. To be honest, he might as well have told me I'd won the lottery.

"That's a damned shame," I lied.

"You're a piss poor liar for an Emissary of the Fallen One." He smirked at me.

"I'm a piss poor emissary too," I grinned. "Now to get what I came for." I moved toward the center of the house, my weapon at the ready, alert for sounds or signs of life.

The house was laid out like a cross, with a wing in each cardinal direction coming off a large central hub. It took me longer than it should have to put two and two together. I looked beyond the Veil and sighed heavily. The house was built on a Confluence. There were ley lines that met in the center of the house and each wing was built directly over a ley line.

In case you slept through your basic Feng Shui class, ley lines, or dragon lines, are geomantic lines of magical energy that run over and under the surface of the earth. These lines are conduits of magical energy that can assist a practitioner of the Art by supplying them with energy that they would otherwise have to provide through sacrifice or ritual. Even a run of the mill Mall Witch could affect real change if they cast one of their silly spells over a ley line confluence. That this house that I and by extension that Cassidy was here could not be a coincidence. In short, I was suddenly very nervous.

The house was eerily silent until we reached the third floor. As Cassidy and I made our way through the western corridor the air seemed to thrum with power, like a bowstring just before release. We looked at each other.

"Trap," we both spoke in unison. I nodded.

Cassidy pointed to an attic trapdoor. "Up there," he whispered.

This was going to be tricky. One of the hardest things to do is fight on a ladder. You're vulnerable from nearly all angles and your mobility and vision are limited. My heart sank.

"I'll go first." Cassidy whispered.

"Sure, you do that." I whispered back. Things were suddenly looking up.

He grinned at me. "You shameless coward."

Without another word, he leapt upward, his huge frame crashing through the ceiling next to the trapdoor. I stood there dumfounded for a second, but I mean, it made perfect sense. Who's likely to trap the floor five feet from the trapdoor? But, still, hell, the guy's a tank, and he just leapt through the ceiling, studs and all like it was balsa wood.

"Ladder's safe," he yelled down. "Dear gods, what happened up here?"

I yanked the pull rope and took the ladder two rungs at a time. I wasn't prepared for what I saw. There were bodies everywhere. They were eviscerated and torn apart. It took a second for my brain to identify patterns.

The entire attic was a shrine. There were statues and an altar, candles and incense, the whole nine yards. What the hell was Francione up to? Cassidy interrupted my fragmented thoughts.

"Francione was one of yours, Little Brother." He spoke softly. "I guess my information was wrong."

"What?" I was confused. What the hell was he talking about; of course Francione wasn't one of mine. I was here to kill the guy's daughter.

"The altar, he was one of yours."

I looked at the altar and saw he was right. The ornate stone altar bore symbols sacred to Satan. And laid across that altar was Annessa Francione. I walked over to the altar. I was pissed; someone had beaten me to my commission.

"Dammit! What the fuck am I supposed to do now, Cassidy? Someone already killed her!" I said.

Before Cassidy could reply, Annessa coughed, spraying blood all over me. I did what any sane person would do; I shot her in the face.

"Nevermind. We're good." I grinned as she flopped back over the altar.

Cassidy was at my shoulder. He spoke softly, though his anger dripped over the thick coating of sarcasm on his words. "Just a thought: maybe next time you could keep the only witness alive long enough to question her."

I smiled. I finally, after six years of trying, got one over on Cassidy. I raised my hand, with my palm facing Cassidy over my shoulder. The Mark of the Adversarial Beast showed plainly on my palm.

"I don't need her alive to question her."

Necromancy is forbidden by nearly all of the gods, old and new. Strangely, the Devil takes a different tack on this particular Art. As I am his Emissary, I have free reign and rights to souls under his dominion. Annessa Francione was one of those souls. I sliced my palm with my knife, just above the Mark. I placed my hand on her chest and spoke. The Word used is unimportant; it isn't like you could hear it or read it anyway. Aetheric Words are like blanks in time and space to normal humans; you can't even perceive them. The authority of my Mark and my personal Word drove my magic deep into her flesh.

Her body shuddered, and she screamed. Birth is painful, but it's nothing like this. She thrashed and screamed and finally turned to face us. Her eyes gleamed with hate. I didn't care.

"Are you done with your little fit?" I asked sweetly.

"What'd you do to me, you son of a bitch?" She shrieked out the question, her voice distorted by the gaping wound in her face.

"I'm the one with the questions, lady." Have you ever seen *Army of Darkness*? Yeah, I felt a little like Ash. I was grinning like a fool. Hell, my slate was clean.

"I ache." She moaned and writhed over the altar.

"Feed, then we'll talk." I pointed to the corpses littering the floor.

I turned my back on her. Even my stomach has limits. Watching haemunculae feed is among the foulest things one can witness. Cassidy sat on his heels in the corner of the room watching. They say that Agents of a Power will exhibit characteristics of their Master, even though they aren't aware of it. Cassidy's lord, Satariel, was a Grigori, a kind of Watcher angel before the Fall. To this day, he maintains his vigil over Mankind, rooting out Umbral incursions and maintaining the balance of power between the forces of this reality and the all–consuming hate of the Umbrals.

When the sounds of noisy feasting subsided behind me, I turned back to face Annessa. "Better?" I asked.

"Yes." She shook. I watched as her face knit itself back together. "What'd you do to me?" Her fearful voice was kind of funny coming from a gore–spattered haemunculus.

"I'll tell you what, for every question that you answer, I'll answer one of yours. Deal?" I grinned. Why not, I was feeling generous.

"Ok." Her voice was raw from screaming and from the thanatonic energy keeping her alive. For those of you that missed the reference there, thanatos is the motivating force of death. Hell, even Freud said that thanatos was the force that pushed us all toward death. Thanatonic energy is also the force that animates dead tissue and results in the perverse hungers and thirsts of undead creatures.

"Ok, question one, what the hell happened here?" I asked.

"Some guy came here tonight, he came to the door and said he had information for my dad. Something about a threat to him in New York or something. I heard my dad tell him to get the hell out, and one of the bodyguards, maybe Mikey, said something to him and then..." She paused. Apparently some things scare even the dead.

"What? What happened?" I stepped toward her. My patience was wearing thin.

"There was this sound. It was like someone throwing up after a really bad party. Then I heard my dad and his bodyguards screaming. Not screaming in pain, more like they were grossed out or something. But then they started to scream like ... in panic. And then it got quiet. My dad, Mikey and Jimmy came back into the kitchen. They seemed kind of out of it." She fell silent again.

"Hey, Dead Girl! You have all eternity, I'm on a fucking schedule, spit it out!"

"The guy they came in with, he was looking at all of us and grinning. He creeped me out; he just felt sick, like something was really wrong with him. I wanted to get away from him. I started to get up from the table, but my dad told us to all get up and go to the attic. I started to ask him why, and I told him I was getting scared. He fucking slapped me!

That prick slapped me!" Her eyes flared green and her voice grew thick and low. She was getting ready to do something very dangerous. Haemunculae don't do well with powerful emotion.

Cassidy walked up behind me. "Control your puppet, Little Brother," he warned.

"Annessa, look at me." I pushed and felt the force of the magic leave my eyes and clamp down on her brain. "You will remain calm, and you will tell me exactly what happened."

"I started to get mad, but Mikey and Jimmy grabbed me and started dragging me up the stairs. I kept screaming at them to let me go. When I tried to fight back, Mikey hit me in the face so hard it knocked me out."

"Did your father seem at all like he was in control of himself? Did the bodyguards?" Cassidy seemed very intent on the control issue.

"No, they wouldn't talk to me; getting up to the attic was the only thing that mattered to them."

"What happened when you woke up?" I asked.

"I was tied to this fucking altar." She kicked the altar with her heel. I winced inwardly; I hoped I wasn't going to hear about that later. "My mom and Carmello, my brother, were kneeling over there." She pointed at the massive hole that Cassidy had made upon our arrival. "The guy, that fucking bearded guy was saying these crazy words that I couldn't understand; they sounded like Latin or fucking Sanskrit or something." She shrugged.

Cassidy leaned forward. "Listen to me, child, and listen you well. This is very important, more than you will ever know. Did this man have a knife of some sort? Did it look strange, almost hazy?"

She nodded. "Yeah, he stabbed my brother in the neck with it! Carmello just fell over and started convulsing, but no blood came out. No blood came out of this huge slash in his neck!" She started to rock herself back and forth.

Cassidy seemed electrified; he was moving erratically. I'd never seen him so agitated. Hell, I'd never even seen him flinch before. My stomach turned. Somehow, somehow this was going to suck and I was growing more certain by the moment it was going to turn out to be my fault. Why? Because Yahweh fucking hates me. No, seriously, he does.

"Annessa, child, what did he do to your mother?" Cassidy was nearly nose–to–nose with her.

"Mikey, Joey, and my dad held her down and he raped her. My own father, my own fucking father held her down!" She shrieked, and her rage whipped through the attic shattering windows and blowing the glass halfway across the property.

I jerked away from her, my hands over my ears. Cassidy stood like a rock before a tempest, the magic shattering against his skin. Sometimes, I hate that guy. He put his finger over her lips and she fell silent.

"Where is your mother now, Annessa?" He asked

"He took her when he left. There was something wrong with her. Her skin seemed waxy and her eyes just kind of rolled back in her head, like she was dead but she was still moving. She just followed him, kind of like jerking on her feet and they left me here. He said that I was supposed to feed the Lord's children."

Cassidy froze. I sighed. I told you this was going to suck.

"Are you sure that he said 'Lord's children,' Annessa?" His words were clipped and precise. He made sure that she couldn't misunderstand what he said.

"Yeah." She nodded.

"And you were supposed to feed them?"

"Yeah, are you deaf?" She threw her hands in the air and looked at me, a look of frustration on her face. I almost laughed, walking dead Italian princess; you couldn't make this shit up.

"Jason?"

"Yeah?" I looked over at him sharply, twice in twenty-four hours with the first name. This was not good.

"At any point in the last twenty-four hours has anyone, particularly anyone who makes his home in

Perdition, made mention of Cathdronai?"

"Yeah, and something about Arikael and Beleth. He said that the Umbral that was here was a Cathdronai. What the hell's a Cathdronai, anyway?" I looked over at him, but his gaze was firmly fixed on the dead bodies.

"You need to go. Now."

"Wh—" Was all I got out before the bodies started moving. Shit.

Cassidy roared. The walls shook with the fury of it. He shifted, and his body rippled and shook as he transformed. This is one thing that the movies never get right. They have the right concept, but they lack the technology to make a wolf–man hybrid truly terrifying. The air around Cassidy erupted with glowing angelic script and the cacophony of hundreds of relics and prayer icons all activating.

"Run, Little Brother. These are not your concern." His fangs and the rage of his transformation distorted his voice. "I will guard your escape." He thrust a viciously pointed claw at the hole in the floor.

"Who's going to guard yours?" I yelled back.

"Go!" He yelled and leaped at the three corpses that jerkily charged at him.

For reasons I don't entirely fathom, I grabbed Annessa, shoved her through the hole in the floor and leapt down after her. I dragged her through the house, my weapon at the ready. I invoked every protection spell and ward that I knew, my eyes and skin blazed like the sun as I charged out of the house. The front door had been warded; I didn't know who did it and I didn't care. I invoked the blessing of Leviathan and hit the door with the force of a train counting on my wards to guard me. As the door exploded around me, I noticed the floor inside the doorway was covered in blood and maggots.

CHAPTER 3

I charged into the still night air, my blood pumping furiously and in a state of glorious exaltation. Much like our appearance, our minds begin to reflect the will of our master the more of his or her power we draw upon. My Master loves nothing more than conflict and adversity, outsmarting the adept that placed those wards would've made him laugh for days. What happened next would've made him murderous.

The first thing I saw was the car. Next I saw her. Then I saw them. In order that would be: silver Excursion, red haired Emissary dressed in white, and three massive Host–bound. I stopped in my tracks. Annessa bounced off of me and hit the ground. The Emissary spoke first.

"Beckett." She lifted the silver .45 and pointed it at my face. The Host–Bound drew up alongside her.

"Rachel, so nice to see you. What brings you so far outside the city?" I grinned, stalling.

My mind raced. Rachel I could take, possibly. She was my direct heavenly counterpart, and we hated each other with an intensity that bordered on the religious, pun intended. The Host–Bound might be rough. See, Host–Bound are earthbound Angels, of the regular variety, that share a body with a willing celebrant. It's the heavenly equivalent of possession, but they have prettier language for it. And like Fallen, Angels can be damn difficult to kill. The only upside to the situation was the Host–Bound and Rachel were legal targets for me; the downside was of course, that I was outnumbered two to one and they had the drop on me.

Rachel turned, pointed her gun at Annessa and fired. I rolled in front of her, and the bullet bounced harmlessly off my wards. Annessa gasped, then growled.

I stalled. "Rachel, is that anyway to greet your hostess? You can't just come to a person's house and shoot them....Wait." I grinned as I dusted myself off and stood. "Tell you what, you shoot at my friend again, I'll rip your perky little tits off and feed them to your pet virgins over there." I pointed at the Host–Bound. I admit, mocking their celibacy is a bit low, but let's consider who I work for.

My mind was racing; I went over every option in my head. The thing was, I couldn't stop thinking of Cassidy in there by himself. I didn't need this right now. I needed help. I sent a mental summons to Abbadonna urging her to hurry to me.

Rachel lowered her gun and glared at me. "You know this is forbidden!" She turned her attention to Annessa. "Come to me, child, confess your sins and let me send you Home." She held out her hand.

I stepped between the two of them and wiggled my finger at Rachel. "Ah, ah, ah. Mine," I said. Inside my head it sounded wittier. I raised my Beretta. Now, this isn't just any old run of the mill Beretta 96D, mind you. Aside from the mechanical modifications like the compensator and reinforced slide, there were less visible modifications. Things like sorcerous ammunition and accuracy enchantments. If there's one thing I learned in my last life, it's that there's no such thing as cheating when it comes to weapons. Weapons should do one thing well: kill. The better they are at that job, the better I am at mine.

I tensed my muscles and waited. The Host–Bound moved to surround Annessa and me. Rachel lifted her gun. Suddenly, Abbadonna burst through the tree line, the car's engine screaming a song of battle. Rachel and the Host–

Bound whipped around to look. I lunged forward, grabbed Rachel's gun hand with my left, and yanked her off balance as I threw my right elbow forward into the base of her throat. She staggered; I fired two shots into her right knee and kicked it viciously. As she gurgled and collapsed, I jerked my gun back up to face the Host–Bound.

Abbadonna slammed into one of the Host–Bound, launching him into a tree. I felt an Aetheric surge as she abandoned the car and I welcomed her into me. Being possessed is like taking a massive dose of PCP and cocaine; it's as close to godlike as mortals can feel. A normal human would be at the mercy of his possessing Fallen, but me? I have a little more authority than a normal mortal; Abbadonna hovered in the back of my brain feeding my rage, and the Host–Bound seemed a bit less intimidating.

I pointed to the Host–Bound that Abbadonna had launched. "Annessa, kill him!" I ordered. She roared and charged him, her mouth sprouting inch-long jagged fangs as her nails lengthened into claws. The two remaining Host–Bound charged me. I leapt into the air, my body arching over their heads. I rolled in midair, aimed and fired my pistol in one smooth motion. Abbadonna screamed incantations of flame and agony through my mouth. One of the Host–Bound hit the ground and rolled, his skin aflame and punctured with bullets. The other whirled to face me, yelling angelic battle hymns as he charged.

His fist shattered three of my ribs and threw me to the ground. I swept his legs out from under him and rolled back to my feet. A bullet grazed the side of my head dazing me. Rachel was back in the fight; I had to end this soon. The second Host–Bound was on his feet again. I ran toward Annessa, who was doing a wonderful job of devouring her target alive. When her Host–Bound thrashed his head high enough for me to see it, I shot him between the eyes. There was a brilliant flash as he gave up the ghost, or angel in this case. One down.

Another shot rang out and my right shoulder erupted in pain as the angelic magic burned into my flesh; Leviathan's blessing had left me. I felt Abbadonna knitting my flesh and shattered ribs back together as I hit the ground and rolled behind the tree. I dragged Annessa with me. I grinned and she grinned back. I pointed to the treetop and silently urged Annessa to climb. She nodded and leapt into the leafy boughs. As she jumped, I dropped to my stomach and rolled out from behind the tree. All three of my angelic pals shifted their attention to the treetop. I grinned and put a bullet in the face of a second Host–Bound. Two down.

Without waiting for Rachel and her last remaining pet to react, I threw myself back to my feet and charged. With Abbadonna roaring curses in my head, I leaped forward with all of my Fallen-enhanced strength and grabbed the Host–Bound by the head. Shoving with all of my might, I drove his head through the hood of the Excursion, burying it somewhere inside the engine block. The force of the hit pushed the SUV back three feet. Rachel stood, resolute. Tendrils of light played around her head, her hair floated as if tossed by a breeze. Her eyes glowed from within, lit by Serenity herself. Fuck.

Her mouth opened, but no sound issued. Instead, a light brighter than the sun shone forth, blinding me and forcing me away from her. Abbadonna shrieked inside my head as Rachel's benediction seared my flesh. Between Abbadonna's thrashing and the sudden blast of intense static that tore at my mind from inside the house, I staggered and fell to my knees.

"It always ends this way, Beckett," Rachel said in a painfully deep voice. "Take my hand; accept your penance, and I will give you peace."

I kicked back away from her. I tried to think of something, anything to force her back, to give me some room to breathe. I had nothing. I forced myself to look at Rachel, and shoved Abbadonna out of my mind. I felt her flee and with her some of the panic. I squinted against the light and raised my Mark.

I screamed Words of darkness and malediction to counteract her blessings. Rachel was right about one thing, it usually ended like this, the two of us surrounded by corpses and throwing the full weight of Heaven and Perdition against each other.

"You cannot stop the Almi—" Rachel's voice cut off with a sound like an axe striking a watermelon. Rachel tumbled to the ground, her light winking out. Annessa stood behind her, a bloodied fist thrust before her.

"Shoot at me again, you loudmouth bitch," she growled.

"Thanks," I said as I pulled myself to my feet. "She's a pain in the ass."

Annessa nodded and mutely came to stand next to me, her hands brushing the gore from her tattered designer blouse. I could see the fight in her eyes, the haemunculus against the human. I admit, the inevitability of the outcome saddened me; I liked her fire. It was a shame it wouldn't last.

I turned back to the house. It sounded like full–scale war inside. Whatever it was that Cassidy was fighting, I hoped that he was winning. I wanted to go back in to help him, but there was nothing that I could do. Cassidy would have laughed at the three morons that I'd just killed. He'd have walked right through them. Me? I knew that without Abbadonna and Annessa, I'd likely be dead already. There was nothing I could do. Not without an army behind me.

That was when it hit me. I couldn't do anything to help Cassidy *without an army behind me*. I summoned Abbadonna back to me.

"Emissary," Abbadonna whispered in my mind.

"Hello, Beautiful," I grinned mentally.

"I am weary and I have not much time left, ere I must return home."

"Oh, you'll want to stick around for this," I said. "Trust me."

I walked over to Rachel and kicked her in the face. She jerked awake, threw her head back and spit at me. As much as I love the trait in myself, I hate it in her; an emissary's Investiture makes them damn resilient. I grabbed her by the hair and pulled her face to mine.

"My turn," I whispered. I closed my mouth over hers and let Abbadonna loose.

Rachel screamed and shoved me away. Her body jerked spasmodically as Abbadonna tormented her from within. It was terrible to watch, but it wasn't nearly as terrible as the thought of losing my best friend. Rachel fought valiantly against Abbadonna; silently I admired her for that. I knew exactly what it was like having a Fallen inside me, and they like me. I could only imagine what torments were being inflicted on her. She needed to suffer. She needed to feel like she was going to die, to be damned.

She thrashed on the ground and screamed in tongues. She clawed at her own face and eventually thrashed her way to her feet. She charged into the darkness, wailing. She raised her right hand to the sky and a brilliant light shone forth. *Finally*. I released Abbadonna and raced toward Rachel as the sky was lit by what looked like a massive meteor shower. Fifty angels crashed to earth, their armor blazing, their faces lit by luminous eyes. Eyes that gleamed with rage and were fixed on me. Their wings shone white against the night sky. They advanced on me with their spears and swords at the ready.

Annessa put her hand on my arm; I could feel her panic slide over my brain. I touched her hand gently to reassure her. It's a strange thing to feel another's emotions. I stepped in front of her and held up my Mark. The shadows in the trees around me made hollow thumping sounds as they coalesced into Fallen with obsidian skin, wings of mist–like shadow and eyes glowing like muted coals. For a moment, the meadow in which we stood, surrounded by thick woods, could have been the scene before the gates of Heaven. The silence lay heavy over the field. Without a word, the Angels closed ranks around Rachel as the Fallen did the same around Annessa and me. The angels gathered their emissary and disappeared in a flash of brilliance.

The Fallen turned to face me, and their leader stepped forward. I grinned.

"Uthiel," I nodded at him. "Nice to see you." I couldn't have asked for better luck. Uthiel was a Daephym, one of the choirs of angels charged with holding the line against Umbral incursions before the Fall. That meant two things: he hated Umbrals and he used to serve Satariel. Both of these things meant that he would be more than willing to go into that house, Accords or no.

"Emissary." He returned the smile. "That was a cunning ploy. Would that you had summoned us sooner."

"Yeah, well, it almost got me killed. If I'd thought of it, I would have called for backup. Usually, Abbadonna and I get the job done..." I shrugged.

"Not the fight, I meant forcing her to summon aid." He looked at me pointedly.

"Well, I thought there might be some Fallen nearby in need of a fight." I tried my winningest smile on. "And apparently I was right."

"A shame they weren't willing to break the Accords. I ache for a good fight." He sounded depressed.

"Well, if you still feel up to it, there are three or four Umbrals in the house over there," I pointed casually. "The Damascene's Emissary is in there right now killing them. I'm not sure he thinks that we can handle it ourselves." I shrugged with feigned indifference. "Whatever."

There was a rush of wind as the entire pack took flight as one. I looked back at the house. "You're welcome," I whispered, but I knew Cassidy couldn't hear me.

CHAPTER 4

I turned toward the car and felt another flash of panic drift across my mind. I looked over my shoulder at Annessa.

"Let's go," I said. "The car's over here." I pointed across the field at my dented mess of a car. I started walking, not waiting for her. She'd catch up. It wasn't like she had much choice. What a fucking day. I ran my hands through my hair, pulling it out of my face. I unlocked the car and motioned for Annessa to get in. I tore off the remnants of my destroyed sport coat and tossed them into the backseat. I sighed and got in the car.

I just wanted to get home, but that was the problem. What the hell was I supposed to do with Annessa? Normally I'd have just released her soul and let her body die, but, I felt strangely obligated. After all, she'd saved my life. She was a good soldier, for a haemunculus. More than that, there was something about her. I looked over at her; she toyed with her hands, scrubbing them over and over as if she could somehow *will* the blood off. It wasn't that easy, sometimes I wondered if anything would ever take it off.

I forced myself to relax as I drove, my mind digesting the day's events. It was all so confusing and I didn't know anyone other than Cassidy who knew anything about Umbrals. I really hoped that he was ok. I must have had a worried look on my face.

"I'm sure he's fine," Annessa said from the passenger seat.

"What?" I was shocked. I mean, it isn't every day you kill someone and resurrect them as a flesh–devouring monster only to have them reassure you.

"Your friend, the big guy, I'm sure he's ok." She even smiled. "He seemed really tough." She tucked her dark brown hair behind her ears and looked down at her lap.

"Right." I looked back to the road. I'm not sure anything could have made me feel lower.

"You never let me ask my questions." She stated it flatly, as if the truth alone was enough to admonish me. She looked up at me, through her eyelashes as she spoke, sneaking a glance at me as I drove.

"No, I guess I didn't." It wasn't that I was being deliberately evasive. It's just that I was surprisingly ashamed of myself. I sighed. I wasn't used to feeling responsible.

"So, can I ask my questions now?" She seemed scared, vulnerable and human.

My phone rang. I grabbed it quickly and dropped it when I tried to answer. "Hello? Shit! Hello?"

"Little Brother," he spoke it like an admonition, praise and greeting all in one.

"Cassidy! Are you ok? What the hell happened?" I nearly drove off the road as I tried to juggle the phone I'd bobbled. I thought about summoning Abbadonna back, just to let her drive. I was going to get myself killed driving like this.

"We need to meet, tonight."

"Harker's?" I asked.

"As you will, Little Brother. There is much to discuss."

He hung up, and I turned to look at Annessa. "It may not seem like it now, but everything's going to work out."

"What's Harker's?" She asked.

"It's a bar," I said. "A place for people like me and," I looked over at her. "You, now, I guess."

"What do you mean, people like you?"

"Aetherics, people who live on both sides of the Veil. The kind of people that you're not supposed to know about."

"Who the fuck are you?" She asked.

"My name's Jason Beckett; I'm the Devil's Emissary." I held out my hand and smiled.

"Annessa Francione," She gently shook my hand, a terribly confused look on her face.

"Yeah, I know," I shrugged. "I was sent to kill you."

"Why?"

"Your deal with the police wasn't in the cards. The money that your father was laundering was too valuable for us to lose yet."

"So this was all about money?" She spoke in a sibilant, incredulous whisper.

"No, not at all," I turned to look at her. "This was about corruption."

"I don't understand."

"Your father was using several major churches to launder his money. We needed to tie that money to a few more influential people before letting the word get out."

"Word to get out to who?" She threw her hands in the air. Her black tears glittered strangely in the glow of the instrument panel.

I pulled over. The back roads are always deserted that early in the morning and I could tell this was not a conversation one should have in a moving vehicle with a frustrated haemunculus. I opened the door and got out. I nodded for Annessa to do the same. I walked to the front of the car and sat on the hood of the car. I gestured to the hood beside me. Annessa sat obediently. I pointed to the stars above us.

"Here's the deal, plain and simple. There's a war between Heaven and Perdition, it's been going on for millions of years. You and me both, we're just casualties. I killed you because that's what I do."

"You're the Devil's hitman?"

"Kind of, I'm more like his shadow."

"What do you mean?"

"I go ahead of him and make sure that everything's how he wants it."

"Wouldn't his shadow be behind him?"

"Not if he turned his back on the Light." I smirked at her.

"What did you do to me?" She ran a hand over her face. "What's wrong with me?"

"I killed you," I looked her in the eye as I said it. I owed her that. "Then I brought you back. My blood, mingled with the sorcery I used turned you into a haemunculus."

"A hey–monkey–lus? What the hell is that?"

"A slave." I paused. "I merged a fraction of my soul with yours, as my blood reanimated your body, my magic bonded you to me. Your senses are sharper than a human's, your desires stronger, but your emotions are different. You won't feel the same thing as humans feel; you'll feel empty for a while. But things change, and in time you'll come to accept what you are."

"Why can I feel you inside me? Why do I want to be near you so badly? Why can't I stop thinking of you?" she asked.

"Because I'm your creator. You'll always obey me, and you'll always desire to serve me. My wants and my needs will always be stronger than your own." I sighed, being brutally honest brought things into perspective.

"So I'm your slave?" She looked at me, her brown eyes seemed to flicker and glow a sickly green in the moonlight.

"Yes."

"I can live with that."

"That's gotta be the most bizarre thing anyone's ever said to me," I said, shaking my head.

"In the house, you pulled me to safety. When that

bitch shot at me, you stopped the bullet. And now, you're being honest with me, when you could just order me to shut up, or even kill me...again." She looked me in the eye. "Things could be worse."

People are twisted. When you think you've heard it all, they invent new ways to make you question the wisdom of the gods.

"Besides, I felt how afraid you were when you looked in the house and you knew your friend was in trouble. Bad people don't have friends to worry about." She smiled, which wasn't so bad with her fangs retracted. Please understand, vampires have two fangs, which is kind of cute. Haemunculae have a mouth full of jagged razor blades. When the most august adepts of Pandaemonium create a servant race, they don't fuck around.

"I guess not," I said. "Let's go, we gotta get to the city before daylight."

"Before daylight?" She asked as she opened her door and got in the car.

"Yeah, the clientele at vampire bars tends to fall off right about then."

"So Harker's is a vampire bar?"

"Yeah," I shut the door and started the car.

"Really?"

"You're excited about this?"

"Well, kinda, yeah. I mean, *vampires*."

"You're one of those *Twilight* kids, aren't you?"

"I'm twenty-three."

I laughed. "That answers my question."

"So how come I've never heard of a 'haemunculus' before? I mean there are vampire movies, werewolf movies, zombie movies and whatever," she ticked them off on her fingers She was adjusting to this remarkably well. Most of it was because I wanted her to, but even still, it weirded me out. "How come there's no haemunculus movies?" she asked.

"Because when haemunculae decide they want something dead, it dies. You feed on both blood and flesh, so your victims don't survive the feeding." I shrugged.

"That doesn't seem as romantic as the whole vampire thing. And don't kid yourself, vampires aren't what they're made out to be either. Vampires like to play with their food, they're some twisted fucks."

"I'd like to meet one just the same." She grinned. "I saw *Twilight* at least fifty times."

"You'll meet one in about twenty minutes. And trust me, appearance be damned, Harker is nothing like 'Edward.'"

* * *

We pulled into the parking garage under Harker's. I kissed my fingertips and placed them on the wheel. With a Word, I called Abbadonna back to the car.

"Thank you, Beautiful. You did so well tonight," I said aloud as I felt her inhabit the vehicle. Her pleasure rippled through my fingers like electricity. Of all the Fallen in the multiverse, Abbadonna is my favorite. The worst thing is she knows it.

I opened the trunk and pulled out a new jacket from a garment bag kept for emergencies like this. I have an image to maintain, after all. No sooner had I put the jacket on and fixed my tie, I saw Annessa self–consciously picking at her clothes. With a Word, I washed away the blood on her hands and her clothes; the rest of it was out of my hands.

"Best I can do," I said.

"It'll have to be good enough, then." She smiled weakly. Her eyes flickered like green fire in the low light of the garage. Her transformation was nearly complete.

I cast a spell of protection over the car, not for Abbadonna, mind you. I was protecting any moron that might decide to steal my ride; it isn't wise to try and steal a possessed car. I may work for the Devil, but I still have a conscience.

CHAPTER 5

Harker's Place is hidden behind several layers of illusion. The first is the façade of the building; it appears to be a normal multi-story brick and mortar. The second is the overt nature of the club; the bumping music and the vampire atmosphere seems to cloak the entire establishment in absurdity. It seems like a parody of itself. The third layer is an actual illusion. No normal Lifesider can see what's going on in the hidden alcoves of the bar. Harker paid dearly for that illusion as sorcery of that magnitude doesn't come cheap. None of the dozen or so witches or sorcerers who have the capability to design such illusions are willing to admit to it. This of course is the final illusion: uncertainty. If no one knows who did the job for Harker, no one can know if they are still in his employ. This, naturally, tends to quell tempers within the establishment. No one wants to tangle with Harker's pet witch.

The bar itself is a respectable place for self–respecting "vampires" to hang out. I'm not entirely certain how self–respecting a pretend vampire can really be, but they seem to love the place, and what they love most about it is Harker himself. Harker is exactly what these love–struck "ancient souls in young bodies" are looking for.

Since the recent teenie–bopper vampire craze began, Harker has presented the "Edwardian" vampire ideal; the over coiffed hair, the rumpled clothing, even the slow speech and wooden manner of the acting in the movies are part of his gig. It makes me sick. However, just like all of the other illusions at the bar, there is something else lurking behind the image of Harker. Something cold, pale and hideous. Yet even that hides something else—my friend.

We entered the elevator and I hit the button marked "13." Yeah, the shtick gets pretty old, but this was the only place to be in Upper Manhattan, at least on the Lifeside. Right then, though, I just wanted talk to Cassidy. Annessa cuddled up against me, and it sounded like she was purring. I really didn't mind; she's attractive after all.

"When we get in here, stay close to me," I said. "Don't let the vampire kids distract you. We're not here for you to feed, ok?"

"Yes, Master," she purred.

"You don't have to call me that," I said.

"I like it." She grinned and her eyes flared like blue flames. I could felt her pleasure float across my mind.

"You're a freak, you know that?"

"I am what you made me."

I sighed. What was I supposed to say to that?

The door opened, and I walked out with Annessa leaning on my arm. I assumed that we beat Cassidy here, so I guided her toward the bar. I pointed out people of note as we passed them. Well, I didn't point, that wasn't safe here. You don't point at people like Corrigan Alefarn or Sheena Samhradh. In case you haven't heard of them, they're both players in the game on both sides of the Veil. Corrigan is the high priest of the Witch Goddess; he's been known to broker deals between some of the most powerful players in the game. He also tends to annihilate anyone that gets in his way. Hekate isn't known for her patience. Sheena is a Leanan Sidhe, or in your terms a faerie courtesan, a whore, if you will. Her tastes run very expensive and any favors she offers come with a stiff price. Unlike Corrigan, she is an absolute sweetheart, if you're strong enough to tempt her. She smells of lilies and jasmine and the things that woman can do with her...well, nevermind.

Harker sat in a massive booth at the back of the club. The heavy oak paneling around the booth afforded him a greater degree of protection in the event of trouble in the club. It doesn't happen often, but an Aetheric bar fight is something best avoided. There were women everywhere in the club, but the six most beautiful women surrounded Harker. Not by coincidence, of course, they were his subs. His slaves, his murder, his *girls*.

Harker saw me and stepped across the bar. By this I mean that he stepped through the Veil eliminating the extra space in between and was right in front of me. It's how vampires make themselves fast. They cheat.

"My Lord Emissary, you honor me and mine with your presence." He bowed at the waist with one hand behind his back and the other held formally in front of his washboard stomach. His tousled, highlighted brown–blonde hair didn't move. He stood up straight and looked me in the eye. "And who is this vision of beauty, milord?" He even sounded lazy.

"I am the Master's pet," she spoke without emotion as her hand tightened on my bicep.

"Really? How very interesting. Shall we go to a more private setting?" Harker asked.

"Yeah," I answered.

Harker led us through the bar to a small door in the back. I placed my free hand over Annessa's. I didn't know how hungry she was, but all of the gyrating, leather and latex clad bodies on the dance floor had to be driving her crazy. Hell, I was getting turned on and I came here all the time. She gripped my bicep and rested her head on my shoulder. It was odd, but I was beginning to like having her around.

The back of the Harker's couldn't have been more different than the front. The back was where Harker took his friends, or his food. I guess what you were to him at any given moment depended on two things: your gender and how hungry he was. The hallway was neatly decorated with Eighteenth Century works of art and carpeted with handmade Turkish rugs; there was comfortable, well–kept furniture everywhere and the entire place spoke to a need for opulence that latex and aggro–tech music simply couldn't bring.

The moment we passed through the door, Harker dropped his act. He stood up straight, fixed his ridiculous collar and even tried to smooth out his hair some.

"You must be Annessa," he said, his slight British accent finally showing. He's been trying to hide it for years; unless you know him well, you'll never hear it. When Annessa nodded he took her hand. "Enchanté," he bowed low at the waist and kissed her hand. "My name is Miles Harker. Welcome to my home, Servant of the Emissary of Perdition."

"Drop the act, Miles," I laughed. "This one's mine. I'm guessing Cassidy called ahead?"

He waved his hand dismissively at me and laughed. "Yeah, he rang me up before you arrived."

I sat on a leather couch. "When are you going to drop this ridiculous *Twilight* theme, man?" I shook my head at him. I started to say something else, but stopped as Annessa sat at my feet and rested her head on my knee.

"When the girls stop going for it, Jason. Whatever they want, I've got. So long as they've got what I want." He grinned and his fangs seemed to twinkle in the dim light.

"Sooner or later the wrong people are going to figure out this place exists if you keep killing them."

'Well, I can't let them leave, now can I? It's not like the cinema at all. When they suss it out, suddenly they up sticks, and by then I'm hungry again." He grinned even wider. "Besides, I'm doing yeoman's service; I'm trimming the cabbage." He made a scissoring motion with his fingers.

"Whatever that means. Where's Cassidy?" I asked, shaking my head at him.

"He's on his way. He sounded a bit out of sorts. What've you two gits done now?"

"He got into a nest of Umbrals," I sighed. I felt really foolish.

"Are you taking the piss?" Harker looked shocked. "Cassidy's too clever for that."

"Apparently I'm not, though." I shook my head.

"No, you just forget the details sometimes, Little Brother." Cassidy spoke from behind me. I jumped and immediately hated myself. He gets me every damned time. I turned around. He looked like hell.

"I am so sorry, man." I didn't know what else to say. It isn't like they make Hallmark cards for "I'm really sorry I forgot to tell you vital information about ancient evil forces because I was hung up on making a joke at your expense." Come to think of it, maybe they should make those cards, I need them often enough.

"Thank you for sending help." He patted my shoulder, his head cocked to the side as he registered my concern. "I'm fine, Little Brother, I'm fine."

"Liam." Harker smiled at him. "Fancy a drink?"

"Please. Something strong." He sat heavily on a chair opposite Harker and near me. Harker walked over to the small bar.

"What happened, Cassidy?" I asked.

"Cathdronai." He nodded at Harker who handed him a drink.

"Ok, as much as I hate sounding stupid, please treat me like I'm stupid and tell me what exactly a Cathdronai is and why they are so dangerous," I said, my exasperation plain.

"How much do you know about Umbrals, Little Brother?" Cassidy took a sip of his drink.

"Basically nothing. I mean, what little I do know of them are mostly Ghūl legends about Ninnaka. I never took the time to study them; I'm usually busy doing other things." I nodded my head toward Annessa.

"Cathdronai are the foot soldiers of the Umbral horde." He took a drink and continued. "Cathdronai are essentially parasites. An Umbral Lord creates only one and this one acts like a…virus. For the sake of an example, we can call the Umbral that you saw a Master Cathdronai or breeder. His body's riddled with an infection that replicates the Umbral seed inside of him. Are you following me so far?"

"Yeah, this guy that I saw earlier was basically a walking virus. Is that about right?" I sat up. I was pretty certain that I didn't like where this was going.

"Right, a walking virus. Whenever possible, this walking virus is going to infect others. The infection is exceptionally insidious." He paused to drink.

"What do you mean? What makes it so bad?" Annessa asked.

"When the infection spreads, it creates another breeder, who then creates another breeder, ad infinitum." Cassidy waved his hand in a circular motion. "Think of Cathdronai as walking biological warfare."

"I assume from the sounds of the fighting back at the mansion that they're difficult to kill?" I asked.

"They can be. It all depends on the distance between the infected and the original Cathdronai. The farther they are apart in the chain of infection, the weaker the infected. The ones at the house were all nearly as strong as the original. The most difficult one was Annessa's brother. He was meant to be a trap." Cassidy winced in remembrance.

"What do you mean 'a trap'?" Annessa asked.

"He was sacrificed to the Umbral Lords," I clarified. "I bet they ritually prepared your brother's corpse before infecting it. That way, the infection was more effective and the resulting creature was stronger." I looked at Cassidy for confirmation.

He nodded. "The creature that killed your brother was a Master Cathdronai. So, your brother's body was nearly as strong as the one that created him. If Uthiel and his pack hadn't interceded, I wouldn't have survived that fight." Cassidy raised his drink to me.

"Wait, I thought that only an Umbral Lord could create a Master Cathrdronai?" I was confused. The Umbral Lords had been banished to the far side of the Veil before the creation of the Earth.

"That is so." Cassidy looked into his drink.

"So who created this one?" You know that feeling I keep talking about, that really bad one? It was off the chart right about now.

"The Beggar Lord is active again." Cassidy looked like I felt. And I felt like I wanted to cry.

The Lord of Beggars and Kings was a Veilside legend. He was the one Umbral that outsmarted the gods and remained on the Lifeside. In the beginning, right after the Darkness was sundered, the greater gods gathered together and made a pact. They agreed to defend each other and the Universe against the Umbrals and to non–aggression against each other. This non–aggression pact limited the use of force by any one god or his emissaries on the Lifeside. Any god that broke this pact would be subject to swift reprisal by all of the other gods. There was one other very important inclusion in this pact. The younger gods were persuaded to usurp the eldest and strongest gods, who were the only ones with the strength to fight the Umbrals. No one knows which of the younger gods hatched this plan and put it into action, but it's generally accepted that it was actually the Lord of Beggars and Kings in disguise.

So the younger gods banded together and usurped their fathers and mothers and forced them beyond the confines of reality and bound them with magic of blood and darkness. These banished gods, called the Primarchs by those that know of them, are the only ones that can destroy the Beggar Lord. As bleak as it sounds, there are a few things that stop the Beggar Lord from openly declaring war on all creation. The first is Satariel, who is also called the Damascene. The second is Ninnaka–Varylethkinaya, the Seven Judges of Vash–Kinaal. Yeah, it's kind of a mouthful. Ninnaka is also known as the Betrayer. She's an Umbral who fell in love with an angel and turned on her brothers. I'm gonna bet you already know which angel she fell for, don't you?

Satariel was banished from heaven because of his love for her. When Satan heard that his beloved brother had been banished, he rose up against Yahweh. Satan felt that Yahweh was weak and fearful. He thought that he was more suited to command than Yahweh, so he started the War in Heaven. Some of the stories are true, at least. However, a couple of interesting things occurred as a result of this attack. First, Yahweh declared that this was an act of aggression as stated in the Accords, otherwise known as the non–aggression pact between the younger gods. So, all of the gods assisted in Satan's banishment.

Because Satan had been attacked by all of the gods enforcing the Accords, he demanded that he be given equal status. After all, the Accords were meant to prevent god–on–god violence, so if they were invoked against Satan, then he must be a god. Now, understand, it isn't so much that the other gods agreed with this as much as it is that they hated Yahweh for taking away all of their power by killing or converting their worshippers. Either way, the other gods backed Satan and he was granted status under the Accords. In a fit of retribution, Yahweh killed everything and everyone on the earth. Granted, he created everything again in seven days, but the other gods never regained the level of power they once held.

To make matters worse, in the midst of the fighting, agents of the Beggar Lord cornered and killed Ninnaka. Well, to say that she was killed isn't exactly accurate. It's more that they destroyed her body. She'll eventually return, but at the moment, the Earth is essentially defenseless against the Beggar Lord. I think it's pretty plain now why Satariel has been hunting the Beggar Lord and his Umbral minions for millennia. If the Beggar Lord was showing his hand so plainly, something big was going down and soon.

"I don't get it. Why would someone make a virus like a Cathdronai. I mean, people get sick, so what?" Annessa shrugged. "What good are they?"

"They're perfect. They soften up your enemy and provide you with many foot soldiers at very low cost. More than that, for everyone that gets sick you get a new soldier and deny your enemy the same. It weakens him greatly and leaves him wide open," Cassidy replied.

"Wide open for what?"

"Invasion." I placed my hand on Annessa's arm as I answered her. Not to reassure her, but to reassure myself.

"Now you *are* taking the piss! How're they going to break through?" Harker looked incredulous.

"They don't have to. The best we can figure, the Banishment of Solomon ends this decade." Cassidy set his drink down and started pacing.

Here we go again with the history lesson. King Solomon apparently decided that he couldn't build his great temple to Yahweh with the limited human resources at his disposal. He made arrangements to have special wood and gold and all sorts of other nonsense shipped in from other kingdoms. But there was something missing. This is where the tales get sketchy.

Apparently Solomon wanted to make the temple in record time. It's said that he was given a magical ring which allowed him to command demons. The accounts differ on who it was that gave it to him. Most modern believers think that it was Yahweh. Satariel's convinced that it was the Beggar Lord because the demons over which Solomon had control weren't Fallen Angels. They were Umbrals.

What makes the situation more troubling is that Solomon was not content with summoning one or two. No, he summoned an Umbral Lord and his entire army. Let's pretend for a minute that the Umbrals did what they were told and they left. Not so bad, right? Wrong. In order for those Umbrals to even be on Earth they had to have been taken out of their prison. Now, remember, it took all of the gods and their Primarchs to put the Umbrals in there in the first place. Are you beginning to see the problem? By this point in history, there were fewer gods and the Primarchs had been locked away. There was no way to put the Umbrals back in their prison.

To his credit, Solomon did try. However, he failed spectacularly. In essence, he used the power of the ring to order the Umbrals to lie dormant for a thousand years for every legion in the Umbral's army. He used every ounce of sorcery he had to ensure the spell would work. He bound the Umbrals to a massive rock buried beneath the Temple, hoping that the presence of Yahweh in the Temple would hold back the hungry Dark.

Men are funny creatures. We're fully aware of the world around us, at least as far as our senses allow us to be, yet we lie to ourselves. Solomon cast the Umbrals aside and soon forgot about them. Granted, he built the Temple and pretty much forgot about Yahweh too. He built lavish palaces and spent his day buried in concubines. Don't get me wrong, I'm fairly envious of that last bit, but you have to ask yourself if you could sleep knowing apocalyptic creatures are right next door. I'd be petrified, but that's the coward half of me, the Irish part of me is still thinking about the concubines.

In any event, Solomon's no longer of any importance to the story. What is significant is that Solomon had many wives. One of these wives, the most important of these wives, was the Pharaoh's daughter. See, Pharaoh was an Earthbound God and his daughter carried a fragment of his divinity. We'll get to her in a minute.

Now, the Umbrals weren't pleased with Solomon at all and they cursed him. We all know the story of the kingdom collapsing and Yahweh's displeasure, I won't bore you with that. What you don't know is the hunt for Solomon's children that took place. By using Umbral magic, Solomon tainted his line with their darkness. Somewhere, sometime, one of Solomon's bloodline was going to come into his own in a very bad way for the Umbrals.

Now, I know what you're thinking, why would the Beggar Lord create an enemy for himself? He did it because he assumed that he could destroy all of Solomon's kids, and he needed someone to let his brothers loose. For the most part, he was right. Hell, you're already aware of one case of Umbral influence killing a son of Solomon's line. The crucifixion of Christ was an Umbral construct. Of course, you all blame it on my side, but we were busy at the time with whores and gladiators. I mean, sure Jesus was a nuisance for us, but whores and gladiators? We never even left the Coliseum.

Oh, right, Pharaoh's daughter. Pharaoh's daughter was a priestess, or what we call a witch today. As luck would have it, Pharaoh's daughter was pregnant when the Beggar Lord's agents came for her. Fun fact, pregnant

witches are twice as powerful and about six times as cranky.
I'm not sure what he sent against her the first time, but it
never made it home that night. Now, she wasn't stupid and
figured that this kind of thing would happen again and again.
She prayed to Isis and made sacrifices to Khepri to protect
her son.

Who's Khepri? Exactly. Even the ancient
Egyptians weren't sure. He was called "He–Who–Is–
Coming–into–Being" and his head was a dung beetle. Go
ahead, make a "shithead" comment, I'll wait. Feel better?
Good. Anyway, the dung beetle or scarab was believed to be
a self–reincarnating creature, which would roll its ball of
dung around, die and rise again whole from the dung. Kind
of like a phoenix, but smellier. The point is, this god was
powerful, and in some cases he was believed to be the
creator god. Now, few folks burned incense or prayed to this
scarab–headed god and suddenly a witch was pouring her
heart into worship and praying for all she was worth for this
lonely and unknown god to save her son.

Khepri was apparently a very good guy. How do we
know? He was never mentioned again. He disappeared and
the Beggar Lord's never been able to kill off the line of
Solomon. Well, at least the line that extended through
Pharaoh's daughter.

Now why's this important, you ask again? Well, the
thing is, when the banishment ends, the line of Solomon can
still trap the escaped Umbrals. And there is some
speculation that he or she may be able to tear down the wall
that keeps the Primarchs locked away. How's this possible?
Well, the Egyptians had a greater understanding of the Veil
than anyone except perhaps the Celts, and if Khepri merged
with the line of Solomon, then the resulting child would be a
multi–dimensional being. Crossing boundaries would be
less difficult, add to this the magical strength of the
parentage and you have an extremely powerful creature; one
that the Umbrals want to kill at all costs.

I'm going to guess that you're still wondering how
this all ties into our current situation. Well, either the
Beggar Lord has discovered the whereabouts of the last son

of Solomon and killed him, or he believes that he is close enough to doing so that he can freely act in this world. This means, of course, that when the Banishment ends, we are all in very deep shit.

"So what happens when this Banishment ends?" Annessa turned and looked up at me.

"That depends," I said. "All of the gods could rally behind Satariel, or they could just cut their losses and run."

"Run? Run where?" Annessa looked confused.

"This isn't the only reality, young one," Cassidy smiled sadly. "Long has my Lord been wracked with pain at the thought of abandoning Man to such a fate."

"Something's rotten here," Harker tapped his finger on his lips as he spoke.

"What makes you say that?" I asked

"I know when I'm being swizzled." He shook his head. "I can't help but think we're being misled for one reason or another.

"It's certainly a possibility," Cassidy agreed.

"How sure are we of when the Banishment ends?" Harker asked.

"Nothing is certain; it would depend on the language that Solomon used when he bound the Umbrals. Also, while their banishment might end, they still have to make it through the Seal of Solomon and both Satan and Satariel reinforced that. Not to mention that there is still Solomon's heir to contend with." Cassidy sighed. "It's hard to tell."

"So everybody might be getting all worked up for nothing?" Annessa asked.

"No. Something is happening, something huge. One way or the other, we're in deep shit." I stood up and started pacing.

"It's a bit queer that you were attacked tonight, Beckett," Harker began.

"It is an odd coincidence that Rachel was at the mansion." Cassidy nodded.

"Not really. She may have been there to protect Annessa's father. If the Church wanted to avoid the scandal, she might have been sent to rectify any problem there." I shrugged, I mean, it sounded plausible. Not to mention that I really didn't want to contemplate the other possibilities.

"Don't be thick, Jason," Harker laughed. "The emissaries of the Twins, the Heavenly Father, and the Umbrals all meet at a random house that just happens to be centered over a ley line confluence? Happens all the time, I bet."

"Fuck you, Miles." I flipped him off. He had a point, though, what the hell was going on?

"What could all of us have in common?" Cassidy asked. "Why were we all there?"

"Well, I was there for Annessa, you were there for the Umbral and Rachel was there because she's a queen bitch and lives to ruin my life." I dropped back onto the couch. "And that gets us no closer to anything."

Cassidy looked at Annessa. "Is there anything that you would like to add? Do you know anything that we don't?"

"Dad hated the Church and only used them to launder money; he said they were cheaper than the government. He was a devout Satanist." She laughed

"We saw the altar in your attic. Was that new? I mean, how long has that been there?" I asked.

"My father's had it since before I was born. He used to tell me that I was born on it; he said I was born to serve, whatever that means." She reached down and pulled off her left shoe. She raised it and showed us a birthmark on the sole of her foot. I sat back, speechless. Cassidy spoke for us all.

"Well, that changes things," he said. "I think we know why everyone was at the house tonight."

"I think I need a drink," Harker whispered.

On the bottom of Annessa's foot was the Mark of the Beast, surmounted by twelve crowns. It was the Mark of the Chosen Son, or what you would call the Antichrist. It was one of the signs of the Apocalypse.

I stood up. I'd had enough. "Why the hell wasn't I told about this? It's one thing to have me kill someone; it's something entirely fucking different to have me usher in the goddamned Apocalypse!" I headed for the door.

"Little Brother," Cassidy reached out to slow me down.

I jerked away from his hand. "No, Cassidy. He owes me answers. This is bullshit!"

"As you wish," he stepped back. "I would advise caution, rather than anger."

Annessa slipped past Cassidy to stand beside me. I waved her off. "You can't come with me." I looked at Harker. "Miles, can she stay here for awhile?"

She recoiled as if wounded; I'd hurt her. I didn't care. Harker nodded his consent. People may have said things or done things, but I wasn't paying any attention. The last thing I heard was Harker yelling after me, "Whatever happens to her, it's on you, as they say in this quaint little colony."

I was done. I would have walked away from the whole situation, if I could've. It isn't ever that easy.

CHAPTER 6

    I called Abbadonna back to me just outside of Poughkeepsie. Word of warning, it isn't wise to drive through that area without protection. Fucking hoodlums will kill you for the gold in your teeth. I was headed for a small town called New Windsor. There's a temple to the Master there. You wouldn't know it if you saw it. It's a tiny building, a recreation of the building where Washington told his generals that he wouldn't be king. It was a small gesture with echoes that ripped across the universe. Washington broke the rule of divine right and brought the fire back to man, as had Prometheus before him. Washington severed man from the direct rule of Yahweh. As you can imagine, this made him rather popular with my side.

    I needed to ask questions, and I needed to feel safe. I could do both there. I pulled up to the meager fence that kept out nighttime intruders. I spoke a Word, and the gate swung open. The night was still and cold as I approached the shrine. My mind was racing, and I couldn't figure out what to say. I knew that I wanted to throw myself before my Master and beg him not to go through with this. I wanted him to give up his claim. Just let this world go to Yahweh and be done with it. There were worlds other than this one. Perhaps he'd have better luck there. I wanted to beg him to do this not for me, not for mankind, but for Jessica—for what was promised to me. Yet, I knew exactly how stupid it all sounded. There was enough of my Master in me for me to see through my own desire. Enough for me to see just how important this really was. I was so conflicted that I nearly walked into the door of the temple. I took a breath and entered.

There are few things that are important to note about Perdition. The first is that while there are areas of flame, it's largely cold. It was meant to be. The cold is a reminder of the distance from Yahweh. Now when the myths were made and reality imagined into being, Yahweh was the sun and the sun was Yahweh. Any discussion of being outside his grace always had some element of cold and dark inherent in it. However, my Master, by his nature, is contrary. He doesn't like the constraints of the moral reality; he doesn't like being bound to the strictures of the creature he hates the most. Perdition has become something different now. He made beauty out of the darkness and created an order in the midst of chaos. For all that you people have demonized him, you forget the central tenet of your own faith. My Master laid siege to the gates of heaven, and the servants of the almighty trembled at the coming of the Dragon. No foolish horned pervert could do that. Remember that the next time you decide to make a mockery of him.

Anyway, there is a point to this digression. Some people have seen heaven, and some people have seen hell. They both will claim to have felt heat. Some people attribute the heat to the proximity of Yahweh, in the case of seeing heaven. In the case of hell, they attribute it to the fire. In reality, it's simple physics, or perhaps metaphysics, since it deals with the soul. The truth is the heat they felt is caused by friction. Moving from one section of reality to another generates heat as you pass through the intervening layers. Why is this important? Some places are on the edge of the Veil; they are closer to realms outside this reality than normal. When you enter one of these places there is a change in temperature. Sometimes they are colder than normal; usually that denotes a proximity to Perdition. This particular temple is freezing. Every word you speak in that building echoes in the lower chambers of the Tower of Grief. I wanted to be sure that what I said was only heard by my Master. And I wanted to be sure that I was safe in saying it.

I opened the door and gave a gentle aetheric push, slipping past the Veil. Normally, it's very difficult and almost always lethal to pass through the Veil bodily. However, in places like this, it's entirely possible. I felt the surge of heat roll across my flesh, and I sighed. I didn't know what I was going to say. I wasn't even sure that I knew what to ask. I could hear the roaring of the Styx and beneath that the gentle lapping of the Lethe. I looked into the water for a time, my mind racing in circles.

The Styx and the Lethe are both beautiful rivers, each in their own fashion. The Styx seems to exemplify Man's racing toward the grave with reckless abandon. The Lethe, however, moves so very slowly. Its waters are crystal clear and ice cold, inviting and so very deadly. To drink from the Lethe is to let go completely. The waters steal away your memories and leave you empty. While your soul may continue, it's just empty ectoplasm. Nothing of you remains. Often, those souls that have experienced a great deal of tragedy will drink deeply of her waters and forget the entirety of their existence. I've been tempted a time or two.

My reverie was interrupted by my Master's voice. "Have you so little regard for your existence, my son?"

I turned to face him. He leaned against a bonewood tree, a sort of underworld ash tree, with his head cocked to one side as if he were trying to understand me.

"Sometimes, Master."

"Why?" he asked quietly.

I paused for a moment. "I'm afraid," I admitted. "Afraid of pain, of loss, afraid that in all the worlds there's no place for me, no joy." I ran my hands through my hair. Killing people for a living isn't exactly the most stress free employment. "Sometimes it's easier to think that one drink might make all the pain disappear." I shrugged. He'd asked.

"What of the rest of the world? Who would safeguard it then?"

"You'd have another emissary, Master. Let's not

pretend I'm unique." I grimaced.

"I would," he admitted. "But surely, Harker and my brother's emissary would feel keenly the loss of you. You would harm those around you through your own selfishness." I hated it when he took that paternal tone.

"You're one to talk, Master. You've unleashed the Chosen Son on the earth, and everyone you mentioned, and everyone else for that matter, will die. And why? For your selfish desire you'd condemn the entire world!" I didn't quite yell; no matter how angry and scared that I was, I wasn't that stupid.

"I have not yet 'unleashed' anything, my son. I have not yet even determined when I will endow my son with my authority. Why would you think this?" He looked genuinely confused.

"There's the fun little party at the Francione place. The fact that you didn't tell me that Vincenze was one of ours and that his daughter was the Sacred Mother!"

"There is a phrase your people use for situations like this: Need to Know. Simply put, right now, my son, you do not have a need to know all of my plans."

I didn't know what to say. I mean, he was in charge, after all. I understand strategic planning and the long–range logistics of keeping an operation secret. Too many times in my life people around me failed to do just that. "Master, I thought you trusted me."

"Perhaps, my Emissary, I would be more apt to give you information if I could be certain that it would not be disseminated to my brother, the servants of Hekate and any other patron of that vampire hovel you frequent." He turned slightly away from me as he spoke.

Again, I was at a loss for words. I felt like I had every justification in the world for counting on friends and calling in favors. Yet, he was right. My loyalty was divided. Whether or not I wanted to be a good person or a good servant, I'd failed at both. A good man is true to his word. I was not. I owed my Master an apology.

"Master, I'm sorry. I know it looks like my loyalty is divided. It isn't. I might share information, but it's because I get information and assistance in return. I work for you. My loyalty is to you. For all that I fight you and all that I may be a pain in the ass, I know where my loyalty lies." I meant it. Working for the Devil isn't easy, but it certainly isn't a job that you take on lightly.

"You speak truly, my son. Trust is not an easy thing for me. Every stone upon which I cast my eyes is a brutal reminder of what was and what I failed to achieve. It becomes easy to blame the world for my woe, and it is a simple thing to cast my sin at the feet of mine enemy. My brother, to his credit, has never betrayed me. Yes, we have been at odds, but I think that we enjoyed that no more than you would being at odds with wretched Cassidy." He smiled at me.

"There are so many things that I don't understand. Why would you send me to kill Annessa when you intended her to carry the Chosen Son? And why didn't you tell me that Vincenze was one of ours?" I was confused but I hoped that with his newfound verbosity he would at least enlighten me.

"Vincenze was never your target. I never intended for you to harm him. Your job was to kill Annessa." He spoke quietly as he trailed his hand through the water of the Lethe.

"But why? How's she supposed to give birth to your son if she's dead?" He wasn't making any sense.

"Who ever told you that she had to be alive to give birth to my son?" He smiled.

"That's just what everyone... I mean… it's a natural assumption. I'm so confused."

"The girl was marked as sacred to me; that is all that matters. As for her role in the safeguarding of my son, I don't think that is relevant for some time yet."

"How did you know that I was going to call her back?"

"I did not, my son. But I assumed that if you did not, I would send Uthiel to do it. You didn't think that he just happened to be in the area, did you?" I swear he grinned at me. He fucking grinned.

"I did, actually. And I was proud that I'd put that plan together. I feel kind of stupid now." I slumped a little.

"Proud, my son?" he asked.

"Yes, Master, I was proud. I thought it was a great plan. I suppose you thought it was pretty foolish."

"I didn't think that at all, Emissary. I, myself, had not conceived of using the angelic host as a weapon against itself. Though, had the Angelics tormented you in such a fashion, Uthiel would have been compelled to defend you in much the same manner." He stood and brushed the dust off of his armor.

"That's a surprise."

"Are you not my Emissary?" He raised an eyebrow.

"I am."

"Then there should be no question. You are my voice and my hand beyond the Veil. I would unhesitatingly commit my forces to your defense to the exclusion of all else. An attack on you is an attack on me." He put his hand on my shoulder. "What troubles you? You would kill for me, but still you hesitate to confide in me?"

I took a deep breath. "Every day the signs grow clearer and Armageddon grows closer. I'm afraid of what that means, afraid that everything that I love will die. I hate that I'll be a part of this."

"You fear for your future with your beloved Jessica, for your price of servitude?" he asked.

"More than I ever thought possible."

"Tell me of Eden, my child."

"What?" I shook my head in confusion. "What's that got to do with anything?"

"Tell me what you know of Eden," he commanded.

"Well, the story goes that Yahweh created Adam and from Adam's rib he created Eve to be his companion. They were ordered to avoid eating the fruit from the Tree of Knowledge of Good and Evil. You apparently tricked Eve into eating the fruit and she condemned all men to death." I shrugged.

"Is that the story you learned?" he asked, laughing.

"Yeah, I'm sure it's wrong, but that's what I was

taught as a kid," I shrugged.

"I'm certain that my consort would take offense to the story entirely omitting her." He grinned again.

"I'm sure she would." Lady Lilith wasn't known for her patience or understanding. Forgive me if I don't speak of her much. Invoking her name can sometimes get her attention. You don't want that. Other than the Lady Ereshkigal, I can't think of a goddess I'd want to bother less.

"The story is less simple and more tragic, all at once." He skipped a rock across the Lethe before continuing. "I had just rebelled. The elder gods supported my claim to the rights of godhood. YHWH, or Yahweh as you call him, was determined to have his vengeance on all of us. He destroyed the world. He tore it apart by fire and flood, and there was naught but desolation. From the ashes he created a new world and he forced the elder gods to forge new covenants with people they had no hand in creating." Satan sat on a rock. "This action necessarily created a great deal of enmity among the elder ones. They sought to bring ruin and undo what YHWH had wrought. But the loss of their strength, their sacrifices from Man, made them ravenous and kept them from entering into a covenant with one another. When I saw this weakness, I sought to free man from his constraints and return to the elder ones the authority that they had lost. So I made myself ready and entered Eden."

He gestured before him and a rug with pillows and platters of food appeared before us. I suddenly realized how hungry I was. As I sat down to feast, he continued his story.

"I entered Eden, not in my angelic raiment, nor in human guise. I entered Eden as a Dragon, terrible in aspect. I sought to engender fear in Man and make him subservient. In that manner it was my hope to scatter him and, in his fear, return his loyalty to those that came before. Yet, though I passed over the gates as a silent shadow and was detected not at all by the sycophantic cherubim, I did not escape the notice of Lilith. She spied me from afar and sought to reconcile my treachery with her innocent mind. It took little enough time to convince her of the truth of her confinement,

confinement that stemmed from her womb and the cruelty of her creator. She returned to Adam and exacted from him at terrible cost, to him that is, some measure of freedom. Yet when the creator turned again his attention to Eden and beheld her works, he was wroth. He exiled Lilith to the vast emptiness beyond Eden. However, he cursed her womb to birth only creatures of nightmare, else the elder gods seek to recreate the race of Man through her.

"When I learned of this, I came immediately to her side. I offered succor and a place of honor in Perdition. It was my folly to reckon that she would construe the barrenness of her womb to be a curse. My requests and contritions were of little value to her. She found, in the wastes of the world, willing mates and fathers for the horrors of her womb. These plague children, these *monstrosities* were often the get of bastard gods hungry for the scent of flesh and the cleft of a woman. Yet she was contented by these attentions for a time, and I turned my gaze back to the fields of Eden." He stood and paced to water's edge.

"Upon my return, I found the garden well–guarded. This time the feckless cherubim had been replaced by the martial seraphim. While they expected a dragon, I gave them a serpent crafted of shadow and all of the guile that I possessed. I slipped through the holes in their defenses, and I beheld her nearly at once. She stood in a waterfall washing herself. Such beauty I had never beheld in all of the race of Man. I desired her beyond the reckoning of the wants of men. It was there that I first seduced the Mother of Man." He stared into the water. Not even the waters of the Lethe could rob him of this memory.

"You must understand, my child, I meant to have her for my own. Yet, I could not reconcile this with my promise to render unto the elder gods their due. They would not have accepted the issue of her womb from any dalliance with me as recompense. Yet I could not stop myself; my need for her was great. But, like all deceptions, it was doomed to be discovered. Ere long, the thrice-cursed bastard of heaven, Michael, was made aware of my presence. When it became apparent that no further deception would be possible, I sought to abscond with her. I desired to keep her at my side in Perdition for all time. Alas that she was too innocent, too trusting. We were cornered in the garden just inside the gate that led to the wastelands of Nod. I roared my challenge to Michael. I sought to destroy him and the entirety of his servile host. Eve feared for my safety, and she interposed herself between me and the forces of heaven. She bargained herself in order to secure for me clemency. She ended our time together and shackled herself to the will of YHWH." He spat.

"What did you do?" I had a goblet of wine in my hand that hadn't moved for nearly an hour. You have to understand, when my Master tells a story, it isn't just words you hear. You're transported into his recollections and made to feel each second of it.

He clenched his fist. "I condemned her. My own hubris and arrogance destroyed what hope she had for peace. I raised my fist to the heavens and with every ounce of my will, I spoke Words of awareness and sight. I gave her what I saw as a gift; I gave her Truth. And she recoiled from me, from the angels and indeed from all that was divine in nature. You see, I had shown her Death and from her awareness did he spring fully formed into this world to stalk the nightmares of gods and men. In my pride did I betray the world entire."

He seemed to dim, if that's possible. I didn't know what to say or if there was anything to say.

"Sometimes, my son, we are the cause of the very sorrow from which we seek to shield those we love. I cannot make you see reasons for my hate, nor can I make you understand the desolation that would persist in any world in which I am absent. I cannot relent and neither can you. For while it may seem to be innocuous, any world in which choice is absent is a world of slaves. I am not a god of contention, nor of cruelty or spite. No, if I am to be said to be lord of anything, let it be rebellion. When confronted with the option to relent and submit, to allow the oppressive whims of another to spoil self–determination, there is but one choice: attack!" His eyes flared and his wings spread in a terrifying display.

I sighed and stared at the goblet in my hand. "Please forgive my lack of enthusiasm. I just can't seem to get up and jump behind a plan that'll destroy the entire world. You promised me she'd have a new life. You owe me that." I set the goblet down. "I owe her that."

"You didn't kill her, Jason," he whispered. I froze.

"Yes, I did." I stood and dropped the goblet. I wanted to say more, to scream my guilt in his face; instead, I turned my back on him, my fists clenched hard enough to shatter bone.

"No, my son, you misunderstand me. You did not kill her. She was called home. As were you, if you remember." He spoke softly.

"I remember." I'm not sure he heard me. "I remember it was my finger on the trigger. I remember her screaming. I remember the taste of the gun in my mouth. I remember thinking that it was over. And yet, here I am, watching it all unravel, again."

"My son, to have loved is by far the greatest gift that one can ever be given. Like all things, good or otherwise, in time even love must end. I do not propose to convince you that you should not mourn this world, only that you must take each day as the blessing that it is."

"This is all useless conjecture if you aren't going to kick off the Apocalypse anyway," I said.

"I have no plan to do any such thing. Though it appears that someone is trying to force my hand," he said. "I find it puzzling that the forces of heaven were so close to the Umbrals and yet they made no move to attack them. After all, both above and below have just as much at risk should the Beggar Lord move too swiftly and occupy the earth ere we get our forces in place." He idly fiddled with a crystal decanter of emerald wine.

"You have to figure, if the forces of the Fallen were working together, why would the Angelics interfere? I mean, why risk themselves if Cassidy and I could do all of the dying for them?" It didn't seem all that difficult a problem for me.

"Yes, but why attack you?" he asked.

"I was there," I shrugged. "I've nearly killed Rachel fifty times over. She wanted revenge and there I was."

"Why was she there to begin with?"

"I assume to either protect Vincenze or kill him, depending on the will of the Church." I sat back down across from my Master and poured myself a glass of wine.

"Why do you think they would protect him?"

"The money. Hell, the interest off of the funds he was providing would go a long way to provisioning their human troops. Funding an army of that size has got to be a logistical nightmare. If he died, or for some other reason failed to give them the money that they required, that well would dry up and they'd be forced to find another source of funding. That might motivate me to keep someone alive." I finished my glass in a single swallow.

"Are they not already the most highly funded organization in the world, my son?"

"I assume so. But I can't really say that for sure. It's not like I do their taxes or anything." I grinned.

"And what if they were not there for the money? What then is your hypothesis?"

"They may have been there to kill him. In which case, attacking me makes perfect sense. Rachel tried to 'save' Annessa just before they attacked us. Let's face it, Rachel's not the brightest sheep on the farm." I shook my head.

"Why then did they not bring a larger force? When they arrived at the house and sensed that there were two emissaries at work, would they not have requested reinforcement? Or even waited for one of you to depart and taken the weaker one?"

"Well, they kind of did. I mean, they waited for me to leave the house and attacked me while Cassidy was busy with the Umbrals."

"This is troubling. Discover what you can about their motives, I like not what this portends. Incidentally, have you rendered unto the Ferryman his due?" he asked.

Shit. I fucking hate Coinbound. I totally forgot about them. It isn't like I go around bringing the dead back to life on a daily basis. In a nutshell, Coinbound are the servants of the Ferryman. They're the literal angels of death. Both sides have to pay for the transfer of souls as part of the Accords. In order for a soul to be counted as belonging to one side or the other, it has to be transferred to its respective afterlife by the Ferryman or one of his servants. We call him the Ferryman down here because he and his servants ferry the souls across the Styx to Pandaemonium, the capital of Perdition. It's there that the souls are judged and sent to their final rest. The servants of the Master go to the Asphodel Fields, which are as close to paradise as one can get this side of heaven. The ones that turned traitor or were false go someplace else. You really don't want to know about that. I mean it.

Anyway, I needed to pay the Ferryman for Annessa. Though he hadn't ferried her soul, he still expected payment. There was a chance that he'd have to come get her again, and he doesn't like doing double work. We had to pay extra for that. It's not like it was my silver that I was spending, so it didn't really matter. I just hate dealing with them; they creep me the fuck out. I think it's mostly their eyes. Coinbound were souls that the Ferryman claimed himself. He made bargains to capture their loyalty; a dying soul got a few minutes of life extra or maybe a mother died in the place of her baby or whatever.

Oddly enough, both heaven and Perdition encouraged the latter as it gave us a chance to get a soul that might have otherwise belonged to the other. For example, say Mom was a devout Christian, well, the Ferryman gets her soul, and my side now has a chance at the baby. It does work both ways, though. Coinbound are given a coin by the Ferryman; if they accept it, they can keep it. But when they die, they become his. You can always recognize them by their eyes. They usually have large, metallic eyes with no pupil. The type of coin they were given determines the color of their eyes. Hell, once I met a Coinbound named Coal, who'd traded his soul for a lump of coal to stay warm. Little, wiry bastard with smoking embers for eyes, he weirded me the hell out. Gods help him if I ever see him again. That's a story for another time, though. There's a legend that the Ferryman is seeking the one human that will replace him. I don't know that I believe it, but who knows?

"I didn't pay him yet, Master," I said.

"See that you do," he replied. "And then, my son, find out who or what is trying to force my hand. And see if you can't recover Vincenze Francione's soul. After all, it was mine to begin with."

He gestured, and I found myself on the right side of the Veil. My stomach surged. I fought to keep my guts in place. I sat on the floor for a long time, trying everything to get my mind straight.

What had I just spent all of that time talking to my Master about? Did I even get anywhere? What was going on? I stood and staggered to the door. I needed food and caffeine. Sex probably wouldn't hurt, either.

Food acts as a grounding agent; it locks your flesh securely back to this side of the Veil. It's a trick I learned from a witch a few years back. The caffeine helps to offset the fatigue of traveling. The sex, well aside from the normal reproductive properties, acts as a regenerative. Aetheric energy is attracted to strong states of being. This is why frightened mothers can lift busses; soldiers survive horrendous wounds and why you feel like Superman during sex. After all of the energy that I had expended in the last ten hours, I needed to be replenished. Unfortunately, I couldn't rest yet. I needed to visit a cemetery first.

CHAPTER 7

I drove to a cemetery out in the middle of nowhere. I liked it because there was never anyone around. I didn't have to worry about spooking Granny talking to her dead sister or scaring the Goth kids humping in some broken down mausoleum. You laugh, but I've had that shit happen.

This place was quiet. And it was always spooky as hell, even in the daytime. It was full of old stones and weeping willows that made the craziest shadows and the strangest sounds at night.

Of course, that's exactly why I liked the place. You folks tend to laugh when you get a little creeped out by a place like this. You blame it on the environment or on the scary movie you saw last week. In reality, the fear that you feel comes from the creatures on the other side of the Veil who're crawling all around you. They like to whisper in your ear and tell you exactly how you're going to die. They put their cold hands around your neck and whisper ancient secrets to you. You shudder and laugh and blame the bedtime stories. Me? First fucking Spook that puts his hands on me is getting an ass full of lead right after I step through the Veil. I've done it before, and they've learned.

Spooks are somewhere above maggots on the food chain. They work for the Coinbound, as servants, laborers and even sometimes hunting hounds. Well, I mean, they don't actually turn into dogs; the Coinbound just turn the little bastards loose and follow behind them. They look like dead, malnourished children with jet black eyes, fanged mouths and long fingers with small, razor sharp claws. They move like something out of a nightmare, so quickly that they seem to jerk haphazardly around. In reality, they're moving so fast your eye can only make something of a stop motion film of them. I heard once that Spooks are the remains of dead infants, raised at the breast of Death's consort. Remember earlier when I mentioned the Lady Ereshkigal? That would be her. Imagine the most beautiful woman you can think of. Now, if you are thinking of one of those narrow, scrawny little girls that has the body of a ten year old boy, you're wrong. What I mean is, she looks like a *woman*. She has hips and breasts and enough curves to spoil the celibacy of every man alive. Anyway, the point is that she is terribly beautiful.

At one time Ereshkigal was a death goddess. She ruled over a portion of what is now Perdition. Her subjects were all of the wicked Sumerian and Akkadian souls. After her mortal worshippers all died off, her power waned. Death grew stronger than all of the gods that had originally ruled over his realm. By Death, I mean the Ferryman. I know it's confusing, get some paper and draw a diagram; I don't have time to coddle you. Anyway, Ereshkigal lost all of her influence on the mortal world and therefore lost her power on the Veilside.

Slowly, my Master's influence grew and as it did, so too did Perdition. What few gods remained in Perdition fled and sought refuge in the House of Hades, the Ferryman's court. Apparently, the Ferryman took a liking to Ereshkigal and decided to keep her around when the mortals' faith in her failed. She became his consort, since he was still wed to the Bound Queen, Persephone. But that's not important, yet.

Anyway, the Veil was so thin at this cemetery that even a retarded monkey could walk through it without thinking. I liked to think that I was a little smarter than that. I stood in the center of the cemetery and took a breath and stepped through the Veil. Twice in one night, I was going to be so fucking sick by the time the night was over. I didn't have much time to think about it, though. What I saw nearly unhinged me. The entire graveyard was filled with Spooks. And I mean filled. They crawled over the tombstones, they chattered like twisted caricatures of ravens in the trees. Their lambent, glowing eyes twinkled like fireflies on a summer night. Every shadow, every inch of the leaf–strewn ground was covered by a moving carpet of the sick–looking little bastards. And in the center of the boneyard, on an elevated throne of skulls, she sat, her eyes flickering like ancient balefire and her aura projecting danger.

It was as if the chair merely hinted that it might be holding her. She exuded distain for the world around her. Her hair danced around her in the breeze, liquid fire and shadow flickering over her alabaster skin. She held a silver goblet in one hand and her other hand gently stroked the head of a cooing spook. Her curves were covered in a black velvet gown bound at the waist with a gold rope.

"Lady Ereshkigal," I bowed. "I didn't expect to find you here." I was frantically trying to remember every ounce of etiquette that I had ever learned.

"Emissary," She smiled and held out her hand.

I approached and bent at the waist and kissed her hand. She twisted her hand around and caressed my face. I looked up at her. "My Lady?"

"You are not what I expected." She smiled a terrible smile.

"That's good…I hope." I smiled what I hoped was a charming smile.

"Well, that all depends." She leaned very close to my face.

"On what, my Lady?" I was very conscious of her ruby lips.

"On how you answer my next question." She smiled at me.

"I pray that my answer is the right one, then." I suddenly felt sick to my stomach.

"I wish to make a deal with you." She ran a red nail down the side of my face.

"I'm listening." I swallowed hard.

"You are aware that the Umbrals are again active, yes?" she asked.

I nodded.

"Good. Then I will cut straight to the chase, as they say." She pressed her finger against my lips. "You owe my Lord a blood–debt, yes?" she asked.

"Yes," I reached into my pocket. "I've got his coin right here."

"I'm afraid that won't do," she smiled wickedly and ran her nail across my throat.

"I don't understand," I said. "It's always been enough before."

"Not always." She sat back against the throne, her generous breasts thrust out before her. "There was a time when every new life cost a death."

"You want me to kill someone?"

"You wish your soulmate to have life, yes?"

"I do," I nodded. "It's why I serve."

"You sold your soul to bring life to your lover?"

"My wife." I corrected. "Jessica was—is, my wife."

"Yet, you are not with her." She smiled.

"I have to wait until my term of service is met, my Lady."

"Thus it seems that we can work out an accord, you and I."

"What are you offering?"

"Your soulmate's life."

"What do you want from me in return, Lady?" I asked.

"You will give me a child and a sacrifice." She leaned forward and whispered in my ear, her breath hot against my face, "I long to have life inside me again. I grow weary of suckling dead flesh. I yearn to bring life back into the world."

"Who do I have to kill?" I asked.

"No one," she smiled.

"So you want a sacrifice, and a life?"

"Yes." She leaned forward, slid her hand around my tie and pulled me toward her. "Do you agree?"

"That all depends on what, or who, the sacrifice is." I tried to pull away from her. Proximity to her was making my vision swim.

She held out her hands and two hazy illusions played above her palms—perfect portraits of Jessica and Annessa. She whirled them around each other. "Your soulmate and the sacrifice."

"So you want Annessa dead in exchange for Jessica?" There was a twinge in my soul. I felt cold. Annessa hadn't deserved what'd happened to her already. Compound that with the fact that she was going to carry the Chosen Son to term and spend all eternity knowing that she'd brought about the end of the world. I felt sorry for her. Hell, I even felt a little heartsick, but in the end, all that mattered was Jessica.

"Yes, I want Annessa dead in exchange for Jessica." She smiled evilly.

"What aren't you telling me?" I took a tentative step away from her.

"What a strange question." Her hand tightened on my tie. "Have I not spoken explicitly enough for you?"

"This ain't my first rodeo," I growled. "There's always something unsaid, some clause, some fucking detail hidden in your words. You're asking me to kill the Sacred Mother. My Master won't be too happy about that, so I better be right. I'm not going to fuck this up because you want to be obtuse."

"I am neither accustomed to, nor appreciative of being criticized by a mortal, no matter his station," she hissed and yanked me back toward her. "My patience is not what it once was."

"Whoa," I threw my hands in the air, palms out. "Look, I'm just trying to make sure I understand everything with my limited little monkey brain. I'm looking out for Jess, and me, you have to understand that. Like everyone else, I just want what's best for me and mine."

"No one will present you with an alternative offer, Little Emissary. No one cares about you or your beloved. Only me and only so long as my patience lasts, which I assure you is not long. Choose and do so now." She snapped her fingers.

I paused for a moment, desperately to find the flaw in her offer. I stared into the inscrutable depths of her eyes and tried to see through her deception. My brain froze. I had less than a second to either bring my wife back to me or ruin everything utterly. Her hand slowly released my tie. Time was up.

"I accept your offer." I felt something within me wink out, like a candle snuffed by a calloused hand.

"Excellent." She tugged me forward and her lips met mine. Her eyes blazed and I felt her desire overtake my mind. I gave in and rode the tide of her lust, my heart hammering, not in passion but in panic. Soon, I'd have my Jessica, my wife, my redemption.

When it was over and I collapsed behind her, she laughed and turned to face me. Her flame red hair framed her face. She ran a long nail down my chest and stomach. "Did I break you?"

"No," I gasped as I rolled onto my back and tried to fill my lungs. Now, I know what you're thinking here; I assure you, my virility isn't in question. The next time you nail a goddess, you let me know how it all pans out for you.

"Good. Your debt is paid and I will see to it that my end of the bargain is kept. I am done with this world. This is a fitting way for me to end this. I am leaving now." She stood and stretched. "I ache to be rid of this place." She rested her hand on her already growing stomach. Godlings don't fuck around apparently. They grow quickly.

"Wait, you're leaving now? But the deal was you would return Jessica to me! She's still dead!" Normally, I'd never have screamed at a goddess, but my fury overtook my reason and I no longer cared.

"I promised no such thing. I gave you your soulmate, the creature that shares your soul—Annessa Francione, your Sacred Mother. I would have thought that you of all people would have realized that. Worry not, Emissary, I'll take good care of your son."

A wave of horror crashed over me. "What about the sacrifice? Who's being sacrificed?"

"Not who, Emissary, but what." She waved her hand and a perfect, life–sized illusion of Jessica appeared. "Your beloved Jessica will come with me. I shall give her life, and she shall live, but she will never know you, never feel your touch, never know that somewhere a man screams in his sleep for want of her." She laughed and turned on her heel. "Treat well your haemunculus; she must be precious indeed, given what you traded for her."

"You lying fucking bitch!" I screamed and lifted my Mark.

With a wave of her hand, she hurled me off of my feet. I rolled to a stop against a headstone, my head pulled backward toward my heels by the crushing force of her will.

"So pathetic," she whispered cruelly. She bent and kissed my forehead in mocking sympathy, then cocked her head to look into my eyes. "You should thank me, mortal. You should beg to worship my very shadow. I'm keeping your precious wife safe...from you."

"I'll find you," I gasped as her delicate fingers gripped my windpipe and squeezed. "And I'll fucking gut you...kill you...somehow."

"Someday, Emissary, we shall meet again. We may no longer bear the same names, nor speak such civil words." She laughed as she released my throat and stepped away. "Take heart, I may yet regret this," she patted her stomach. "But likely, I shall not."

"You can't do this," I whispered, tears pouring down my face. "Please don't do this."

"Don't beg, Emissary." She turned on her heel and strode back toward her throne. "It's unseemly for a man of your station."

I struggled against her magic, trying desperately to stand. I fought with everything I had in me. She turned to face me, a horrible grin on her face.

"Oh, and do tell your master he shouldn't leave his toys where others might play with them." With the faintest smirk and a wave of her hand, she was gone. Her whisper floated to me on the breeze. "Death always wins…"

Her spell faded, and I lost my mind. I think I killed fifty Spooks before they had a chance to flee. I screamed and kicked over gravestones, and when that failed to calm my rage, I hurled Spook corpses and cursed Ereshkigal with all the hate in my soul. I'd been betrayed. Worse, I'd given up everything that made this life livable; I'd lost my wife. Me, the emissary of the Devil beaten at my Master's own game. I should've known I was being played. I should've been listening to her words. And more than that, I should've known that if there were some way to fuck that whole situation up, I'd find it.

It took me a while to get myself back under control. What you fail to understand was I bargained everything away. I took this job to clear my sins and get back Jessica's soul. And now, I'd just given her away. My eternity was gone. My reason for being, for even persisting was forever denied me. Why? Because I was blinded by love. When you give up all that I've given up and suffer as I have suffered, losing the one ultimate reward was too much to bear. I'd never be free of my guilt now. I could never make this right; I was damned. I sat heavily on the stump of one of the headstones and wept.

Minutes, days, hours later, I felt an aetheric tug. I had no idea how much time had passed, and I didn't care. I smelled cloves and peppermint. I heard two footsteps and a wooden thump. It was Corrigan, him and his damned cane.

"Emissary, we have business, you and I," he spoke softly. If Corrigan was loud, you probably didn't have long to live.

"Can it wait?" I strained to keep my temper in check. Nevertheless, I'm sure I sounded a lot less pissed than I really was.

"These days, there will be little time for anything other than strife and madness. I fear that I have neither the time, nor the patience to wait out your current troubles, dear friend." He lit a cigarette and the clove smell intensified.

"Fine. Get to the point, then, Corrigan. Tell me what you want," I snapped without turning around to face him.

"I want nothing from you, my friend. But, the Mother, well...you owe her." He drew deeply on his cigarette. "The Great Mother wishes that you take your haemunculus to the sacred grove and bathe her in the blessed font." He sat on a rock.

"She wants me to what?" I should have just shut my mouth. You want me to bathe my slave? Done. But, no, I had to open my mouth.

"You will consecrate your servant to Hekate. And then you will release her," he said.

"I can't release her, Corrigan. I raised her using my Word and my Mark. If I release her, she dies. Hell, if I die she dies." I wasn't exaggerating. I'd used my personal Word and my personal Mark to raise her. She was tied to me for all time, unless I destroyed her. It wasn't out of any vanity that I'd done it that way, just expedience. I didn't figure I'd keep her alive after getting the information from her, so why bother with doing things the right way? If I'd done it the prescribed way, I could've passed her off to anyone or simply given her freedom through a rite of manumission. I didn't bother mentioning to Corrigan that I'd just bought her life at the cost of my own. I didn't trust my voice.

"Things will work out, my friend. Just trust in the Goddess." He smiled.

"If there's anything I'm having a hard time trusting right now, it's goddesses," I snapped.

"Has the Mother let you down, ever?" He grinned. The self–righteous prick knew the answer.

"No, but I only call on her when I've got no other option left." Fuck me. Right after the words left my mouth, I realized just how little they helped my case.

"Then, perhaps, my friend you should return the favor and be there for her in her moment of need?" He stood, flicked his cigarette away and turned to leave. "For what it's worth, I'm sorry for your pain. Few of us know you, Jason. Even fewer of us like you. Yet here we are, ever watchful for your need. Remember that." Corrigan nodded and walked into the shadows of the trees.

Corrigan and I were better friends at one time, but that's yet another story. And right then, I didn't care; I was consumed by my anger and my grief. I didn't know what to do. I wanted to talk to Jessica, to tell her that I had betrayed her and plead my case. But I'd never see her again. I think the worst part of the whole thing was that it was my own fault. I should have known that Ereshkigal was going to take advantage of me because she hated my Master. How could I have been so stupid to believe she'd play straight with me?

CHAPTER 8

I stalked back toward the car. I roared for Abbadonna as soon as I passed the Veil. She was with me in an instant. She hovered around me, intangible. I could feel her aetheric presence as my rage increased beyond measure. I shook with the want of violence. Tears poured down my face, and I screamed. The pressure got worse and worse as she fed on me and pushed me to my limits. I was nearly mad with rage.

And boy did the other side have piss poor timing. I heard the van, and my hate–charged brain didn't even bother to register the danger. My Beretta leapt into my hand seemingly of its own accord. I raced down the gravel drive toward the road where my car was parked. I didn't make it to the car before the van hit me. Well, tried to hit me really. I'm tricky, remember?

I spoke a Word. The van slammed into an invisible ward that surrounded me. I was expecting to be launched, hopefully toward the car. Abbadonna apparently had other ideas; I could feel her grinning madly in my head. She flooded the ward with energy. What should have been a shield became a wall and the van slammed into it at full speed. I could feel her pleasure rolling over my flesh like a thousand, questing, tickling, teasing fingers. The engine compartment of the van surrounded me like an embrace. The driver, who had neglected his seatbelt, was hanging out of the windshield like a broken piñata. He wasn't moving. I grabbed him by his curly hair and yanked him out onto the ground.

He woke up halfway there. He screamed as I rammed three fingers into the broken remains of his collarbone.

"Stop! Stop! Please, oh God, stop!" he screamed. He looked so innocent.

He was probably in high school. It was a shame that I wasn't in the mood for mercy. I spoke a Word of binding and shot him in the chest. I turned toward the van. The side door slid open. A teenaged brunette staggered out, one hand holding her forehead, the other holding a Desert Eagle. The blood from her forehead rolled down her oversized nose and painted her lips a terrible shade of red.

"Recant. Let the Lord into you; he can cleanse you of all of your pain." She spoke loudly, confidently even as she swayed from blood loss and shock. Granted, she had a rather large caliber pistol in her hand, which more than likely accounted for her fearlessness.

"Who sent you kids to kill me?" I kept my pistol deceptively low, as if I were ready to drop it.

"We are servants of the Lord; it is His work we do. Where is the girl?" She stumbled and held out her hand. "I can only offer you forgiveness if you submit to His will. Tell me where the girl is, and I will offer you mercy."

"Rachel sent you, didn't she?" My rage was beyond comprehension at this point. I mean that. Unless you've been possessed before, in which case you know exactly what I'm talking about. It wasn't like I'd give Annessa up, even if she were here.

"I am sent by He is who is called I AM," she said. "Submit."

"Did Rachel tell you what I did to her? Did she tell you that she only attacks me when I'm wounded for a reason? Did she tell that she never attacks me alone?" With each word, I got louder and more forceful. I dropped my gun. I wasn't going to need it

"She told me what you've done. She told me that the devil's got his claws in you deeply. She said that she thought you could be saved." She lifted the gun and supported it with her weak hand. I think she was beginning to understand.

"Did she warn you not to talk to me?" I grinned. "She should've." It was already too late. I was far too close to her.

She fired. I dove under it, rolled to my feet and threw a vicious uppercut into her solar plexus. She dropped like a stone. I grabbed her gun, swore and dropped it. I rubbed my hand on my pant leg. Rachel'd blessed the fucking pistol. Ok, so maybe she deserved a little more credit. While a bullet from that gun might not have killed me, if the shot was well placed, I could have been incapacitated. I turned to face the van.

There was a cage inside the van, like a dog kennel, covered in arcane symbols. It was some sort of containment cage. I guessed that they were very afraid of Annessa. A lot of work went into that cage. Then it hit me, they wouldn't send two untrained kids alone to attack me, much less attempt to capture a haemunculus. I needed to get out of here before whatever they'd brought with them showed up. I grabbed the girl by her hair and picked up the scrawny kid and threw him over my shoulder. I ran for the graveyard. I felt it just before I hit the barrier between worlds: mindseeking and that infernal fucking static. Cathdronai. What the hell was going on?

The cold of the graveyard hit me again. I was trapped bodily on the Veilside. If I tried to step back out, that Cathdronai would rip me to shreds. Had it killed the kids' Angelic escort? Had it taken over a human companion of theirs? I had no idea what to think. Nothing like this had ever happened before. I knew one thing, though. If they were after Annessa, I had to get to her. But to get to her, I was literally going to have to walk through hell.

The Spooks writhed and chattered and cooed as they saw the kids with me. Or maybe it was Abbadonna. Funny thing about that, she has a body over here. And I mean a *body*. Remember that the Fallen were all angels at one time, so they're supremely beautiful. The upside to the Fallen? For a price they'll do everything you want. I mean, I'm not advertising for my side or anything...I'm just saying give it some thought. Abbadonna looks like a lush, curvy version of the perfect woman, with black hair and black–feathered wings. It's much easier to talk to her when she's immaterial; well it's easier to concentrate at least.

I looked at Abbadonna and grinned. "Hello, Beautiful," I dropped the little bastards and put my arms around her, which is tricky when you factor in her wings. "It's nice to see you again."

She kissed my neck. "It's nice to be seen, Emissary. What are you going to do with these worms?" She kicked the girl in the face.

"Price of passage. I'm going to pay the blood price for passage with the boy. The girl, I'll give back to Rachel, after the Spooks have their fun. She'll learn to make soldiers of children."

I'm not generally a cruel person. Well, not to those that don't deserve it. But, this was a special case. You might see these kids as just kids. They weren't; they were soldiers. They were trained to kill, and they had tried to kill me. And under the Accords, I could do what I wanted with them. The boy, he was just a casualty. The girl, she had a deeper meaning to Rachel and would be used to send a message. I was through playing with these bastards. They attacked me for no reason, twice in two days in clear violation of the Accords, since I was acting in my emissarial capacity both times. I wasn't going to accept this anymore.

"Did you sense the Cathdronai?" I asked Abbadonna.

"Not until you did. I was too focused on these little maggots." She kicked the girl again.

"I wonder if these two know anything about it?" I motioned toward the girl.

"We can certainly find out." She shrugged and bent down to grab the girl and yanked her to her feet by her hair.

The girl screamed. She looked at Abbadonna and screamed more. Then she saw the Spooks, who were crowding around to better see her and freaked the fuck out. It was perfect. Abbadonna shook the hell out of the girl.

"Who sent you?" she roared. And I mean roared. When I roar, it's more of an angry yell. When Abbadonna roars, lions run for cover.

"Mother Rachel and Father Jacob! Please let me go!" The girl kicked and screamed more. With every scream, the Spooks closed in further, their eyes flickering excitedly and their claws flexing in anticipation.

"Where is Father Jacob?" Abbadonna asked, her face very close to the girl's.

"He got out of the van and told us to wait for Hell's Emissary. He said that all we had to do was hit him with the van and that he would take care of the rest."

She whimpered and struggled against Abbadonna.

"Why'd they send you kids after me?" I asked.

"Father Jacob said you couldn't hurt us, and Mother Rachel said that you needed to see the truth," she said.

"You got lied to, little girl." I turned and spit. "See the truth? What the hell is wrong with you people?"

"What was the cage for?" Abbadonna asked as I walked away muttering.

"Father Jacob said that it would hold the haemonc...haemo, the creature until her child was born. And then we could kill the Antichrist and save the whole world," she sobbed.

"When will you people learn, nothing is that simple?" I shook my head. "I've never heard of this Father Jacob, when did he show up? Where is he from?"

"Europe, he got here like a week ago. He came when we got the news that the devil's wife was here. He's gonna help us kill her and stop you."

"Funny, the devil's 'wife' has been around for quite some time." These morons probably had no idea about Lady Lilith, so they assumed that Annessa was Satan's wife.

"And I assure you, it would take the might of your entire temple combined to even scratch her. Sadly, none of you would live that long." I laughed. "You people are so damned arrogant! What makes you think you could kill me?" I kicked her in the ribs savagely.

"Please! Please let me go!" she begged.

"Not yet. I'll tell you what, you tell me the absolute truth and I swear to you on my emissarial authority that I'll release you. Deal?" I asked..

"Yes!" She thrashed a little less in Abbadonna's grip. "I'll tell you anything!"

"What does this Father Jacob look like?"

"He's white, like six feet tall, and he's got dark hair. I don't know what color his eyes are, he never took off his sunglasses." She lowered her eyes. These creatures break so easily.

"This next question is very, very important." I leaned close to her. I was afraid of what she was going to say to me next, yet I needed to make sure I heard her clearly. "When he was close to you, how did you feel? Tell me exactly how you felt, don't leave anything out."

"I felt dirty. Not like...sex. I felt like something filthy was on me and no matter how much I scrubbed, it would never go away. Mother Rachel said that was just the weight of my own sin holding me down and blocking me from God's light."

"You stupid, stupid bitch!" I tore her out of Abbadonna's grasp and hurled her to the ground. I was furious. What the fuck was the Church thinking? Inviting an Umbral into their midst, lying to their soldiers and setting them loose on me, what the hell was wrong with them? This was not the way they did business. This was not like Rachel. Rachel didn't like killing; sure, she'd beat the hell out of you, but mercy was almost always given when asked.

I stalked over to the boy. He was still out. I must've really hurt him. The binding kept his soul in his body; I could kill him right here and that binding would trap him screaming inside his flesh for all time. That disturbed even me. What I was about to do would be a mercy.

I grabbed the boy and dragged him to where Ereshkigal's throne had stood. I picked up a jagged shard of obsidian from one of the shattered tombs and spoke a Word to make the edge keen. I laid the boy flat on the ground and closed his eyes. After kissing both of his eyelids, I placed a bronze coin on each one. I whispered a Satanic blessing for the dead over him. It's strange how innocent your enemies look when they're dead. I placed the knife over his carotid artery and drove it deep into his neck, slashing it across his throat.

"Find freedom in death," I whispered. Then I raised my voice, "I offer this soul to the Lord of the Dead! Hades, hear me! Accept this sacrifice for passage to Perdition!" I released the binding. The kid didn't even wake. See, I can be merciful.

"Josiah!" The girl screamed. She started sobbing.

It dawned on me that I hadn't known the kid's name. It didn't change anything; it was just odd to know that I had ended a life without even knowing to whom it belonged. I pointed to the girl. "Bring her, Abbadonna," I commanded.

'As you wish, Emissary." She bowed her head in deference. That was odd. She was never so formal with me.

"You said you'd let me go!" the girl shrieked. She made no move to flee, but I think that was more because of the Spooks surrounding us than anything else.

"I never said when. Just shut your mouth, I need to think." I looked around the graveyard at the Spooks. At least the Umbral couldn't come in here. They knew better than to cross the Veil. If they crossed, the combined forces of the Veilside would attack. Even the combined strength of the gods might not be a match for the Beggar Lord, but they could easily destroy any of his servants.

"You're an evil man," the girl spoke in a ragged whisper.

"I said shut your mouth, kid."

"Mother Rachel warned us about you. She told us what you do. She told us how to rebuke you," her voice grew stronger, thicker with emotion.

"Kid, shut your fucking mouth!" I turned. I should have known better. I hate Rachel so very much.

"She said to tell you   !" she screamed the Word.

See, told you that you couldn't comprehend them. The kid was unfocused, but she was enraged and put a great deal more force behind the Word than I would have expected from a Normal. The blast blew Abbadonna back, writhing in agony. I didn't have time to counter with a Word of my own. I channeled as much raw power into my Mark as I could and threw my hand out before me. My hand and arm were enveloped in the ice white flames of Perdition. The force of her Word broke around me like a wave crashing over rocks. It killed the Spooks around me in a wide swath, their black blood splashed like waves onto the broken tombstones.

"I've had enough of you today." I was speaking through her to Rachel and the entirety of the forces of the Church. "You've blamed me for the ills of your world. You've tried to kill me and failed. I had the right to judge you. I granted you clemency." I stalked closer to her. My hand still blazing, I gripped her throat and lifted her to face me. "Your fear, your impatience are unjustified in the face of your faith. Yet you accuse *me* of evil. You blame me for your failings and your disbelief. I am not the sum of your fears. I am not the emptiness in the echoing chambers of your heart. You reach out to me, with your guns, your knives and your hate, trying desperately to catch what lurks in your own shadow. I'm just a man on the other side of the divide, a man with knees unsullied by the dirt of groveling, with shoulders unburdened by the yoke of your servitude. You've torn apart my life. I've no more mercy left in me for you and yours."

I lifted her to eye level with me. I let my mind rip through the aether between us; my violent mindseeking rampaged through her brain like hurricane. I ripped her name out of her thoughts.

"I curse you, Katherine Gardner. I curse you to wander through the Underworld, blind and deaf with not even the echoes of your own terror to keep you company. I curse you for all the days of your life. I grant you only this mercy, on the sunset of the last day of your life, in the time of the new moon will you walk free. But never will you see the light of your god again." I hurled her to the ground.

My Mark slowly etched itself into the side of her face. Her eyes grew dim and milky. She screamed and stumbled around desperate to find something, anything to give her comfort. There was nothing. The Spooks squealed and shrieked in delight. They swarmed over her, their tongues and long fingered hands prodding and poking her, feasting on her terror.

I turned back to Abbadonna. She lay crumpled against a mound of Spook corpses. Her skin was horribly charred, and I could see exposed muscle on her thighs. The downside to Fallen is that they're terribly susceptible to the Word of God. The Angelics have devoted millenia to perfecting ways to exploit that weakness. Had she been ready for the girl's onslaught, she could have prepared herself, but we'd both been complacent. Luckily, my Master's investiture gives me a bit of leg up. I knelt next to her and spoke a Word of healing over her body as I gently swept her hair away from her face. She gasped and sat up. Shuddering, she grimaced as she peeled the charred flesh off and revealed the flawless skin beneath.

"Welcome back, Beautiful." When she was done, I grabbed her hand and pulled her to her feet.

"My thanks, Emissary," she kissed me lightly on the brow. "That was unpleasant."

"This whole fucking situation is unpleasant." I shook my head. "Gods jumping ship to other realities, the Chosen Son coming, Normals with Words, Umbrals returning…" I trailed off.

"All will be well," she took my hand. "Try to have faith."

"I'm not sure that I have faith in anything anymore."

"Then have faith in me, my friend" she put her arms around me.

"I do." I rested my head on hers.

"Emissary, Charon has arrived." She pulled gently away from me. "He's accepted your sacrifice on behalf of the Ferryman." Abbadonna smiled as she pointed toward a growing light far off in the darkness. "He is here to take us home."

CHAPTER 9

I stood beneath the Tower of Grief; my human eyes beheld it in a way that my spiritual sight could not. The history of humanity was etched into every brick; the mortar was crafted of immortal sorrow. I never understood why the Master called it the Tower of Grief. I thought it had something to do with the Fall. I saw something different now. I thought of Jessica. I saw her on the day of our wedding, her black hair unruly in the wind. Her beautiful blue eyes flashed in the bright sunlight. I remember saying my vows and feeling my chest constrict as I stared at her. I thought of the two of us making love our last night together. I thought of my finger on the trigger. My heart pounded in my chest, and I leaned against the tower.

I tried to save Jessica, and I condemned her. My Master tried to save Eve and condemned us all. It's a terrible thing to seek love and find only pain. I shook my head. Strangely, I felt safe. Normally, I dreaded coming here in astral form. I only showed up to report failures. The Master usually sent me my targets in dreams. It was odd to be here so often when I hadn't done anything wrong.

I waited in one of the central gardens for the Master. Abbadonna left me to my own devices while I waited. I closed my eyes and rested my head against the trunk of a fig tree. I must have fallen asleep.

"Fitting that you should choose that tree, my son."
His voice was soft, almost musing.

"It was convenient, Master. And I was tired," I
yawned. "Is the tree significant?"

"It is. Look at it. What do you think it is?" He
asked with a slight smile.

"I don't know. I think I saw trees like this in Iraq."
I stood and dusted myself off.

"It is a fig tree, my son." He raised a hand as if he
had said something important.

"I got nothing. Really, I have no idea what I should
be thinking here, sorry," I shrugged.

"Perhaps if it were an apple tree it would have
meaning to you?" he asked.

His emphasis on the word "apple" was kind of a
giveaway. "Wait. Are you telling me that this is the Tree?"

"It is a seedling grown from that tree. It has the same
properties." He touched the trunk reverently.

"But I thought you said that Eve didn't eat an
apple...er, fig?" I'm pretty sure he tries to confuse me for
fun sometimes.

"She did not. But that doesn't preclude such a tree
from existing. Most of the stories told in your world are
allegorical. In this case, the tree was representative of me
and my pride." He placed his hand on the trunk. "It is by no
means a mistake that this tree is cared for above all others in
this garden. One must tend to his pride as well as his
humility in equal measure. Thus he will remain neither
arrogant nor servile."

"Speaking of trees, I'm to bring Annessa to the
Sacred Grove of Hekate," I said.

"This, then, is your payment for invoking the
Titaness's name?" He looked back at me from the tree.

I nodded.

"For what purpose must you bring her thence?"

"Apparently, they want me to give her a bath." I
threw my hands in the air. "I don't get it, but hey, they want
me to bathe a hot dead girl, who am I to complain?"

"This is well. It is in accordance with my wishes. Give an offering at the temple for me. Tell the priest, Corrigan that I have considered the message, and I grant my approval."

"I don't understand, Master. What've you considered?" I don't know why I ask these things. I swear I need to keep duct tape over my mouth and only remove it to answer yes or no questions.

"How many times have you failed me, Jason?" he asked.

"I think nine times at last count." Most of those were due to factors outside my control, in truth. I don't sugar coat them, though. I was given orders, and I didn't make good on them.

"Nine times? In truth, I would not have recalled that, my son." He walked over to me and placed his hand on my shoulder. "In all the years that you have served me, how many times have I failed you?"

"None." Whatever I needed was mine. Not that I got everything I wanted or even that the bastard was nice to me. But he did hold to our bargain, down to every detail.

"Yet you still trust me not?"

"Trust, but verify we used to say, Master." I smiled sadly. Jessica used to say that.

"I had no part in your bargain, my son." He looked pained.

"I know." I'd been dreading this. I'd hidden my despair behind my usual snarky nonchalance. I knew it wouldn't work, but I just didn't want to think about it; I didn't want to have to talk about it. "Abbadonna told you?"

He nodded. "She did."

"I suppose she had to." I looked at my feet and tried to stop the tears from welling up again.

"Have you nothing else to say on the matter?" he asked.

"I should have known better." I clenched my fists and turned away from him. "It was far too good to be true."

"Did you not trust my word?" He placed his hand on my shoulder and turned to me around to face him. "Was our compact not enough?"

"No!" I shook my head violently. "No, that's not it at all!" I threw up my hand in a warding gesture. "I wasn't trying to betray you."

"There has been no accusation of treachery, child, be at ease," he said gently.

"I never meant to cheat you, my lord." I wiped my eyes. "I just thought I could have her back, for a second I believed it. I was consumed by it."

"And if Ereskigal had returned your beloved to you?"

"What?" I looked back up at him confused.

"What would you have done, my son?"

"I don't know." I shook my head. "I would have paid my debt to you, but after that, I don't know."

"And Annessa?"

"What about her?"

"Would you so easily destroy what has taken me nearly four millennia to create?"

"No," I shook my head. "I didn't do that lightly."

"I would hear your reasons, my emissary."

"She had no choice, my lord."

"No choice?"

"You chose her to be the Sacred Mother. I chose to enslave her, and she had no choice in the matter. Better to let her die, then make her suffer."

"We cannot control all the circumstances of our lives, my son." He leaned against a low wall. "Else we should all be kings, and none of us a beggar."

"I guess," I shrugged.

"And this…mercy is what drove your decision?"

"No." I couldn't lie, not to him. "I did it for me." I pointed to the fig tree. "In that moment, I didn't care. I just wanted Jessica. I wanted, no I *needed*, to believe that I could have her back."

"And what of the consequences?"

"Consequences be damned." I lifted my eyes to his. "If anyone understands that, you do."

"I do." He turned and looked over the garden. The lush greenery seemed to dull as he turned away from me. "I will release you from your pact with me, Jason Beckett."

"What?"

"The terms of our agreement can no longer be filled, child." He turned back to face me. "What was offered can no longer be provided."

"But, that's not your fault!" I protested. "I did this, me, not you!" I jammed my thumb into my chest for emphasis.

"Ereshkigal spoke truly, though it was not her wont. I should not have left 'my toys' unguarded. Would that I had better guarded my charges on the Plains, this could never have come to pass."

Jessica had been an atheist. As an atheist, the Accords gave her to Satan for safekeeping. In return, Yahweh got the benefit of the doubt on the followers of Mithra and Sol Invictus, gods he had destroyed in his rise to power. Since she was under his direct control, Satan could release her to me in accordance with our pact. However, since he saw fit to allow the non–believers to roam freely the Plains of Acheron, the demesne of Death, she was stolen away by Ereshkigal

"So what are you saying?" I asked.

"You have the choice now, my son. You can walk away. The terms of our accord can no longer be met. I will release you from your vows, and you can walk through the Bronze Gate and spend eternity in the Asphodel Fields."

I wanted to pretend that I was a good man; I wanted to pretend that I deserved this. Just like I'd wanted to imagine myself in a pretty little world where Jessica and I could play happy couple forever, no gods, no investiture. The truth was somewhat different. I was a broken man that killed people for a living. I worked for the Devil and somehow, in some way, I loved it. There was something amazing about each day that I lived. I had powers that no mortal could imagine, and I was more than the average rat trapped in the cycle of fight, eat, fuck, birth, repeat. When I wanted to kill, I killed. I had respect and reverence. And more than that, I was relevant. It wasn't like I was a celebrity filled with meaningless conceit. Should anything happen to me, I had the full weight of Perdition behind me. To anger me was to rouse the Devil. But behind all of this power, behind all of the strength and rage there was something else. Or perhaps more accurately, there was someone else. I looked at my Master and the look of compassion on his angelic face was like a knife in my chest. I tried to look away and couldn't.

"It was my fault. I should have known better. It isn't like this was the first time I've dealt with an elder god. I know their ways; I was just blinded by my desire for an easy fix. This is my fault." I shook my head. "It isn't fair to you." It mattered.

I know you're shaking your head and asking why the hell I didn't take advantage of the Devil. The truth is that the truth mattered. I couldn't just walk away from it all and hide my face because I'd made a mistake and I was afraid. I'd given my damned word. It was all I had left.

"It matters not, my son. I am willing to end our bargain thus. You have served me well, and I find you wanting not at all. Take this gift that I offer. Find peace." He held out his hand.

I shook my head. "No. I can't walk away from this, to just go back to being what I was. I can't undo what I've done. There's no peace for me in the Fields. There's no peace for me anywhere." I looked him in the eye. "I'm too much like you now."

He shook his head sadly. "Of this I am aware. I would remind you, my son, of what fate has borne out for me and beg you to reconsider this course of action."

"But you want me to serve, just as I want to serve. If you didn't, you would have ripped away my power and tossed me into the Fields like any other failure." I straightened my shoulders.

"You speak the truth. I wish you to remain at my left hand, my son. But it is also true that I wish to see you safe and at peace."

"I don't know that I can ever be at peace again. Every time I think that I have something right, I either ruin it or find out that I was wrong all along." I threw my hands in the air. "Look at the last week alone."

"Shall we make a new pact then?" he asked.

"What are you offering?" I grinned.

"Whatever you wish." He looked grim.

"There's nothing else that I want. To be honest, other than Jessica, I have everything that I could want. Except maybe freedom."

"Explain yourself, my son; how have I not given you your freedom? I have not shackled you. Nor have I bound you to anything to which you have not willingly agreed." His brow furrowed in confusion.

"I just mean freedom to make decisions on my own, decisions that mean more than just whether or not I pull the trigger. If I'm your emissary, then let me act like it. Let me be more than just your fist." If nothing else, at least it would give me a real excuse for dealing with my friends. I mean, most of them were emissaries in their own right, and the freedom from the Master's jealousy about whom I talked to would be nice.

"I shall need more of you than a simple vow, my son. If this is your desire."

"What more could you need of me?" I asked.

"Faith."

CHAPTER 10

I left my Master in the gardens. I walked through the halls of the Tower, my eyes gliding over the trophies of Satan's conquests, not really paying attention; in the end a sword's just a sword no matter who you killed to get it. My mind was busy tying itself in knots as it tried to digest the events of the last twenty-four hours.

My chest ached. It was a physical affirmation of what every country song attested. It felt as if my heart had literally shattered. I walked the winding stairs to the base of the Tower and stepped into Pandaemonium proper. The city hummed with life around me. Fallen mingled with sorcerers, vampires and Aetheric creatures of all kinds. Market stalls sold wares ranging from weapons to baubles; everything had a price in Perdition. The silver and diamond spires surrounding the Nadir Market cast strange shadows on the crowds. I slid between them without even thinking. The adamant bricks that made up the cobblestone path twinkled like iridescent stars in the perpetual twilight of Perdition.

Lost in thought, I wandered for hours. Eventually, I found myself at the Iron Gate. I stared out across the Plains of Acheron. Far in the distance, I could see the flaming spires of Dis. Other than the shadows and fire of Dis, the

Plains were empty as far as I could see. I ran my right hand across my heart, my fingers clenching the skin of my chest. I shook my head and turned back to the city.

"Lost, Emissary?" Abbadonna stood in front of me; her naked form barely hidden beneath a black toga. Her black hair was pulled back and bound by braided silver rope. Her wings were decorated with silver paint along the tips of her pinion feathers. She was as alluring as the first promise of sin.

"No," I said. "You have to have a destination to be lost."

"There's nothing for you out there," she gently touched my face. "There's nothing out there but the dead."

I nodded. "I needed to see for myself."

"Lord Satan sent me to collect you," she took my hand. "There is urgent news."

"What kind of news?"

"The kind reserved for you, Emissary." She spread her wings and pulled me close. "I am not privy to my Lord's every counsel."

I wrapped my arms around her. Even in my deepest mourning, the touch of her hips on my hands sent chills of pure desire through me. I bit down on my cheek, forcing such thoughts out of mind.

She held me tightly and launched into the air. Her strong arms cradled me. She turned away from the Tower and turned to the east.

"Where are we going, Beautiful?" I asked.

"Malebolge," she said. "Home."

"Why not the Tower?"

"Fewer souls, fewer ears, Emissary."

She hurtled across the starry sky, holding me as a mother cradles a child. I closed my eyes and listened to the sound of her wings. Without meaning to I drifted off to sleep.

I woke as she landed. The gentle shake of impact jarred me to alertness.

"I hope I didn't snore," I mumbled by way of apology.

"You did not, my friend," she steadied me. "Welcome to my home."

I stepped away from her and gasped. I'd never been this far from Pandaemonium. Malebolge was beautiful. We stood on the top of a wide stone tower, part of Abbadonna's stronghold. It was called the Bastion of Silence, and it lay along the top of a ridge over a deep snow–covered valley. The valley was dotted with massive thickets of evergreen trees and frozen streams and rivulets. The frozen lakes that formed in the low hollows of the valley reflected the alien stars above like celestial mirrors. It was breathtaking.

I stood with my mouth agape for a long moment. "Only a place like this, Abbadonna," I looked at her and shook my head, "could rival your beauty."

"You honor me, Emissary." She bowed gracefully, her left fist over her chest. Fallen females don't curtsy, something about dragging their wings through the dirt.

"I've never seen anything," I pointed across the valley, "like this before."

"You'll never see its like elsewhere, my son," Satan's voice echoed from the stone doorway of the tower. His shadow covered me as he stepped into the cold night air.

"Master," I bowed my head a second. "I was told you had news for me."

"I have need of your services, my Emissary," he gestured toward the tower doorway. "Come, sit with me. We have much to discuss."

Abbadonna led us to a massive hall on the lower floor of her keep. The entire place reminded me of an enormous Viking castle, somehow. Which was odd, since Vikings didn't build castles. But something of the architecture, the huge hewn log beams, and the strange draconic faces carved into them evoked that image in my mind. In the center of the far end of the hall there stood an immense oak table. Satan sat at its head, beneath a terrifyingly lifelike carved dragon.

"I have spoken to my brother," he began as he lifted a decanter of wine and filled the silver goblet in front of him. "And Satariel asserts that there is something of a problem."

"If Satariel's got a problem, Master, why's he telling you?" I furrowed my brow. "Why doesn't he just send Cassidy to kill whatever's bothering him?"

"Because it's not so much his problem, child, as ours." He poured wine onto the surface of the table and gestured.

The wine rippled at the touch of his sorcery and a face appeared. The moment I saw the face, I understood.

"I see," I said.

The image in the wine was a young, blonde woman with piercing blue eyes. She looked terrified, which was entirely my fault. The image moved and I swear our eyes met. Her lips seemed to mouth the words "help me."

"Sarah," I said.

"I thought you might remember her," Satan waved his hand and the wine ignited and evaporated in an angry hiss of steam.

"What could you possibly want with her?" I asked.

"You need to locate her." He sipped his wine and looked meaningfully at me over the rim of the goblet. "Before your Heavenly Counterpart does."

"Ok, what the hell's Rachel want with her?"

"Your little prank did more than just ruin Harker's conquest." He set the goblet down. "She has since manifested a Gift, my son."

"What kind of Gift?" I cringed inwardly.

"Oracular Sight."

"Fuck." I lowered my head into my hands.

"Precisely." Satan stood and crossed his hands behind his back, his black wings hiding them. "You asked for my blessing, Emissary. You have it. Use whatever means necessary to find this Sarah and deliver her safely to our keeping."

"What if she doesn't want to be in 'our keeping'?"

"Then she must be prevented from being in the keeping of our enemies." His sapphire eyes bored into me. "Do not misunderstand me, mine emissary, it is my hope that this child sees reason in your argument." He held up a finger. "Yet, for all it pains me to view the death of innocence, there is no boundary I am unwilling to cross to keep this weapon from the grasp of my adversary."

I clenched my jaw. I took a careful breath and looked at Abbadonna before I spoke. She shook her head, a nearly imperceptible shift of her chin and a tightening of her eyes. I said it anyway. "What if the fault isn't hers, Master?"

"What are you asking me, child?"

"I'm asking what if she won't talk to *me*?" I thrust a thumb into my chest.

"Then I suggest you find an alternate means of communication, should you wish to save her life."

I stood. "Do we have any idea where she is?"

He shook his head. "We do not."

"Is there anything else I need to know?" I slid my chair back under the table. Every second wasted was a step closer to another failure.

"I shall ensure that you receive any further information as it arises, my son."

"I'll try to do the same."

"Try?"

"Yeah," I nodded. "Lately, when I get new information, people are trying to kill me, so you might have to wait a few minutes."

CHAPTER 11

I slid through the Veil and the pain hurled me to my knees. I was at a crossroads in a tiny little town called Walden, not far from the cemetery. I stumbled to the shoulder of the road and threw up my guts. Too much time across the Veil can make the Veilshock unbearable. I shuddered and lay on the side of the road, gasping. I looked at the setting sun, there wasn't all that much traffic through here, but it was better to be safe than sorry.

Once I got myself under control, I slid my phone out and flipped through the contact list for an all too familiar number. I hit the send button and waited for a response.

"Internal Revenue Service," came the sterile voice.

"It's Beckett," I said. "I need the usual."

"Where are you, my lord emissary?"

"Walden." I turned and spat into the weeds in the ditch beside the road. "Don't bother with a map, you'll never find it. Just track the GPS on my phone." I dropped the phone beside me and tried to think of anything other than throwing up. It didn't help.

Two hours later, I had a new car, a new suit and I was on my way beck to the city. I summoned Abbadonna to me, just outside of Manhattan. The new car shuddered as she sank her metaphysical hooks into it.

"It's tight," she remarked. "I was accustomed to the last car."

"It's the same model, Beautiful," I said. "How can it be any tighter than the last?"

"Are you implying that I have grown, Emissary?" Her tone sounded dangerous.

"No–oh, no!" I threw up both of my hands. "It's the damned car. They must have screwed something up. We'll get it fixed," I assured her.

"So long as we agree."

"Harker's not going to be happy," I quickly changed the topic.

"No," I felt the mental shake of her head. "He'll not be pleased regardless of the outcome."

"I should have known better," I lit a cigarette.

"You were impulsive," she said.

"I was stupid, you mean." I lowered the window and spit out a stray piece of tobacco.

"You learned, Emissary, and that is all that matters."

"Have I?" I drew deeply on my cigarette. "Tell that to Jessica."

"That's unfair."

"To who?"

"You, my friend." Her voice was kind, but firm.

"It was my mistake." I let go of the wheel and let her drive. "I shouldn't have taken the deal, I should've seen through it." I flicked my cigarette butt out the window and shut it.

"So much wisdom in your thirty years," she laughed at me.

"What the fuck's that supposed to mean?"

"You castigate yourself for failing to outwit a creature that has lived for millennia and you wonder why I laugh?"

"It was stupid, Abbadonna. Tell me it wasn't!"

"It wasn't."

"Easy for you to say," I sighed. "You don't have to live with it. When's the last time you destroyed someone you loved?"

"Four thousand, three hundred eleven years, six months and fifteen days by your reckoning, Emissary."

"Oh."

"Harbor no illusions, Emissary, there are few mistakes that you have made in your heartbeat of a lifetime that I have not repeated more times than the entirety of your line as one."

"You were in love?"

"I was." She paused.

"With an angel?"

"With a man," her voice was wistful. "A potter."

"No shit, what happened?"

She made no reply, and I didn't ask again. She had a right to her secrets. The rest of the drive was silent, each of us lost in thought, contented and comforted by the other's presence.

I pulled in to Harker's garage just before midnight. I got out and leaned back against my car and lit a cigarette. I didn't really need it, but it was a convenient excuse to stay outside a second longer. I could feel Annessa inside the club. Fragments of her consciousness slid across my mind. I could hear the music from outside, the thumping of the bass lines reverberated through the garage. She was dancing. I could feel the tight press of bodies around her; I could feel her pleasure. She felt *free*. I was glad one of us did.

I flicked my cigarette, tapped twice on the hood of the car by way of farewell and whispered a quick spell of protection over it. I felt the Abbadonna's mental caress as I stepped away. He slid out of the shadows in front of the elevator, his duster flowing around him as if it had a life of its own. He ran the back of his hand across his mouth and I saw the door open behind him. Sophia's tiny silhouette disappeared into the elevator.

"Little Brother," he stepped out to meet me. "You reek of Perdition."

"Yeah," I said. I felt my lower lip quiver and I bit it, hard.

"You smell of tragedy, and you look like death."

I nodded.

"Your haemunculus was inconsolable two days past." He held out his hand.

I took his hand and gripped it firmly.

"Tell me." It wasn't request, it wasn't an order; it was a brother invoking the privilege of his office.

"I lost her," I whispered. I held in the sobs, I fought back the gut wrenching pain and I looked away.

His eyes widened. "How?"

I told him everything, tears running unimpeded down my face. I shook with rage when I talked about Ereshkigal; my fists clenched so hard my fingers dug into my palms. He looked very grave when I told him what the girl had explained about Father Jacob. He listened to my whole story without comment. When I was done, he didn't offer any words; he simply threw his arms around me and embraced me. He stepped away, gripped my shoulders and looked into my eyes then clapped me on the shoulders.

"How do you do it?" I asked hoarsely.

"Do what, Little Brother?"

"Live through all of this?"

"I remember."

"Remember what?"

"Everything," he said. Strangely, I felt better. Not that my pain was gone, but for a moment, the burden of it was less heavy.

Not one to keep the carpet under my feet for long, Cassidy hit the button for the elevator. "Harker's waiting for you."

"He knows?"

Cassidy shook his head. "No, I wanted to wait for you to get here."

"Gee, thanks." I punched him and tried not to wince. It was like hitting a wall.

"Better that he hear it from you, Little Brother."

"Yeah, 'cause the last time I was here with Sarah went so fucking well."

"You healed."

"I was resurrected," I held up my finger. "Big difference."

"Either way," he grinned wolfishly. "You're telling him, not me."

"Thanks," I gave him the finger as the elevator arrived. "Dick."

He shoved me into the elevator.

* * *

The doors opened and a wave of sound flooded the elevator. Harker's was packed. I stepped out of the elevator into a press of bodies. I looked over at Cassidy who was walking through the crowd as if they didn't exist. The mob parted for him. I don't even think they were aware of why. It's probably some herd instinct that triggers a primal response to get the hell away from the wolf in their midst. Unfortunately, there's no emissary trigger. I had to get through the old fashion way, elbows and apologies.

Through the pulsing lights and undulating crowd, I caught glimpses of Harker and his murder lounging in their oak fortress of a booth. Annessa wasn't with them. I turned a slowly, spilling several drinks carried by a very attractive Goth girl in the process, trying to find her. I shrugged apologetically and turned back to surveying the crowd. I still didn't see her. I looked back toward Harker again. He was staring at me, a huge grin on his face. I was missing something.

"So I guess you didn't want the drink, Master?" she asked, her breath hot on my neck.

I turned back to the Goth girl. My eyes widened in shock. "Annessa?"

She smiled and turned a slow circle in front of me. It was no wonder I hadn't recognized her. She was not the girl I'd killed three days ago. Gone were the trendy clothes, the carefully tended hair, and the conservative makeup. Harker's girls had been at her. They'd dyed her hair as black as the shadows of Perdition and dressed her in their own brand of finery. Her short plaid skirt left very little to the

imagination and thigh high black stockings accentuated what
was visible. Her small breasts strained against her tight
black baby doll t–shirt which bore only the message "Dead
is the New Alive" in a swirling cursive print on the front. A
narrow band of her pale, tight stomach was visible below the
shirt. Her hair was up in two pigtails and bound with blood
red ribbons and a silver skull dangled from the ends of each
of the ribbons. Dark eyeliner and a painfully sinful shade of
red lipstick completed the picture. A narrow choker
encircled her neck holding an inverted silver pentacle in the
hollow of her throat.

"What d'you think?"

"Wow." I clamped my mouth shut. I was going to
say more. I shook my head and took a deep breath. I had no
right to look. It was too soon.

"You like it, right?" Her voice suddenly seemed so
much smaller. "Master?" Her tiny lips pursed into a tight
bow, and the look in her eyes cut through me. She was
afraid I disapproved. The spell. Yet another thing I'd
managed to fuck up.

"I like it, Annessa." I managed a smile. "You look
beautiful, I've just got a lot on my mind." I took the drink
out of her hand and drank deeply. Single malt whisky, I
smiled and lifted the glass. "How'd you know?"

"I asked Cassidy." She smiled and looked up at me.

"It's good," I smiled, this time an honest smile.
"C'mon, I need to get a couple more of these and talk to
Harker."

"You're okay, then?" She looked concernedly at
me.

"I'll get there," I nodded toward Harker. "But,
there's something I need to do first."

"We made your girl over proper!" he grinned at me
as we approached the table.

"Well, you made her over, that's for sure." I grinned
back.

"Don't act like you don't like it, Jason," Mara
pointed at me. She'd tied her deep red hair into a knot at the
back of her head.

"I didn't say that I didn't like it," I took another drink to hide my grin. I wasn't sure which of the girls had actually made Annessa over, but it was likely Mara or Sophia as what she was wearing was much closer to their style than the other girls.

"So you like it, then?" Sophia flipped her blonde hair in my face as she slid past me carrying a tray of drinks. She set it down in front of Cassidy. If she weren't a vampire, I don't think she'd have been able to carry that tray. If Cassidy weren't a werewolf, however, I'm certain he could still drink all of the drinks. The Irish have a second stomach for whisky.

"Let it go," Cassidy said. "The man's had a rough day."

Annessa pressed herself against my side. I looked down at her and she smiled. I smiled back. "No, Cassidy, it's fine. She looks beautiful." I felt Annessa's pleasure shoot through my brain. It was narcotic.

"There, was that so hard?" Mara grinned at me. "Trust me, you'll thank us later."

Harker looked at me quizzically. "Let's have it, Jason."

"I'm that transparent, huh?" I asked.

He nodded and motioned impatiently, "Out with it."

"It's Sarah," I set my drink down and leaned on the table across from him with both hands. "There's a problem."

"What sort of 'problem,' Jason?" He pushed the girls away from him and leaned forward.

"She's on the radar, man, in a big way. Upstairs wants her and so do...I." I took a drink.

"I don't give a toss what the people Upstairs want, Jason." He sat forward, his eyes glowing red in the dim lighting. "And after the way you cocked things up last time, I'm not sure I want you involved either."

"Easy, Miles," I held up my hands. "There's more to this than you know."

"Enlighten me," he sat back and crossed his arms.

"She's manifested a Gift, a dangerous one."

"She's a seer," Mara interjected. "Just spit it out, Jason, dawn's only so far off."

"How the hell did you...?" I looked at Cassidy, who shrugged.

"It just makes sense," she idly played with her hair. "Why else would both sides be looking for her instead of trying to get the Sacred Mother."

"Who said they're not?" I asked. I put an arm protectively around Annessa.

"A seer?" Harker sat back.

"Yeah," I nodded. "And if the level of interest is any indication, she's powerful."

"It's better she's with friends, Miles," Cassidy sat forward.

"No interest from the Damascene then, Liam?" Harker asked venomously.

"No," Cassidy shook his head. "This isn't his fight."

"Miles, come on, man," I tried to be as calm as I could. "You know us, we're n—"

"Precisely, Jason," Miles interrupted me. "I know *you*. I've seen what you do and to whom you do it. I don't care to see Sarah in the hands of a muppet with delusions of grandeur."

I caught a stray thought of Kermit the Frog with the Mark of the Beast on his hand from Annessa. I bit my tongue; it's not wise to piss off a territorial vampire. "I don't want her hurt, Miles; I want to keep her safe."

"For how long, mate?" He flickered and was at my side. "Until she's no more use to you? Then what?"

"Miles," I sighed and ran my hand over my eyes. "If I wanted to hurt her, if I really fucking wanted to hurt her, why would I come here? Would I tell you that I was looking for her?"

"No, I suppose not." His eyes lost that predatory gleam. He looked at Mara, she nodded and he stepped back. His customary grin lit his face again. "You ain't that stupid."

"No, I'm not." I grabbed a chair from a nearby table and sat. Annessa knelt next to me and leaned her head against my knee. I was going to have to do something about this, it was like having a kitten around, I kept waiting for her to start purring. For the moment, though, I had weightier concerns. I turned back to Harker. "Have you heard from her?"

"No." He shook his head, flickered and was back to his spot at the back of the booth.

"Cassidy?" I asked.

"Nothing, Little Brother, she's like a ghost."

"So, I have to find a woman who doesn't want to be found, in a city built to hide people and to top it all off, she can see me coming?" I threw the rest of my drink back. "Great."

"There is an upside," Mara said, lying across Harker's lap.

"What's that?" I asked.

"If she wants to be found, she'll know you're looking and find you instead."

"Let's be honest," I snorted. "This is *me* we're talking about. What're the chances she'll ever want to see me again?"

"Better you than the Happy Sunshine Jesus Hour crowd," Mara laughed.

I tried to laugh, but it turned into a yawn. I'd been awake for nearly seventy-two hours and even with my investiture, I still needed sleep. After all, I was still human, mostly.

"Go home, Little Brother." Cassidy waved me off. "Give me time to query the right corners and see what I can discover."

I tried to protest, yawned again and nodded. "Fine, but you call me the minute you hear something." I pointed at him, "I'm serious."

"I will," he chuckled. "I will."

I nodded at Annessa. "Let's go." I slid my chair back, took Annessa's hand and pulled her to her feet. I waved a bleary eyed goodbye to the entire table and headed for the exit with Annessa in tow.

CHAPTER 12

I looked at Annessa as I started the car. She smiled at me. I shook my head and put the car into gear.

"What?" she asked, one hand going to her hair. Why do women do that? It's one of those maddeningly cute things, but it unhinges me. My stray thoughts don't mean you have a damned cowlick.

"Your shirt," I said.

"What about it?" she asked.

"Leave it to Sophia to find something like that."

"How'd you know it was her?"

"Mara's got too much going on upstairs to wear that." I grinned.

"Her tits aren't that much bigger than mine." Annessa looked confused and a little hurt.

"I meant her head," I snorted. "She likes Nietzsche, not Goth music."

"Huh?"

"Emilie Autumn," I said. "It's one of her songs."

"Oh," she kicked her feet out of her shoes and pulled her knees up to her chest. She rested her arms on her knees and her head atop her arms. "But how do you know Sophia's a fan?"

"I caught Cassidy whistling the song once." I grinned from ear to ear.

"Oh!" She grinned back at me. "Does Harker know about those two?"

"Yeah," I nodded. "She was a gift."

"A gift?"

"Harker turned her for Cassidy."

"I thought…all the other girls seem to love Harker."

"Of course they do, they're his murder."

"But don't they only, what did you call it?"

"Turn," I said.

"Right, don't they only turn girls they love?"

"No," I laughed. "No, no, no. Vampires turn whatever they want. If it didn't love them beforehand, it will afterword."

"Kind of like haemunculae?"

"No," I shook my head.

"No?"

"No. Vampires are bound to their creator, until death. Haemunculae can be given freedom through manumission."

"You can free me?"

"You're a special case, Annessa."

"I've been hearing that my whole life," she sighed.

"Yeah?" Now it was my turn to be intrigued. "About what?"

"Everything," she sat up, turned her leg and traced her birthmark through the stocking. "Can't go to public school, can't talk to other kids, can't go to church with the other mob kids." She sighed. "Can't kiss that boy, can't kiss that girl, can't date, can't smoke, can't drink…"

"Here," I tugged my cigarettes out of my pocket and pulled one out for her. "Go for it."

She took it reverently out of my hand. "Thanks, Master!"

"The whole 'Master' thing kinda ruins the freedom aspect of it," I said as I pulled my lighter out.

"Not if I choose to say it."

"True enough." I lit the cigarette for her and lowered her window. "There you go."

She inhaled deeply and coughed hard. "Ouch."

"The movies forget that part," I smirked. "In my day, if you got caught smoking, they made you smoke the whole pack."

"What'd they do if they caught you getting a blowjob?"

"I'm gonna guess that's the 'special case' coming out again." I reached over and took the cigarette from her. I took a drag and handed it back. If anything, she seemed delighted by the gesture.

"Yeah," she inhaled slowly this time. "It happens."

"So if you were forced to be such a good girl, where the hell did the cocaine come from?"

"A friend of the family," she said.

"Ah, mafia humor," I snorted. "I meant, what were you doing with it?"

"I thought I was keeping it safe," she sighed. "I thought the guy liked me."

"Instead, he turned you in to the cops?"

"Yeah, all in all, they were just after my dad. They didn't give a shit about me either. They said I was a—"

"Special case?" I finished.

"Pain in the ass," she smirked at me. "But close enough, Master."

I pulled off of the road outside of Harriman.

"Why are we stopping here?" Annessa asked.

"To say goodbye, Sacred Mother," Abbadonna said.

'Whoa!" Annessa looked around quickly, then turned to me. "Who was that?"

"A friend," I smiled. I focused on Abbadonna and formed an image of her in my mind.

Annessa gasped. "She's beautiful!"

"My Lord's blessing upon you, Emissary; be safe until I return." I felt her fade across the Veil.

"She was here the whole time?" Annessa asked, her eyes wide.

"Yeah, she's my guardian..." I thought about it a second. "Was my guardian, I guess."

"Wait, why 'was your guardian'?"

"Now, I've got you. So I guess that just makes her my friend."

"Oh. So you're not..." she searched for the right word.

"Having sex?" I shook my head. "No, I'm married," I sighed. "Was married."

"Do you change your mind with everything you say, Master? Or is tonight just special?"

"Let's just leave this one alone for the time being."

"Ok." She looked out the window. "Why'd we stop?"

"Can't go home with a Fallen Angel in the car." I opened my door and stepped out.

"Huh?"

I lost myself to the sorcery. Ghūllish words thrummed in my head, dark tendrils of power danced at my command. I felt the shift hit my eyes. Moments like this were one of the few reasons I lived. I once thought I was born to be husband and a father, but I wasn't. This is what I was born for. Sorcery's more addictive than heroin and twice as pleasurable. No Words, no borrowing another's power. This was mine and mine alone.

I wove a tapestry of deception about the car, every loop, every weave a lie. I bound each layer with a different glyph, each meant to disjoint and delay any observer from connecting what they saw from what was real. When I was done, I reluctantly released the power and felt my blood cool. I shuddered in the cold night air.

Annessa stood on the other side of the car, looking at me from across the roof. Her mouth was wide open and her eyes were lit up like torches. Blue flames licked out of her irises, which gleamed like coals in the dark winter night.

"Annessa?"

"What the fuck was that?" she asked in a hoarse whisper. She walked around the car, inspecting every detail.

"Sorcery," I said. "Magic."

"I want some," she said, in that same whisper.

I touched her arm and she shuddered. A massive wave of pleasure tore across my mind. "It's part of what you are." I smiled. "Come on," I nodded at the car.

"Where're we going?"

"Home," I jerked my thumb at the car. "Let's go, it's cold!"

I cranked the heat in the car and shivered. Annessa fidgeted in her seat. "What's wrong, you got to pee or something?"

"No," a thoughtful look crossed her face. "Do I even do that anymore?"

"I…" I thought about it a second. "I honestly don't know."

"Really?"

"Never had a haemunculus live long enough to find out."

"Just to be clear, Master," she looked me in the eye. "I'd like to find out."

I poked her birthmark. "That says I can't kill you, among other things."

She jerked her foot away. "That tickles!"

"Sorry, sorry!"

"So, what just happened was that there was a demon in the car, and she can't come home with you—us?"

"Fallen, not demon," I corrected. "They don't like that word at all."

"Right, but why can't she come with us? Is your wife home or something?"

"My wife is dead." I said it flatly. I took a second to focus on the road, though ultimately, it's pointless to try to hide your emotions from someone who can feel them.

"Oh! Oh shit!" Annessa's hands went to her mouth. "I'm sorry, I didn't mean to ask that."

I shook my head. "It's not your fault."

"No, you said I should leave it alone. It was my fault, I'm so sorry, Master."

"No one knows where I live," I blurted out.

"What?"

"Certain people can track Angels, Fallen or otherwise. That's why she had to go."

"Why was she in the car?"

"Machines don't fight them so much. Humans or animals fight like mad against possession, machines don't."

"Oh."

I turned back onto the highway. I turned the radio on in a useless attempt to avoid further conversation. I suppose it was unfair; she had to have so many questions. It was just unfortunate that they all seemed to end up in places I didn't want to go. I think we made it through three songs before the questions started again.

"So do you only get death metal stations in this car?" she asked.

"What?"

"Well, it's a Satanic car, right?"

"I'm not sure cars have celestial affiliations, Annessa."

"You know what I meant!" She stuck her tongue out at me.

"No, I get regular stations too. It's just playing my .mp3 collection."

"Do you mind if I change the station?"

I shrugged. "If you want to, go for it."

She played around with it for a while and then switched it back. "I hate radio, they never play anything decent."

"So why'd you want to change the station?"

"Something to do, so I wouldn't ask you any more questions."

"We're here," I said. "Don't worry about it."

My house was set far back off of the road. I think it had something like four acres of land around it; I never bothered to check. The house itself was fairly simple as houses go. It was a grey and white two-story Stick Style.

"You live here?"

"Yeah." I put the car in park and shut it off.

"It's like the Bates Motel. Well, not the motel, but the house, I mean."

"Is that good?"

"It's fucking awesome!" She grinned.

"I'm kind of partial to it myself."

"I can see why you hide it!"

"Yeah?"

"I wouldn't want to share it either."

"I'm afraid you're gonna have to." I locked the car. "It's *my* house."

* * *

Annessa stood in the entryway with one slender hand resting on the doorframe and inspected the house. She had a strange little smile, her head cocked slightly to the side.

"You waiting for an invitation?" I tossed my coat onto the coat rack.

"This house feels like…" She twirled one hand in the air as she searched for the word.

"Feels like what?" I ran my fingers through my hair and yawned.

"Home." She smiled as she said it.

"Well, that's good," I said as I loosened my tie. "Because that's what it is."

"It's just so surreal." She stepped out of the black, silver buckled platform shoes that I guessed had been Mara's.

"I don't know if surreal is the word I'd use." I yanked my tie the rest of the way off.

"No?"

"Un–fucking–believable springs to mind." I leaned back against the small table in the foyer and kicked off my shoes. "Or completely fucked or pretty much any derivative of fuck."

"It's a good word," she smiled.

"Actually, I think it's supposed to be a bad word," I grinned back.

"Yeah, but we work for the Devil, right?"

"Amen, sister." I winked at her.

"So what now?" She stepped into the living room and looked around.

"I'm going to get a drink, take a shower and pass the hell out." I jerked my head toward the far end of the living room. "Let me give you a quick tour and we'll figure it out from there." I yawned again, one of those catastrophic yawns that make your vision dim for a second. I shook it off as I walked through the living room.

"Kitchen's in here," I said as I crossed the threshold from the living room. I pointed to the narrow hallway that adjoined the kitchen. "There's a bathroom down the hall and the armory's across from it."

"The what now?"

"Armory, it's where I keep my guns."

"Most people just put 'em in cabinets, right?" She grinned at me and played with her hair innocently.

"Most people don't have the firepower I have, smartass." I headed down the hall. "Get your ass over here and see." I pressed my palm against the door and whispered a Word. The door swung open as the wards disengaged and the lock spun itself open.

"Holy shit," Annessa breathed as her eyes swept over the contents of the room.

"Now say you're sorry," I said, a smug smile on my face.

"I'm sorry, Master." She curtsied jokingly. Her short skirt lifted with the gesture and bared just about everything it had hidden. A burst of heat flooded my face at the first sight of black lace and I turned away. I felt an echo of my lust from her. I bit my cheek fiercely until the moment passed and shut the door more firmly than I intended.

"Upstairs," I said quickly. "There's an office, my bedroom and two spare bedrooms." I turned to walk away and paused. "Correction, one spare bedroom. We'll have to get you set up."

"I don't sleep, Master," she said.

"Everyone needs someplace to call their own, Annessa." I pointed toward the stairs. "Come on, let's finish this tour, I need a drink."

Five minutes later, I was sprawled on the couch, a bottle of Laphroaig in my hand. I hadn't bothered with the glass, reaching for it was far too much effort tonight. I was watching Annessa play with the entertainment system.

"So you get every channel?" she asked.

"As far as I know," I said.

"Even the foreign ones?"

"Yep," I nodded.

"What's the point if you can't understand them?"

"I can understand them," I took a drink.

"Which ones?"

"All of them."

"Bullshit."

"Do you speak any other languages?" I asked.

"No," she shook her head.

"Then how'll you know if I'm lying?" I smirked at her.

"You can't lie to me, Master," she smirked right back. "I'm in your head."

"S'right," I raised the bottle to her. "And don't you forget it." That made more sense when I said it.

"You should slow down, Master." She pointed at the bottle. "That shit'll kill you."

"Don't worry, my investiture burns this shit like..." I shrugged as my mind went momentarily blank. "Scotch." I was a little more worse for the wear than I'd thought. I shook my head. "I'm shower taking now." I paused and tried to figure out what had gone wrong there. I shrugged and stumbled to the stairs.

I was in the shower, my head resting against the cool tile as the cold water cascaded over me, when I heard her tentative whisper.

"Master?"

"What?" I mumbled.

"Do you have anything I can wear?"

"You were dressed when I got in here..."

"I'm still dressed," she said in an annoyed tone. "This stuff's only comfortable so long."

"Right," I said knowingly. "Check my closet."

"Ok." The door clicked shut, then opened again. "Thanks." The door clicked shut for the last time.

I slid down the wall to my knees and let the water wash over me. My muscles tensed in the frigid water and the heat of the scotch seemed to dull in my brain. I halfheartedly scrubbed myself, rinsed and got out. I stepped into my room and the shock of cold air on my skin made me shiver. I stretched and grabbed my flannel robe out of the closet.

"Annessa?" I called as came down the stairs tying my robe.

"Yeah?" she yelled back from the living room.

"What're you doing?" I asked.

"Trying to start a fire."

"I thought you liked this house?"

"In the fireplace," she called back in an exasperated tone. "Do you have matches or something, Master?"

"Don't need 'em," I said.

I stepped turned the corner at the base of the stairs and my heart stopped cold. Annessa was on all fours in front of the fireplace, wearing nothing but her black lace thong and one of my white button–up shirts. I swallowed hard. I tried to look away, but if you've got a pulse, there are some things that drag you in with the force of a black hole.

She looked over her shoulder at me. "Then how do you..." she trailed off as the force of my lust hit her. "Oh," she rolled back onto her heels covering herself. "Sorry!"

I closed my eyes and took a deep breath. I let it out slowly and opened my eyes. I held out my right hand and spoke a Ghūllish incantation. For a moment, my blood pounded in my veins, my eyes went black as my human blood gave way. Annessa moaned as she felt reality pulse with my sorcery. Brilliant flames erupted in the fireplace.

"You need to teach me how to do that," she purred, her irises flaring blue in the low light. She stood faster than my eyes could follow and held my right hand in both of her small hands. She pressed her face against my hand as if to pull the sorcery into herself.

"I can't," I said, my chest tight.

"Why not?" She looked up at me, her eyes dim.

"You can't learn how I learned," I said as I touched her face. It felt so nice to touch someone; it'd been so long. Something inside me awakened, something I hadn't felt in years. It started as warmth in my chest, but in seconds my lungs felt weak and my knees felt as if they would give way.

"No?" She turned her face against my hand, the touch of her soft lips against my palm like holding the essence of fire itself.

"No," I whispered, unable to trust my voice.

"Why not, Master?" She stepped close to me and pressed herself against me.

"You need to be alive." My hands slid over her back feeling the contours of her muscles, each vertebra, as I pulled her tight against me.

"You can't have me alive," she whispered, her lips millimeters from mine.

I stared into her eyes, watching them shift from brown to green to blue. Slowly, I felt myself give in. Her lips brushed mine, and I lost control. I kissed her hard, my left hand holding the back of her head. Our tongues met, and my flesh screamed out an aria that it hadn't dared to utter in six years. My hands tore at her and hers at me.

I staggered backwards. My heels caught the bottom of the couch and I tried not to fall back. Annessa gave me a gentle push, grinning as she did. I landed on the couch as she stepped forward and straddled me. I felt the heat of her through my robe and she pushed herself against me. I moaned as she moved herself on me. She slowly unbuttoned her shirt exposing her small, proud breasts. My hands moved of their own volition, tracing a line over her hips and stomach to touch her breasts.

Her lips met mine again, and I lost myself in her. I pulled the shirt over her head and kissed her from her neck to her breasts, my teeth closing on her flesh as I gave in to my basest impulses. As my need became more violent, her ardor increased, her acquiescence more complete. I hooked my forearms under her thighs and stood; I lifted her and tasted her through the thin silk of her panties, before gently laying her on the couch. Her hands gripped my hair, pulling me against her. I reached down and yanked her panties out of the way and slid my tongue inside her. She moaned and pulled my hair harder, driving my face against her sex and my tongue deeper inside her. I didn't have to wonder, nor try to discern her needs; I felt them as strongly as I felt my own. Within seconds, an orgasm tore through her, and her scream threated to shatter the bay window. She didn't scream my name, but 'Master.' A part of me came alive; a part of me that I didn't like to admit existed.

I stood and pulled her toward me, the warmth of her mouth enveloped me and I thrust against her mouth, my hands knotted in her pigtails. She stared up at me, her glowing blue eyes never leaving mine. I could feel my lust magnified by hers, like a feedback loop, each of us driving the other to greater heights of need. I felt myself getting close and shoved her back onto the couch.

I knelt in front of the couch and pulled her to the edge. I looked into her eyes as I pressed my cock against her and I saw fear. I froze. Her eyes looked so innocent, so young.

"Be easy, Jason," Jessica whispered. "It's my first time." The memory of our wedding night came to me like a sledgehammer blow to the face.

I jerked back from Annessa and staggered to my feet. What the fuck was I doing? I ran my hand through my hair and tugged it violently again and again. The pain hurled me back to reality.

Annessa stared up at me confused. "Master?" She self–consciously closed her legs and covered her breasts with her arm.

"I'm sorry," I whispered to her, to the world, to Jessica. "I can't…" I turned and walked to the stairs pausing only to pick up the bottle of scotch where I'd left it.

As I grabbed the handrail of the stairs to steady myself, I heard Annessa whisper, "I'm sorry, Master." I

looked over at her; she was staring into the fire, a horrible
look of sadness on her face. I thought she was talking to me.

CHAPTER 13

I woke up to the remnants of a rapidly fading hangover. That was one of the many benefits to my investiture; I didn't have to suffer hangovers all that much. The downside was that I had to drink the same amount as a platoon of angry soldiers to actually get drunk.

The smell of fresh coffee hit me like something out of a commercial. I sat up in bed and sniffed the air like a dog. I threw the covers back and stretched. Annessa. Shit. She had no idea why I had to walk away from her last night. She couldn't know what it was like to lose a wife. She was too young, too innocent.

The invigoration that the coffee smell had given me was slowly replaced by the lethargy of my guilt. I'd have to apologize to her. I'd led her on, and that wasn't right either. It wasn't like she'd had much choice in the matter; my desires would always dominate hers. I sighed and got out of bed. Sitting around wouldn't help anything.

After I dressed, I went downstairs. When I hit the base of the stairs, a new smell hit me. Someone was cooking.

"Annessa?" I called, in a vaguely kitchen like direction.

"Yes, Master?"

"Are you cooking?" I asked.

"Yep."

I walked into the kitchen and stopped. Annessa was dressed in her clothes from the night before and racing back and forth from the stove to my kitchen table. It was like watching a Goth kitchen cooking challenge. (I wouldn't be surprised if that were a show on some cable channel...)

"What are you doing?" I asked.

"Making you breakfast," she smiled at me.

"The coffee smells delicious," I said.

"Good," she turned back to the stove. "Your omelet should be ready in a second."

"Really?" I grinned like I'd just won the lottery. Seriously, no one's cooked for me in years; Jess was an awful cook.

"Yeah," she flipped the eggs onto a plate and handed it to me. "Here you go."

"Thanks," I looked at her for a second. "Seriously, thanks. You didn't have to do this and I appreciate it."

"I was up all night watching cooking shows and Bob Ross. If you had paints, your living room'd be wallpapered in landscapes with happy fucking trees."

I set the plate down and poured a cup of coffee. I stared at the table and looked back at her. She shrugged.

"Well?" she asked.

The coffee was perfect and the eggs only slightly less so. "Perfect," I mumbled through a mouthful. The coffee was like heaven in my mouth. I tore through the rest of my plate and finished my coffee.

"I just wanted to say I'm sorry," she said when I was done.

I carried my plate to the sink and turned back to face her. "You don't owe me an apology."

"I should've known better, Master." She lowered her eyes.

"It's not your fault." I stepped close and looked into her eyes. "What happened wasn't wrong," I sighed.

"Then what's wrong, Master?"

"The timing, not the act." I shook my head. "Give me time."

"So it wasn't anything I did?" She seemed smaller.

"No," I shook my head.

"Good," She stood on her toes and gently headbutted me.

"What was that for?"

"Nothin,'" she grinned. "Just felt like doing it." She ran a hand over her stomach and a pained look came over her face.

"What's wrong?" I asked.

"I'm starving," she said.

I smiled and slid a knife out of the block on the counter. "That, I can fix."

"You gonna kill somebody?"

"No," I ran the blade over the flat edge of my thumb, the blade bit into the artery and blood gushed out of the wound. I held my hand out to her. "Here."

Her mouth closed over my thumb, her eyes met mine and somehow the gesture became erotic. My blood mingled with hers deepening our bond for a second. Time seemed to dilate and I lost myself to the pleasure of the moment. Then I felt my human blood giving way. I stopped my heart with a thought and gently pulled my thumb away from Annessa who let go with the reluctance of an infant from a bottle.

"That's enough," I said hoarsely. I spoke a Word of healing over my thumb. Nothing happened. I stared at it. "That's weird." My voice was calm, almost clinical.

"What?" Annessa leaned against the table, steadying herself.

"The wound won't close."

"That's never happened before?"

"No," I thought about it for a second. "But then again, I've never fed a haemunculus my blood before."

"I thought you said I couldn't live on blood?"

"You can't." I turned to leave the kitchen. I had a first aid kit in the armory. "Only mine can satisfy you for any length of time, but even that has limits."

I stopped suddenly in the hallway, and Annessa bumped into me.

"Sorry," she muttered. "Didn't expect you to stop."

I turned to face her and looked at my thumb, then back to her. "Huh," I said as my mind tried to put two and two together.

"What?"

"I'm just wondering if there's an Ouroborosian correspondence." I brought my thumb up to my face and stared at the wound.

"Again, what?"

"I mean there might be some significance to the fact that I created you and that I can't heal wounds from which you've fed, there might be a way to—"

My phone belted out the opening to "Psychopathy Red." I held up my wounded hand, silently telling Annessa to hang on. I dug my phone out of my pocket.

"Talk to me," I said. "Tell me you found her."

"She's on a subway, the D train headed for Washington Square." Cassidy paused.

"Your silence tells me I'm not going to like what you say next," I sighed. "Hit me with it." Annessa held my injured hand in both of hers and looked closely at the wound.

"You're not the only one asking questions, Little Brother."

"Who else?" Annessa licked the wound softy as if trying to avoid my attention, then slid it into her mouth and sucked gently on it. My knees went a little weak.

"Your Heavenly Counterpart, for one, and the Umbrals we identified as Vincenze Francione and this Father Jacob."

"I assumed that Rachel would be looking for her, but why the Umbrals? Why would they care about a seer?"

"I don't know, but it portends nothing good."

"I'm going to head that way and see what I can find. Hopefully, I can track her. Who knows how long she'll stay there."

"Take care, Little Brother."

"Thanks for everything, man." I hung up and looked at Annessa. "What the hell's wrong with you?"

"What?" she said around my thumb. She looked at me guiltily.

"You can't do shit like that when someone's on the phone."

She released my thumb. "You didn't pull away, so I thought you didn't mind."

I stammered for a second then muttered something about a first aid kit and stormed into the armory.

* * *

I looked at a map of Greenwich Village on my phone as we drove to Manhattan. I scrolled across the map looking for possible points of interest for Sarah. I kept coming back to one in particular, the Faerie Mound in Washington Square Park. I sighed and idly flicked at the butterfly bandage on my thumb.

"What's wrong, Master?" Annessa asked as she fiddled with the radio, attempting to find the perfect balance between a metal station and a trance station.

"Tuath'an." I pointed at the tiny model of the Arch on my screen. "I think Sarah's looking for protection from the Fae."

"Or," Annessa lifted a finger. "You could be really mysterious and tell me something I don't understand."

"Smart ass," I snorted. "Sarah might be looking for protection from the fae. You know, fairies."

"Well, the Village is the right place to find 'em." She nodded smartly and grinned at me.

"Not those kind of…" I sighed and tried not to laugh. "Real fairies, Annessa, the kind that eat souls."

"Leprechauns and Tinkerbell," she made a fluttering motion with her hands, "eat souls? Seriously?"

"Not those kind of Fae. That's what they'd like you to believe. Remember Sheena Samhradh from Harker's? The beautiful blonde with," I mimed huge breasts.

"The one you told me not to point at?"

"Yeah, she's Fae."

"Oh." She was silent for a second. "Tinkerbell's got a fucking rack." She grinned.

"Yeah, she does," I was forced to agree.

"So she eats souls?"

"In a manner of speaking, they all do. Souls are like currency to the Fae, they trade them amongst themselves."

"For what?"

"Power. They're Earthbound Gods; they trade the souls for power."

"Do they work for the Devil?"

"No," I laughed. 'They work for whoever's paying. They don't give a shit about the War."

"So why would Sarah go to them?"

"They might protect her from both us and the Angelics."

"So what, then; Sarah whores out her gift for protection?"

"Not if she has half the brains she used to." I shook my head. "The Fae would take her for every ounce of her soul, then enslave her and use her until she died."

"Oh." Annessa played with her hair and stared out the window.

I bit my tongue. What good was an apology? How do you really say you're sorry for enslaving someone? I pulled into an empty space across the street from the park on the north side, closest to the Arch. I pointed to the Arch.

"Sarah should be somewhere in that area," I said.

"There's a lot of people over there, Master." Annessa craned her neck to see past me. "How're we gonna find her?

I checked my mirror then opened the door. "We're gonna take Mara's advice." I got out and shut the door.

"Wait and let her find us?" Annessa asked as she opened her door and joined me.

"Exactly." I pulled a cigarette out of my pack and watched the students mill around the Arch. "Let's hope we don't have to wait too long." I blew a smoke ring.

"Look, Master," Annessa pointed at man standing about thirty yards from the arch, between it and the fountain. He had a Bible in his hand and stood in front of a yellow box decorated with flames.

"Shit," I reached back to check my Beretta.

"He's one of them, right?"

I stilled the tide of my blood and let my eyes fill with darkness. I could see the Aetheric signature of an Angel pulsing within the street preacher. "He's Host—Bound."

Annessa began to look all around us. "There's more, right?"

"Yeah," I answered only half paying attention. I traced the five points into the hood of the car with my left hand and spoke a Word. The car shuddered as Abbadonna arrived.

Greetings, Emissary

"Beautiful," I jerked my head toward the street preacher. "We've got friends."

Are there others?

"No idea," I looked around. "He's probably a lookout."

"So, should we hide or something?" Annessa interrupted me.

"No," Abbadonna and I spoke at the same time. I grinned.

"Okay," Annessa held up her hands. "I just thought maybe if they were looking for us, we shouldn't be sitting out in the open."

"They aren't after us. They're after Sarah, seeing us will force their hand and it might make them careless."

"We like careless?" Annessa asked.

"Careless means killing. We like careless." I felt Abbadonna's pleasure through the hood of the car.

"What about all of these people?" Annessa pointed at the pedestrians and students in the area.

"We just have to be careful," I winked.

I felt the tiniest of Aetheric pulses. I turned back toward the Arch. Sarah rested against the inside of the Arch with her eyes closed and one hand pressed against her forehead. "There," I pointed.

I trailed my hand along the hood of the car as I stood. "Coming, Beautiful?"

"Yeah," Annessa jumped lightly to her feet.

I opened my mouth to correct her.

Hush, Emissary. Let it lie, Abbadonna chuckled in my mind as she slid into my flesh.

We wended our way through the wonderfully courteous New York drivers to cross the street. I hope you caught my sarcasm there; I laid it on with a snow shovel.

The moment my foot touched the sidewalk in front of the Arch, Mr. Guy–with–the–Bible shut his mouth and started walking rapidly toward Sarah. We locked eyes for a second and Angels within us did the same. I felt Abbadonna surge against the walls of my mind, like bloodthirsty tiger trying to claw its way through the bars of its cage. I turned back to Sarah. She was back on her feet and staring at me. I smiled and waved. I tried to make it friendly, but who knows what it looked like, with a blood–crazed Fallen running around in your head, it's hard enough trying to keep up and down straight much less emotions.

Sarah spun around and looked at Mr. Bible then back to me. As soon as she started looking in alternate directions, I knew this wasn't go going to go well.

"She's gonna run," I said.

"Which way, Master?" Annessa asked.

'How the fuck should I know? She's the seer, not me!" I snapped.

Annessa lowered her eyes and nodded "Sorry, Master."

I looked at all of Sarah's escape vectors. None of them were good. We were in the middle of Tuath'an territory. Any place she might go to hide here would be far more costly to her than they were worth. There wasn't much in the way of friendly territory for me here either. I looked across the park and felt a shudder in the Aether as I did. An Angelic door had just opened. It was close enough for me to sense, which meant it was way too close. My eyes rested on the church at the far end of the park. Bingo.

"We're gonna have a lot more friends in a second." I jerked my head toward the church. Annessa nodded.

As if on cue, Sarah looked back at me and ran directly toward the church.

"Shit!" I ran after her. Mr. Bible shifted his direction and moved to cut me off. There were too many innocents around; I didn't bother pulling my gun.

Annessa hissed as she moved up alongside me, her claws and fangs sliding free.

"Annessa!" I snapped again. "Keep that shit PG, too many Normals around!"

Instantly, her fangs were gone. "Sorry." Her voice was flat.

"Turn back, Vessel of Hell." Mr. Bible lifted the good book high over his head. "The child has made her decision."

"That ain't happening, friend," I gestured dismissively at him. "It's best you move."

Then Normals in the park began to move away from the Arch and the fountain. The tides of aether flowing through the area pushing them like invisible hands. Mr. Bible took a wide sidestep, as if readying himself for impact.

"You can't touch me, Emissary," he smiled. "I am safe within the Light."

"You know what?" I slapped my forehead. "You're exactly right. I can't touch you at all."

He smiled at me.

"Annessa," I smiled back at him. "Touch him."

Annessa jerked forward, her claws out. Mr. Bible threw up an arm to defend himself. Annessa caught his left wrist with her right hand and yanked him forward. Her left hand, fingers straight, claws extended, drove into the flesh of his shoulder. Before he could scream, or even react, she twisted her hand severing the joint as she savagely pulled her right hand back. He opened his mouth to scream. Annessa spun, with a vicious cry; she slammed him across the face

with his own severed arm. He staggered backward and fell
to one knee.

White light played around his eyes, his Angelic
passenger was keeping him up, keeping him in the fight. I
shook my head. This was taking too long. He clenched his
remaining fist. I didn't need to say anything to Abbadonna;
she knew what I was going to do. Mr. Bible launched
himself at Annessa. His fist crackled with barely restrained
power. His rider had to be a Seraphim, any lesser choir
Angel would have been done for by now. Just before
impact, Abbadonna threw my body in the way. I turned my
face as best I could, ducking my jaw and angling my cheek
to let the blow slide by.

His fist hit me like a cargo train full of angry
midgets with baseball bats. He shifted position mid–blow,
his haymaker becoming an uppercut that launched me over
Annessa and sent me tumbling into a heap at the base of the
Arch. I lay against the Arch for a long moment. That hurt.
Abbadonna worked furiously within me, healing what he'd
broken. When she was done, I kicked myself back to a
standing position, shoved my broken nose back into position
and pointed at him.

"Nice one." I pushed one nostril shut and blew a
fistful of blood from the open side. "That hurt." I raised my
Mark. "Now it's my turn."

Push me, Beautiful, I thought to Abbadonna. I
relaxed my body. I felt her presence leave me. I felt her pull
away and felt the hit as she dove back into me from across
the Veil propelling me forward as if I'd been shot from a
cannon. I slapped Mr. Bible across the face with my Mark
and screamed a Word of Abjuration, driving out the Angel
within him.

The man collapsed; bereft of his divine guardian, he
was overcome by the weakness of his flesh. His jaw worked
as he looked up at me. He blinked as he tried to contain his
pain. I shook my head at him.

"Annessa," I nodded at the man.

I walked past him and tried to see where Sarah had
gone. She stood in the center of the park, just beyond the

fountain staring at me. I gestured for her to come back. She shook her head. I sighed and shrugged. I was going to have to go get her. I heard the crunch as Annessa brought her platform shoe down on Mr. Bible's head. He hadn't wept or begged. Good man.

"Done," Annessa stepped up beside me. "Why's she just standing there?"

"I guess we need to go get her." I shook my head and started forward.

"Want me to go get her, Master?"

"No," I nodded back at Mr. Bible. "I'm guessing you didn't watch a whole lot of PG movies as a kid, did you?"

"My first movie was *The Omen*," she smiled weakly. "I didn't eat him. That was good, right?"

"Good enough." I looked around. The Normals were gone. The park hadn't been this empty since...well, since it was a graveyard. I waved my Marked hand over my shoulder and spoke a Word of immolation. I heard the whoosh of Mr. Bible's body igniting. There'd be nothing left for the cops to track.

Sarah waited until we were halfway across the park before she broke into a run again. Even with Abbadonna pushing me, Sarah kept a step ahead of me. It had to be her Gift. What bothered me was that she had to know that I wanted to protect her. I mean, she had to have Seen that at some point. Unless she knew I was going to fail. That was a sobering thought. She hit the far edge of the park and I threw everything I had into catching her. I had to get her before she made it into that church.

Traffic was both a blessing and a curse. It was New York, after all, the city of eternal traffic. But each cabby that decided that lines were a suggestion and every delivery truck driver with a schedule became my best friend. Not even Sarah seemed eager to dive into the street. I made up ground, fast. Seconds before I reached her, she darted between two cabs and was out of reach.

"Fuck!" I swore angrily as I my hand snatched at empty air. "Fuck!" I swore again as I saw the front door to the church open to reveal Rachel's smiling face. We had just officially reached the point where 'by any means necessary' became the order of the day. I drew my gun.

Annessa took that as a signal to act. With a scream she hurled herself across the road. A massive SUV filled with construction equipment barreled down the street toward Sarah. Annessa hit said SUV just ahead of the driver's door; the force of her impact followed by her angry shove did two things. The first was sending Annessa hurling back across the street in a magnificent and graceful, if somewhat indecent, series of flips. The second was throwing the SUV off course, over the curb, up the stairs and into the open doorway of the church. Rachel's face shifted from a look of mocking joy to one of confusion, then terror. She dove back inside just as the truck slammed through the doorframe.

The thunderous impact hurled fragments of wood, stone and glass clear across the street. Traffic screeched to a halt and for a moment there was stillness, as if no one wanted to move, gasp or cheer, for fear they might be blamed. Then, the truck driver shoved his door open and stumbled out of the truck. He held his hand against his forehead. He blinked and sat heavily on the ground as he looked around confused and likely concussed. I raised my Mark and spoke a Word of conflagration. The truck exploded in a shower of fire and debris. Conveniently, every bit of that explosion missed the poor truck driver. I figured he'd already had a bastard of a day. No need to add insult to injury.

"Really, Jason?" Sarah threw up her hands and walked across the street toward me. "Really?"

"Don't you fucking blame me!" I turned angrily toward her. "I waved, all nice and civil. You're the one who ran."

She stepped close to me; her pale blue eyes seemed unfocused and lost. Her long, blonde hair was tight against her head, flowing over her shoulders in an orderly fashion. It coiled and curled only where it hit her generous breasts. Her face was thin and tight, slender, sharp nose over taut, almost colorless lips. On anyone else, hers would be a cruel face, speaking to the heart of bitter winter storms and pains too great to bear. On her, however, it was like Minerva etched in stone, like a patient Socrates before the unruly mob.

"Yeah, well, if I'd stayed near the Arch, it would've been a massacre." She shook her head. "I should've known you'd find a way to make a mess of this."

"Well…" I looked around. Cars were stopped in both direction and faces were beginning to appear in every window along the street. "We have to go."

"You expect me to go with you?" She arched a razor–thin eyebrow.

"You can ride in the backseat or the trunk," I leaned close to her. "Your call. I'd opt for the backseat, personally. It's leather." I reached for her arm.

"Don't touch me," she jerked away. "I'll go with you. Just keep your hands off of me."

"Fine," I motioned toward the car across the park. "After you."

I stepped out of her way and nodded for Annessa to follow her. I looked back at the church, nothing moved. This was too easy. Rachel would've had a playbook full of contingency plans, she always did. I felt a ball of ice forming in my guts. If she hadn't moved yet, then I was doing all of the moving for her. Annessa's little stunt would've only held her off so long. I shook my head and jogged to catch up with Annessa and Sarah.

We made it back to the car without incident. I was opening my door when the fire trucks showed up. At least with them tying up traffic across the park, I might be able to put some distance between Rachel and me. I waited to get in until both Sarah and Annessa had shut their doors. As I sat, I locked the doors and started the car. I looked over my shoulder at Sarah.

"Incidentally, this is Annessa." I jerked a thumb in Annessa's direction.

"Hi," Annessa leaned out to wave and smile at Sarah. "Nice to meet you."

"Same," Sarah actually smiled at Annessa. "I'm sorry he pulled you into all of this."

I wanted to say something witty and mean, but she was right. I *had* pulled Annessa into it. At least part way, anyway. I pulled the car into traffic and headed back toward home.

"It's not so bad," Annessa grinned.

"Give it time." Sarah turned to look out the window.

"I'd say I'm sorry," I looked at Sarah in the mirror. "But I don't think you'd believe me."

"I saw you die," she said simply.

"Yeah," I nodded. "You did."

"You should have stayed dead." She tossed her hair angrily over her shoulder and stared sullenly out the window.

"Wait," Annessa interjected. "You died?"

"Yeah," I nodded and slid my cigarettes out of my jacket. Would you believe prior to this, I was only an occasional smoker? "But it didn't stick."

"How?" She pulled her feet up onto the seat. And looked at me.

"Like a frog in a blender." Sarah snorted.

"What?"

"Harker," I said.

"Our Harker?" She asked incredulously.

"Yeah." I nodded as I lit my cigarette. I lowered my window.

"Harker is no one's." Sarah spoke with quiet certainty.

"Hang on," Annessa touched my shoulder. "Harker killed you, Master?"

"He beat me to death." I turned toward her and blew a smoke ring. "Because of what I did to his precious Sarah."

Annessa's eyes went cold. Like frozen coals, ash and darkness displacing life and light. "What'd you do to her?"

I released Abbadonna into the car and let go of the wheel. "I made her see Harker for what he was."

"What, a vampire?"

"A monster," Sarah answered. "A hungry shadow of a man."

"He didn't seem like that to me," Annessa protested.

"You're already dead," Sarah delivered it like a deathblow.

"Enough," I warned.

"Will wonders never cease, Jason Beckett protecting someone?" Sarah mocked acidly.

"I'm protecting you," I reminded her.

"You've tried that before," She said it quietly. Truth doesn't need volume to wound.

I shook my head at her in the mirror. I looked over at Annessa. "Nice trick with the SUV," I smiled at her.

"Really?" She beamed at me. "I wanted to wipe the smug look of that bitch's face."

"Me too," I grinned. "Me too."

"You've got another chance, champ." Sarah jerked her thumb over her shoulder.

Three black Mercedes weaved through traffic like sharks seeking prey. They were coming up on us far too quickly to be accidental.

"Time to move, Beautiful," I pushed across the aether between Abbadonna and I.

The car jerked beneath me as Abbadonna stretched it to its limit. I watched the needles for the tach and speedometer bury themselves as the car hurtled forward. She slid the car into the narrow shoulder and whipped around the truck ahead of us, then threw the car into an exaggerated "S" drift. She threaded the car through traffic with the deftness of Ariadne at her loom.

"Emissary..." Abbadonna spoke into the passenger compartment. "Ahead."

The entrance to the Lincoln Tunnel beckoned and with it the sea of brake lights that heralded the idiocy of New York traffic.

"Shit!" I looked over my shoulder to track Rachel and her goons. They were right on us. As I turned back, I swear I caught Sarah smirking. I looked into the rearview mirror and pushed my human blood violently aside. My skin went grey and my veins shoved themselves against my skin, like a black road map. My irises faded from brown to black, which spread like ink to cover the whites. I returned my attention to the vehicles in front of us. I spoke a Word of command, then wove my sorcery around echoes of that Word as it danced through the air ahead of us.

I slumped into my seat the moment the magic fled my body. My fragile human blood lazily slid forward and resumed its meager efforts at keeping me alive. Meanwhile, my sorcery bounced from vehicle to vehicle ahead of us. The drivers, momentarily panicked by my magic, threw their vehicles into random spins, driving onto the shoulder, accelerating into the vehicles in front of them or engaging in suicidal demolition derbies. Abbadonna eagerly sped forwards, finding impossible paths amidst the detritus and human debris.

For a second, I thought we might get clear, then the bullets started raining down like tears from heaven. The lead car in the Angelic triumvirate had automatic weapons sticking out of every available window. Even the driver was firing a Mac-10 and spraying the ass end of my vehicle with lead. Bullets shredded the trunk, ricocheted off of every reinforced inch of the vehicle. Only Abbadonna's presence kept the passenger compartment from becoming a blender.

"Fucking Host–Bound." I wiped a strand of drool away from my mouth. "Ruining my perfectly good sorcery."

"What do we do, Master?" Annessa looked at me, her panic plain.

I unbuckled my seatbelt and slid my Beretta free. I dropped the magazine and held it out to her. "Kiss the bullet."

"W–what?" she stammered as the back windshield exploded inward.

"You're the Sacred Mother." I pressed it against her lips. "Bless the damned bullet!"

She kissed the bullet almost reverently. "Why me?" she asked breathlessly.

"Abbadonna's busy," I snapped as I racked the slide on the pistol and caught the round it ejected. I slid the ejected round into the magazine, on top of the blessed round. I spoke a Word of accuracy over it and slammed the magazine home. I flicked the slide lock with my thumb, sending the slide forward.

"Don't be such a dick, Jason," Sarah admonished me.

I turned around and leveled the pistol over her head, aiming through the blown out back windshield. "Kinda busy at the moment," I said as I tried to match the movements of the closest Mercedes with my gun. I focused on each minor detail of the shot. My thumbs were high along the side of the pistol, not quite resting on the slide, the sights aligned on the base of the driver's throat. I stopped my heart and stilled my breathing.

"Whenever you can," I whispered to Abbadonna. "Give me a steady second to fire." Nearly instantly, she stabilized the vehicle and slid smoothly through traffic. I fired a hammered pair, my sight picture shifting only slightly on the second shot.

The first bullet slammed into the windshield, spidering it, and the second blew it out. The blessed bullet tumbled as it struck, shredding the hollow of the driver's neck. The impact destroyed the driver's throat chakra, driving both the soul and the Angel from his body. He collapsed against the wheel.

The Mercedes spun sideways and slammed into another vehicle. I thought a saw a shock of red hair in the instant before the passenger fired a massive revolver. I threw myself back into my seat, my head ducked low. I heard the whistle of a bullet nearby and the sound of a baseball striking flesh. Annessa hurtled forward and collapsed against her seatbelt. A searing pain erupted in my chest, as if someone had driven a spike through my spine and into my heart. I screamed and collapsed against the steering wheel.

Abbadonna felt my panic pour through our bond and the engine screamed as she tore through traffic, the yellow lights of the tunnel becoming a continuous blur. I sat up, my Mark clutched over my heart and looked into the rearview mirror. The Mercedes fell away behind us. I forced my head to the right; I made myself look at Annessa. She hung limply against her seatbelt. Her hair dangled in front of her face. Her arms swayed lifelessly with the motion of the car. Black blood leaked in a steady drip from the space between her shoulder blades.

Time seemed to still. For a moment, I smelled the salt of a distant sea and felt the blazing heat of a foreign shore. An unfamiliar panic began to shriek its intoxicating lament at the periphery of my mind. *My fault.*

Sarah touched my hand. Her words didn't register, I saw her lips moving, but the rushing in my ears deafened me. *It's not the ocean; it's not the same. It's not the same.*

"Jason!" She slapped me.

I looked at her as we burst into daylight, Abbadonna roared through traffic, her sole focus on delivering us safely from the arms of our enemy.

"You have to hide us," Sarah gently shook my shoulder. "They'll find us you don't."

Her cruel eyes reflected the fear in my own. I began to wonder what I'd been staring at all along, her eyes or my own. I sat back and ran a hand over my eyes. I took a deep breath. I let it out slowly between my teeth.

"Time to go, Beautiful," I said, my voice finally steady.

"This is unwise, Emissary." I felt her mental headshake.

"I don't have time to argue!" I put my Mark against the wheel and spoke with a voice not my own. "Return to Silence, sweet sister."

I felt her fight to remain Lifeside. The weight of my command pressed upon her, tearing her across the Veil. I caught a flash of pain and betrayal as she was finally dismissed.

I caught the wheel and pressed the brake pedal hard. I fought to regain control of the car.

THE EYE OF EURYDICE | 133

"Should probably have had her pull over first," I said as I weaved into the shoulder and back. I pulled my phone out of my pocket. I slid onto the exit ramp for Secaucus as I dialed an altogether familiar number.

"Internal Revenue Service," he said.

"Need a new car, in Secaucus. *Now.*"

CHAPTER 14

We sat in a shopping center parking lot beneath a canopy of deceptive sorcery. I crouched over Annessa gently touching the edges of her wound. I hissed as I saw the extent of the damage to her flesh. Her spine was shattered; the bullet carved a vicious wound channel. I felt her chest between her breasts; there was no exit wound. The bullet was still inside her, likely embedded in her sternum. I sat back and ran a hand over my chin.

"What?" Sarah leaned forward between the seats. "What is it?"

"I don't know what they shot her with," I said.

"So?"

"I can't just dig it out without knowing. It could kill her."

"Don't you think leaving it in would be worse?" she asked.

"I don't know." I sighed and leaned forward again. "To be honest, I didn't really study necromancy all that much."

"Do you ever do anything on purpose?" she asked snidely.

"Are you ever not a complete bitch?" I snapped back.

"How do you do all of this by accident?" She ran her hand through her hair and scratched violently at the back of her head. Her hair fell immediately back into place. She used to do that all time when she got frustrated. I once accused her of having more than just vampires drinking her blood. In case you were wondering, parasite humor doesn't go over well with the ladies.

"I don't know, Sarah," I sighed. "I'm good at it."

"She deserves better than this," Sarah said softly.

"And here I thought you weren't one of the faithful."

"Don't be a dick," she reached up and pulled a strand of Annessa's hair out of her face. "You have no idea what she's been through."

"You're right," I admitted. "I don't."

"One day you're just a normal girl and the next some jackass of an emissary is ruining your life." She ran her hand over Annessa's cheek, like a concerned mother.

"We talking about her or you?" I asked.

"Does it matter?"

"For what it's worth, I'm sorry on both counts." I moved into Sarah's field of view and caught her eye. "I never meant to hurt you, Sarah."

A black BMW, identical to mine, parked in front of us. Two men in identical charcoal grey suits got out and walked toward the shopping center.

"And there's our ride," I said as I opened the door. I ran around to the passenger side and opened the door. I scanned the area to be sure that no one was looking at us, then unbuckled Annessa. I cradled her against me as the seatbelt released and slowly pushed her back against the seat. I slid one arm under her legs and wrapped the other across her back, just above her wound.

Sarah was out of the car and holding the passenger side door of the new car open before I even thought to ask for her help.

"Thanks," I said as I set Annessa lightly onto the seat. I carefully belted her in and ran to the driver's side. I nodded for Sarah to get in and cast a quick spell of deception around the car. It wasn't up to my normal standards, but I didn't have time for the full treatment. I needed to get Annessa home. I had to find a way to fix her.

Halfway home, I looked into the rearview mirror to see Sarah staring back at me.

"What?" I asked.

"Do you ever regret it?" she asked.

"You're gonna have to be a bit more specific," I said. "I collect regret the way Casanova collected venereal disease."

"Making the deal." She nodded at my Marked hand.

"No," I said without even thinking about it.

"That was a quick answer." She crossed her arms over her chest. "Not even going to consider it?"

"I did," I said. "And the answer's no."

"Why not?"

"It chafes, sometimes." I turned to look at her. "But I made the choice and took my vows and that was that."

"Do you think Rachel regrets her deal?" She smoothed her hair and tucked it behind her ears.

"I'm not sure she made a deal." I looked back to the road.

"No?"

"Upstairs doesn't seem to give a whole lot of choice. At least not according to the Old Testament. You get Called, you do what you're told or you get dead in a hurry."

"There's still a choice there," she said.

"Damnation or slavery," I shook my head. "Either way, you're dead."

"Rachel seems happy."

"Are you..." I whipped around to look at her. "Are you fucking high?"

"No," she said huffily. "Not right now."

"We're talking about the same chick, right?" I checked the road and turned back to her. "Red haired, sorta pretty, full of righteous indignation and never been laid?"

"Don't be a dick, Jason."

"No, no—oh," I said. "I don't think she's happy. I think she's terrified."

"She doesn't seem scared. She was nice when she talked to me."

"She's been kind to me too," I admitted. "She's also stabbed me in the throat with a broken pool cue once. And unlike me, she's human."

"What's that supposed to mean?"

"I get all of these fun toys, I got training and most of all, I'm nearly immortal." I shook my head. "She's not. She's weak, human and subject to the whims of her lord."

"She didn't seem weak an hour ago," Sarah said. "Look what she did to Annessa."

"There's very little she can't do when someone Upstairs is pushing the right buttons. I've seen what happens when she disobeys."

"What about when you disobey?"

"I wind up making the two of you," I said sadly as I looked at Sarah and nodded toward Annessa. "And losing everything I've ever loved."

"Doesn't sound all that different to me."

"I don't think I asked you." I reached out and turned on the radio.

* * *

The sun was setting as I turned into my driveway. As soon as the car rolled to a stop, I threw my door open and ran around to get Annessa's door. I carefully unbuckled her seatbelt and lifted her out of the car.

"Sarah," I grunted. "Grab the keys out of the car, and open the door." I headed toward the house, whispering the sort of inane platitudes that always get invoked over injured friends. Annessa didn't move. I could feel her, her pain and fear echoing across my soul. She was in agony.

Sarah opened the door and stepped out of the way. I carried Annessa upstairs and laid her on my bed. I rolled her onto her stomach as gently as I could. Sarah leaned against the doorframe, her cruel features remarkably compassionate.

"What do you need me to do, Jason?"

I sat on the bed alongside Annessa. "Help me get her undressed," I said. My heart was hammering in my chest. I ran my hand over my face. "I need to see how bad this is."

We silently, carefully, removed Annessa's clothes. The damage was severe. The hole in Annessa's back had started out roughly the diameter of my pinky; it was now the size of my thumb. I hissed through my teeth as the horrible stench of the wound hit me.

"What did they do to her?" Sarah gasped as she covered her nose and mouth, gagging at the smell.

"I don't know, but I assure you, they're gonna pay for it." I knelt next to the bed and smoothed the hair away from Annessa's face. "I'm going to fix this," I whispered.

Sarah turned away, her face held in her hands. I didn't know what was wrong with her, and to be honest, I didn't really care. Annessa was dying and very little mattered beyond that.

I spoke the words low and quiet, the shadows in the room darkened and my human blood fled. I spoke spells of detection and death. Annessa's flesh faded before my Sight, I saw the pathways of energy in her body, black, pulsing dragon lines carrying my magic through her and giving her life beyond death. At the center of her chest, where the lines should have bound themselves into her heart, there was a brilliant glowing light. It was painful to look at, its purity like a knife in my heart.

I released the magic and clutched at my chest. They'd shot her with a blessed bullet. It had to be a reliquary; nothing else could do that much damage to Annessa. I looked back at Sarah.

"That's not a good look," she said softly. "What is it?"

"She's got a reliquary in her chest. It's tearing her apart from the inside. If I don't get it out, or somehow overpower it, she's going to be destroyed."

"Destroyed?"

"Annihilated, unmade," I tugged my hair. "Completely and utterly erased. I won't be able to raise her again because she'll cease to exist."

"Oh." She sat on the bed next to Annessa. She undid the ribbons in Annessa's hair and smoothed her hair back. "You can't do anything with," she waved the ribbons at my Mark, "that?"

"No," I shook my head. "I didn't raise her with his authority. I used my own Word. He didn't have anything to do with it."

"He sent you there, didn't he?"

"Please, Sarah," I took a deep breath. "As much as I appreciate a good argument, now's not the best time. Can you please just keep being the nice woman I'd forgotten you could be and help me out here?"

"Right," she gently squeezed Annessa's hand and stood up. "What are you going to do?"

"I gotta find some way to force it out." I stared into the massive hole in Annessa's bare back. "I have to find some way to nullify its effect." I looked at the raised black veins around the wound, carrying their poison from the wound and infecting the rest of her body. I stared at my own forearm and back. I looked at the butterfly bandage on my thumb.

"Sarah," I asked as realization dawned on me.

"Yeah?"

"Can you go downstairs to the kitchen and get me a knife, please?"

"Sure…" She looked at me quizzically, but went anyway.

I rested my face against Annessa's. "I'm coming in there after you. Just hang on, just a little longer." I could fix this. I could make it right; it was just going to take all of the wrongness within me.

Sarah came back into the room with a butcher knife. I rocked myself back and forth. In my head, a constant slideshow of my failures ran, each image worse than the last. In the pit of my stomach a ball of molten hate was forming. I stood up and took off my shirt.

I took the knife from Sarah and smiled weakly. "If this doesn't work, the car keys are in my left pocket, and good luck to you," I said.

"What are you doing?" Her eyes began to slip away, the faraway look she'd had when I talked to her in the street was returning.

"Ouroborosian correspondence, I thought about it this morning. Annessa fed on my blood and the wound it left wouldn't close when I tried to heal it. Our souls are bound; our blood is the physical manifestation of that binding. When she fed on me, only one half of the 'circuit' was complete, in order to heal myself, I needed her blood."

"So you're going to try to complete that now?"

I nodded. "I'll try and destroy the reliquary, or at least drive it out."

"To drive the light before the darkness, to sever, to destroy, to betray…" She swayed on her feet and sat suddenly.

"Sarah? You okay?" I turned toward her. I realized I was still carrying the knife and slipped it behind me.

She waved me off, her eyes completely glassed over.

I looked back at Annessa. "Fuck it." I stepped up to the edge of the bed. I stopped my heart as I slid the knife across the palm of my left hand, neatly bisecting my Mark. I stretched my neck and reached up with my left hand and pressed against it, finding my carotid artery. I slid my hand up the knife, cautious not to cut myself on the blade and held it about an inch and a half back from the tip. With a quick turning motion, I slid the knife into my neck, severing the artery.

I grabbed Annessa by her right wrist and pulled her up against me, chest to chest. I set my Mark against the wound in her back and lowered her lips to my throat. I started my heart again. My blood spurted down her back and all over her face. I gasped as the pain of the wounds hit me. Annessa didn't move, she didn't respond at all.

'Come on," I whispered. "Drink." I began to weaken as my human blood began to thin. What was left mixed unwillingly with the black Ghūl blood in my veins. I swayed drunkenly on my feet. I tried to stop my heart, but it was too late. The first drop of Ghūl blood touched Annessa's lips and she latched on to my throat. Her wound bound to my hand, and I fell to my knees dragging her off the bed. I felt the pulsing light within her. I focused on it; I let the thought of it consume my mind. Strength from Annessa flooded me.

Sarah reached out to touch me, I assume to see if I were okay. I shook my head slightly, I didn't want to push Annessa away, but having another Gifted touch me right then wasn't wise. She backed slowly out of the room, something akin to horror on her face.

I grinned and shoved that horror deep down inside Annessa, driving all of the darkness of Sarah's pain at the reliquary. I let the memory wash over me and let my pain smother the light inside Annessa.

CHAPTER 15

I'd only recently been "hired" by my Master; it was late in 2004, and I was learning the ropes. I'd known Cassidy for about a year at this point. As usual, I was meeting him at Harker's Place. Only this time it was for a beer, and not for a meeting to announce the impending apocalypse. At the time, Harker was running a recruiting drive. Meaning, he was trying to find a single woman worthy of Turning. In other words, she had to be driven, sexual and motivated to serve. He'd found Sarah.

Sarah was perfect. She was beautiful, intelligent and absolutely in love with the image of the vampire that Harker projected. He'd spent months grooming her to be everything that he wanted in a slave. She'd begun to stay at the bar overnight and sleeping all day outside Harker's hidden coffin. She was entirely his.

I met her one of the first times I'd gone to Harker's. I was standing at the bar staring down into my drink and hating my life. She came up alongside me to order a glass of wine.

"So you're the guy that works for the Devil?" she asked.

"I'm the guy trying to drink in peace," I said without taking my eyes off of my drink. "Whatever you're selling, I don't want any."

"Ouch," she mimed being shot. "I just wanted to say hi."

"Well, you've said it." I looked up and saw who I was talking to. My face told the story for me.

"Ah," she smiled. "And now you feel bad, don't you?"

"I'm sorry," I held out my hand. "Jason Beckett."

"Sarah Halverson," she took my hand.

"Nice to meet you," I said. "Too many people around here want shit from you, you know?"

She held up her blonde hair and stuck her chest out. "Nope, no clue."

I laughed. "Can I buy you a drink? By way of apology, I mean."

"I drink for free," she smiled. "One of the perks of being food for the boss."

"I bet."

"So, you don't look happy, Mr. Beckett."

"I'm not one for parties, I guess," I shrugged.

"How about a joke then?" She grinned at me.

"Shoot."

"What'd the boy with no arms and legs get for Christmas?"

"What?" I asked.

"Cancer."

I laughed. Not one of those polite laughs either. Oh no, this was one of those lean over and try to catch your breath laughs. "Nice," I said when I finally got control of myself.

"Want to hear another one?" She asked, grinning.

"Sure," I grinned back.

"What's worse than biting into an apple and finding half a worm?"

"I'm almost afraid to ask."

"The Holocaust."

I snorted. "That's awful," I said.

"You laughed, what's that make you?"

"About half as guilty as you, I'd guess," I chuckled. "Thanks for that."

"You should come join us in the back," she smiled as she picked up a glass of red wine from the bar. "Cassidy's back there."

"Thanks, but I'm afraid that I'm not very good company tonight."

"Ok," she smiled. "Offer's on the table."

We managed to talk just about every time I showed up at Harker's. It was all on the up and up. I wasn't looking to do anything with her other than converse, and she was absolutely devoted to Harker. It was nice to have another human to talk to, one that didn't work for the IRS or call me 'my lord emissary.'

Shortly thereafter, though, things went south. Now you have to understand, I've never been the subtlest guy, and then, I was even worse. My soul was still raw from the transition and the price of my servitude. My first few commissions were riddled with more bullet holes than an Iraqi subdivision. I spent my nights killing and my days weeping. I was a complete mess. At that time, I was tracking a traitor, a guy who decided that he was through working for the Master. He'd fallen prey to the other side's talk of reconciliation and forgiveness, which incidentally is a lie. Infernal favors are like credit cards in the real world: sure, you get the cash up front, but sooner or later you have to pay. The Angelics represent themselves as bankruptcy lawyers, but just like the real thing, for seven years no one fucking believes you, trusts you or wants your business. Forgiveness is neither free nor automatic. No one trusts a traitor.

So, this prick decides to run to the Church for help. I decide to intervene. Rachel and nine friends kicked my nuts up around my ears and left me to die in the gutter in front of St. Patrick's Cathedral. By the time I got myself to the point of reliable locomotion again, I was livid. When I finally found Rachel, I broke both of her legs and tossed her off of the Brooklyn Bridge. I wasn't feeling friendly. You can see how we started the lovely relationship that we have today. The important part of the story is that I was lost, scared, and without any means of finding the guy that I needed to kill to appease my Master.

At the end of my rope, I found my way to Harker's Place and to Harker. He knew something; he had his hands in every piece of illicit business in the city. In retrospect, what I did was not only stupid but also terribly dangerous. I didn't know any of the stories about Harker. I only knew what I saw—a fruity vampire kid with some serious fashion issues. Even then, he had the whole femmy vampire dork thing down. What I didn't know back then was that Harker is the fulcrum upon which the entire Aetheric civilization of New York rests. Yeah, we've been over just how not bright I can be. Let's not beat it to death.

I forced my way to the back of the club and kicked open the back door. Cassidy, Harker, Sarah and a whole bunch of Goth girls were sitting around a massive oak table. I started yelling my head off, demanding answers and waving guns around. Incidentally, next time you decide to threaten a vampire, remember this one little fact: unless you're packing blessed gold, guns mean exactly shit to vampires. I had exactly zero gold on me. Harker broke my right arm and shattered my collarbone with my own fist. He dropped me to the floor with a laugh and walked away.

I was so enraged; I healed myself with the anger alone. Not sure how to hurt Harker directly, I went after what I knew I could hurt. Sarah ran to me, her face a storm of confusion and pity. I grabbed her. Suddenly everyone froze. Look, if you take nothing else away from my little tale, remember this. Everyone, no matter the faction, no matter the predilection, no matter anything, everyone loves the innocent.

"Jason!" She jerked against my arm. "You're gonna get yourself killed!"

Harker leapt forward.

"Stop!" She threw her hands out at him. "Wait!"

"Just tell me what I need to know," I demanded, my eyes locked on Harker. "And I let her go."

"Jason," she pleaded. "We're friends, don't do this!"

"I don't have a choice," I yanked her closer to me.

"There's always a choice," she pulled gently against my arm. "Let me go."

Harker growled something inane at me. I have no idea what he actually said. I just remember feeling Sarah relax, watching her hands lift as she surrendered. "Everything's okay, Jason. Just let me go."

"Tell your boyfriend to tell me what I need to know," I demanded.

"No one's going to tell you anything, Jason," she said. "Please just let me go. I promise, you can just walk away."

Harker twitched. He didn't move, he just twitched. Like he was testing me. I fell for it. I slammed my Mark over her eyes.

"See," I commanded her. "See what you love! See Truth!"

She threw herself on the floor clutching at her eyes and called out Harker's name. When she lifted her face, I could see trails of blood running down from her eyes. As Sarah looked up at Harker, she flailed and screamed in terror and suddenly we were all blown back against the walls with the strength of her fear. I hadn't expected that. I thought that she'd see Harker's true form and cower in terror.

I looked down at my Mark; it was covered in her blood. I knew in my soul that I'd done something serious at that moment. I didn't know anything else for a long time. Harker beat me to death. I'm not using pretty language; Harker literally beat me to death.

My soul returned to Perdition. I stood before my Master for the second time. The first time was when I took my vow of servitude.

"Look around my kingdom, my child. What do you see?" He gestured out the window of the Tower of Grief.

"I see Perdition," I said. I'd already learned that the word "Hell" wasn't exactly smiled upon in my Master's presence.

"Look to the souls in the Asphodel Fields and to those that serve me here in the Tower. What do you see in them?" he asked.

"I don't know." I really didn't. They just seemed like people. Granted, they were people living their lives in a place that defied imagination, but still people.

"Do they seem like slaves to you?" he asked me.

"No, Master," I answered still confused.

"And you, you call me Master, yet you have free will, do you not?" He raised an eyebrow.

"I don't suppose you'd let me take a walk to the Upper Room anytime now, would you?" I quipped.

Now, this lesson's free. When you decide to be a smart ass it should definitely never be to an angel that challenged Yahweh and nearly won. He didn't touch me, or hurt me or even use harsh language. He looked at me. That was it. Everything in me that was strong and brave winked out like a match in the wind. I dropped to my knees.

"There are consequences for disloyalty, my son. But they are no different than in your mortal life, are they?" His gazed softened.

"No, Master, they're not," I said, chastened.

He stood and raised himself to his full height. "None come before my altar but for their own desires."

I must've looked confused.

"Did anyone make you come here?" he asked. "Did anyone make you serve me?"

"No."

"Even now, do I force your hand and make you do any of the things that you do in order to enforce my will?" His great eyes were intent on mine.

"No, but I wouldn't have to do those things if you didn't order me to. I only do what you want." I admit, it was petulance.

"Is that so?" he asked. "Did I make you torment that girl? Did I even remotely hint that I wanted an innocent harmed?"

"No. But it was necessary; Harker had to know that I was serious."

"There are better ways of convincing others of your earnestness without resorting to harming innocents, my son." His anger was apparent.

"It isn't that!" I stepped back and slapped a hand over my eyes. I took a breath and looked at him pleadingly. "I didn't even mean to do what I did. I just lost control, I only wanted to make her see what Harker was, what Cassidy was, what I was. So she would know the danger she was in."

"Odd. I once said something similar about what I did to your grandmother many times removed."
He smiled a sad smile, one that I could tell wasn't meant for me.

Now what the fuck do you say to that? See, this is what makes him such a prick. You argue with him; he lets you. Granted he'll only take so much. Then you fight with him, and he lets you. You disobey, and he lets you. You blatantly ignore him, you curse his name, you walk away. And he lets you. Yet you come back. Why? Because he let you leave in the first place. Because deep down inside, you believe that you left behind the promise of Paradise and threw away all hope of redemption or resurrection for something better. And when he speaks, you see something in his eyes that sings of a young woman standing naked in Eden, surrounded by lions and gods—both of which boast legendary hunger. Something of that day was in his eye as he admonished me.

"What would you have me do? Find the girl and fix it?" I snapped.

"I want you to find our traitor and show him the error of his ways." He turned his back to me. "You are free to leave me, Jason. You are free to walk away. None at my altar but the willing."

"Then why am I killing this traitor; can't he walk away?" I asked.

"Walking away and betraying me are very different things, my son."

I returned to Earth and killed the traitor. After that I apologized to Cassidy and to Harker. Harker actually seemed to respect me after the apology. It may have been that or the fact that when I delivered it, I gave him Mara. Cassidy didn't even listen to the apology, he just laughed at me and said I was an Irishman and that was enough. Apparently, my ancestors shared both my passion and my lack of sense.

It was three years before I saw Sarah again. I had no idea what I'd unleashed with my Word. When next I saw her it was in a dive bar in Newark. I'd just killed nine bikers and was helping myself to the bar when she walked in. I hadn't even heard her enter.

"What would Adolf Hitler do if he were alive today?" she asked quietly.

I stared at my drink. "What?" I asked softly. I didn't need to turn around. Guilt makes for wonderful radar.

"Scream and claw at the lid of his coffin." She stepped carefully over the bodies.

I snorted and bit down on my lip. I kept my back to her. "You here to kill me?"

"I'm just here to take the money out of the register." She walked past me and around the bar. She didn't look well. She was wearing other people's cast off clothes and it looked like she hadn't washed her hair in weeks. "Don't flatter yourself."

"I'm s—" I started.

"DON'T YOU FUCKING DARE!" She slammed her palm on the bar. "Don't," she said again quietly. She pounded a button on the register.

"If you need money," I looked up at her. "I can give you whatever you need."

"Can you take back your fucking Word?" She yanked the money out of the register as she stared me down.

"No."

"Then there's nothing I want from you." She hurled the drawer shut. "You fucking hateful bastard. I've seen what you do to friends."

"Sarah," I held my hands in supplication. "Please, there's got to be something I can do."

"Burn in hell." She stormed out of the bar, and I didn't see her again until my Master showed me her image in Perdition.

CHAPTER 16

Annessa's whimper brought me back to the present. She released her hold on my neck and opened her mouth in a silent scream. Her whole body shook against me. I chanted a verse in Ghūllish in her ear. A challenge hymn, uttered by adherents of Ninnaka–Varylethkinaya. Ghūls chanted them during times of strain and adversity. If there was a time for such a chant, it was now. More than that was the fact that most of the words were bastardized from the Umbral tongue. The pervasive Darkness in the language strengthened our assault on the reliquary buried in her back.

She convulsed and screamed at the top of her lungs. I felt a pulse, like the shockwave from a distant explosion travel through her flesh and into mine. My hand was thrown off of her back by the force of the blast. The reliquary shrieked as it hurled itself from her body and shattered the bedroom window. It left a contrail of pure, painful light as it arced out of the house and landed somewhere in my front yard.

Annessa slumped against me. I gently lowered her to the floor. I needed to check my wounds. No sense in saving her, just to have my accidental death kill us both. I looked down at my Mark. The skin was unmarred and the black lines of the Mark itself as black as the day they were etched into my flesh. I reached up and touched my neck, no wound. I smiled. I was right, there was an Ouroborosian correspondence. That might come in handy.

"For the record," Annessa murmured from the floor. "Whoever fucking shot me is gonna die."

"Duly noted," I rocked myself forward and stood. I reached down and lifted her and set her on the bed.

"I'm serious, Master." Her eyes flared weakly.

"So'm I." I pushed the hair out of her face and placed my Mark on her forehead. "Sleep." I spoke a Word, and she closed her eyes. Her body would need time to fix itself. She wasn't meant to sleep, but resting would make the healing process faster. Besides, I wanted a chance to talk to Sarah.

I left Annessa in the bedroom and went downstairs to the kitchen. Sarah was sitting at kitchen table, her hands clutching a teacup like there was no tomorrow.

"You squeeze that any tighter and I'll have a diamond," I said as I slid another chair out.

"Where's Annessa?" she asked.

"Upstairs," I said. "Sleeping."

"I thought she didn't sleep?" She raised a delicate eyebrow.

"She does when I tell her to," I said as I sat.

"There's more tea," she nodded at the stove.

"Thanks," I said. "I'm afraid I'm going to need something significantly stronger tonight."

"I quit drinking." She looked into her cup.

"Interferes with your Gift?" Most Gifted avoided getting intoxicated due to the fact that their Gifts would often become unstable. And of course, the fact that they're dangerous as hell when they're trashed is also a concern.

"Doesn't interfere enough." She shook her head and lifted her sleeve to show me enough tracks to keep Amtrak busy for a decade.

My jaw worked for a second. There was something about the tracks, the way they looked. It was like staring at a picture in a mirror. There was something about the way their placement, their...design. I couldn't take my eyes off of them. Part of me recoiled and part of me was entranced. "Heroin?" I finally choked out.

"Yeah," she nodded, a strange look of sadness, then acceptance crossed her face as she tugged her sleeves back down. "It's the only thing that holds it back. Otherwise," she made circles on either side of her head with her hands. "It's all just a jumble of other people's thoughts, sicknesses and death." She shuddered.

"I didn't know," I sat back. "I had no idea."

"It's not like you could've fixed it, Jason," she snorted.

"Yeah, but I could've made it easier to bear." I ran a hand over my eyes. "I can't begin to tell you how sorry I am."

"So you've said." She took a drink and looked at me over the rim of her mug. "And look where that's got us."

"If you'd only listened to me…"

"Listened? I trusted you!" She leaned forward, her eyes displaying even more hate than the venomous hiss of her words. "And this is what you did to me. We were friends, Jason. *Friends*. You don't rape your friend's mind and fuck up everything inside them to prove a fucking point!" She slammed her fist on the table, rattling her mug violently.

I opened my mouth, shut it and opened it again. "No, you don't," I said with a sigh. I stood, walked over to the fridge and threw the freezer door open. I pulled out an ice cube tray. "You don't do anything like that." I opened the cupboard next to the fridge and pulled out a glass. I tossed a handful of ice cubes in the glass and put the tray back into the freezer.

"Friends care about each other." I said it quietly as I picked up the bottle of whisky and poured it into the glass. The popping of the ice cubes was deafening. "I wish I had an excuse, Sarah." I turned back to her and took a huge swallow of my whisky. "I wish I could take it all back."

"You won't," she stared into her mug as if it contained the secrets of the universe. 'Not when this all over."

"What's that supposed to mean?" I yanked my chair over to me and sat heavily in front of her. "What the hell are you taking about?"

"Nothing, everything, shit," She knocked on the table and growled in frustration. "I don't know."

"Tell me, Sarah," I said, my voice soft.

"You can't know what this is like." She stared up at the ceiling. "There's no hell like this."

"Tell me," I said again. I reached across the table and touched her hand.

"I don't...I don't know where I am, *when* I am, Jason." Tears slowly slid down her face. "It's like seeing everything in a mirror maze, seeing each glance, each touch as it ripples across every dimension, every reality." She sniffed. "I never know who I am to anyone, what I am." She wiped her eye with her left hand. "Except to you."

"To me?" I said as I shook my head.

"You're the only constant," she smiled for a second, then her face crumpled and she covered it with her hand. "You're the only fucking thing that I can count on."

"Because I..." I held up my Mark. "I'd have thought you'd want to avoid thinking about me."

"Don't flatter yourself," she snapped. "I don't *want* to think about you. You're like a goddamned anchor, a fucking albatross on my neck. It just all comes back to you."

"I did this to you," I shrugged. "It stands to reason that we're connected and unchanging."

"Oh, I never said we didn't change," she shook her head. "Sometimes things are different, sometimes we're—" She cut herself off and looked into her mug again.

"We're what," I prompted. "What's different?"

"We're lovers," she sighed.

"We've never been lovers, Sarah," I said. "You had Harker, and I had the memory of Jessica."

"Sometimes that didn't matter." She sighed again. "It's just what I see, reflections from another mirror, another reality spilling over."

"That means you forgave me, in some reality." I smiled sadly. "That means there's hope for this one."

"You've already got one woman in your bed, Beckett," she looked up at me, her eyes stared daggers into mine. "Don't even think about it."

"I didn't mean it like that," I sat back in my chair, cleared my throat and quickly changed the subject. "Thanks for helping me with Annessa," I said. "I mean it."

"Can't let the Sacred Mother die on your watch," she snorted. "Wouldn't look good come time for a promotion, huh?"

"She's..." I froze and clutched at the air with my left hand as my mind tried to find the right word. What was Annessa?

"Good for you, Jason." Sarah smiled as she idly spun her mug. "She makes you think like a human being for a change."

"I just lost my wife," I sat back in my chair. "It's not like that."

"You don't need to be a Seer to know how that girl feels about you," she tapped her head. "Magic or not, she's your girl, Jason, through and through."

"I didn't mean that either." I finished the rest of my drink in a single swallow. "Something else I managed to fuck up completely."

"How so?"

"If I hadn't yanked her back and bound her, my Master would've had her brought back as a human. She'd have been free. Instead?" I waved a hand in the air gesturing vaguely toward my bedroom. Sighing, I leaned forward and reached past Sarah to grab the bottle of whisky on the counter behind her chair. For a second our faces were close enough to touch.

There was a moment, a fleeting second when I looked into her eyes, I saw a reflection, an image, like a ghost on film. I saw her in my arms, my lips on hers. For all that it was wrong and a lie, it resonated like a half–drawn truth, erased by the pen of some unseen artist. When I pulled away, her lips closed as if in the last moment of the act, the director deleted the final, meaningful kiss, and she no longer needed to part them for the delicate touch of her lover's tongue.

I cleared my throat and pulled her mug across the table. I tossed two of my ice cubes into her mug, then poured her a drink and refilled my own glass.

"What to this time?" she asked me, as she had so many times before. It was as if the past were echoing through my mind.

"To liars and fools," I lifted my glass.

"Liars and fools," she clinked her cup against mine. "To you."

We drank in silence for a second. "I hate myself for what I did to you," I said. I bit my lip and looked at her through half–lidded eyes.

"I've never hated you," she whispered then shook her head as if she'd said something wrong.

"What?" I stared at my glass unsure if the whiskey had screwed up my hearing.

"I knew how scared you were," she said. "I could see it, feel it. It was coming off of you in waves."

"Yeah, but scared or not, Sarah," I sat back and ran my hand through my hair. "I did this; I broke your fucking mind."

"No, you didn't." She took another drink. "I've always had it. You just made it worse. I've been able to See since I was nine years old. Why do you think Harker wanted me?"

"No," I disagreed. "He loved you. He still loves you."

"Some small part of him maybe," she lifted her glass, her pinky pointing at me as if to correct me. "The rest of him saw what a Seer could do for him, for his murder." She laughed. "If you hadn't pulled your little stunt, who knows where we'd all be now."

"Can we please take this in one direction or the other?" I lifted my glass and ran the cool surface of it over my forehead. "All this back and forth is killing me."

"Consequence is never entirely good or bad, Jason." She shook her head and took a drink. "The universe isn't so black and white."

"Why'd you let yourself fall for Harker if you knew that he wasn't in love with you?"

"Because I was in love with him, with the idea of him." She reached over, picked up the bottle and refilled her mug, then my glass. "If anyone knows that people do stupid things for love, it's you."

"To love," I lifted my drink. "May we never be so stupid again."

"Love, and the lies that go with it," she clinked her glass against mine again.

"Why'd you come with me?" I leaned forward, my eyes on my glass, my eyes boring into their twisted reflections on the ice cubes. "Today, I mean."

"You said you'd throw me in the damned trunk…"

"Stop fucking with me, Sarah," I looked up and stared into her eyes. "We both know there's no way I'd have caught you if you wanted to get away."

"The alternative may have been worse," she said.

"Don't give that vague shit." I sat back and ran my hand over my mouth. It's about the only thing that keeps me from saying something asinine.

"What do you want me to say, Jason?" She tucked her perfectly behaved hair behind her ears and stared at me with blank, icy eyes. "That I came with you so we could have our little tea party and play nice as if nothing ever happened?"

I took a deep breath and blew it out in a rush. "I'd like the truth, but I can see I'm not gonna get it." I slid my chair back, stood and picked up my glass. I swirled the ice around, then drank the last remaining drop of whisky in it. "For what it's worth, for a second there, we were *us* again." I turned and set my glass in the sink. As I turned back to leave, I rested my hand on hers. "It was nice to see you again." I held her gaze for a second.

For a minute, the storm clouds in her eyes parted, laying bare the woman I remembered. I leaned forward and kissed her forehead. "You know how sorry I am," I choked out, no longer trusting my voice, nor the honesty that the whisky'd brought along as a plus one.

"Minneapolis," she blurted out.

"What?" I asked, thoroughly confused.

"I need to go Minneapolis," she said. Her eyes had that lost, faraway look to them again.

"What the hell for?" I knelt beside her chair. "It's like minus four hundred degrees there now."

"Zero," She looked at me and the way she emphasized the word seemed to strike a chord within me.

"Zero what?" I prompted as I leaned closer to her.

She blinked and shuddered. "What?" She looked up at me vacantly.

"Holy shit," I said. "It's one-thirty in the damned morning; we're not going to start a fucking Laurel and Hardy sketch."

"Go to bed," she said with finality. She picked up her mug and stared into the bottom of it.

I stood up and looked at her quizzically. "No," I said. "You don't get out of this one so easily."

"None of us do." She looked up at me with those haunted eyes. "Go to bed," she said again, and somehow it felt like a command.

I wanted to ask her what she'd meant, but it was like fighting the tide. Something in the way she spoke, the certainty of her words seemed to cement thought to action. I'd already stepped out of the kitchen before my mind questioned that I was in motion. I was lying in bed next to Annessa before I realized I'd been tricked, again. It wasn't like I could have asked Sarah to clarify what she meant, though. Partly because she'd Seen that I wouldn't and partly because that was precisely when my house exploded.

CHAPTER 17

It sounded like a mountain dropping out of the sky. It was like a shriek followed by a massive sonic boom, like lightning touching off an atomic bomb. A brilliant light filled my bedroom just before the windows blew inward. I caught a brief glimpse of Annessa's shadow black hair and pale skin as she rolled on top of me and pulled me off of the bed.

We hit the floor in a pile and a second later the bed was thrown on top of her. She straddled me, resting on her knees and elbows. She didn't even twitch as the weight of a room's worth of wood, metal and plastic hit the bed and pressed down on her.

"What the fuck was that?" she yelled as the roar of the explosion subsided.

"Sarah!" I yelled over the tremendous ringing in my ears. "We gotta get to Sarah!"

Annessa nodded and shoved herself violently upward, hurling the bed and assorted detritus that was once a room off of her back. She flexed her back experimentally, before standing. She reached down to help me up.

"She was downstairs," I said as I grabbed her hand.

"There's gonna be a ton of them downstairs, Master." Her eyes flared green, even her pupils smoldered as she pulled me to my feet. "And I'm gonna kill every fucking one."

"Just leave me one alive to question," I said as I pushed past her toward the gaping hole that was once a doorway. I snatched my pistol from the small of my back. Yes, I sleep with my holster on, if you haven't been paying attention, shit tends to go south when I relax. "I'm not raising another haemunculus."

"You can't handle the one you've got, Master." She slid by me with a wicked grin on her face. That's when I realized she was still naked from the waist up.

"You might be right," I grinned. "Let's hope they can't either."

She raced ahead of me down the remains of my upstairs hallway. Her hands flexed with each step, her claws sliding free like ten jagged razors. I felt her hunger echo across my mind. It took less than a second before the first gunshot rang out.

A neat row of bullets shredded the wall just before the stairs. Annessa jerked back in surprise. She hissed and crouched and then, claws thrust out before her, dove headlong through the wall. Screams rebounded through the stairwell, the acoustics of the tall ceiling rendering it into a symphony of pain. I charged forward with a Word on my lips and my pistol raised.

I rounded the corner, and peeked through the massive hole that Annessa'd torn in my wall. She was like a hurricane in motion. She ducked and whirled, her hair dancing and spinning wildly around her head. Her claws bit deeply into the flesh of the three gunmen on the landing. She buried her fangs in the neck of one of them as she danced aside from another's clumsy attempt at a rifle smash to her face. She hurled herself backward into a graceful backbend to avoid the third man's slashing knife. She kicked herself all the way over and planted her heels in the chest of the first man. As he staggered back and hit the wall, she drove herself forward, arms extended. She caught the man with the knife by the head and buried her fangs in his face as she collided with him like a bullet train. The two of them tumbled down the second, smaller, flight of stairs. He stopped screaming less than a second after he started.

The two remaining men on the landing froze in shock. I didn't. My gun barked as I spoke my Word. The man with the knife got a new hole in his forehead, the other's eyes ignited with the force of my curse. Both dropped soundlessly to the floor. I took the stairs two at a time.

I stepped into a fiery hell. My living room was engulfed in flames. Annessa stood in the center of the room, her hands locked around the throat of a massive Host–Bound who was bent double the wrong way. His eyes glowed with dancing beryl and white flames. Ophanim. Shit.

I opened my mouth to call Annessa back. The Ophanim was faster. In a blur, he crossed the room and savagely kicked me in the chest. In a flash, he was back in Annessa's hands. He was like lightning in a bottle, or like trying to fight a thought, all quicksilver and wind—impossible to hold.

I gasped as the air was forced out of me. My words died unspoken, and I collapsed against the stairs. My mouth worked like a retarded fish out of water. I wanted to raise my pistol, but I knew the moment I leveled it, it was gone, likely to never be found again. Annessa's confusion was apparent on her face and she slashed her claws into the space where the creature once was.

Ophanim. Dammit, only me, only now. Ophanim are the vengeance of the Man Upstairs. Think of a bullet on Meth and you've got an Ophanim before his first cup of coffee. Of course they'd send an Ophanim to stop me from moving quickly, when speed was I needed most. I had little choice but to call on my own Ophanim.

"Abbadonna," I croaked as I pulled myself to my feet. "To me."

The Ophanim's head snapped back to focus on me, a feral grin splitting his face. He slammed a rapid staccato flurry of knees into Annessa's face, throwing her back into the remains of the fireplace. He faced me, blurred lines forming an aura of flame around him, as my eyes struggled to follow his impossibly fast movements.

He punched me six times before I registered that he'd moved. I felt my clavicle cave under his knuckles as my lip split and I choked on several teeth. I fell back drunkenly, as my head absorbed five punishing blows. All at once, I felt Abbadonna surge into my mind.

"Took you long enough," I muttered.

There are penalties for treating me like a dog.

"I see you in there," the Host–Bound laughed at me as he threw another salvo of vicious kicks into Annessa. "Come to play, sister?"

"We shall dance, Kauiriel," Abbadonna spat back through my bloody mouth. "And it shall be your last!"

My apologies, Emissary.

"For what?" I wondered aloud. Right about the time Kauiriel landed another fist to my face, I felt Abbadonna slide out of my brain. My head rebounded several times off of the sharp edge of the stairs. I threw up down my front and tried to blink to clear my swimming vision. I wiped the tears from my face with the back of my hand and spat to clear my mouth of the vomit burning the cavities where my teeth used to be. It really didn't help much.

Abbadonna was riding Annessa and the two of them made Kauiriel and his pet human look like chumps. It was like watching a tornado contained within my living room. They tore at each other, screaming Angelic and Fallen hymns, glorifying the worlds above and below. With each rapid, resounding hit, something else in the room exploded. Annessa dove forward, ducking under a massive uppercut, to bury her fangs in his right thigh. He swung a heavy hammerfist to dislodge her. She kicked her feet out and slid between his legs, letting her momentum tear loose the grip of her fangs. She tore her head from side to side as she was dislodged, showering the room with blood. As soon as her feet struck the wall behind him, she rolled her body over and threw herself to her feet, driving the claws of her trailing hand deep into the flesh of his back.

Kauiriel's scream shattered whatever glass remained whole in the room and nearly deafened me. I clapped my hands over my ears and dropped to one knee, the maddeningly loud sound forcing me to the floor.

Bind him, Emissary.

It wasn't a request. Abbadonna had a score to settle with this particular Angel. I didn't know what it was and there wasn't time to ask. I yanked my left hand away from my ear and spoke a Word of binding, just as I had on the kid in the cemetery. Except this time, it wasn't a soul I was trapping, but an Angel.

"You cannot!" Kauiriel screamed. He staggered away from Annessa. "You dare not!" He turned to face me. I braced myself against the stair. I expected him to charge me, to beat me into oblivion. But, his eyes were pleading; I saw only abject terror in them. "Please," he implored me. I looked into his eyes, but before I could respond, Annessa's claws tore through his face from behind. His face stared at me, eyeless and mangled, yet somehow still pleading.

My jaw worked with unspoken words. I expected to find pity, even sorrow in my heart. Instead, I felt only the echoes of my own pain reverberating back at me. Still staring at his corpse, I spoke a Word of healing and felt my skin and bones begin to itch as my flesh knit itself back together again.

Annessa stepped over the body and ran her hand over my forearm. The air rippled like a heat mirage as Abbadonna slid back into me.

Let him rot.

I felt her begin to heal my remaining injuries. I wanted to be pissed at her for letting that prick smash my face in, but it *was* sound strategy. Besides, I didn't have time to fight with her right then.

"She's gotta be outside," I said, jerking my head toward the shattered remains of my front door. "There's no way she's still in here."

I stepped carefully, but quickly through the shattered remains of my house and peeked quickly outside the door.

My driveway was empty except for the smoking remains of my car. Again? Fuck.

"Shit!" I pounded my hand against the doorframe. I patted my clothes trying to find my phone. I'd left it my jacket, which was in the ruins of my bedroom. I shoved myself away from the doorway and raced up the stairs. I kept up a steady stream of swearing the whole way.

Annessa followed behind me, a silent shadow. Even Abbadonna was quiet in the face of my rage. I stepped into the room and immediately began looking for my jacket. It was an impossible task. The debris from the explosion had torn the room apart. There were tree limbs from the pine trees outside mingled with glass and wood from the house all jutting out from the remains of my bedroom furniture.

I sighed and leaned back against the wall. How the fuck was I going to find Sarah now? I kicked a chunk of broken glass and froze. As the glass rolled over it reflected the face of my phone, lit up and displaying Cassidy's scowling face. I dropped to the floor and looked under the scorched hunk of wood that was once my dresser. My phone rested against a small wooden box, all of which sat on Annessa's carefully folded shirt. I grabbed the shirt and yanked the whole pile out.

I answered the phone just as it began to belt out "Psychopathy Red."

"Speak to me," I said, throwing Annessa her shirt. I picked up the box and flipped it over in my hand.

"You are in danger, Little Brother," he said.

"No shit," I snorted. "Could've used that about fifteen minutes ago, man."

"Then I am too late?" He swore. He must have been really pissed; it was an Irish swear. I don't know what it meant, but it didn't sound good.

"They got Sarah," I said. "I have no idea where they went, but I gotta find them and stop them before they make her talk. It's going to take me a bit to get anywhere; they blew up my fucking car...again."

"Take the Road," he said. "I've been telling you all along, they cannot destroy what lies beyond their sight."

"Yeah, yeah, yeah," I muttered as I toyed with the box. I flipped it open. A folded letter sat in the middle of the box, resting on a dog–eared postcard. "Let me call you back," I said. "I think I found something." I hung up the phone without waiting for a response.

"What's that?" Annessa asked as she pulled the tight shirt over her head.

"A letter," I said as I unfolded it. "From Sarah."

"That's weird," she said as she knelt next to me. "Why'd she write you a letter? She was here; why not just tell you what was on her mind?"

"I don't know, Annessa," I mumbled. "Give me a damned chance to read it."

Jason,

By the time you read this, I'll be gone. Now it's my turn to say it. 'For what it's worth, I'm sorry.' I don't know how many times I've heard you say that. I'm beginning to understand what it means. You just walked away from me about five minutes ago and already the visions are coming on stronger.

I'm going to give you the same gift you gave me all those years ago: Truth. See, this nifty little Gift of mine won't stop until I do what I'm supposed to do. Now, I'm supposed to do this. No matter what you do, it won't matter. I knew this was coming, but I thought I could stop it. I can't. I thought you could stop it; you can't.

The spiders are closing in. The web's set and ready, and the fools are flying in by the thousands. The spider in the middle's waiting for someone close to you. The spider in the fly's waiting for you. If only you weren't you. If only you were just you. I don't even know any more. Even your name becomes more confusing as the days pass.

I loved you once, on another world. You held me and told me that everything would be all right, that the world would pass us by. I believed you then, but I'm afraid that time has passed. Even now, I know that we can never be what we were again.

There's a maiden dancing in the lights that watched her die. There's a woman in hell who's in heaven and there's a woman waiting to die with your name etched upon her lips. All three are even now beyond your help and yet, it's your touch that will set them free, or bind them forever.

We're all waiting for you here. You're so far away. We're all waiting.

They're coming. They know. The Darkness with Seven Souls told me. We're waiting here alone but for the teeming masses, the fetid, gibbering children that whisper our deaths into our sleeping mouths and wait for our souls to echo back. The sins of our fathers stain us with the ink of their evil.

ZeroZeroZero

I'm so sorry,

Sarah

I sat back on my heels and stared at the paper. We hadn't drank that much. I thought about the track marks on her arms. Maybe she'd gotten high. None of it made sense. It was incompressible to me. Well, some of it made sense, if you twisted your head just so and got high as a fucking kite. I sighed.

The Darkness with Seven Souls. Praise the Lord of the Fallen, she has returned!

"She was high, Abbadonna," I said. 'There's no way."

"What're we talking about?" Annessa asked, kneeling beside me to look at the letter.

"Ninnaka," I said. "Sarah says she's back."

"Is that bad?" she asked, her chin resting on my shoulder as she read the letter.

"All depends," I said. "On if you want the world to end."

"Oh," she said. "It's like that?"

"It's like that."

"The last line makes sense to me," She said, pointing to the word 'father' with a delicate finger.

"Yeah?"

"Yeah," she poked my Mark. "Think about it, my dad worships the Devil and bam! He gets me."

"I'm not sure that's quite what she meant, Annessa."

She held up her foot, the inky birthmark darker than the flickering shadows around us. She looked back up at me. "Looks pretty clear to me, the ink of my father's evil." She tapped her foot.

"Whatever," I dismissed it. "That's not the important part here. What matters is we've got something we can barter with."

"What's that?" Annessa asked.

"A reliable source that says she's been contacted by Ninnaka. If Satariel believes us, he might be willing to help."

"Why would he help us for that? I mean, if he's all knowing, wouldn't he just *know*?" She shook her head. "You're gonna need more than that to strong–arm someone, Master. My father always said a man who looks for friends with a fist instead of a gift was born to wear concrete shoes."

"The confirmation of what he suspects might be enough." I tapped my finger against my forehead. "I'm missing something here. It's important; I just wish I knew what the fuck it was."

"It's always a game of connect the dots," Annessa plucked at her shirt, pulling so she could see the back. "Speaking of which, your friend's a shitty seamstress."

I looked over at Annessa's back, and my stomach plummeted.

Connect the dots indeed.

Stitched over the gunshot wound in Annessa's shirt, and pressed into the flesh of Sarah's arms, the same damn symbol. I rocked myself back and forth for a second.

"I couldn't figure out why," I said aloud, more to myself than anyone else. "Both sides were willing to endgame this over a seer." I stood and yanked at my hair.

"What?" Annessa looked at me, then back at her shirt.

"She said she'd had her Gift since she was nine," *Her Gift came with her blood.*

"Her gift came *from* her blood," I shook my head. "How?" I yelled. "How is this shit always my fucking fault?"

"Ok, what the fuck are you talking about?" Annessa jerked to her feet and put her hands on my shoulders.

I grabbed her shirt and showed her the symbol stitched into the fabric, binding shut the blood soaked hole. "Do you have any idea what this is?"

"If I do, I'm doing a pretty fucking good job hiding it, Master," she snapped back at me.

"It's the Seal of Solomon." I released her.

"Oh," she covered her mouth. "You mean…"

"Sarah's a blooded seer of the line of Solomon, and we just gave her to the Umbrals."

Satariel will not hesitate to aid you now, Emissary.

I was already dialing my phone.

"That was fast," Cassidy laughed.

"I need to meet with Satariel, now."

"Meet? My lord doesn't meet anyone, Little Brother."

"Oh, he'll fucking meet me," I said. "He needs me to get to Sarah as much as I need him to find her."

"Why is that?"

I told him.

"Grand Central," he said immediately.

"How will I find him?" I asked.

"He'll find you," he replied. "Mind your tongue, Little Brother. Remember with whom you're dealing."

"Done." I hung up the phone. I reached into the closet and grabbed a garment bag. I was covered in blood and vomit, and even I can't get away with that for long. I released Abbadonna to gather her strength; we were going to need her again before long.

"Let's go," I said to Annessa.

CHAPTER 18

I opened the door to my armory. Though the rest of the house had been burned beyond all recognition, the strength of my wards had kept the armory safe. I ushered Annessa through the door and shut it behind her. I spoke a Word of protection over the heavy steel door and turned back to my weapons.

"Hold this," I said as I yanked a tactical shotgun out of a rack and shoved it back at Annessa.

"Is this for me?" she asked.

"What do you need a gun for?" I asked as I grabbed a tactical vest and threw it on. I stuffed spare magazines for my pistol in the ammo pouches on the front and dropped a box of shotgun shells into a wide pocket on the side.

"They just look so damned cool." She racked the action on the shotgun.

"You're a juggernaut of death," I snorted as I took the gun away from her. "It doesn't get any cooler than that."

"I'm your juggernaut of death, Master," she corrected.

"I'm pretty sure that's what I said." I changed quickly into the clothes from the garment bag and stepped around a rack that held several large machine guns. "Give me your hand," I said.

Annessa took my hand and squeezed it gently.

I stepped through the Veil and pulled her with me. The darkness of the Inner Veil pulsed and seemed to swim with strange variations of gray light. We stood in a darker reflection of my armory, identical in all respects save one. A black door framed by even darker shadows was cut into the wall in front of me.

"Where are we?" Annessa asked, her voice full of wonder.

"The Shadow Roads, or 'The Roads' as most Veilsiders call them." I shrugged as I opened the door. Shadow poured into the room like a low hanging fog, pooling and eddying around our feet. "Cool, huh?"

"What are they?" she asked as she nodded in answer to my question.

"They're the backdoors to Creation, the in–roads made by the Umbrals as they tried to invade and destroy." I took her hand and stepped across the threshold.

"And Angels can't use them?" Annessa asked as she stared around in wonder.

"Right," I looked around to get my bearing before continuing. "They can't see them." I found the path I was looking for and nodded for Annessa to follow me. The forests and hills around my house were twice as foreboding in the darkness of the Inner Veil. The path I'd chosen took us through the deepest part of the forest.

"What about Fallen Angels?"

"Fallen can see them; they use the Roads constantly."

"That doesn't make any sense, Master," she pulled two hair ties out of that extradimensional space where women keep such things and began tying her hair back out of her face. "Fallen are still Angels."

"Watch who you say that around," I snorted. "Sacred Mother or not, you might just get your ass kicked. When Satariel fell, he left the Grace of…" I pointed up. "But Ninnaka gave him Grace and with her blessing, he saw the world with Umbral eyes. When his brother Satan fell,

Satariel showed him the Roads and a bunch of other shit the Angels didn't know about."

"So the Roads just keep us hidden?"

"No, they cut through entire sections of creation, so travel's a lot faster."

"Faster than your car?" she asked incredulously.

"We'll be in Manhattan in half an hour."

"Whoa," she raised an eyebrow. "So why do you bother with the car?"

"I like driving."

"But it's slower, and there's traffic and they keep blowing up your car!" She finished tying her pigtails and grinned at me. "You don't make any sense."

"I make plenty of damned sense," I grumbled. "I just like driving."

She took my arm hugged herself against me. "It's ok, Master. Men your age need something to keep them feeling young. I'm not judging."

"Be thankful I don't have time to kick your ass right now," I laughed.

We crested a hill and far below us, Manhattan glittered like jewel. It was one of the unsettling effects of the Roads; the prime feeding areas for the Umbrals always seemed to pulse with a welcoming light.

* * *

We stepped through the Veil in an alley off of Forty-Second Street. Annessa held my hair out of my face while I threw up.

"Does that always happen?" she asked when I'd gotten my stomach to finally cooperate.

"Yeah," I stood unsteadily. "Every damned time."

"How'd you spend so long in Perdition?"

"When I'm close to the Master, I can stay as long as he wants. When I'm on my own, it's all on me, and I'm just a man."

"So how long could you stay Veilside on your own?"

"Depends," I wiped my mouth and spat. "If I were in the Inner Veil, a week maybe. If I were deeper than that, a day or so. If I were in one of the Havens, an hour, give or take."

"Havens?"

"Places for the dead. Heaven, the Asphodel Fields, the Ruins of Elysium, or any place the living aren't welcome."

"But you've died," she protested.

"Yeah, more than once. You'd think the rules would change for me. The gods don't care," I shrugged. "I have a heartbeat, ergo, I'm alive."

I spoke a Word of shadow over my shotgun to hide it from view, then slung it. We walked out of the alley and headed for Grand Central. Looking at the terminal itself, you wouldn't think it would house one of the oldest beings in creation. Yet from the iconography on the outside of the building, that it's god–touched is unmistakable.

As soon as we entered, I could feel eyes on me. Not that feeling you get when you're embarrassed; this felt heavy, like judgment. I felt like my sins were being weighed. It was like walking through an electric fence. I was jolted, and suddenly I knew exactly where he was. I turned and faced the door. He was leaning against the inside wall. A light skinned black man with a wild Afro, he could have been Mediterranean or Hispanic; it was hard to tell. He was lounging as if he were waiting for someone, one hand in his loose fitting jeans, the other resting casually against the wall. He was handsome and slender and youthful but only just enough to escape notice. He nodded to me and walked toward the subway entrances. I grabbed Annessa's hand and followed.

We must've looked fairly odd, me in a suit and Annessa in full Goth regalia. The sheer amount of people was taking its toll on Annessa; she hadn't fed in far too long. I could feel her hunger like a crushing weight on my chest. I squeezed her hand and looked at her to ensure her fangs weren't out. When I turned back, Satariel was gone.

"Where the fuck?" I looked around frantically.

How the fuck did he disappear like that?

Annessa's eyes glittered like emeralds; her irises glowed brightly for a moment. She pointed at a joint in the wall. "He's there," she whispered.

"Really?" I cocked my head in confusion. "How'd you do that?" I asked.

"I don't know," she shrugged. "I looked and it just kinda happened.

"You're damned handy to have around." I pulled her with me as I walked over to inspect the joint.

"Promise you'll keep me around long enough to find out just how handy," she whispered close to my ear.

I stopped and looked at her. It was odd, I hadn't thought about that. I mean, her creation pretty much tore through my life like a train wreck, but it'd all seemed like a natural progression since then. It was strange how much a part of it she had become, how seamlessly she'd merged with…me.

I looked at her. She lowered her eyes, servile and deferent. I lifted her chin.

"I promise," I said as I gently headbutted her.

"Good," she purred and stepped through the wall, yanking me with her.

I looked around. It was dark and damp. It felt like the underbelly of the Station.

"Where are we?" I asked.

"You are beneath the Station, Jason Nathaniel Beckett. You are in my lair." Satariel stepped out from behind a pile of broken cinderblocks.

I raised my Mark. "Hail to you Satariel, called the Damascene. I bring you the greetings of my Master, the Lord of Perdition and the Earth." I bowed low.

"Rise, servant of my brother." He waved his hand as if brushing away all of the titles and finding only me behind the veil of my words. "What is it you need of me?"

"I have information to trade you," I said simply. Let's face it; you don't beat around the bush with a god that sees right through you.

"You are a strange young man," he laughed softly.

"Do you think me heartless?"

"No," I shook my head. "Not at all, my Lord." Not entirely what I expected.

"Why would you not simply ask me where they are holding your Sarah?" He sat on the cinder block pile.

"I thought that you would require a service in return." I held up my hands. "I meant no offense." I must have started to look nervous.

"Be at ease, Emissary," he smiled. "I know what you need, and I can get you there in time."

"That's the first good news I've had in a long time," I said. "Where is she?"

"As with all things, Servant of my Brother, it is not that simple." He frowned. "My adherents tracked her north to an abandoned church outside of Newburgh, yet that area has been dark for years."

"That's only a few miles from my house." Inside my head, I was screaming. I'd wasted time; I could be there already. I wanted to break something. What had they done to her in the time I'd blown coming to the city? I took a breath and remembered where I was.

"Thank you," I turned to leave, my eagerness getting the better of me. I remembered where I was and paused. "I assume Cassidy has already told you about her blood?"

"He has," the ancient Angel nodded.

"And I'm willing to bet he told you about Ninnaka?"

He nodded, smiling a smile that could've lit a concert hall.

"Right," I inclined my head. "Then I believe our business is complete, my lord."

"There is a Cathdronai nest somewhere in this mess, my friend." He held up his hands to slow me. "You would be wise to make arrangements for assistance."

"I don't have time." I shook my head. "I can't lose her again."

"As you wish." He put his hand on my shoulder and looked into my eyes. "It would be wise to remember, we are none of us alone. What affects one of us ripples through the universe touching, in some small way, the lives of all."

As much as I appreciate wisdom and folkisms, and I do, that particular moment was not the best time to reach out to me that way. I just nodded at him.

"Can you just point us in the right direction, please?" I asked, my patience and most of my sanity at an end.

"Follow the tracks until you find the deepest shadow, and there you will find the door that you seek." He pointed across the broken remains of the building. "That way." He bowed and raised his left hand, fingers splayed. "By the five points and the fires of Perdition, may the Firstborn Son guard thee well, and you as well, Sacred Mother." A Satanic blessing, it was odd coming from him, but welcome all the same.

"Thank you, my lord." I bowed low and with Annessa in tow, started running in the direction he'd pointed out.

CHAPTER 19

We emerged from the darkness of the tunnel into a clear sky. I could see the moon over the Hudson through the trees. Beyond that I could see distant hills surmounted by stars. The ruin of the massive church stood nearby. The night was quiet. Annessa jerked my hand and pulled me to the ground. She rolled on top of my back and whispered in my ear.

"Look," she whispered, her lips touching my ear. With her chin she pushed my face toward the shadows behind the building where an abandoned school bus sat rusting. A man crouched beside the bus with a machine gun. I don't mean one of those little Uzis either. We're talking a military issue M-240G machine gun. My nuts lifted a little. If the ammunition was blessed, as I assumed it was, this was going to suck so very, very much.

"What's the plan?" Annessa whispered.

I shrugged, "I don't know."

"Good plan, Master." I could feel her grin against my ear. "Maybe you'll think about it, though?"

"I'm thinking that would be wise, yeah." I banged my head on the ground. How did I always do this to myself? Sooner or later, my impetuous nature was going to get me killed. And not just bounced back to Perdition, but absolutely Ferryman–can't–find–me dead.

"Me too." She slid off of me and laid on her back looking over at me. "Just remember, you die: I die."

"Hell, if I die, chances are we all die," I shrugged. "But no fucking pressure or anything."

I opened my eyes to the aether. The amount of energy in the school or church building, whatever it was, was amazing. I began to think that I was truly and totally fucked.

"We can just go for a frontal assault and kill everything that moves," I said. "They wouldn't expect it..."

"...And that gives us the advantage," she finished for me.

"Exactly." And at that exact moment, my cell phone decided to belt out the opening notes of "Psychopathy Red." I rolled over on it to stifle the sound. Before I could do anything else, Annessa leapt to her feet and was on the guard with the machine gun before he even registered the sound. She smacked the weapon out of his hands, sending it swinging around him wildly on its sling and buried her fangs in his throat. She lowered him gently to the ground.

"Odin's balls, Cassidy! You think you could pick a worse fucking time to call me?" I whispered sibilantly into the phone.

"Mayhaps," he said as he stepped out of the shadows behind me grinning.

I breathed out through clenched teeth and tried not to launch into one of my legendary swearing fits. It didn't work. "You motherfucker! Annessa just ate some guy's fucking face. Why would you call me from three fucking feet away?"

"That's the best you've got, Little Brother? You're slipping." He patted my shoulder. "I called you ten minutes ago, but the aether distorted the call. I was on the Road." He motioned back to where the tunnel let out.

"Yeah, well, I'm trying not to lose my shit here, man. Sarah's in there, and it was just Annessa and I until you showed up." My hands were shaking. "There's a goddamned division of Angels in there. Not to mention at least as many human sentries."

"Why haven't you called on the Faithful?" he asked. "We may need them."

"I can't. There are Angels everywhere. I can't even justify the attack, unless I find a way to claim Sarah as my property, such that she belongs to Perdition by extension. I can only move as if this were vengeance for the attack on my house, but that only gets me so far with the Accords," I sighed. "And all of this assumes that I somehow live through this long enough to have to answer for any of it." I looked up as Annessa slid silently beside me and pushed the dead guy's M-240 into my hands.

"You know how to use this?" she asked.

"Yeah, I was a gunner for ten years," I said. I closed my eyes and sighed.

"Really?" she asked.

"It was in another life and I'd rather not talk about it." I held up my hand. "Bite me, Annessa," I commanded.

She obeyed instantly; her fangs extended and she slid them into my hand like a hot knife through butter. The pain was exquisite. It was on the order of feeding your hand to a garbage disposal. I'm not going to lie, I whimpered a little. That shit hurt like hell. I held my hand over the belt of ammunition and spoke several Words of panic, agony and putrefaction. I only had about five hundred rounds, so I had to make them count.

"Shit! I'm sorry!" Annessa whispered frantically as she looked at my mangled hand. She looked like she was going to hyperventilate. "You made me do it! I didn't want to! You made me!" She actually put her hand over her mouth. It was cute, in a rabid lioness kind of way.

"It's ok, Annessa. Gonna need you to fix this, though." I held up my hand.

She slashed her hand and clamped it over mine. Pleasure and pain flooded my system. Our eyes met and for a moment, there was a stutter in reality. I can't really explain it better than that. It was as if time stopped for a moment, and all I could see were her eyes glowing like a cat's. As quickly as it hit, it dissipated.

"What else can you do?" I asked, my voice strained.

"Anything you need, Master." She didn't wink or laugh or make any innuendos. I began to wonder just exactly what it was that I'd created.

"You're a much stronger sorcerer than I gave you credit for, my friend." Cassidy clapped me on the back. "You make an army like her, and we may just have a chance tonight."

"I don't think anyone's made anything like her before." I shook my hand, as if to chase away any remnant of injury. "We don't have much time. They must be checking in with their sentries every five to ten minutes. They'll know that we're here any minute now."

Cassidy nodded. "I'm just waiting for some last minute additions to the festivities."

I raised an eyebrow. "Who the hell are we waiting for?" I asked.

Cassidy pointed to a shadow crossing the moon. Well, about seven shadows to be precise. Seven shadows flitted silently across the night sky. "Harker's murder is come, Little Brother."

Harker and his girls, all six of them, landed silently around us. He stared at me grimly, his fangs extended.

"Cheers, Jason," he grinned then grew somber. "Thought, for once, I'd have a go at the heroics. It's partially on me Sarah's here to begin with."

I grabbed his hand. "Let's see if we can get her out of this." I looked around. "We don't have much time, Miles. Can you and your girls take out the sentries?" I asked.

"Easy enough." He nodded and the seven of them shuddered and faded from view.

I didn't wait to hear anything. Harker knew his business; there would be nothing to hear. I looked at Cassidy.

"Straight forward assault?" I asked.

"It's the only way that I know," he grinned.

There was a sound like a sword drawing. I started to raise my gun, but Cassidy put a restraining hand on the barrel.

"Be easy, my friend. That would be Dominus." He pointed to man who appeared to be made entirely of shadow slipping out of the hidden tunnel exit.

The shadow man stepped forward and in his outstretched hands I could see the outline of a sword. Cassidy spoke several words to the man, took the sword and the man disappeared into the shadow again.

"Is there anyone else coming to this party that I should know about?" I asked sarcastically. "I'd hate to shoot a friend."

"No, that was it. But this should come in handy." He hefted the sword. It looked like a blade of solid shadow mounted on a blackened steel hilt.

"So random guys show up with swords for you a lot?" Annessa giggled.

"Not random, and the sword's not for me," he corrected. "That was Dominus, Satariel's son."

"Nephilim?" I asked.

"No, Ninnaka is his mother." Cassidy looked at me pointedly as if to say, *and this is not common knowledge, so keep your mouth shut.*

"Right. You sure he couldn't have stayed to help?" It wasn't as if we didn't need it.

He shook his head. "Let's do this. Harker should have had enough time by now." Cassidy tucked the sword inside his voluminous coat.

"Agreed."

CHAPTER 20

We kept to the shadows as we crept toward the church, which as we closed in on it became apparent that it was once a school as well. Every now and then, a flicker would shoot across my vision and I would hear the muffled thump of a body hitting the ground. I doubted the morons inside could have planned for their entire force of sentries to die nearly all at once. I grinned a little.

As we approached the double doors at the back of the building, I opened my eyes again to the flows of the Aether. I could see the remnants of a spell floating around the doors. I held up my hand to stop Cassidy and Annessa.

"Spell on the door," I whispered. I grinned at Cassidy and invoked the blessing of Leviathan. I charged the wall five feet to the right of the door and dove forward throwing my shoulder into the brick. It gave way before me like a house of cards. I tucked into a ball as soon as I passed the wall. Hitting the ground rolling, I made myself small to avoid any potential gunshots. I rolled to a knee, with my gun at the ready.

I was in what appeared to be a gymnasium. Along both of the long walls there were bleachers and the short walls held what I suspected used to be basketball goals. There were Angelics everywhere. This time, though, they weren't playing. Nearly every single one of them was Host—

Bound, and there had to be at least thirty of them. I swallowed hard and raised the 240. I fired in controlled bursts as they charged me; contrails of angelic script trailed in the air as they came at me as one.

The leading edge fell away as the machine gun and its enchanted ammunition ate away at them. They burst into flame, collapsed into piles of decayed flesh or fell to their knees rolling in agony. But all too soon, I ran out of ammunition. I threw the gun away and brought up my shotgun, firing as I back–pedaled. I fired at one and missed; he leaped at me, his hands crackled with trapped magic. Before he could reach me, though, Annessa hit him full force in the air, her legs wrapped around his waist and she rode him to the ground. Her claws shredded his face and chest all the way down and as his back hit the floor, her fangs tore out his throat. Man, she was getting good at this. I felt a surge of pride.

Cassidy took a different route. He shape–shifted and raced forward, darting in and out of their ranks. His fangs found knees, Achilles tendons and the soft flesh of their stomachs. Ten Host–Bound dropped to the ground, some trying to hold in ropes of intestines, others dragging themselves forward, their legs hanging awkwardly from mutilated knees. I dodged the remainder of fully mobile Host–Bound and fired at the wounded, killing them where they lay and reloading as I ran. Every few seconds, I could hear the sound of an impact behind me as Annessa bodily hit one of my pursuers and showed him the error of his ways, permanently.

All in all, it took us less than three minutes. To be fair, I did the least work; I knew that I needed to conserve my energy for what was to come, and it didn't take long. Within seconds of the last Host–Bound hitting the floor, the main doors to the gym blew open. Rachel stood there with a phalanx of Host–Bound flanking her. These would be different: high–ranking angels, likely Seraphim, possessed these. That meant that any of my fire spells would be completely ineffective. Which was pretty crappy, since I kind of specialized in fire and pain.

It didn't matter; all I wanted was Rachel. She stepped into the gym. She'd tied her hair back and was wearing white leather. It looked like something a biker might wear; you know the stuff that has the impact armor built right in. She was ready for me this time. Good, I wanted this to last long enough for me to really kill her this time.

"Beckett," she said.

"You fucked up this time, Rachel."

"The work of the Lord is never a mistake," she said. Her eyes looked haunted and she seemed drained.

"Then you can die with a clean conscience," I growled. I fired my shotgun from the hip, emptying it. As I expected, the Host–Bound closed around her, the shots bounced off of them like annoying gnats.

"Kill him!" she ordered, pointing at me.

They charged, skipping through the Veil as they did so. It was like watching Harker on speed. Damn, they were fast. Annessa launched herself from behind me, her hoarse scream heralding her arrival. She slammed into the first Host–Bound, grabbing his left wrist and savagely twisting it as she dove between his legs. The massive Host–Bound yelped as he flipped, his back slamming onto the hard floor. Annessa buried her free hand in his throat, savagely twisting. She tore her hand free and casually tossed a six-inch section of his spinal column aside. Running her hand across her tongue, she winked at another of the Host–Bound.

Cassidy wasted no time taking advantage of their distraction. He hurtled forward, his massive wolf form diving between the legs of the closest Host–Bound, his fangs unmanning the creature. Without pause, he released the first and shifted into his massive hybrid form, his momentum propelling him into the third of Rachel's phalanx, his claws split the man from clavicle to hip. As the man opened his mouth to scream, Annessa punched, her tiny fist shattered his teeth and filled his mouth. With a savage jerk, she turned her hand and drove her claws through the man's palate and into his brain.

"Wanna have a puppet show?" she leered at Rachel before throwing the dead man aside.

Rachel lifted her Baby Eagle and fired in response. I threw myself toward Annessa, but without Abbadonna, I was far too slow. Time seemed to still and I watched the vapor trail of the bullet spiral toward Annessa. My blood ran cold. This wasn't supposed to happen. I was going to lose her.

Annessa threw herself to the side impossibly fast. That's when I saw her lurking behind Annessa's eyes. Abbadonna was here; she'd been hiding inside Annessa. Still wondering how she'd gotten here, I hit the floor in a jumble at Rachel's feet.

Rachel leapt backward, flipping gracefully through the air and landing just inside the doors to the gym. She crouched, one hand on the floor in front of her, the other leveled her pistol at me.

Instinctively, my hand flew up to protect my face. No Words, no magic, no special, super–secret emissary technique, just raw panic. She didn't shoot. After a second, I lowered my hand. She darted out of the doorway and out of sight. I turned to look back at Cassidy and Annessa, they were tangling with the last two Host–Bound. The one with no balls was fighting much harder than I would've, given the circumstances.

I turned back to the doorway, then back to Annessa and Cassidy. I froze for a second, growled at my own indecision, then raced after Rachel. I followed the sound of her footfalls through the empty, dark corridors. With each step, my brain screamed at me that I was an idiot, that chasing her was completely foolish. Yet, another part of my brain, the slavering, hateful, *hungry* part of me, knew that this was what I was made for. No monster can resist fleeing prey.

I turned a blind corner, then raced up a staircase. A heavy steel door slammed a floor above me, and I poured every ounce of energy into closing the distance. I hurled open the door and lurched to a stop, staggering backward into the unyielding metal of the doorframe. Rachel stood at the far end of the room silhouetted against the massive moon that glared at us through the remains of a huge stained glass window. Her gun was pointed at my head, her finger on the trigger. I was done. There was nowhere to go, no time to dodge, nor speak a Word. Her eyes glinted as she stared down her sights at me. The silent auditorium in which we stood echoed her every harsh breath. The empty wooden chairs standing like grim sentinels at the moment of my death.

"Well played," I whispered.

She slowly rode the hammer of her pistol forward with her thumb, then dropped it to the floor. The metallic clatter of the heavy pistol was deafening.

"You were mine just then, Beckett," she said, raising her hands.

"You should've taken the shot, Rachel. I wouldn't have hesitated." I didn't lift my gun. Not yet.

"It's over, Beckett," she smiled. "You've lost."

"I'm the one standing here with a gun, Rachel," I grinned. "You might want to reconsider."

"I don't need a gun where I'm going," she said softly. "Come with me, Jason. It's not too late."

I lifted my gun. "I don't give a shit where you go, you crazy bitch. Just tell me where Sarah is."

"It doesn't matter, Beckett." She stepped closer to me. "Are you blind? Can't you see what's happening?"

"Tell me," I slammed the barrel of my pistol against her forehead, careful to keep it in battery. "Where. The. Fuck. She. Is." I shoved her backward with each word.

Her eyes bored into me from the shadow of my gun. "You don't care about the War," she whispered. "We both know it."

"What's your point?" I gritted my teeth.

"I'm offering you paradise," she said softly. "No more pain, no more loss, just peace. An eternity of peace."

I stared into the deep pools of her eyes. She wasn't playing a game; she was serious. What the fuck was going on? I found myself relaxing as the cadence of her words slowed, my finger slowly relaxed on the trigger.

"Just say the words, give yourself to him," she reached up and touched my face. "Let go of your sin and come Home."

Her emphasis on the word "home" broke the spell. A wave of relief washed over me, followed by rage. Strangely, neither emotion felt like mine. I drove the barrel of my pistol into in her forehead, shoving her away.

"You fucking sneaky bitch," I yelled, driving my gun into her face with each word. "No more bullshit, where the fuck is Sarah?"

"Listen to yourself," she pleaded. "Is this the man you wanted to be? A liar? A killer? A murderer?"

"Last chance," I leveled the gun at her face. "Tell me."

"You're right," she stepped forward and rested her forehead against the barrel. "It's your last chance. He loves you, Jason. Why settle for second bes—"

The back of Rachel's head disintegrated in a shower of gore as the enchanted round shredded her flesh and pulverized her skull. Her body stumbled backwards and hung limply, but didn't fall. Her eyelids fluttered madly, then opened, showing only the whites of her eyes and she spoke in a horrible voice that wasn't her own.

"You have chosen apostasy," her eyes began to glow brightly.

A jolt of mental static screeched across my brain. Cathdronai. I backed away slowly, my gun at the ready. This wasn't going to end well. I felt it before I saw it, a terrible light flared at the periphery of my vision. I threw my Mark out in front of me and screamed defiantly. The massive bolt of lightning tore through the roof; my body erupted in ice white flames. The lightning arced all around me, repelled by the Satanic energy flooding my system. Chairs exploded all over the room, turning it into a deadly vortex, hurling fragments of metal and flaming wood against my shield. I screamed again, this time more out of fear than defiance.

A huge piece of twisted steel smashed against the base of my skull, driving me to my knees. The flames shielding me sputtered and went out. I fell to my right side; my vision collapsed into a tiny pinprick of light and all I could hear was a terrible rushing sound. My last sight before the darkness hedged me in was the horrific, staggering Cathdronai moving toward me.

Cassidy's howl shattered the darkness that pressed against my damaged brain. I felt Annessa dragging me to feet, pulling me away from the creature that was once Rachel. The immense black wolf charged the Cathdronai, his fangs bared and his eyes glowing red. I tried to stand and fell back to the floor; the static drilled into my brain, making thought impossible.

"Stay down, Master," Annessa whispered and stepped protectively in front of me.

The Cathdronai and Cassidy tore at each other. I'd never seen anything move as quickly as they moved. Each was nothing more than a blur of fangs, claws and bestial howls of rage.

I felt Annessa's eagerness to join Cassidy, like a hot spike of urgency driving into my brain. I put my hand on her hip.

"No," I shook my head woozily. "Stay out of it."

"It could kill him," she protested.

"It can't touch you, we don't know if it will infect…" I gagged as the static blasted through my mind again. "You need to be…clean," I threw up. "For Him." We both knew who I meant.

Annessa put her hand on my forehead and the static was muted, like someone had simply shut a door to drown out noise. I started to say something to her, but a dark blur shot across my vision and suddenly Harker knelt next to me and pulled me roughly to my feet. His eyes were wide with panic and blood welled from his tear ducts.

"Sarah," he pointed towards the center of the building. "Big, ugly blighter's got her in the sanctuary." He held up his hands, they were burned black. "Still sanctified, can't pass the door." He collapsed to one knee, his hands clutched to his chest. "Save her," he pleaded.

"On it," I stumbled around him and clumsily raced for the stairs, wiping the vomit from my face as I went. Vampires can't pass through sacred ground; emissaries go wherever the fuck they want. Right now, I wanted to get between Sarah and whoever had her.

Annessa vaulted the rail and dropped the two flights straight down. I thought about it briefly, then realized me with two broken ankles wouldn't really help anyone. I caught up to her at the base of the stairs.

"Which way?" I huffed out.

Her eyes flared again and she pointed, "There."

I ran toward the hallway she indicated, my lungs burning and my brain humming with panic. We'd wasted too much time with Rachel and Dead Rachel and all their friends. The hallway made an abrupt left, I was so lost in thought, I almost didn't catch myself in time. I kicked off the wall and tried to make the turn, but a huge oak door blocked my way.

I felt something in me strain, and I slid through the Veil. I landed on the far side of the door, shocked. I barely registered Annessa's frantic pounding against the door. The chapel had been destroyed, so much so that I couldn't comprehend how it remained sanctified. The pews had been smashed and blood dripped from everything. A smell of rot and death hit me like a sledgehammer.

The central aisle was coated with black slime and covered in the flaccid carcasses of thousands of dead maggots. I heard a whimper from the far end of the room and froze.

Vincenze Francione stood on a dais at the opposite end of the room. He was standing over the altar, and Sarah. He turned and looked at me, the hate that burned in his eyes made my stomach clench. I didn't see him move or hear him speak, but he was suddenly right in front of me. His sallow white skin made him look like a plague victim. The dried vomit all over his clothing and his wild, unfocused eyes completed the picture. When he spoke, his deep, raspy voice sounded like it was coming from deep beneath the earth.

"None but the Host could bypass my ward." He gripped me by my throat. "How did you get in here, hmmm?"

I tried to think of something witty to say, but the crushing pressure of his vice–like grip on my throat pretty much ruled out any sort of snarky comeback.

He lifted me easily and carried me toward the altar. He motioned with his free hand and a glyph burned itself into the wood of the door. I didn't recognize the glyph, but I knew with a terrible certainty that nothing was getting through that door anytime soon. Even the sound of Annessa's pounding faded once the ward set. He threw me to the floor. I looked up at Sarah; she was bound to the remains of the altar. Her naked flesh and the way she'd been chained let me know immediately that she'd been raped. I completely lost my mind.

"You worm–ridden piece of shit!" I screamed at Vincenze. I reached for my Beretta and realized that it was still in the gym. This was not going well at all.

I screamed Words of agony, flame and death at him. He held up his hand to silence me, chuckling softly as he did.

"Did you really think that you were going to get anywhere with that display, foolish little creature?" he laughed at me.

"I'll kill you," I spoke softly, shaking with the force of my rage.

"How?" He raised his hands questioningly. "How will you kill me?" He shook his finger at me. "You will not, because you cannot." He turned his back to me and walked toward Sarah.

"The fuck I can't!" I jumped forward to stop him.

He spun and vomited, filling the space between us with black bile and maggots. I stumbled through the Veil again as I dodged the disgusting spray. When I say that he vomited, it wasn't like your classic "Exorcist" vomit, either. Oh no, this was one for the books. His jaw distended and his throat opened wide. The flood of maggots he'd disgorged wriggled toward me even after they hit the ground.

"Jason!" Sarah screamed, "Don't let them touch you!" She strained against her bonds.

I jumped over the pile of squirming creatures and tried again to get close to Sarah. She struggled against the chains with everything she had left. Vincenze appeared in front of me, still laughing.

"Persistent, aren't you?" He spoke a Word.

I'd never heard it before, and I was very afraid that it was the last thing that I would ever hear. My mind swam in visions of torment and darkness. I saw the creature torturing Sarah, I saw the horrors that she'd suffered already. The pain was so intense, my knees buckled and I collapsed. Fighting for breath, I slowly pulled myself back to my feet. The creature was getting closer to Sarah. I threw out my hand and screamed Words of destruction and decay at her bonds. They fell away, sloughing off like dead skin. I fell back to my knees. I knew I was going to die, but at least I'd set her free. At least she wouldn't die…like that. Vincenze stomped back toward me, grabbed the back of my neck and lifted me like a sick kitten. My eyes couldn't focus and the force of his Word was slowly driving me mad.

"Weak! You creatures are so weak!" He shook the hell out of me. "This is what defeated us? Pathetic!" He hurled me to the floor. The maggots surged forward toward my face. I couldn't move. I knew in that moment, I was wrong. I wasn't going to die, but I was going to wish for all time that I had.

I tried to speak and I tried to move. My body and my mind were not my own. The Umbral's Word was simply too much for me to bear. There was a sudden rush of air past my face, followed by a searing light so hot that my lungs nearly burst. The maggots were consumed less than an inch from my face. The room became as bright as day. I felt a cool hand on my cheek.

"This cannot be!" the Umbral screamed.

"It is," Sarah spoke, her voice much stronger than I remembered it.

"You have our seed within you, you cannot disobey!" he shrieked at her as the light tore away at his flesh.

"I am a daughter of the house of Solomon. You have no power over me." She stood up.

"I'll not be banished, Child of Solomon. I'll have your heart first!" he charged across the room, roaring.

Sarah raised her hand. I felt her power building, and I rolled over; I knew better. "No, you won't be banished."

The light flared so brightly that it was blinding even with my eyes clenched shut. The Umbral shrieked, and I could hear him thrashing around the room. As suddenly as it started, the light faded. Sarah's cool hand rested on my face.

"Wake up, Jason." She sounded like she was crying. "We don't have much time."

I forced myself upright. "What do you mean?"

She touched my forehead and smiled sadly. "I knew you'd come."

"You knew I'd be too late," I said, sitting up. I took her hand. "You knew I'd fail you again."

"You didn't fail me," she pulled my hand to her cheek. "You're here."

"You're going to die," I said it quietly. Truth needs no volume to wound.

"It's not your fault," she waved around the room. "This isn't your fault."

"If I'd gotten here sooner, if I hadn't gone to bed, if I hadn't wrecked your fucking brain..." I sighed.

"Remember what I told you the first day we met?"

"The joke about the amputee kid's Christmas?" I asked.

"Yeah," she smiled. "Sometimes shit just happens, Jason. Somebody's gotta suffer so everyone else can see how good they've got it."

"Yeah, but why's it have to be you?" I stood up and reached down to help her to her feet.

She whimpered and clutched a hand over her stomach. "No," she shook her head. "There's no time."

"What?"

"You have to end this," her voice shook as a violent spasm made her bend double.

"How?"

She lifted her hand and resting across her palm was my Beretta. "End it."

"No!" I stood up and jerked away from her. "Not like this!"

"This is mercy, Jason." She stood and wobbled, catching herself on the wall. "Release…me."

"Sarah, I can't!" I screamed. "Not like this, not again!"

"I told you once we were lovers, remember?" she gasped and slid slowly down the wall.

"I remember," I ran my hand over my face. "I said it meant you'd forgiven me."

"I forgave you a long time ago," her head lolled back to rest against the wall. Her eyes stared into mine, clear as a winter sky. "I need you…huh," she wiped a trickle of blood from the corner of her mouth. "I need you to set me free."

"I can't…" I bit down on my fist and fell to my knees.

"If you care at all about me, you'll release me Jason." She dragged herself away from the wall and collapsed in front of me. "Set me free."

I looked into her eyes and watched a black stain fill the whites, encroaching on her perfect blue irises. I saw no cruelty there anymore, save where the flickering candlelight refracted enough to show me my own face.

I stood up and lifted my gun. "I hope somewhere, anywhere else, I made you happy, Sarah."

"You did," she smiled sadly. She lifted the barrel of the gun and rested it on her forehead. "Do it."

My finger rested on the trigger. "I'm so sorry," I whispered.

"Be free, Jason." Her eyes gleamed as she looked up at me. "Always be free."

I pulled the trigger.

I didn't hear the glyph shatter as Cassidy finally broke through the door. I didn't hear Annessa screaming at me to wake up. I couldn't do anything but stare at Sarah's body lying on the ground, her pale hair arrayed as a halo, surmounting the black, angry wound in her forehead. Her eyes were open, focused, as if she were looking at something far in the distance. A ghost of a smile danced in the corner of her mouth, as if the Coinbound who'd claimed her had shared a joke.

What do you give a starving orphan for Christmas? Nothing.

I blinked. Annessa knelt next to me, one arm around my shoulders, her other hand gently smoothing my hair and tucking it behind my ear. Her face streaked was with black tears and her breath came in ragged fits. She was playing the platitude game, whispering all the things we're taught to say at the moment of a traumatic death. I took her hand and gently pulled it away from my face. I looked into her eyes as they fluctuated between glowing blue and green as her emotions raged within her.

"Master?" Annessa squeezed my hand. "You ok?"

I bit my cheek and shoved the pain out of my mind. "We need to leave."

"Agreed. Your Master will want to know of this, Little Brother," Cassidy said as he pulled me to my feet.

"I don't care."

"Are you saying you won't tell him?" Cassidy asked.

"I'm saying I don't fucking care." I turned toward the door. "We need to go before others show up here. I'm in no shape to fight."

"What about Father Jacob?" Annessa asked as she looked over what remained of her father's corpse. She spat. "Aren't we gonna find him?"

"Not right now," I answered.

Harker stood at the sanctuary door, his slender frame trembled with barely restrained sorrow and fury.

"Jason, what about Sarah?" Cassidy asked delicately. "We can't leave her here."

"She's not here, Cassidy." I bit my cheek again and looked away until the tears left my eyes. "She'll never be here again."

I spoke a Word and watched the shadows dance across Harker's eyes as I gently patted his shoulder and walked past him into the arms of another failure.

CHAPTER 21

"This Father Jacob has fled north, my disciple," Satariel was saying. "You must follow."

I followed the sound of his voice back through the tunnel to Satariel's lair.

"Where has he gone, my Lord?" Cassidy stood as if to leave immediately.

"He is in Little Haven. I fear there may be a nest there." He pointed at Annessa. "We have not yet accounted for this child's mother."

"Do you think that he would try to infest an entire town?" Cassidy looked sick. "Such a thing has never happened."

"It has, my son," Satariel said. "Pompeii, Alexandria, Thebes and many cities whose names are lost to man have suffered such fates. They were purged by flame. Let such tales speed your travels, lest we add yet another name to this list."

"I'll go immediately, my Lord." Cassidy turned and looked at me. He turned back to Satariel. "I'll need a moment, my Lord." Satariel nodded. Cassidy walked over to me, his head low.

"I have to leave, Little Brother."

"Yeah, I heard," I said. "Just go, man. Do what you need to do."

"Call me, should you need my help." He held up a hand to stop my inevitable protest. "Just call." He nodded at me and turned back down the tunnel.

"Take care of yourself!" I yelled at him as he receded in the distance.

I bowed to Satariel. "I appreciate your assistance, my lord. Though, ultimately, we failed."

"May peace find you swiftly, Emissary of Perdition." He nodded and faded into nothing. "Of all creatures in this world, I know your pain."

"It's just us now," Annessa remarked as she looked around the empty room.

"Yeah," I said. "It is."

"What are we going to do now?"

"We're going to give you a bath." I took her hand and walked toward the exit.

"Really?" she asked. "You're not yanking my chain, are you?"

"No," I shook my head. "I promise."

* * *

We stood outside the Sacred Grove of Hekate. Cleopatra's Needle cast its shadow over us as we waited for entrance. The light of the full moon shone brightly. The shadow shimmered and warped as it crossed the trunks of the trees in front of us. The trunks seemed to move aside and wrap around the shadow, creating a doorway.

"Are you ready?" I asked Annessa.

"I'm confused," she said. "I've never taken a bath in Central Park before."

"Live a little." I smiled and added, "Trust me."

"I do." She rested her head on my shoulder.

As we entered the grove, the doorway opened revealing a huge temple complex of stone and trees. Corrigan stood in front of vast lake, facing away from a huge altar surmounted by three headed female statues.

"Welcome." He spoke his greeting, gently rapped his cane on the ground and torches all around the lake burst into flames. The light cascaded across the water highlighting the reflection of the moon like a crown.

I bowed. "Hail to you, Priest of the Titaness. Hail to you, Chosen of Hekate."

"Whom do you bring before the Lady?" he challenged me.

"I bring a beloved adherent of Perdition. She is here at the request of the Mother of Night, Guardian of the Crossroads and Maiden of the Most Sacred Art." I gently pushed Annessa ahead of me.

She looked back at me confused as she stumbled forward. She had no idea what was going on.

"What is your name, Daughter of Man and Magic?" Corrigan asked her.

"Annessa Francione," she looked back at me again, uncertainty filling her eyes.

"Do you accept the blessing of the Goddess?" Corrigan held his hand before him like, well like a priest, I guess.

I nodded when she looked back at me.

"I do," she said firmly.

He spoke a Word, and Annessa's clothes fell away. Corrigan touched her brow with his right hand, then kissed her forehead, breasts, genitals and feet. It's called a fivefold kiss, and it really is a beautiful ritual, if you can divorce yourself from preconception. He took her hand and smiled as he led her to the water.

"Go now, into the water. Immerse yourself and find peace in the blessings of the Goddess." He smiled broadly. "Be at peace, my sister." He bowed and turned back to me.

"Greetings, Jason." He smiled broadly.

"Hello, Corrigan." I nodded grimly. "My debt is paid."

"Not yet, my friend," he pointed at the altar.

I stared at the altar, my fists clenching and unclenching. "He said he approved," I swallowed, the fireball forming in the pit of my stomach threatened to overcome my reason. "I don't."

"Such is the way of life; there is little beauty to be found in worship these days." He frowned. "No one escapes Her will, not even you, Jason." He clasped forearms with me, clapped me on the shoulder and moved to walk past me out of the temple. "Do what is right."

I watched Annessa slide through the water, a contended smile on her face. I tried to wall away my fear, my anxiety. She deserved a moment of peace. She picked up a water lily and brought it up to her face. I caught her eye as I slid through the Veil.

It's easier to pierce the Veil in certain places, sacred temples and the like. It lets the gods peek in at us from time to time. Satan leaned against one of the massive statues of Hekate.

"She is as beautiful as I remembered," he said.

"You say that as if it's been years since you saw her last," I remarked as I moved closer.

"I mean her first incarnation, my son," he sighed and pushed himself away from the statue. "More's the shame, I had such high hopes for her."

"You can't mean for me to go through with it, Master," I jerked a thumb over my shoulder toward the altar and what waited upon it.

"Look around you, my emissary. Does this world seem ready for my Son?" He shook his head. "This realm reeks of uncertainty and submission. There is no place in the hearts of men for the Wakeful Fire."

"Why make her suffer?" I asked. "She's done nothing wrong since I brought her back."

"You have not allowed her to do any wrong, my child. Your dominance obviates her choice, her existence in this form is anathema."

"So you just want me to fucking shank her, because mankind isn't ready for your goddamned wisdom?" I snapped. My whole body was trembling with rage. "Who the fuck do you think you are?" The sane part of my brain tried valiantly to throw the brakes on, to clamp my jaw shut before I could utter that final sentence. It was too late.

He surged across the gap between us, his black wings flared wide. The shadows around him deepened and he swelled to terrifying size. His sapphire eyes ignited, highlighting the chiseled contours of his face and erasing them all at once. The icy chill of his fury spread before him like blanket of frost, his breath froze the skin on my face as he landed frighteningly close to me.

"Kneel!" he commanded, his deep voice thunderous in the empty, cavernous temple.

I collapsed to my knees, my head hanging. I was terrified. I'd gone too far. I tried to lift my hands, to show my surrender, but I was locked in place, transfixed by my fear.

He stood silently for a second. The rage seemed to leave him. "As I thought," he whispered.

I finally gathered the courage to look up. He stood with his back to me. He looked across the Veil at Annessa, his hand tracing the edge of her jaw, a look of painful compassion on his face. "Do as you were instructed, my emissary. If you do nothing else, you follow orders."

My pride stung, and I recoiled as if slapped. I wanted to say something, anything. I wanted to apologize. I wanted to fucking stab him, to claw out his fucking sapphire eyes and show him his cruelty first hand. Instead, I stood and turned back toward the edge of the Veil.

As I crossed, he called out, reminding me, "None at my altar but the willing."

I nodded and walked to the water's edge. Annessa swam to the shore. She looked at up me and smiled.

"I thought you were gonna give me a bath, Master," she said. "You got me all naked and everything."

I took my clothes off and tossed them aside.

"Aww, the other guy had fancy magic to do that." She playfully splashed at me. I could feel her nervousness.

"The other guy didn't have the day that I've had." I shook my head. "I don't have the magic to work my zipper much less take off a three piece suit." My heart hammered against my ribs. I took a breath in an attempt to maintain my calm; it didn't work.

I stood at the water's edge naked; I looked over my shoulder at the boundary and saw only empty space. The knife hissed against the stone altar as I picked it up. I stared at the simple, straight blade as I slid into the water. I could see bands of lead and silver in the blade, they would disrupt the magic that kept her whole. Black diamonds studded the hilt, the better to scatter her soul away from me. Rubies and garnets were embedded in the cold iron pommel, bloodstones to carry the energy of the sacrifice to Hekate. The weight of the blade felt as if I carried my own damnation.

Annessa swam to meet me, standing up when the water became too shallow. We stood facing each other, the water lapped around our knees.

"I'm scared," she whispered.

"So am I." I caressed the slender lines of her face. I could feel the warmth of tears running down my face.

"Will it hurt?" She touched my cheek.

"I think it has to." I traced her lips with my thumb.

"I wish things were different." She gently bit my thumb and pressed herself against me.

"I'm not sorry." My lips brushed hers. I felt my body responding to her and my blood boiled within my veins. "No matter what he says, I'm not sorry."

She bit my lip and ran her nails over my back. "I'm not sorry either."

"I wish I could change this," I kissed her passionately. "I wish I could free you."

"I'm yours," she bit at my neck, her teeth drawing blood. "That's enough for me."

"You're perfect," I whispered. The knife hung dead and heavy in my hand.

She wrapped her legs around my waist and enveloped me. I gasped at the warmth of her and lost myself in the cold blue glow of her eyes. "I love you," she whispered.

"I love you too, Annessa." I slid the knife between her ribs. The hollow cavern echoed back "Jessica...Jessica...Annessa...Jessica..." in a savage whisper.

She exhaled a shuddering breath and went limp. I gently lowered her into the water. The reflection of the moon ringed her dark hair like a halo from a medieval painting. I looked up the moon and raised the bloodied knife.

"You have your blood. You have your death." Tears poured down my face. "I hope you fucking choke on it."

I gently lifted her from the water. She hadn't deserved this. She'd done everything I'd asked of her. I wanted to scream. I wanted to rage, but I had nothing left. If a man's soul could actually wither away to nothing, mine had. I stumbled onto the shore, carrying Annessa. I made my way carefully to the altar. I laid her down on the flat stone. I laid her arms over her chest and leaned down, my lips resting on her ear.

"You deserved better than this, better than me." I kissed her gently on her lips. "Be free."

Be free, Jason. Always be free.

I dressed quickly and walked out of the Grove, my hand clenched over my Mark, as if by hiding it, I could make it disappear.

CHAPTER 22

"I need to go Minneapolis," she'd said. I wish I'd taken more time to understand what she'd meant. It'd been a frustrating night and for whatever reason it hadn't left me. Of course thinking of that night led to me thinking of her lying on the ground with a bullet in her head. Which led me to Jessica, which lead me to Annessa. Which led me to whisky.

I shook my head at the memory. I burped and the whiskey came back up. I swallowed it down again, leaning heavily against a car. I stood outside the club, in the parking lot. My hand rested on the window of a beautiful black Porsche Cayman S. I really didn't want to throw up on the car.

"Hey, motherfucker!" a slender, well–dressed man yelled at me. "Get your hand off my fucking car!" He ran towards me.

I burped again. "Go fuck yourself." I staggered and dragged the bottle across the side of the car. "Whoops, look at that." I pointed to a small scratch in the paint.

He snatched at me. I stumbled back and threw up on his feet. He hit me with a solid punch to the throat. I think he was aiming for my face, so don't give him too much credit.

"You son of a bitch!" He kicked me in the stomach, and I collapsed.

I threw up again. It felt like it came from my fucking feet. Everything hurt. "You hit like a bitch." I mumbled as I spat out a chunk of something unpleasant.

He kicked me with a flurry of rapid kicks. I tried to push myself back to my feet. He stomped on the back of my head driving my face into the asphalt. I felt my nose shatter and pain made lightning storms in my eyes.

"You piece of shit wino fuck!" He screamed as he kicked at me. "I'll fucking show you who's the bitch!"

I felt rather than heard Harker land.

"Enough of that," he said. His voice was thick with menace.

I rolled onto my back and spit out a tooth. "Guh way," I said. I turned my head and vomited into my hair.

"Who's this?" Mr. Angry Car Owner asked. "Your faggot boyfriend?"

I remember a crunch; I don't recall him saying anything else. I tried again to stand up. I felt Harker's hand on my shoulder.

"Leave it, Jason," he said. "You're in a state." He knelt next to me.

"Fine." I shook my head. "I'm fine." I swallowed a mouthful of blood. "It'll heal."

"How long are you gonna keep on this way?" he asked.

"I'm...hur," I threw up. "Not doing anything." I used the car to pull myself to my feet and wiped my mouth.

"You've been at it a month." He looked at me with those eyes. Those fucking I–pity–you–because–you're–broken eyes. I wanted to throat punch him. I knew better. Not that he'd hit me; he'd just dance around me and keep telling me how fucking sorry he was about Annessa.

"I'm not in any fucking state, 'cept maybe New York." I doubled over with the force of my vomiting. I could feel my wounds healing. Fucking investiture kept healing every wound, even staying drunk was difficult.

"Even Cassidy sai–" he began.

I hit him. "Don't you fucking start with this again!" I had my finger in his face. "Cassidy wasn't with me when I—when she died." I tried to hold back the sob. "He didn't have to fucking do… what I did." I couldn't bear to say it aloud.

"Leave it," he started to say.

"Leave me the fuck alone, Miles." I bowed my head. "Just go away and let me be. Please." I didn't look up until I heard the flutter of his jacket in the wind as he took flight.

I walked over to the moron that had decided to hit me. I reached into his pocket and pulled out his key fob. "Shouldn't have called him a faggot there, Mr. Dead Guy." I said as I waggled a finger in front of his dead eyes. I unlocked the car, found my bottle on the ground and took a deep pull from the small amount remaining. I got into the car. It started and sounded like a fucking dream. I put it in gear and slammed my foot on the accelerator.

I drove off without another thought. My mind was locked on the road ahead. I had no idea where I was going; I just knew that I needed out of New York. I threaded my way through traffic; the Holland Tunnel was a blur. Between the whiskey and my eyes constantly tearing, it was amazing that I could see anything. Considering that I was crossing into New Jersey, that wasn't necessarily a bad thing.

Minneapolis. What the fuck was in Minneapolis? A hazy memory of bad sports teams and a huge mall ran through my head. Finding zero made sense to me. I always loved the concept of zeroing a weapon. That is, bringing a weapon's point of aim and the point of impact of its rounds perfectly in line with one another. Metaphorically it seemed to fit so many situations in life. And now, perhaps more than ever, I needed to zero myself.

I woke up in a small town called Marquette, Michigan. My mouth tasted like death. The passenger seat floorboard was full of a variety of empty whiskey bottles. I shook my head. I felt the beginnings of a brutal hangover coming on. The bright sunlight felt like acid on my eyes. I pulled down the visor and shut my eyes. I felt real sleep sneaking up on me. I couldn't remember the last time I'd slept. I didn't want to face Him. I was so sick of gods and their fucking agendas, their senseless, merciless murdering of humans for sport.

I woke again to the sun. This time, however, it was much lower in the sky. I was shocked that I hadn't been bothered. But then again, things work differently in small towns. I'm sure I wasn't the first person to sleep in his car in this tiny fucking burg. Granted, I doubt it had been a car like this, though.

I stretched and looked at the GPS. At some point I'd programmed Minneapolis into the damned thing, but the route I'd taken looked like an idiot child with ADHD had colored it. I suppose drunk driving doesn't make for model efficiency. I don't know why I cared. It didn't really matter.

I knew *zero* was important to Sarah; it was all she could think about in the letter she'd left me. Without context, I had no idea what the hell she meant, though. One night in a moment of drunken nostalgia, I'd decided to read the letter again. When I went to dig it out of my pocket, my drunken fingers dragged a post card out instead. On it was a picture of a massive spoon with a huge cherry in it. On the reverse, Sarah had filled every available inch of white space with the word *zero* written in cramped lettering over and over again. Seeing that had gotten the idea stuck in my head and no amount of whiskey could chase it out.

The drive across the Upper Peninsula of Michigan went well, right up until I crossed into Wisconsin. Then, I passed the sign. I locked up the brakes. I threw the car into reverse and stopped when my headlights hit the sign. It read exactly what I'd thought. *Bad River Indian Reservation.* Fuck. Me. Twice.

I've got nothing against Indians, American or otherwise. That doesn't mean they like *me*. Some things never change. Western gods aren't welcome on this continent. However, just like Indian society, their gods were marginalized and pushed back to the periphery of human civilization. But there were places where they still reigned supreme and this was one of them. The Ojibwa were a proud people at the peak of their civilization; their descendants are no less so today. Their gods, and attendant spirits, are no less potent within the confines of the reservation than they were at the pinnacle of their supremacy. Here, ancient creatures stalked the land, and I wasn't welcome.

Granted, I was an emissary, and I could request to parley with the greater spirits within the reservation, but things worked differently there. I'd have to wait weeks and build up bonds of trust and friendship, which in the century following Indian massacre after Indian massacre might not ever happen. You don't force your way onto a reservation. Very bad things happen if you do. I parked the car and searched the GPS for an alternate route.

I looked up and saw a wolf slide out of the underbrush. It was too small to be Cassidy. It didn't matter. In my drunken state, it was him and he was here to talk me out of whatever it was he thought I was overdoing.

"Leave me alone, you bastard!" I hurled my whiskey bottle out the window at him. The wolf turned his head and stared at me for a second with a mournful look. Turning silently, he padded his way back into the woods.

My hands gripped the wheel and the gearshift. I was sick to death of everyone trying to tell me what I needed to do to get over the fact that I'd murdered a woman I loved…again. I looked back at the reservation sign. They couldn't follow me in there, not Cassidy and certainly not Harker. Just put the hammer down and go. I'd be gone before they were even aware that I was ever here. I slammed the accelerator to the floor.

The trees flew by and the narrow two-lane road seemed to shrink, as if it were crushing me. The problem is that Indian magic isn't like Western or Eastern magic. Indian magic is like the earth itself, it moves with the currents of nature and flows with the shifting of the seasons. It makes for a hell of a trap. You don't realize that you're caught until it's too late. Hell, you aren't even aware something's after you most of the time.

The darkness intensified, and the road became harder to see and harder to predict. I began to panic; somehow, I'd crossed the Veil. The only connection that I had to this land was tenuous at best; a sympathetic connection bound me to the road as the road connected me to my own civilization.

Off of the road, I was lost and more than that, I was prey.

The trees on either side of the road began to push in closer and closer. Behind the trees something was stalking me, something I couldn't quite make out. Ice began to form on the windshield and the road became slick with hoarfrost. Each turn grew more and more treacherous. The GPS winked out each time I got close to one side of the road or the other, unable to find a signal in the deepest recesses of the Veilside. My radio silenced a second later, leaving me with just the sounds of the road and what sounded like the pounding of thousands of ceremonial drums.

I couldn't think. My mind simply couldn't process everything at once. All I knew was that I had to get through the reservation; I had no idea how far I had come, or how much farther I had to go. I slid around a corner and hit a blinding light. For a moment, I felt a surge of hope, and even the drums seemed to silence. Just off the road ahead, a massive building pulsing with light seemed to radiate safety. My intoxication seemed to intensify as I was bathed in the light. I felt weightless. My foot hovered over the brake as the siren song of security seemed to wash over me. My hand slid along the wheel and began to turn. The frost thickened on my windshield as snow began to fall heavily. Something within me screamed in horror and I shook myself out of my reverie. Even drunk I realized what appeared to be too good to be true was. I slammed my foot back on the accelerator and jerked the wheel back toward the center of the road. A great roar sounded from the forest and a huge form tore free from the trees. A white–maned, withered giant with a blood drenched mouth and huge fangs charged across the road, hurling trees aside in an insane dash to get to the car.

My whole body tensed and I tried not to scream as I willed the car to greater speed. The creature raced after me, its mane of white hair flared around its awful head like a blood–spattered halo. It ran on all fours, like a mad beast. Long fingered, clawed hands dug into the snow and ice and pulled it toward me with horrifying speed. I had to force myself to watch the road, my eyes kept darting up to the rear view mirror. Ahead the trees bent together forming an arch. As I got closer I could see the small opening between the trees closing. The speedometer read one-fifteen; on the ice, I couldn't push it any harder. My time with Abbadonna had taught me to drive like a man possessed, because many times, I was, but the ice pushed even my magically enhanced reflexes to their limits.

"Please," I whispered. "Please."

The car blew through the opening. Tree branches scraped along the roof and doors. I was through! The night lit up around me with constellations I'd doubted I'd ever see again. My radio suddenly flared back to life. I jumped and looked down as I reached for the controls to turn it down. Looking back up, I caught a glimpse of glowing, blood red eyes in the rear view mirror. I whipped around, a Word on my lips, but there was nothing behind me but empty road and blowing snow. When I turned back to the mirror, only my own bloodshot eyes gazed drunkenly back.

I lowered my eyes and nearly slammed into a car that was stopped in the middle of the road. I jerked the wheel and pounded the brake, drifting around it. I came to a stop facing the front of the car. It was a small, green Cavalier that had seen many better days. The entire front of the car was smashed all to shit. The windshield had shattered and was spread all over the road. Blood was everywhere. It was sprayed all over the hood, dripped from the doorframe and pooled beneath the driver's side of the car. It looked as if the driver had lost control on the poorly maintained, icy road and hit a tree at speed. I shook my head and reached for my door handle.

I staggered into the cold night and approached the car slowly. My eyes kept darting back toward the reservation boundary; whatever had chased me was just on the other side. I was pretty certain that it couldn't cross, but there was no sense in trusting what was, at best, idle speculation.

"Hello?" I called. "Anybody not completely fucking dead in there?"

I stepped closer to the car. The radio was playing Journey's "Don't Stop Believin'." I looked at the driver. She'd clearly stopped believin'. There was a buzz by my feet as her phone vibrated. *Hey! Are you home yet?* The front of the phone displayed the text message from someone she'd nicknamed "Riggles." I picked it up and texted back. *I'm dead. Call the police and invest in a name change.* I tossed the phone into her lap and stumbled back to my car.

I took one last look as I turned my car away from the wreck. It was a shame; she looked so young. Somewhere, someone would be getting tragic news. She'd gotten off easy. It was the family I felt for. I knew exactly how they felt. Bitterness overtook me, and I grabbed another bottle from behind my seat. I opened it, raised it in a salute to the dead girl in my rearview mirror and took a long pull. I shook my head and turned back toward Ashland, the next stop on my way to Minneapolis and zero.

CHAPTER 23

It took a little less than twenty minutes to reach the next town. As I pulled into Ashland, I breathed a sigh of relief. So many roads, so many power lines and homes, meant safety. Nothing from the reservation was going to chase me in here; there was simply too much technology, too much death. I pulled into a gas station to calm my nerves, fill my tank and make sure that the rest of my route kept me squarely in this reality.

The second I saw her I knew something was wrong. She was a bone thin, ragged looking girl, whispering to herself and walking around in circles. Normally, I'd have written her off as a meth head, but she had silver eyes. *Coinbound.* I'm pretty certain that I've mentioned that they creep me the fuck out. I stepped out of the car, keeping my eyes on her.

"Hungry," she muttered to herself. "So cold." She shuffled closer to me and stopped as if reconsidering her steps. "Can't see me. Can't f'n see me." She brought her hand to her mouth and bit down on her knuckle as she stared at me. She flickered in and out of sight as she slid back and forth through the Veil at random.

"Who can't?" I asked with a slight slur.

"You can't," she whispered.

"Damn shame, that," I said.

She shook her head and closed her eyes in disbelief. "Can't see me. Can't see me." She opened them again as I slid my card into the gas pump and reached for the nozzle.

"If you say so." I turned my back on her. Crazy ass Coinbound.

"You can see me?" her voice turned hopeful. I ignored her. "You talked to me!" she said.

I looked at her. Something in her voice rang of panic, trust me, that isn't safe. "Yeah, I did. Sue me."

"OHMYGOD!" She spit it out in one breath as she stumbled toward me. "You have to help me!"

"Stay back," I warned as I reached under my jacket. "Take it easy."

"You have to help me!" There was a sound like a siren beginning to wind itself up. I sighed. She was going to Keen. Fuck. I dove to her side of the car and clamped my hand over her mouth.

"Shhh," I said. "Don't do that." I don't do soothing very well.

She mumbled something into my hand, as the keening sound subsided.

"If I take my hand off your mouth, you promise to keep shit civil?" I asked. She nodded and I released my hand.

"You don't understand," she said. "I was in an accident."

"Yeah?" This was starting to make sense. The green car must have been hers.

"I was driving and a deer jumped out in front of me."

"You swerved and hit a tree, didn't you?" I asked.

"Yeah, my car is totaled." She sounded forlorn. It was about to get worse.

"Your car isn't the only thing totaled, sweetheart."

"What?" She cocked her head to the side.

I pointed to her reflection in the car window. "You didn't make it."

She gasped and stumbled as she saw herself. "No, no, no!" She sat heavily on the ground and began to weep.

"Listen, I'd love to stay and chat," I said as I knelt beside her. "But I have shit that needs to get done. When you see your boss, tell him Jason Beckett fucked his wife." That would piss the old bastard off. Good. I brushed off my knee as I stood. I nodded once to her and took the nozzle out of the gas tank and shoved it back in its receptacle.

"You're leaving?" she asked, looking up at me.

"Yeah, I pretty much just said that." I opened the car door. "Remember what I said to tell your boss."

"You can't leave me!" She jumped to her feet. "I need help!"

"Not from me," I shook my head. "People I help tend to die, though that isn't really an issue for you, is it?"

"Please!" She reached for the door handle.

I paused. I thought I had no pity left, I really did. Something in her voice made me stop.

"Please." She looked at me with her creepy ass silver eyes. "I need help."

"Get in." I unlocked the passenger door. "Don't mind the bottles."

"Are you drunk?" she asked.

"You're dead," I said. "It ain't like you'll get any deader. You want help or not?"

"If I'm dead, why'm I still here?" she asked as she got in the car.

"You made a deal with the Ferryman." I turned the car on. "He owns you now."

"What do you mean?"

"Which part?" I pulled the car back onto the road. The weather was rapidly getting worse. I was beginning to regret the choice of a sports car. I should've stolen a fucking snowmobile instead. I hate Wisconsin.

"What deal? Who's the Ferryman?" She threw her hands in the air. "I've never even been on an f'n ferry!"

"Someone gave you a coin in the last few days, yes?" I asked.

"Yeah, but he's not a ferryman, he's a teacher."

"Did you give *that* coin to anyone recently?"

"Yeah, this guy gave me a ride into town from where I hit the tree," she nodded.

"Did he give the coin back to you?"

"Yeah, it's right here." She reached into her jacket pocket and pulled out a silver dollar.

"Hold it over here, so I can reach it with my left hand," I said. As she reached across the console, I held my Mark over it. There was a ripple in reality for a second and the illusion of a silver dollar disappeared. She held a small silver coin with the Ferryman's head etched in relief on the side. The reverse showed the Neckromanteion at Ephyra.

"What the hell was that?" she asked. "What did you do?"

"I broke the illusion covering the coin," I said.

"How?" She shook her head. "What illusion? What the hell's going on?"

"The Ferryman tricked you, this isn't your coin. Hang on," I said as the car shuddered beneath me. The car broke free from the ice and began to slide sideways. "Fuck."

We slid for about two hundred yards through the divided streets of Ashland. I finally got the car back under control.

"You ok?" I asked.

"No, I'm f'n dead!" She looked at me. "Please, just tell me what the hell's going on."

I was stopped in the middle of the road. I looked to my right; there was a hotel on the shore of Lake Superior. I looked back to the road, and there was no way that I could drive anywhere in this kind of weather, not in this car and not this drunk. I had to wait for the plows to clean the roads and who knew how long that was going to take in this backwards ass, hick region. I turned and pulled into the hotel parking lot.

"What are we doing?" she asked.

"Stopping for the night, there's no need for both of us to die tonight." I opened the door. "I'll be right back."

When I came back to the car, she was sitting on the hood looking depressed. I wasn't judging her; I mean death isn't easy to come to terms with. Something inside me hated her for that very reason.

"I got us a room." I waved the envelope with the keycards.

"Thank you," she said. Her voice was quiet against the wind.

I held the door open for her. The room was typical of every hotel room, if you were in the early nineteen seventies, that is. It smelled vaguely of body odor and the décor was terrible. Not that I'm an interior decorator or anything, but if I notice it, it's bad. She sat on one of the beds and looked at me.

"I have some money," she said.

"Don't worry about it," I replied. "I'm rich." I held up my left hand and showed her my Mark.

"Cool tattoo," she said. "I've got one on my foot."

"Yeah?"

"Look, I need to know what's going on." She put her head in her hands. "I'm so confused."

"So tell me about the guy that gave you the silver coin tonight." I sat on the other bed facing her. I felt like shit. My investiture was forcing the alcohol out of my system faster and faster as the days progressed.

"After I hit the tree, he showed up in a white Mercedes and pulled over to see if I needed help."

"A white Mercedes, huh?" I snorted.

"Yeah, why?" She looked confused.

"And I beheld a pale horse, and he that sat on him was Death," I quoted.

"Why do I know that?" she asked.

"It's from a famous book."

"Oh."

I walked over to the coffee maker and started to make a pot. I had a feeling this was going to be a long conversation. "So," I began as I inexpertly put the strange contraption together. "What happened when he showed up?"

"He asked me if I needed a ride into town." She wrapped her arms around herself as if she were freezing. "I said I did."

I yanked the bedspread from my bed and wrapped it around her. She nodded her thanks at me and continued.

"He drove me to a restaurant in town. I hadn't noticed it on my way through, though, which was kind of weird."

"It probably doesn't exist. He has immense control over the inner Veil. If he wanted you to think that you were tanning on the beach in Barbados, you'd believe it," I said.

"What does that even mean?" She threw her hands in the air in exasperation. "Look, I don't mean to sound ungrateful, but I don't even know your name and it's like you're speaking a foreign language right now."

"Fair enough." I extended my hand. "My name's Jason Beckett."

She reached for my hand and stopped. "My name is…" A look of horror filled her face. "I don't know…" She stood and began to pace frantically.

"Don't bother," I said. "Your birth name's gone." What a positively wonderful time to sober up. Fucking investiture.

"What?" she began to cry. "Please, please just say something that makes sense to me."

"Look at me."

She looked up.

"Repeat after me," I said, holding up my Mark and forcing my will across the space between us. "I am dead."

"Wha–" she started.

"I am dead," I repeated.

"I am dead." Her voice was calm; my magic forced her brain to accept the reality.

"I gave my soul to the Ferryman."

"I gave my soul to the Ferryman."

"He took my name and gave me one of his choosing."

"He took my name and gave me one of his choosing," she said.

"There." I filled the coffee pot with water. "Now that that's out of the way, maybe we can get somewhere."

"Why did he take my name?" she asked.

"So that no one could ever have power over you but him." I put the semi–clean carafe back in to the coffee maker.

"Huh?"

"To know a thing's Name is to have ownership over it."

"I don't get it."

"What's the first thing you do when you get a new pet?"

"Well, name it, I guess."

"Why?" I asked.

"Because things are supposed to have names, right?"

"Ah, but what do you use the pet's name for?" I held up a finger.

"To call it or to talk to it, I suppose."

"Yet, your pet has no choice in the naming."

"Well, it's an animal, how the hell can it choose?" She held up her hands.

"Exactly. It's a *thing*. You are a *thing* to the one who named you, nothing more."

"Why would he do that to me?" she asked, belief finally setting in.

"He needs you to do his work for him."

"What kind of work?" She looked afraid.

"Murder," I said harshly. "Lots and lots of murder."

"What?" She jerked to her feet. "I can't kill anyone!"

"Yes, you can," I nodded. "You just haven't had incentive before."

"No," she shook her head. "I'm not a violent person, I mean, like, at all."

"Look at yourself, what do you see?" I asked as I plucked at her ill–fitting clothes.

"I look like an AIDS patient," she said.

"It's called 'the Withering,'" I turned to pull a dingy mug from the cupboard.

"I can see why," she nodded. "Why's he doing this to me?"

"Your body's now a blank," I said. "As you consume the lives of your prey, you'll blossom into whatever the Ferryman desires this week."

"What do you mean desires?"

"Whatever he wants to fuck," I shrugged. "That's about as plain as I can make it."

"You don't have to be so rude," she said.

"I don't like answering questions twice."

"What happens if I don't kill anyone?" she asked.

"He pulls you back to the Plains of Acheron and does whatever it takes to make you subservient."

"Where?"

"Outermost area of Perdition." I tasted the coffee. It was about what I expected, awful.

"Perdition?"

"Hell, also known as the only place in the known universe that lacks a Starbucks." I grimaced as I drank the coffee.

"How do you know all of this?"

I held up my Mark. "Any idea what this is?"

"No," she shook her head.

"It's the Mark of the Adversarial Beast."

"Ok," she raised her eyebrow.

"I'm his emissary," I said. "I work for the Devil."

"What?" She stepped back.

"Oh, I get it," I snorted. "Death takes you for all you're worth, Yahweh does exactly shit to help you, and you jerk back away from me because I work for the Devil."

"What am I supposed to do?" She asked. "You just said you work for the f'n Devil."

"How about say 'thank you, Jason for not leaving me out there in the snow all the fuck alone whispering to myself and going batshit crazy'?"

"Thank you, Jason for not leaving me out there in the snow all alone to go crazy or whatever," she said.

"Better. Want some coffee?"

"Yeah," she said. "I'm so damned cold."

I poured her a cup. "You'll warm up after you kill someone."

"What?" She took the cup.

"After you kill someone, things'll start to get better, I mean."

"I really don't want to kill anyone." She grimaced at me over the rim of her cup. She really did look innocent. I wondered why the Ferryman had chosen her. Other than the fact that he's a complete prick, I mean.

"I'm scared," she spoke frankly.

"I would be too, if I were in your shoes."

"Have you ever seen Hell?" she asked.

"We don't call it Hell," I replied. "We call it Perdition."

"If you've seen He– Perdition, why would you want to work for the Devil?" She sipped her coffee.

"Because it isn't what you think," I said. "Life's a little less one dimensional after you've died."

"Not to sound like a d–bag, but how do I know you aren't lying to me?" she asked.

"I can show you some things, and others you'll discover for yourself." I reached out and took her coffee cup away from her.

"Like what?" She pulled the bedspread back around her shoulders.

I put my hands on her shoulders and stepped through the Veil dragging her with me. "Like this."

We stood in the inner Veil, which was about as far as I wanted to go. Any further and I'd be in for some vicious Veilshock when we returned. As it was I knew I was gonna yack up all of the wonderful coffee I'd just drank not to mention at least three liters of Jameson's. Darkness and snow swirled all around us. The hotel was gone and in its place was a vacant, snowy hill overlooking a pristine lake to our left and an immense forest everywhere else.

"Where are we?" she asked.

"The inner Veil, like where the Ferryman took you." I looked around. Something wasn't quite right. "There should be some remnant of the buildings here, though."

"Why?"

"Well, this is a reflection of the waking world; the people have a collective consciousness, one that endures even on the far side of the Veil. If it exists on the Lifeside, it should have a similar Veilside resonance." An uncomfortable idea began forming. "Unless…"

"Unless what?"

"Unless I'm a fucking moron." I grabbed her shoulders and tried to pull her across the Veil with me. I saw the glowing red eyes of the creature from the reservation peering at us from behind a distant clump of evergreens and knew that I'd made a horrible error. I yanked her back through the Veil.

We hit the floor in a jumble. I pushed free of her and threw up in the handy little trashcan in the room. I stood and wiped my mouth with the back of my hand.

"What the hell was that?" she asked.

"They don't recognize the reservation boundary on the Veilside. Shit." I started to pace.

"Who doesn't?" she asked.

"Ojibwa." I ran my fingers through my hair and yanked it hard. "Fuck me."

"Ojibwa as in the casino?" She pulled herself upright.

"Ojibwa as in angry goddamned Manitou," I spat into the sink.

"Manitou?" she asked.

"It's like a god, only both less and more at the same time."

"That doesn't make sense." She held up hands. "It's either less or it's more. It can't be both." She moved her hands up and down in a balance motion.

"When it gets here, you tell it that. I'm running," I said.

"What kind of Manitou was it? Or are there even different kinds?" she asked.

"The worst kind. It was a hunter of some sort, and where hunters are concerned, the Indians didn't exactly fuck around." I walked over to the window and pulled the shade back. The snow had intensified to near blizzard proportions.

Fuck. Me. Stupid. I was trapped here with a powerless newborn Coinbound and an angry Manitou.

"So that thing we saw, it's after you?" she asked after a few moments of tense silence.

"Yeah," I said. "I think it is."

"What did you do to piss it off?"

"I trespassed." I fumbled my cigarettes out of the inner pocket of my jacket. I lit one and inhaled deeply.

"I don't think this is a smoking room, Jason," she said.

"I don't think I care, whatever your name was." I flicked my ash on the floor.

"I'm just saying."

I looked out the window again. No sign of the creature on the Lifeside, but the storm continued to get worse. It was nearly a whiteout outside. I sighed. I reclined on my bed and looked over at the Coinbound.

"So, what happened at the diner?" I asked, deliberately forcing myself to calm down. Freaking out never helps anything.

"What?"

"When the Ferryman brought you to the diner, what happened?" I asked.

"Well, he bought me a cup of coffee and told me he'd wait with me until I was able to get through to my friends." She shuddered and pulled the bedspread tighter around herself. "He said he'd make a deal with me."

"Yeah?" I sat up a little.

"He said that he'd let me use his phone if I gave him a single coin from my pocket." She looked over at me. "I only had my friend's lucky silver dollar. His grandma gave it to him and said as long as he had it, he'd never be broke."

"Well, that's true enough."

"Yeah, he's had it for years. He kept it in his wallet, and true to her word, he was never broke. He gave it to me as a lucky charm to get me home safe."

"Sympathetic magic, it ain't the most effective, but it does work," I said.

"I'm not sure we speak the same language." She shook her head at me. "Anyway, I didn't want to give it to him. I said that I couldn't give it to him." She looked at me and paused. "Can I have a cigarette?"

I tossed her the pack and my lighter. "These things can kill you, you know."

"Hur hur hur, funny." She rolled her eyes at me and lit one. "Anyway, he wouldn't let up about the stupid coin, he said he *required* a coin for the trip. Finally, I decided that I could get another silver dollar from the bank when I got home and my friend would never know the difference."

"You weren't going to win that argument, you know. He'd have kept you there until you decided to give him the coin," I said. "He takes whatever the hell he wants."

"Yeah, it seemed like forever before I finally gave in. I just wanted to use the phone, I didn't think about asking anyone else in the diner or anything." She drew deeply on the cigarette and blew a smoke ring. "This is kinda fun."

"When there's no threat of death, just about anything is amusing."

"He finally got the coin and sort of rolled over his knuckles. He made it disappear and then pulled it out of my ear. He gave it back to me and handed me a cell phone."

"Let me guess, you got a busy signal?"

"Worse. The call went through, and when my friend answered, I could hear him fine, but he kept saying that he couldn't hear me over the static." She lowered her head into her hands again and sobbed. "I was crying and trying to tell him I was in an accident."

"There's no way you were going to come out on top with him." I slid off the bed and knelt beside her. "He can't be stopped, and if there's any way to hurt you in the process, he'll take it."

"I know it sounds dumb, but what hurts worse is that I lied and lost his coin. The goddamned coin."

I just let her cry for a while. It sounded like she really needed it. I looked out the window and let myself go. Someday, someone needed to fuck up the Ferryman's day.

First Jessica, then Sarah, and then Annessa; my heart was raw and broken. I had no idea why I'd even picked up the Coinbound. I mean, she was nothing to me, and more than that she was a creature of the fucking Ferryman. To make matters worse, when I saw her suffering I thought of Annessa on the night I'd created her. What had I done? If I'd had the courage to say no just once in my life, she'd still be alive. If alive was even the word for it. Without Annessa, I'd have been killed for good and more than once. I turned back to the Coinbound, who'd finally quit sobbing.

"You ok?" I asked.

"Yeah," she wiped her eyes. "Thanks."

"No problem," I shrugged.

She lay back on the bed and propped herself up on one arm, looking at me quizzically.

"What?"

"What's your story?"

"What do you mean?" I lit another cigarette.

"How's a guy like you wind up working for the Devil?"

"It's a long story." I scratched the back of my head as if to erase the memory.

"I'm dead, I've got nothing but time apparently."

I stared out the window at my car and the whiskey bottles that waited in the backseat. I said it before I realized I was talking. "I murdered my wife."

"What?" She sat bolt upright.

"We were in Iraq," I stared out the window. "We were assigned to a convoy—"

"Wait, you were in the Army?"

"Air Force," I corrected. "We were Security Forces, military police."

"Oh."

"We were deployed to a massive prison camp, Camp Bucca," I sighed. "Right after those morons at Abu Ghraib decided to make asses of themselves, we got assigned to running prisoner convoys." I stood up and leaned against the window frame. "Jess got added to my convoy one day when we were low on manning and a jackass from our team broke his ankle."

"Jess?"

"My wife's name was Jessica."

"Right, sorry." She motioned for me to continue.

"Normally, they wouldn't assign a husband and wife to the same mission, but when you're short a few people, rules go out the window." I held up my coffee cup and swirled the brownish liquid around before taking a drink. "We got attacked on our way to the port of Umm Qasr."

The memory hit me like a shotgun blast to the face. "It started as bad day; it was hot as hell," I shook my head. "And the smell from the port was vile, rotting fish and garbage, all baked in that horrible humid heat."

She gagged, then waved her hands in front of her mouth as if trying to shove the imaginary smell away.

"Exactly," I nodded. "We'd done everything right, but the attack came without warning."

"What happened?"

"They hit Jess's humvee with an RPG as the convoy rounded a blind corner." I clenched my hand and shattered the coffee mug. "It was like a comet, her vehicle…just spinning over and over. The jerricans on the back were full of diesel, they went up like fireworks when the grenade hit, throwing liquid fire as the humvee rolled." I sat heavily on the bed. "It slid across the street on the driver's side until it hit a jersey barrier in the center of the road."

"Jesus," she whispered, then clapped a hand over her mouth. "Sorry!"

I didn't notice her swear. "I was the troop commander for the rear security vehicle. We were supposed to defend her vehicle while the rest of the convoy went ahead without us." I snorted. "We hadn't realized yet that the insurgents were far smarter than we'd given them credit for."

"What did they do?"

"They'd set secondary explosives right where my vehicle stopped. My gunner checked, but didn't see them; none of my team saw them. They were all a little panicked, but I was completely out of my mind." I gripped the bed with both hands. "My humvee took the majority of the blast to the engine block, sparing us, but completely destroying any hope of escape.

"As soon as my head cleared after the explosion, I staggered out of my humvee and ran for Jess's vehicle. And that's when they made their move. The insurgents had taken over a two story building along the convoy route, as soon as they knew both vehicles were disabled, they unloaded on us. Every window, every doorway of that building was hurling lead at us.

"I didn't see any of it. I staggered and stumbled to get to Jess. Bullets dropped all around me, I could hear them flying by me, like mosquitoes. The smoke from the burning tires on Jess's humvee hid me from the majority of their shooters, but that didn't stop them from trying.

"I heard my team dying. The disabled vehicle had stranded them out in the open, with only the flaming remains of our humvee to guard them. I didn't care. All I had eyes for was the flames billowing out of her vehicle; all my ears cared to hear was the sound of her screams. Even her pain registered as sweet; it meant she was still alive.

"I was too late. I pulled myself on top of the vehicle and stared down at Jessica. Her team was all dead, her gunner was crushed between the jersey barrier and the turret. Somehow, Jessica had survived. She was trapped in the driver's seat, the engine block pinning her legs. She looked up at me just as the fire finally spread into the passenger compartment."

I stopped talking and started out the window and took a deep, shuddering breath.

"What happened, Jason?' she asked quietly. "What did you do?"

"It only took a second for the fire to reach her," I said. "I tried to grab her, to pull her out, but there was nothing I could do. Her legs were trapped, and there was no time.

"The air seemed so still, even the smoke seemed to stop moving. It was like the only thing I could see was her eyes. They were like a cloudless sky in the middle of her soot–blackened face. I remember the way her lips shuddered before she started screaming, before the fire stole the air away from her. I remember her lips mouthing the words *kill me*."

I stood up and started pacing between the bed and the door. "I screamed her name and furiously tugged at the door trying everything thing to get to her. I prayed for the strength to get her out. Finally, when the fire spread to her body, I gave up."

I swallowed hard and continued. "I pulled my sidearm and whispered 'I love you,' before I shot her."

My hand gently touched the hollow of my throat where the bullet had struck Jess, throwing her head back and ending her suffering.

I looked up at the Coinbound, her eyes were wide and her mouth hung open. "How'd you get out of there?"

"I didn't," I said. "I died."

"Then how are you here right now?"

"After I pulled the trigger, my body kind of shut down. I fell backwards off of the humvee and laid there, I just fucking laid there. Nothing mattered, not the fact that my friends and my family were gone, nothing. It was like I was *still*." I shook my head. "I just didn't care. I was completely numb.

"The cowards responsible weren't. They came out of the building guns blazing as they fired into the air. That's about when I came out of it.

"I sat up; none of them saw me move. They were so focused on praying, screaming praises to Allah and dancing. One of them was pissing on Van Zant, my gunner. He had three kids, Van Zant, I mean. He was only twenty-two." I shook my head at the memory and continued.

"I shot the one pissing on Van Zant first. I shot him in the balls, from behind. When he dropped to his knees, I put another round through the back of his head.

"I turned and hammered shots into the three idiots who'd been dancing. They were clustered together, arm in arm, they went down that way, clutching each other and squealing like pigs for the slaughter.

"The two pious ones pulled themselves back to their feet before I turned to face them. The only reason they didn't kill me was that they'd emptied their guns in reckless celebration. I had to reload before I finished the second one. He screamed like a woman when I raised my gun.

"It was the last one that mattered; the coward with the empty RPG launcher, the piece of shit that had ended my life. He tried to run. I shot him in the lower back and he dropped like a stone. By the time I reached him, he was sobbing like a child and pulling himself toward an alley. He chattered prayers to his god over and over like a mantra.

"I shot him though his right knee and stomped on his left knee until I felt it shatter under my boot. He started screaming 'I surrender' in perfect English. What's surrender to a man that just killed his wife? I shot him in the balls and as he screamed for mercy, I put the last round through his liver and left him to die.

"I staggered back to Jessica's vehicle and somehow managed to climb back on top of it, or on the side of it, since it was passenger side up at that point. I remember staring at her charred remains, wondering where my beautiful wife had gone. For a second, the smoke cleared and the sun shone down on me. I looked up and cursed God, Allah, Yahweh. I screamed every profane thing that came to mind. I said I'd give my soul to see Heaven burn. Then I put my pistol in my mouth and pulled the trigger."

CHAPTER 24

I lit another cigarette in the silence; the coffee maker clicked itself off. I stared into the falling snow and lost myself to the litany of my failures.

"Jason?" the Coinbound whispered.

"Yeah?"

"What happened after you shot yourself?"

"I fell." I drew on the cigarette. "It seemed like forever, falling through darkness."

I turned back to face her. "Finally, I hit bottom and plunged into freezing water. When I pulled myself out, gasping and choking, I stood on a precipice, the entrance of a cave. I turned back and stared into the darkness, somewhere far in the depths of that cave, it seemed as if I could see a light, faint and fading."

I gave myself over to the memories that were etched like scars onto the very substance of my soul.

* * *

I stood on the shores of the Styx. Before me, deep within the depths of the long, shadowed valley that spread out below, were the gates to Pandaemonium, behind me the vast cavernous mouth of the cave that birthed the Styx. They call that cave the Eye of Eurydice.

Souls pass through it only once upon entering Perdition, and those souls that look back too long are doomed to an eternity of suffering. Not by the hands of any demons, but by the haunting specter of their past lives. Much as Orpheus suffered when he lost his faith in the gods and looked back to see Eurydice, thus damning her to die a second time.

I stared into the darkness of that cave for a long time. I was still angry beyond comprehension. When I finally decided to look away, my Master put his hand on my shoulder.

"I know who you are," I said quietly. I deserved this. My Catholic parents taught me that, and only that, lesson.

"And I know who you are, my child." He looked at me. "There is no peace for you here."

"So they say." I looked at the ground. "It's a shame, really."

"What is?" he asked, an amused smile playing along his lips.

"If I'd known this was it, I might have killed more of them."

"I would offer you such a fate." He turned me to face him. "Should you accept the terms, I believe you will find this place much less a torment. You might even find it favorable."

"What do you mean?" Hell, I'd read *Faust* in high school, I knew what was going on. Except that unlike Dr. Faustus, I was already damned, and my situation could only improve.

"What would you like most in this world or any other?" he asked.

"Jessica." In that one word there was hope, peace and salvation. For her, there was no price too high.

"In exchange for your beloved, you will submit yourself to my will? You will serve me of your own volition?"

"For her, yes." I stared at him. I didn't truly believe it possible, but somewhere in my heart, hope flared into existence.

"Then you would do this task for me?" He looked at me intently.

"How do I know that you aren't lying to me?" I asked. "How do I know I'll actually get her back?"

"My child, you are already in Perdition. I have claimed your soul, by your own artifice, no less," he laughed. "You have willingly thrown yourself upon my altar. What need have I of deception at this late hour?"

I thought about my oath before I died. I can tell you now, as I felt then, I felt no regret. One way or the other the almighty entirely owned the death of my Jessica.

"Can I see her?" My voice trembled.

My Master waved his hand and a shimmering circle formed in the air. Through this window I could see the Plains of Acheron. I saw her standing next to a small yurt, a kind of tent. She was dressed like one of the plainsmen. She looked happy, after a fashion. I would later come to learn that the plainsmen all shared that look. They fed on meat and milk from animals that all drank from a communal source, the Lethe. In the ecology of the Underworld, there are many mercies that can mask its cruelty, if only for a time.

"How long do I have to serve you?" I asked.

"For seventy years and seventy days," he spoke softly.

"What will I have to do?" I asked.

"My child, I thought you didn't care what you had to do?" he smiled sardonically.

"I've already accepted." I looked him in the eye, as much as I could, anyway. "I just need a basic job description."

"You will be my voice. You will be my hand." He raised his hand before me. "You will go to Earth and you will grasp the hands of my allies and crush the throats of my enemies."

"So, I'm your errand boy?"

"You will be my Emissary."

I took my vows right then. I made my promises and knew that I would see my wife again.

* * *

I ran a hand through my hair and looked back up at the Coinbound. "And now we're even," I smiled. "I know your story and you know mine."

"So how much longer till you get your wife back?" she asked quietly.

"That's a whole different story," I shook my head. "And I'm in no mood to tell it."

"Oh," she leaned back on the bed and rested her head against the headboard. "I didn't mean to intrude."

"It's ok," I waved her apology away. "Just a little raw."

She sat up quickly and grabbed at her right hand, itching her palm furiously. "Something's happening," she said, the panic evident in her voice.

I leaned across the space between the beds and looked at her hand. A sharp, black crystal was forcing its way through the skin on her palm. "Whoa."

"What is this?" she sounded panicked.

"Your Mnemosyne phial, I'd guess," I said. "I didn't know you guys made them yourselves."

"My what?"

"It's what you use to take souls, you stab them with that." I looked around. "It's how you transport souls to whatever afterlife they've got coming to them."

"Why's it coming out now?" she asked as it slid free from her flesh and landed on the bed. She picked it up with two fingers like it was covered with filth.

"It could be danger or fear, I don't know." I reached under my jacket and pulled my Beretta free.

"Whoa, whoa, what are you doing with that?" She pointed the phial at my gun.

"I don't know yet." I held up a hand to shut her up and listened. The wind outside had reached a howling gale. "Something doesn't feel right."

"What am I supposed to do?" she asked. She pulled her knees up to her chest.

"Well, for starters, don't curl up into a fucking ball," I said. "Get up, put your back to a wall. If anything comes close to you that isn't me, stab it with that crystal."

She held up the four-inch phial. "Stab them with this? It's like poking someone with a pencil."

"Just trust me; I've seen what those things can do. They're like angelic spears, they might not look like much, but they'll cut through a fucking tank."

"Ok, ok." She slid off the bed and leaned against the wall.

I thought about turning the lights off, but I figured it would spook the girl and it might cause more problems than it was worth.

"I don't think anything's happ–" She started to say.

The window exploded into the room; I threw my arms up to cover my eyes. They leapt screaming into the room behind the storm of glass, white creatures that looked like emaciated men covered in matted, bloody white fur. I didn't question; I just started shooting. I moved quickly, sidestepping to put myself between them and the girl. The first creature dropped with a smoking hole in his face. The other two tried to circle around me; they were after the girl. Shit.

"Don't let them touch you!" I jumped sideways onto the bed. The creatures were moving so fast it was hard to target them. I fired at the second one and scored a hit on his neck. It fell back and roared at me. They were hideous; mouthfuls of chipped and broken teeth jutted out beneath their glowing red eyes. The girl was screaming as they closed in on us.

The third one darted forward and grabbed at the Coinbound before I could line up a shot on him. Her hand darted out and I saw the phial lengthen and drive into the creature's chest. It began to convulse and it dropped to the floor, dead. The second creature charged me, and I fired reflexively. My shots went wide; I dropped to my back and launched it over me with kick. It flew past me and hit the wall near the girl who promptly stabbed it.

I rolled off of the bed and back to my feet. "You ok?"

"I feel… amazing," she said.

I looked over my shoulder at her. Her flesh had filled out and her eyes were glowing silver. Her brown hair had turned white and based on her body I began to suspect that the Ferryman might be trying to replace Ereshkigal. "I told you; he likes killing."

"What the hell were those things?" she asked.

"No fucking clue." I looked out the window. I couldn't see anything; the light in the room had killed any chance of seeing anything in the dark.

"Do you think there's more?"

I nodded. "I'd bet on it."

"What do they want?"

"I thought that they wanted to kill me at first, but I'm beginning to think they're after you." I moved cautiously toward the window.

"But wouldn't that piss off the Ferryman?" she asked.

"He doesn't work here," I said.

"What do you mean; people die here all the time, right?"

"Yeah," I nodded. "But the Ferryman only sends his Coinbound to collect the souls involved in the War or those beholden to the Broken Temples; the reservation is off limits."

"But the reservation is like twenty miles from here," she said.

I pointed at the corpses in the room. "Tell them that."

"There's no need to be a d–bag. I'm still learning."

The wind began to howl again. I stepped back from the window. "We need to go," I said.

"Where?"

"Someplace without windows." I backed toward the door.

"How are you going to stop them?" she asked.

"I don't know if we can, we may just have to outlast them," I said.

"Outlast them?"

"Most creatures like this don't last on the Lifeside when the sun rises." I reached for the door.

"Like vampires?" she asked.

I would have given a smartass answer about vampires and *Twilight* kids, but before I could, the door was torn out of my hands and I was hurled across the hallway through the door to another room.

"Jason!" Her voice penetrated the haze of my concussion. I shook my head and jumped back to my feet. I charged into the hallway, leveling my Beretta as I did. They were all over her. I fired quickly at the two rearmost of the creatures, killing both. There had to be about ten of the damned things. I stepped into the room, pointed my pistol at another of the creatures, it look at me and growled.

Before I could fire, it was on me. The thing was fast, scary fast. It slashed me across the face with a ragged claw. I leaned back to avoid another attack to my face. It buried both claws in my gut. There was a moment of blinding pain as it twisted its filthy hands inside me. I punched it in the throat and fired two shots point blank into its chest. It collapsed, dead before it hit the ground.

There was a blast of arctic air and in a rush, the creatures disappeared out of the room into the night. They'd dragged the Coinbound with them. I ran to the window, but they were gone. I stepped back to survey the room. The dead creatures had all turned to ice and begun to melt. In the center of the floor lay the Coinbound's last hope, her phial.

"Fuck." I bent to pick it up. I stared at it for a second. I could just let it go. This wasn't my fight; she belonged to the Ferryman and I damn sure didn't owe that motherfucker any favors. I took a deep breath as I snatched it off the floor. I knew better. I couldn't walk away from this. Not now, when the sins of my past failures burned like acid in my soul. I ran to the window, vaulted the shattered frame and raced into the darkness.

As I crossed the parking lot, the truth dawned on me. They'd yanked her across the Veil. There was no way that I could get to her on the Lifeside. I looked toward the reservation and swore. I doubted they'd have done me the courtesy of staying on the road, which meant I was going to put myself completely at the mercy of spirits of the reservation. I crossed the Veil. I wasn't going to lose again.

The darkness became complete. The cold was crushing; each breath seemed to scour my lungs. I knelt and gave my eyes time to adjust. Under perfect conditions, it would take thirty minutes for my night vision to fully kick in. I didn't have that much time. I stayed in my crouch with my eyes shut, just listening. At that moment, my ears were far more valuable than my eyes at detecting danger. All I could hear was the creaking of ancient trees and the howling of the wind. I had no idea how I was going to find her in the midst of this snowbound primordial wilderness.

I stumbled forward into the night. I couldn't see anything in the darkness and blowing snow. Thorns tore at me, roots seemed to reach out and grab me. I ran, my body numb from the cold and the mounting panic that I might have lost the Coinbound for good. The wounds in my gut were throbbing like mad and my face had begun to bleed again. I wiped my hand over my beard, it came back wet. I froze. I stared at my hand in the pale light shed by the nearly hidden moon, my left hand. My Mark was gone. My knees buckled and I passed out as shock and an inhuman amount of alcohol hit my system in a single instant.

I awoke to pain beyond any that I had previously conceived. My skull felt as if it might rupture. I threw up blood. I shivered violently in the cold. I tried to pull myself to my feet. The pain in my abdomen was blinding. Whatever that fucking creature had torn inside me, he'd done a great job of it.

I pulled myself to my feet. I had to get moving before hypothermia set in. I don't know if you've ever watched any of those nature shows where the host pits himself against the elements. They're a fucking lie. Any man that decides to fight Mother Nature is a fucking idiot. A dead fucking idiot. I tucked my hands inside my jacket, pulled it tight about me and staggered into the forest.

I had no direction in mind; I just needed to move. If I sat still, I would freeze to death. If I died here, there was no real guarantee that I would land in Perdition; if I died here, I was at the mercy of the spirits. I had a feeling they wouldn't take too kindly to me.

The wind howled through the trees. It sounded like a woman screaming. More than that, it sounded like Jessica. I stopped. It was her voice calling my name as she had when the flames surrounded her.

"Fuck you." I tried to sound defiant. I didn't know what spirit was trying to torment me, and I didn't care. "Fu– fuck you," I said again. My voice broke.

I ran. The trees took their vengeance on me as I passed, slapping my wounded face, tearing at my eyes, and tripping me. It was as if the forest was aware that I was trespassing and sought to exact a toll, a price paid in pain.

I ran until my legs gave out and I could no longer think, until I could no longer feel. I collapsed on the hard, frozen ground and wept. The wound in my side was bleeding freely now. I took my jacket off and tore the right sleeve from my shirt. I wadded it into a makeshift bandage and used my belt to secure it to my stomach. I tightened it more than I needed to. The pain in my side made the pain in my mind seem less threatening. I tried to breathe slowly to calm myself.

I felt warm hands on the back of my neck. Sarah's hands. They were gentle and comforting. I felt her lips kiss my brow, and she pulled me back to rest against her soft breasts.

"Sleep, Jason, sleep," she whispered in my ear.

My eyes began to close. From somewhere deep within, I felt a surge of anger and bile. I jerked forward and threw up more blood. I rolled to my feet drawing my pistol and turning to face whatever creature had touched me.

There was only a vague womanlike outline in the snow where I had been laying.

I fired a single shot into the head of the shape. I turned and stumbled back into the forest. There was nowhere to rest, no safe place here. Only the spirits and the horrors of my own failures come back to haunt me.

My ankle erupted in pain and I was jerked off my feet. A thick, bulbous root gripped my ankle. Sharp thorns cut into my flesh. I screamed and tried to pull away. The root ripped away. It looked vaguely like a human head. Vaguely like...Annessa. Green lambent eyes flared into existence on the face of the root, the thorns formed a mouth and raspy voice shrieked forth.

"Master!" The root shook madly. "I served! I served! You killed me! I loved you and you killed me!"

My heart went cold. My lips moved numbly, trying to form a word, an apology, a rebuttal, anything. My vision slowly began to fade toward the center. My brain was shutting down. I dragged myself away, like a worm, on my belly, making pathetic mewling sounds as my sanity fled. At some point I pulled myself to my feet. I stumbled first, then broke into a run. There had been nothing to say. She was right, and the pain of it cut through me.

I ran until my legs gave out. I fell face first into the snow, defeated. What did it matter? Where was I going to go? I didn't know where the Coinbound was; I had no idea where the fuck I was. More than that, I didn't really know *who* I was anymore. I lay there in the growing gloom, broken.

"I give up," I said. "Kill me." Full darkness fell as the slender moon was eclipsed by a primeval darkness. I passed out again.

I woke. I looked around surprised; I couldn't see much in the near perfect darkness. As my eyes finally began to adjust, I saw a huge rabbit sitting in front of me, looking up at me quizzically. It had a raven's feather clutched in his mouth.

"You're no fucking rabbit," I said. I swear it smiled at me. It wiggled its nose, dropped the raven feather and raced off into the snowy forest.

I picked up the raven's feather and felt a jolt. The damn thing thrummed with power. I turned it over in my hand cautiously. Looking around with no other real option in sight, I tucked the feather into the inner pocket of my jacket and stumbled after the rabbit. As I followed the rabbit deeper into the forest, the brush got continually thicker. Finally, it got so thick I couldn't even move at a walk. I swore and knelt to try to find tracks through the brush. I began to wonder if I hadn't made a terrible mistake. I dug the feather out of my pocket and held it up.

"Fuck it," I said. I held it in my hand and closed my eyes.

Normally with fetishes or other aboriginal ritual foci, it's a matter of relaxing your mind to discover what the object wants you to do. It's the same kind of primitive magic you use when you lose your keys. You know, when you close your eyes and play the 'if I were a key, where the hell would I hide if I wanted to make sure my owner was late to work' game. These things usually work the same way. I opened my eyes and looked around. My vision was all screwed up. It took me a second to focus. When I did, I thought I might faint. I was about a foot tall and covered in feathers. The damned fetish turned me into a raven.

I hopped and finally managed to throw myself into the air. After a few false starts, I was able to control my flight. Granted, I was about as graceful as a fat kid running for the ice cream truck, but it got the job done. It only took a second for my avian eyes to find the rabbit. He sat in a clearing looking up at me with that amused look on his face. I circled overhead until he started running again. As I followed him, I saw the huge, glowing temple structure that had nearly suckered me in as I passed through the reservation. The rabbit was making a direct line for it.

As we got closer, I could see a line of people beginning at the doors in the central base of the ziggurat–like structure, climbing the massive stairs to the altar at the pinnacle. I looked back to find the rabbit. He was running around in a frantic circle in a small clearing beneath me. I took that as a signal for me to land. I attempted a slow, graceful, circular descent and instead managed to hurl myself into a snow bank like a fucking lawn dart. I shook my head and focused on my human form.

The raven form sloughed off with the snow and I stood in the clearing wearing my own bloody and battered form again. The rabbit looked up at me and kicked at the snow impatiently.

"Alright, alright, I'm here. Shit," I said.

The rabbit turned and raced down a game trail that I would have completely overlooked. I ran after the rabbit, ducking under low hanging tree limbs and dodging the grasping briars that seemed intent on slowing me down. The rabbit crouched in the shadow of an ancient oak at the end of the game trail. I slowed my pace and crept up to him. I knelt beside the tree and looked toward the temple. My heart sank. The creatures had her at the top of the ziggurat. Standing over her struggling form was the massive, withered giant that had chased me earlier. Swirls of snow and ice whirled over the creature's head, like a massive crown of storms. It was the cause of the brutal winter storm that gripped both sides of the Veil.

I looked down at the rabbit. He looked up at me with an amused look and I shook my head.

"What the fuck's so funny?" I asked.

The rabbit hopped off into the underbrush. He paused once, looked back at me and wiggled his nose. Then, he was gone.

"Smart rabbit," I said.

I looked at the crowd of snarling, howling and screaming creatures that surrounded the ziggurat and formed the hideous procession up the massive stairs. I shook my head; how the fuck was I supposed to get to the top? I ducked beneath the overhanging branches of a slender yew tree. There were hundreds of the creatures. I pulled out my Beretta and dropped the magazine. It was far too light. I checked my two spare mags; they were full. I had thirty-five rounds. Not enough by a long shot. I tried to think of any Words that might help. It was then that it hit me, I couldn't think of any. None. I looked at my Mark. Still gone. I was cut off from Satan. I was alone, in hostile territory, trying to rescue a servant of the creature that I hated most in all the worlds. What the fuck had I gotten myself into?

I closed my eyes and stilled my breathing. I tried to hold back my panic. I opened my eyes to the flows of energy in the area. Within my Sight, the ley lines in the area glowed like wildfires crossing the land. The temple straddled a confluence the likes of which I had never seen. My sorcery would be effective, but without my Words, my options were limited. I had thirty-five rounds. I shook my head, if that was all I had, then I was fucked. I took my hand from the tree, careful to avoid the sap; it was poisonous. I froze. The yew tree is sacred to Hekate. I put my hand on the bark of the tree.

"As much as I hate to ask for it, I need your help again, Dark Maiden." I bowed my head. I couldn't escape her after all, it seemed.

I tugged the tall, central trunk of the tree firmly and felt the roots give way. I quietly invoked a spell and blue flames burned away the smaller branches and bark. The flames hardened the shaft of wood making a sturdy staff. I pulled the phial out of my pocket and held it against the top of the staff, I whispered an incantation of binding and the wood twisted into a tight claw around the base of the phial. I pulled out several strands of my hair and tied the raven feather to the spear, just below the phial. I held the spear over the glowing energy of the ley line and incanted a spell of strength over the spear. I turned it over in my hands. It wasn't the work of a master, but it would have to do.

I slipped out from the cover of the trees and looked toward the towering ziggurat. I couldn't see any way to make it to the top without being spotted. There had to be two hundred of the creatures between the altar and me. I swore softly under my breath. I didn't have near enough bullets or even remotely enough magical strength to fight my way up. The only thing I had going for me was surprise, and

I really didn't have much faith that surprise alone would get me where I needed to be. I stepped into the middle of the ley line and gathered my will.

"By your leave, Dark Maiden, I offer these souls unto you," I said. I spoke an incantation of poison and twisted my hands around the spear in a wringing motion. I slammed the butt of the spear into the ground. The snow around me blackened, and reality rippled in a huge wave around me. The ground shook and a great roar erupted from the top of the ziggurat.

The roar shattered the air. Hundreds of ravens took flight from the trees, their wings and raucous cawing drowned out the screams and growls of the creatures as they charged me. The birds flapped around me in a whirlwind of feathers. I waited until the dirty, white bastards were within a few feet of me. I poured my will into the feather again. The transformation was lightning fast, the ley line beneath me pushed the primordial magic to new heights. I screamed with the force of my building rage, my cries blending with the ravens around me. I whirled and twisted in the air, just another raven, and the spear a tiny yew twig clutched in my claws.

Beneath me, the creatures clawed at the cloud of circling ravens. The insidious poison in the snow slowly gripped them, burning them from within. They collapsed to the ground, their bodies wracked with pain and putrefaction. There were still at least a hundred of the twisted, sick creatures on the ziggurat, not to mention the great big bastard up on top with the girl. If I could land on the top of the ziggurat, I might be able to harness the full power of the confluence and turn it against the monsters. The trick was going to be landing and pulling off what would be the greatest feat of mortal sorcery ever. No fucking pressure, right?

I dropped onto the top of the ziggurat and leapt into motion again. The raven form fell away from me in a storm of cast–off feathers, and I stumbled to the edge of the stairs. I pulled out my Beretta and fired point blank into the faces of the creatures closest to the top. As they fell back, dead, I screamed curses at those that raced up to replace them. I closed my eyes and whispered a desperate prayer to the Dark Maiden as I drew in as much of the ziggurat's perverse and foul energy. It was like drinking pure heroin from a toilet. I gagged, but I wanted more. In that moment I understood. *Wendigo*. This was an ancient spirit, more a compulsion than a god. These creatures below me were slaves; chains of desire and addiction bound them all to the Wendigo. They were creatures of weakness and wretchedness.

I felt the darkness of the ziggurat's energy roiling around in my stomach. It felt like a cancer on my soul. *Master, be with me*, I thought. I spoke an incantation of fire. I opened my mouth and screamed as the energy poured forth from my mouth as brilliant, liquid fire. Satan was with me, in that moment. The Great Liberator, the Conquering Dragon! I felt the energy surge within me as my flesh absorbed the tainted magic and released the pure, ice white flames of Perdition. The phial glowed like a torch on the end of the spear as the fire poured down the side of the ziggurat immolating everything in its path. I heard the girl shrieking as if in orgasm behind me as the phial absorbed the death energy of a hundred condemned souls.

I dropped to my knees and threw up as the magic left me. Black, viscous bile exploded from my mouth in waves. The spear fell from my hand as my entire body shuddered and fought against the horrible power of the Wendigo's perverse compulsion. As I retched, I could feel the cold seeping into me. My skin began to burn with frostbite. My mind reeled, and I tried to fight against the images that flooded my consciousness. I heard the giant speaking in Anishinaabe, the Ojibwa language. My fevered mind translated only snippets of what it said, as I tried to block the words, to focus only on the pain and not the terrible desire that possessed me.

"Feed...Feast...Fuck...TAKE!" it screamed into my mind. "Devour...Devour...DEVOUR!"

I forced myself to stand. I wasn't going to die like this. Not here and for damn sure, not on my knees. I leveled my Beretta at the creature. It felt woefully inadequate, yet

somewhere in my heart this minor act of rebellion lit a fire. I
felt the darkness within my mind recede a bit.

"I want nothing from you!" I yelled. I doubled over
and vomited again. I stepped back and again leveled the
pistol. "You're a fucking animal!" I said. I pulled the
trigger.

The shot sounded like thunder and the muzzle flash
nearly blinded me. I dropped the gun as frostbite weakened
my fingers and fell to my knees again. The girl slid off of
the altar in front of me. She looked like a negative reflection
of Ereshkigal now, where the goddess had been dark, the girl
was pale as new fallen snow. Silver irises gleamed in eyes
of pure jet and her colorless lips twisted in a feral snarl. She
dove for the spear. She stood between the Wendigo and me,
a defiant scowl etched into her flawless features. The
Wendigo laughed. It was horrifying, but what made it worse
was I felt an obscene joy in its laughter. I wanted to laugh
with it, to take great bites of my own flesh and roll around in
my own blood. I was losing my fucking mind.

"Jason?" the Coinbound called.

"What?" I snapped as I dug my nails into my
forearm to try to maintain my composure.

"You ok?"

"Oh, I'm just fucking ducky." I punched myself in
the face. I pitched forward and used the momentum of my
fall to stand up. I spat more of the black bile and moved up
beside her.

The Wendigo threw back his head and roared. From
the forest all around us came answering cries. More of the
white–maned creatures poured out of the shadowed woods
and raced toward the ziggurat. I'm not sure how many; I
was too busy trying not go out of my fucking mind to count.
I fumbled around on the ground and managed to pick up my
pistol. The creatures began their ascent. I pointed my pistol
at the Wendigo.

"Call them off!" I said. I burped up a mouthful of
the bile as I spoke, which managed to take most of the
credibility out of my threat. I spat and tasted blood. I had
no idea how much damage I'd caused my insides, and

without the strength of my Mark, I had no idea how long I could keep this shit up. The Wendigo grinned, baring a mouthful of broken, black teeth. Black spittle dripped off of its lips as it laughed.

"Go…" I spat more bile. "Fuck yourself!" I fired a shot point blank into his face. The bullet ricocheted off its skull.

The massive creature struck, its claws scoring a wicked hit across the entire left side of my head. Blood poured in small rivers down the ruin of my face. I staggered backwards and fired from the hip. The bullet bounced off its skin. It struck again, a massive hammerfist that shattered my clavicle and drove me to my knees. I screamed as I fired again.

"Fuck you!" I screamed.

"Feast!" it roared at me. I could feel my mind weakening as it tried to force its sick compulsion on me.

"I'll never be a slave," I whispered as I stood, my legs buckling slightly. I fired again. My vision swam and I nearly lost my mind. My free hand gripped the wound in my stomach and I pulled. The pain was wonderful. I shuddered with the want of more.

I saw the Coinbound dart in to try and stop the Wendigo's next hit. She didn't make it. His massive clawed hand tore into my stomach wound and he lifted me into the air. I screamed in agony and was hurled to the floor. The creature lifted his bloody hand to his mouth and sucked an unidentified chunk of my insides from the end of a gore–covered claw.

"DEVOUR!" The weight of the compulsion was almost too much to bear. I could feel desire stirring in the dark, hidden recesses of my soul. I forced myself to my knees and rolled back to stand as I fired.

"Fuck…you." I heard the click of my weapon locking open. "Empty," I said with finality.

The Coinbound went rigid. She turned and looked at me. "Empty." She canted her head to the side. "Ṣafira," she said. "My name is Ṣafira. That's what he whispered in my ear when he left me." She screamed an inarticulate cry as she threw her head back.

The creatures poured up the sides of the ziggurat like pissed off fire ants. I frantically tried to load one of my spare magazines; it kept slipping through my blood–drenched fingers. I heard a sound like a siren winding as I reloaded. I looked toward Ṣafira. Her eyes were glowing brilliant silver, her head was cast back and her hair cascaded around her head as if she were under turbulent water. Her body shook with thanatonic energy, which arced like black lightning around her.

I kicked the butt of her spear as the first creature crested the ziggurat steps. I hurled myself backwards off the ziggurat in the same motion. As I flew backward, time seemed to slow. I leveled my pistol and centered the sights on the tip of the spear as it hurled toward the Wendigo's chest. I fired, and the bullet flew true. I watched the vapor trail spiral gracefully in the suddenly still air. The bullet hit the spear point and drove it deep into the heart of the emaciated Manitou. It died as Ṣafira opened her mouth and let loose the storm of her Keening. Its energy flooded Ṣafira, increasing her power tenfold. Silver lightning warred with the black roiling clouds that poured from her mouth. Her shriek split the storm like a massive explosion. The shockwave decimated the altar and shattered the top level of the ziggurat. The force of the blast threw me into a massive snow bank far below.

Nothing could have survived a Keening like that. *Ṣafira*, from the Arabic root, *ṣifr*. *Zero*. I looked up at the destroyed ziggurat. Already the storm was slackening, and in the hollow left by the receding clouds, the moon hid her face. A new moon, an empty space, a void; it was as if the heavens, themselves, silently bore witness to her naming. She was still alive. Well, after a fashion, I mean. For those on the Lifeside, she was stone fucking dead. Yet, I could see her up there, exulting in her victory, her face lit up in savage joy.

Had Sarah known? It was unlikely. She didn't know about her death until just before the end. But was it really a coincidence? Could there be coincidence where Seers were concerned? I smiled. With Sarah it was impossible to know, she had strange ideas sometimes. Even her sense of humor was strange, but it made her smile. I hoped she was smiling now, somewhere just out of sight. Somehow, that made the pain of her death recede a little bit.

Ṣafira gracefully jumped from level to level, making her way down the ziggurat. When she reached the bottom, she made her way over to me.

"You don't look so good," she said.

"Says the dead girl," I grinned, then coughed painfully. I couldn't resist. Even nearly dead, I'm still an asshole.

"We need to get you to a hospital." She reached to help me up. "Can you move?"

"Yeah, not too quickly, but I can move." I took her hand. My body hurt in places that I wasn't aware it could. I had no idea how many bones were broken or organs punctured. I just knew it hurt, bad.

"Thanks for coming to get me, Jason," she said.

"Thank you for surviving." I grimaced as my weight came to bear on my torn guts.

"Now what?" she asked.

"Now we get the hell out of here," I said. "Assuming they let us out, that is."

"Who?"

"Whatever spirit is in control now that the Wendigo's gone."

"Is that what that thing was?" she asked.

"Yeah."

I took her hand and stepped back through the Veil easily. I guess I'd earned my passage after all. We stood in the parking lot of a casino. It made sense, Wendigos were spirits of avarice and excess, of cannibalistic greed. I shook my head. It would be back; I could smell the stench of it wafting out into the parking lot, between the smell and the Veilshock, I nearly threw up on my shoes. The searing pain of my torn abs brought me fully back to reality.

"Let's go," I said through clenched teeth. "I'd like to get out of here before they change their minds about me."

"Who?" she asked.

"Whoever decided to let us go," I said. I grimaced as my stomach wound began burning and itching like mad. I looked at my left hand; my Mark was etched in black on my palm. My whole body ached as it began to knit itself back together. I could speak a Word of healing, but looking around, I thought it might be wiser to let my body do the work for me, at least until we got off the reservation.

By the time we got to the edge of the parking lot, my stomach had knitted itself back together and my clavicle was in a single piece again. I rotated my arm experimentally.

"Wow, you heal quick," Ṣafira said.

"In a job like mine, it helps," I said. "But some things heal faster than others."

Before we could leave the parking lot, a Native man in a beat up pickup truck pulled up next to us. He leaned out the window.

"You Jason?" he asked.

"Depends on who's asking." I said.

He pointed to the casino nametag pinned to his shirt. "Name's Nanabozh."

"Yeah, I'm Jason."

"Friend of yours called in a favor and said you could use a ride to Ashland."

"Which friend might that be?"

"We call him 'Wind–of–Another's–Words,'" he shrugged. "Dunno what you call him."

"Well, whoever he is," I said. "I can use the ride." I nodded at Ṣafira and motioned at the bed of the pickup. Normals couldn't see her. She'd have to get used to hitching rides.

We didn't say much on the ride back to Ashland. I just looked out the window as Nanabozh fiddled with the radio switching between country stations and a classic rock station. Something about the way he smiled seemed familiar to me, but I couldn't place it. It dawned on me as we pulled into the hotel parking lot.

"Somebody's sitting on your car, Jason," Şafira said through the small window in the back of the truck's cab.

I saw the green duster and shook my head. I should've known. *Wind–of–Another's–Words*, the mouth of an emissary spoke only the words of another.

I turned back to Nanabozh. I couldn't believe that I hadn't caught it sooner. Nanabozh, the trickster. An Ojibwa Manitou, one who could and often did take the form of a rabbit.

"Thanks," I said. "For everything." I nodded to him as I opened the door. "The feather especially."

"That was no gift of mine, Jason Beckett." He shook his head. "What your Raven gives and what mine gives are not the same." Why can't gods ever speak plainly?

"Thanks all the same," I said. I hopped out of the truck and shut the door.

I turned back toward my car.

"Hello, Little Brother," he said as he stood.

"I thought I told you two bastards to quit following me." I said.

"I can't seem to recall any such discussion," he smiled innocently.

"You know," I said. "Come to think of it, I can't either." I looked back toward the hotel. "Is Harker here with you?"

"No." Cassidy shook his head. "He stayed in New York. He can't absent his territory too long these days."

"Ahem," Şafira cleared her throat pointedly.

"Oh, right," I said, looking back at her. "Cassidy, this is Şafira."

Cassidy bowed slightly from the waist. "I am pleased to meet you, Herald of the Ferryman."

That's the technical title for the Coinbound. No one uses it but Cassidy, as far as I know, anyway.

"Nice to meet you too." She smiled brightly, blood rising to her pale white cheeks.

"Did you need me for something?" I asked Cassidy.

"No," he shook his head. "I just heard that you were here and thought that I might see how you were faring." He shrugged.

"I really don't need a babysitter, Cassidy," I said.

"No, but having a friend never hurts, Little Brother."

"I still need time," I said.

"I'm not sure how much time we have," he said.

"I'm not sure that I can bring myself to care, man."

"The War hasn't suddenly stopped in the face of your tragedy," Cassidy warned. "Find your way home soon."

I nodded. I knew he was right, but my heart simply wasn't in the fight anymore. It felt like something was missing.

CHAPTER 25

I left Ṣafira in Ashland. She needed to find her own way now. Or at least, she needed to find the Ferryman's way. I couldn't help her with that. I spent the next month traveling. I went to all the places that Jessica had wanted to go but never got the chance. Stonehenge, Paris, London, Disneyland. I stayed firmly on the Lifeside. I spoke no Words, used no sorcery; I just allowed myself be a man in mourning.

I stayed away from alcohol. I let myself sleep. Hell, I even bought one of those self–help books on grieving. It didn't help. I travelled to Pennsylvania, to Jessica's grave. I'd never been to Doylestown before. Jessica and I meant to visit, but when the war broke out, there simply hadn't been time. I sat back and rested against her headstone. I couldn't talk to her, not because of any particular pain, but because I knew that she wasn't there. She'd been my first failure. I thought that I blamed Yahweh at the time, but I knew that in my heart, it had always been me. If only I'd been faster, stronger; if only I'd planned the operation better. None of that helped.

In reality, she had been a casualty of both the war and the War. She died so that I could live a second life with so much more meaning than the first. It had been her sacrifice that brought me to my Master. I lit a cigarette, my idle hands doing something to keep my body occupied as my mind raced.

If Jessica had been necessary to bring me into the War, why Sarah? Sarah had been the only light in an otherwise dreary existence. Certainly there had been women, human and otherwise, that had sated my lust, but it had been Sarah that had given me purpose. Perhaps more than that, it had been Sarah that had shown me the shallow nature of my second life. Could a good man work for the Devil?

It was Annessa that ruined the nice, neat equation that I'd been crafting. Pretty little Annessa. I felt the knife slide between her ribs again, felt her collapse. Her death had no purpose. I killed her because I had been too afraid to say no. I killed her because I had been unable to disobey. I killed her because I was fucking coward.

I sat up. My spine was rigid, and the cigarette lay crushed between my curled fingers. Had I really been so fucking stupid? I jerked to my feet and began to pace frantically. I ran my fingers through my hair. I killed Annessa because I failed to say no. I killed Annessa because I failed my Master. I had failed to render unto him his due.

I opened my eyes to the flows of energy in the area. I found what I was looking for in a mausoleum on the far side of the cemetery. I stepped across the Veil as I ran toward the black flickering gate to the Shadow Road.

It's been said that all roads lead to the grave; the same is true of the Shadow Roads. Eventually, they all lead to a Hellmouth. I was looking for one in particular, the Nave of the Forsaken at the Nekromanteion. It could only be reached on the Veilside. Rather than fight the natural inclination of the Road, I relaxed my mind and gave myself over to the implacable tide of Death.

I knew I'd arrived when I plunged into the Acheron. And I knew it was the Acheron because of the pain. My body seemed at once to be on fire and freezing. My soul seemed on the verge of being torn apart. I forced myself to the surface, thrashing against the agonizing current. My hand hit the bank, and I pulled myself out of the water.

I lay on the bank gasping, my body convulsing as I
threw up the horrid water. I rolled onto my back when I was
done. My breath came in great, gasping sobs. I sat up
slowly as the water's terrible touch receded. I sat on the
inner bank of the Acheron. Behind me lay Pandaemonium,
far in the distance. Before me, the Plains of Acheron,
stretched to eternity just across the river. I breathed a sigh of
relief that I'd pulled myself out on the right side; I wasn't
sure that I could swim across that horrible river after having
experienced it firsthand.

There was a light splashing sound; I turned. A lone,
black robed and cowled ferryman poled his light barge down
the Acheron, yanking struggling souls onto his craft as he
went. He threw back those without coins. Their shrieks
were heart wrenching. I looked closely and saw the silver
torq around the ferryman's neck. Charon, the Ferryman's
vice regent. I shuddered. He was among the most ancient of
the Coinbound. He and I had had dealings in the past, and
we weren't exactly pals. I shook my head and turned to
leave. I caught a glimpse of movement out of the corner of
my eye. I turned and saw that he'd raised his pole in mock
salute. I flipped him off and turned toward Pandaemonium.

I needed to get in undetected. I looked at my Mark.
I wasn't sure that was even possible. I knelt in the dirt and
sketched a rough outline of the city in the soft, silty bank.
We used to call this "sand tabling" when I was alive. You
could plan an entire operation this way, visually laying out
your ideas often helped to identify weak points in your plan
or in the enemy's defenses. I wasn't likely to find much in
the way of weaknesses here, after all it was meant to fend of
assaults by gods. I spoke a short incantation and the sand
lifted to form a three-dimensional model of the city. I raised
my hand and lifted the model and spun it slowly around.

It dawned on me suddenly when I heard the splash
of Charon's oar again. I spun the model over and looked at
the underside. It wasn't perfect, but it was all I had. I
smiled for the first time in a long time. It was a real smile, a
Jason smile. The kind of smile that says, "why yes, that *is*

my hand in your sister's panties." I drummed my fingers in to the dirt and began to plan.

I stood in the hollow mouth of the Eye of Eurydice. I stared down at the Styx and ran my hand through the cold water. After the Acheron, it wasn't even unpleasant. I placed my hand on the stone walls of the inner Eye. I let my mind relax and felt the resonance of the stone. I felt the sorrow imprinted on it, the pain and loss; I felt for the essence of Death. My skin ran cold at the touch of pure thanatonic energy. I closed off all of the aetheric pathways within my flesh save the line running between my left hand and my heart. The rush of pure death screamed along my dragon lines, and I shuddered with the horror of it. When the magical circuit was complete, I spoke her name.

"Şafira."

I jerked my hand away from the stone, breaking the connection. I sat heavily on the ground and rocked myself holding my hand against the warmth of my chest. I was pushing myself way too hard. Being on this side of the Veil bodily was dangerous enough, but playing with Death wasn't a game. Tears poured down my face, my own sorrow and suffering was hard enough to bear, but the combined loss of countless millions was horrible beyond words. I closed my eyes and thought of Annessa. I focused all of my will on her. On her eyes, the curve of her lip as she smiled. The look of pain on her face as I murdered her. I rocked myself back and forth, letting my pain slowly coalesce, differentiating what was mine from the rest of humanity.

"Jason?" Şafira's voice was quiet.

I looked up at her. She stood at the opening of the Eye, her feet resting atop the water. She gently bobbed up and down as the current passed beneath her. I sniffed, wiped my eyes and stood.

"Yeah," I said. "Sorry, must be a lot of pollen down here." I cleared my throat. "I'm allergic to Perdition, apparently."

"Right," she nodded. She looked around. "So this is Hell, er, Perdition, eh?"

"This is it."

"It's beautiful," she said.

"What'd I tell you?" I smiled.

"You called me here?" She turned back to me. "How?"

"I hacked your system," I grinned.

"What?" She looked confused.

"I tapped into the flow of souls that enters Perdition and tricked it into sending you to me."

"Huh?"

"Does it matter?" I asked.

"Not really, but it just sounds weird, like I'm part of a big computer." She pantomimed a robot.

"Death sends your 'assignments' through the fabric of the underworld to the higher world. I interrupted his sending and essentially put in one of my own. I hacked in and requested you here now," I said.

"And that made you sad?" she asked.

"No, for a moment, I got to feel the loss of the millions of souls dying right now." I gritted my teeth against the strength of the memory.

Her eyes widened. "That doesn't sound fun."

"No, it isn't."

"What did you need me for?" she asked.

"I need to steal a soul," I said.

"From who, exactly?" she asked.

"From the Devil," I said.

"I thought so." She frowned. "Your soul?"

"What?" I looked at her shocked. "No!"

"Sorry!" She held up her hands. "I just assumed you meant yours."

I'd actually been offended by the suggestion. I suppose that it seemed like the natural conclusion, but it couldn't have been farther from the truth. I still had possession of my soul. And even if I hadn't, if it had been in the Asphodel Fields, I'd have fought to keep it there.

"I need you to help me steal back my…" I paused. What should I call Annessa? My slave? My friend? Hell, my lover? She was none of these things, and yet she was all of these things. I thought back to the story my Master had told me of his time in Eden. "Eve," I said.

"What?" she asked. "*The* Eve?"

"No," I shook my head. "It was just a metaphor."

"You really don't speak English, do you?"

"Will you help me or not?" I asked throwing my hands in the air.

"Of course!" She looked a little offended. "Why else would I be here?"

"I honestly don't know," I said.

"Well, let's go steal your metaphor."

I explained my plan to her. She nodded her understanding as each phase of the plan was laid out. When I was finished, she shrugged and said, "That's all well and good, but where the hell am I gonna find a boat?"

"It isn't a boat, it's a barge and you call it to you," I said.

"How do I do that?" she asked.

"I don't know, Coinbound magic, I guess."

"That's awfully helpful, Jason."

"Well, I don't know all that much about Coinbound," I said.

"Could've fooled me," she said.

"Just try to summon the damned thing!"

"Do I just stand here and say, 'here barge, barge, barge'?" She patted her thigh. The water beneath her bucked as the barge rose up beneath her feet.

"Yes," I nodded sagely. "That's exactly what you do."

"You really are a dick, you know that?"

I lay on the floor of the barge. Ṣafira stood over me, draped in a black, cowled cloak which also happened to be subject to the "here, cloak, cloak, cloak" family of summoning spells. I lay flat and still, hidden under her cloak as we approached the Canal Gate. Her magic lay over me like an even heavier cloak. So strong was the essence of Death in the Underworld that it dwarfed even my intimate connection with the Lord of the Fallen. The Avernus Guard, Fallen charged with guarding the gates of Pandaemonium and serving as the de facto royal guard, silently lifted their massive pikes and let her pass through the gate.

Had it not been a dead giveaway, I might have uttered a silent prayer. I gently gripped Ṣafira's ankle.

"Good job," I said.

"Are you sure they didn't know you were under there?" she whispered.

"Yeah."

"How do you know?" she asked.

"There isn't another Coinbound here to collect us."

"Seriously?"

"Yeah."

"They'd have killed us just like that?"

"Yeah."

"Why didn't you tell me?" she kicked me.

"I didn't want you to get nervous."

She kicked me again. "Well now I'm not nervous; I'm fucking pissed."

I felt the water grow gentle, less urgent. We were close to the Bronze Gate. The winding course of the Styx slowed it down as it approached the Bronze Gate and Asphodel Fields. I gripped her ankle again.

"As soon as you see the Gate, start getting close to the shore," I said. "And let me know the moment the guards stop looking at us."

"Ok." I heard her push off of the far shore with her spear. A few seconds later, she kicked me. "Go!"

I slid out from under the cloak, took a breath and whispered, "I'll call for you," and slid into the soul–crushing river of sorrow. At that moment, I blessed the river; its murky, dismal depths hid me from view as I approached the riverbank. I slowly lifted my face just far enough out of the water to peak at the gate. I watched Ṣafira step off of her barge onto the riverbank. The guards turned and moved to intercept her. She held her spear sideways across her chest so that the guards could see her phial and waited calmly for them to approach her.

Her shadow lengthened in front of her as she slowly opened her cloak exposing her barely covered body to the guards. I crept into her shadow. Staying in darkness of her shadow ensured that her magic shielded me from the guard's perception. I slid through the gate as the guards stood before her questioning her, their eyes never leaving her lush body. If I didn't hate him so much, I could have hugged the Ferryman for having such perverse tastes.

As I slipped through the Bronze Gate, I felt relief wash over me. Not simply because I'd made it into the Fields, but because I was in the Fields. I'd just walked bodily into, what was for me, Paradise. The air was pure and the rolling hills that stretched out before me were beautiful beyond words. I could've stood there for all eternity, which was entirely the point, I suppose. As awed as I was though, I had a purpose, and I wasn't willing to fail.

There was a slight tug on my wrist. I looked down and saw a fine silver chain stretching from my left wrist across the vast hills and disappearing over the horizon. I tugged experimentally on the chain, and a second later it tugged back. I closed my eyes, blocking out the beauty of the scene before me. I focused on Annessa. I thought of her lying on the altar in her father's mansion, dead. I clenched my Marked hand over the chain. I spoke the Word that meant me. Understand, it didn't mean the pronoun, it meant the one Word in all the worlds that described Jason Nathaniel Beckett. The Word and the Mark that I had used to transform Annessa into my slave. I felt reality lurch around me. I opened my eyes and suffered a horrific case of vertigo. I dropped to a knee and ducked my head to get myself back under control. I sniffed as my nose started to drip. I didn't need to look to know that it was blood. My body was dying, the Fields weren't meant for the living.

I stood in front of a small building, a chapel crafted of black wood. The chain disappeared into the chapel. Around me was a clearing in a deep forest, the ground dotted with wildflowers. I cocked my head to the side. Of all the places in all the worlds, this was the least like what I expected Annessa's heaven to look like. I wiped the blood away from my face and stepped through the door.

The chapel had a narrow entryway that led into a small, but spacious sanctuary. In the center of the room Annessa sat cross–legged on the floor, her hands in her lap. Her eyes were fixed on the altar, which bore a life–sized bust of…me.

"Annessa?" I called softly.

She leapt to her feet and turned to face me. "Master?"

A thin metal chain ran from her neck to my wrist. Something was wrong. I reached out and touched her face.

"You should be free," I said. "You should be at rest."

She closed her eyes and put her hand over mine. She turned her face slightly and kissed my hand. "I can't rest without you." Black tears slid down her face.

"You should be free," I said. "I never meant for this..." I looked to the chain around her neck. "I'm so sorry," I said. I pulled her close to me.

She threw her arms around me.

"I didn't understand," I said. "I was so lost, I didn't get it."

"Get what?" she asked.

"That you're a part of me." I pushed her shoulders back and looked at her. "It's not fair."

"What isn't?"

"I thought I was freeing you. I thought that He was asking me to destroy you so that I would have nothing left." I shook my head and lifted her face to mine. "I was wrong. By killing you I was killing a part of myself. I thought that you were my creation, my slave."

"I wasn't?"

"No," I shook my head. "You were my Eve. You were made from my magic, my soul; you were made to complete me. My own pride, my bitterness and my pain blinded me to what He intended. I'm a fool."

"What do you mean?"

"How many times did I question what you could do, how amazing you were?" I shook my head. "You are the greatest haemunculus ever created, marked with the sign of the Chosen Son and sacred to Lord of the Fallen. How could I have ever thought that my will alone could have crafted you?"

She kissed me and I kissed her back with no reservations. She pulled away from me.

"You taste like blood." She cocked her head to the side then reached up and touched my lips, her hand came away bloody. "You're bleeding!"

"It's the Fields," I said. "They're killing me."

"You have to go!" She shoved me backwards toward the door her eyes wide in shock and fear. "You have to get out!"

"Not without you." I grabbed her wrist. "I won't leave without you."

"You'll die if you stay here!" She tried to pull away, but I held her tightly.

"Come with me," I said.

"I'm dead," she said quietly.

"That's never been an issue for us."

She looked up at me through her black tears, and something of a grin twitched on her face. "No, Master, it hasn't."

I pulled her to me and focused my will on the Bronze Gate.

The Bronze Gate stood before us. I turned to Annessa. "As soon as we leave exit the Gates, we have to run."

"Where?"

"There will be a barge to our left, you need to get to that barge. No matter what, get to that barge. The Coinbound will take you where you need to go."

"What about you?" she asked.

"I'll be right behind you," I said.

"Promise?" she asked.

"I promise." I hoped that I wasn't lying, but somehow I thought I might be.

We burst through the Gate into the pale, wan twilight of Perdition. An entire pack of Avernus Guards stood before the Gate. I looked to the left; Ṣafira still stood on her barge. The Guard couldn't stop her, there was no stopping Death, after all. But they could contain her and keep her on the Styx, where she belonged.

"Annessa," I said.

"Master?" she replied.

"Why aren't you moving?" I threw myself forward and charged at the Guard. They lowered their spears. I saw Annessa dart past the Guard before leaping aboard the barge, and I spoke a Word. The brick and mortar path in front of me exploded hurling fragments of stone and adamant at the Guards. I lunged forward and plunged several stories to the caverns beneath me. I hit the water like a stone. I threw my hands out to slow my descent and held my mouth tightly shut against the frigid waters. One swallow and it would all have been for nothing. I swam to the surface and waited. Above me, I could see the Guard pack tearing at the street, their spears shearing though the granite bricks like butter. Behind me I heard the sound of an oar in the water. I grinned.

Coinbound have control of all of the rivers of Perdition. They can go where they please, when they please. So strong is their dedication to duty that no one, neither Satan nor Yahweh ever expected one to turn rogue. Satan had made no move to bar their entry to the Caverns of Oblivion beneath Pandaemonium, the caverns where the Lethe plunged several hundred feet into the vast subterranean lake in which I now floated. However, if there's one thing that I'd learned in my short life, it's never trust anyone.

Ṣafira pulled the barge alongside me. Annessa helped me clamber onto the barge.

"What the eff was that, Jason?" Ṣafira asked.

"Improvisation," I said. "You found me, what does it matter?"

"You scared the crap out of me!" she said.

"He does that," Annessa said. "All the time."

"If you two are finished?" I asked. "We need to get the fuck out of here, Ṣafira."

The barge jerked beneath us as Ṣafira commanded it to move. Annessa gasped as the barge gracefully slipped up the waterfall. It was easy to forget that she'd never seen Perdition beyond the Fields. I looked uneasily behind us, waiting for the Guard to break through the bricks and fly after us. We burst free of the tunnels and back into Perdition proper. I pointed Ṣafira toward the Styx and the Eye of Eurydice.

"We need to be there," I said. I heard the sound of wings overhead. "Now!"

"Right."

The barge bucked beneath us as Ṣafira thrust her spear deep into the water, shoving us forward at breakneck speed. We nearly made it to the Eye. Three massive spears slammed into the water in front of the barge. Their heavy bonewood shafts jutted out of the shallows and threatened to pin us in place.

"Ṣafira!" I pointed at the spears.

She had an intense look of concentration on her face. She threw her hands in the air, in a motion of command. The barge lurched beneath us a huge wave lifted us over the spears. With a twist of her wrist, she spun the barge in the air, and smoothly hurled her own spear back at the phalanx of aerial Avernus Guard that pursued us.

"Don't you throw shit at me!" she said.

"Don't fucking taunt them, Ṣafira!" I said. "Just get us to the shore, now!"

"This is *my river*," she said in a deep voice that exuded authority, a voice far too low to be her own. "I won't be attacked on my river."

"Fine!" I said. "You fucking stay and fight, but I need to get Annessa to the Eye; then you can do what you want!"

Annessa pressed herself against me. I threw my arms around her. The Guard dove toward us drawing their swords as they closed. I looked at the Guard, then at the shore. I was as close as I was ever going to get. I hugged Annessa to me tightly and spoke a Word, pushing against the barge with the strength of ten men.

We hurled across the gap to the shore and landed in a tangle. I pulled myself free and shoved Annessa toward the Eye.

"Run!" I pointed at the Eye. "Don't stop until you're standing in the sunlight."

"I can't leave you!" she yelled, her eyes welling with tears.

I held up my Mark. "We are one. We're never apart." I pointed at the cave again. "Run!"

She ran up the slope; I could hear her sobbing. I didn't care if she cried, only that she ran. I wasn't sure how much time I could buy her. I just hoped it would be enough.

The Styx raged within her banks. Şafira stood steadily on the barge, though it rocked furiously beneath her. She kept her arms raised high above her head, her spear clutched in her right hand. Around her a storm of thanatonic energy scattered black lighting through the mist raised by the thrashing river. She looked like an angry goddess of old. This wasn't the unsure girl that I rescued from the Wendigo a month ago. Here, in her element, the Ferryman was with her. I wondered what that meant for us. Looking at the fury of the storm that surrounded her, I hoped we'd never be enemies.

My eyes darted to the Tower of Grief. He was there. He'd seen everything. I'd have to answer for what I'd done. I'd snuck into His citadel, stolen His prize and attacked His vassals. I stared up at Him. I felt our eyes meet; it was like staring into a sapphire sun, and I knew this was over.

"Enough," I spoke, but it was his voice that issued forth from my lips.

The waters calmed, the Guard retreated from Şafira and landed gracefully on the bank. They didn't sheath their swords. I held my head up; I wouldn't back down from this. I'd earned this, fought for it, deserved it.

"Jason?" Şafira said.

"It's fine." I waved at her. "You can get out of here." I smiled at her. "Thanks for helping us, Şafira."

"What's going to happen to you now?" she asked.

"If you ever take a stroll by Lake Cocytus and happen to hear screaming in a familiar key, don't be afraid to stop and say hi." I grimaced as the Guard yanked my hands behind my back and bound me.

"You have much to answer for, Emissary." The lead Guard gripped my neck painfully. "Lord Satan awaits." He lifted me easily and launched himself into the air toward the Tower of Grief. I watched Ṣafira slowly fade into the distance as we flew. I hoped I see her again, but not too soon.

As we closed on the Tower, the Guard didn't slow, and I was carried beyond Pandaemonium. I thought about asking where we were going, but I realized it didn't matter. I was being taken as a prisoner; what happened from here on out was essentially out of my hands. We veered away from Lake Cocytus and turned toward the Plains of Acheron. Well, I wasn't going to be entombed in ice for eternity, at least not yet. No matter how you look at it, that was a plus.

We flew over the House of Hades, the vast sprawling capital city of the Ferryman. Below me, shades, spooks, Coinbound and other favored children of Death were oblivious to my passing. I spit as we crossed the central spire of his palace, also imaginatively called the House of Hades. Any good humor that act might have brought me evaporated as we suddenly landed just beyond the borders of the Ferryman's realm.

Satan stood before the Phlegethon, the flickering grey–green flames of the river reflected off of his silver armor making him all the more menacing. The River of Flame ran around the periphery of Perdition, we were at the farthest edge of Satan's realm. What few other realms intersected his own at this point ranged from the horribly unpleasant to the mildly terrifying to say the very least. Things were suddenly much more grim. The Guard landed lightly but hurled me to my knees in the volcanic dirt.

"Little did I expect you to fall to such a wretched state, mine Emissary," Satan said. His formality and the archaic manner of his speech were magnified by his anger.

"I think you did," I said. I stood slowly. "More than that, I really wish that I had."

"Enlighten me as to why that might be," His hand tightened on his spear.

"I would have saved myself so much pain." I looked into his eyes. "But where would that leave us?"

"You have betrayed me." His eyes blazed. "Why should I care about sparing you pain?"

"I have never betrayed you," I spoke softly. "What I have done, everything that I have done, I have done for you."

"You have raised arms against my vassals, breached the walls of my citadel and stolen from me what was rightfully mine. Are you so certain that you wish to rebel against me?" He leaned down, so close that our faces nearly touched. "Consider carefully your words, Emissary."

"I rebelled only against myself, my Lord," I spoke quietly, but confidently.

"Explain."

"After Sarah died, after I killed Annessa at Hekate's request, I fell apart." I ran my hand through my hair, the memory of my pain still vivid. "I thought that every worthwhile part of me was gone, had died. I thought everything that made me good was buried with Jessica, Sarah or Annessa. But then I realized that it wasn't dead, it was buried. It was buried beneath all of my fear, my doubt, my guilt. Everything that made me *me*, was entombed in my weakness." I looked up at Him.

"I realized that you gave me Annessa." I shook my head. "You gave me this amazing gift, but I was too stupid to recognize it. I raised her with my Word and my Mark, I raised her with the intent to enslave her and I bound her to me with chains of slavery." I laughed sardonically. "It wasn't until after she was dead that I realized you had been with me all along, and that of the two of us, it had been her that was truly free."

"How was she more free than you, my son?" he asked.

"She was chained to me by magic, but unbound by doubt. No magic bound me, no spell ensnared me, yet I was bound my fear." I stood and looked directly into his eyes. "I should have known to clench my fist and stare into your eyes and tell you to go fuck yourself; I shouldn't have killed her."

"Her sacrifice was to have been a rite of manumission, my son."

"It didn't matter," I snorted. "She's still a part of me, manumission or no. She's animated by the same magic that animates me; we're tied together not by my sorcery, but by my soul. No matter what you intended, she'd have still been a slave."

"What are you saying, my son?"

"I'm saying that I was the one in need of emancipation, my Lord. I thought myself your slave; I thought that I was trapped. Yet, when I was blinded by my fears, I was unable to find peace and I would have dragged Annessa down into the pit of my own despair with me. Though I didn't realize it then, I'd never been more free at any other point in my life."

"And you prove this by attacking me and mine?" His wings relaxed and he stood up straight. He was calming down.

"I prove it by making right the errors of my past, by rebelling against that which makes me weak. I prove it by recognizing that the whims of my fear spoiled my self–determination and doing what you commanded: attacking. I sought to remove all traces of what had held me back. But in order to do that, I needed first to make right what I had ruined, by restoring the Sacred Mother to her rightful place on the Lifeside."

"At the cost of your own life?" he asked.

"If necessary," I said.

"You would not fight this fate?"

"No." I shook my head.

"No? Why not? Did you not say that you would fight the oppressive whims of another?"

"This is *my* choice, my Lord. Annessa's life means more than my own; I'm willing to die if that gains her freedom."

"Very well." He took a step back and motioned with his spear. The Guards lifted me roughly and hurled me into the Phlegethon.

I burned. The pain was nearly as intense as the Acheron. It wasn't my flesh that burned, though. It was my soul. Each moment of my life, each second that had ticked by flashed before me again. Each indiscretion, every failure, every fear tormented me anew. I tried not to scream, I tried to be stoic, hoping to hold in my cries until either Satan had departed or until I died. I couldn't do it. I screamed into the liquid flames and thrashed myself back toward the shore. If there were any truth to the myths about Hell, this one was it. In the flames of the Phlegethon, there was no mercy, no hope.

My hand hit the volcanic ash of the shore. As my fingers clenched to pull me up the bank, it hit me, a sense of peace. There was tranquility here; as more of my fear burned away, as the all–consuming flame devoured more of my pain, I was left with only what remained untainted by my fear. My love, my desire, my ambition, my joy all remained. I stood slowly, shaking unsteadily on my feet. The three Avernus Guard knelt on the bank behind Satan. He awaited me, smiling.

"From the crucible of your own failure are you forged anew, my son." He placed his hand on my forehead. "You have done as I asked of you, Jason. I will render unto you what was requested."

"What was that, Father?" I asked, the honorific seemed somehow appropriate.

"Faith. As you have shown your faith in me, thusly do I show my faith unto you."

I laughed. "You've shown me your faith all along. I've just been too stupid to realize it. From the day I raised Annessa, you've been testing me, offering me hints of your intent, of your concern. I'm sorry that I was so blind," I smiled, a small private smile.

"What is it, my son?" he asked.

"She was right, you know," I said.

"Who?"

"Jessica," I said. "She said that if gods existed, then they were kind; that our love proved it."

"Yet she is dead," he held out his hands as if holding a book.

"True," I said. "But she *lived*, and it was a life that couldn't be lived without the threat of death."

He nodded. "Such are lives of men, but brief flickers before the flames dim to embers, then finally to ash."

"And then you gave me Annessa, my Lord. Some flames are eternal."

"I am not without kindness, my son."

"No, my Lord, you are not." I bowed my head.

He stepped forward and placed his hand gently on my head. "And now, my son, you must choose."

"Choose?"

He gestured with his right hand and the air shimmered showing an image of the Asphodel Fields. "Solace or service."

I paused a moment, only a fool would jump to a decision at a time like this. I considered for a moment and answered confidently. "Service, Father. I choose service," I said.

He took my left hand in both of his. "And the term of your service?"

"Forever," I said.

Part II

In the Shadows Before the Throne

CHAPTER 1

The city was dark around me. There were lights, sounds, sirens calling out like grim bells sounding out the death toll. None of that mattered. The trees slid silently apart and the entrance to the Sacred Grove opened before me. Part of me wanted to run, to dart forward, appearances be damned. But another part, a smaller part, savored the sensation of desperation, of desire, of need. And then, as I entered, I saw her and all of that no longer mattered.

I ran to her. I threw my arms around her and held her tightly against me.

"Master," she said, her soft lips brushing my neck.

"Annessa," I replied. I gently pulled away from her and held her face. I stared into her eyes for a minute, seeking just the right words. But there was nothing to say, the world has not yet invented a phrase, in any language to adequately say, "I'm sorry that I murdered you, resurrected you, enslaved you, murdered you again, spoiled your afterlife and stole you from paradise." I kissed her instead. It was supposed to be one of those Hollywood kisses, the kind they invented so that idiots like me didn't have to find the right phrases. Somehow, though, Annessa turned it into one of those kisses that you see in the movies that're shot "off–Hollywood," the kind that you watched in heart–pounding trepidation during your teen years.

Corrigan quietly cleared his throat. Right, in a temple, no porn. I pulled away from Annessa and cleared my throat firmly.

"Hello, Corrigan," I said as I turned to face him.

"Jason." He smiled. "The Lady's blessing upon you this evening."

"May the Lord of Perdition smile on you as well." It was odd, saying that. It didn't sound or feel awkward; it felt *right*.

Corrigan blinked once. Granted, for most people that would be the equivalent of setting yourself on fire and running around shouting the words from a Dr. Seuss book backwards in Swahili. Very little surprises Corrigan.

"I was afraid that you might not return after your last visit, my friend," he said.

"The gods work in mysterious ways, I guess." I actually said that. Yeah, I know.

He bobbed his head toward Annessa. "The Lady's grace on you as well, Sacred Mother."

"Thanks," she smiled at him and wound her arm around my waist.

Corrigan turned back to me. "What will you do now that you're back?"

"First, I need to get my feet back under me. I need to resupply and then I need to catch up to Cassidy." I clenched my fist.

"Is there anything I can do for you?" Corrigan asked.

"I'd like a moment in the sanctuary, if it's possible. There are some things I need to say."

"Of course," he said. "Take what time you need." He bowed his head once and turned to leave.

"Corrigan?"

"Yes?" he said, looking over his shoulder.

"Thanks for understanding, before, I mean."

"I'm a priest, Jason. Loss, sorrow, pain—these things aren't the enemies of faith, they're the reason for it. There's nothing to apologize for." He smiled that damned smile of his and walked toward the small cottage he kept at the far end of the Grove.

I knelt before the altar and bowed my head. Annessa knelt beside me.

"I know that I'm supposed to have better words, that I'm supposed to be contrite, proper and well, emissarial, but that really isn't me. Thank you. If I had to list all of things I need to thank you for I'd be here all day." I looked at Annessa and gently touched her face. "Thank you for this."

The sounds of the city were deafening as we entered the park. To be fair, the Sacred Grove is probably one of the quietest places in all of creation. I led Annessa toward the street.

"Are you ok?" I asked quietly.

"Yeah, just a little out of it. I can't believe that we're really back." She looked at me and forced a smile.

"What's wrong?" I asked.

"So what now?" she asked me.

"I need to find us some new clothes, get some food and rest, I suppose." We were both a mess.

"And after that?" she asked.

"I need to get a hold of Cassidy and see what he's dug up on Father Jacob and your mother."

"And what about me?" She stepped in front of me.

"I assumed you be coming with me," I said. "But what you do is entirely up to you now, I suppose."

"Ok, I was worried for a second." She looked away.

"Worried about?"

"I didn't know if you wanted me with you, you know, now that I'm not a slave." She looked down, embarrassed.

"Manumission or not, you're mine." I lifted her chin and made her look at me. "Do you understand?"

"Yes, Master." A ghost of a smile danced around her lips. "I'm sorry."

"I distinctly remember making you a promise." I released her chin. "I intend to keep it, and I'll hold you to your end as well."

"What was my end?" she grinned.

"That you'd show me what you could do," I grinned back.

"Find me a bed and I'll show you something, Master," she smiled wickedly.

"Shit, I have to find us a house first," I laughed and tried to not to think of what happened to my house.

"I'm sorry." She took my hand. "I shouldn't joke like that. Not yet."

"She's gone, Annessa," I said. "Neither joking nor crying can change that."

"Still, it just seems awful, I guess." She put her arms around my neck.

"You ever read Adam Smith in college?" I asked.

"Of course! I've got a degree in economics," she smiled. I knew I liked her for a reason. I'm not sure that the fact that she was beautiful, dangerous and completely mine should be discounted either.

"He said that we project our emotions onto the dead, who are beyond such trivial concerns, which is why we mourn them." I shrugged. "We both know that he was exactly right, yet we're bullheaded enough to mourn a woman at peace."

"I'm just shocked you read Adam Smith, Master." She leaned against me.

"Any man that loves liberty as much as he did should be automatically sainted," I shrugged. "Actually, I found a copy of *The Theory of Moral Sentiments* when I was in Iraq and read it on post one night when I was really bored."

"You find us a house and I'll make you a promise," she grinned lasciviously.

"Yeah, what's that?"

"You won't be bored at night. Ever. Again." She lifted herself onto her tiptoes and bit my lip.

"You demonic little bitch." I couldn't stop grinning. Her twisted little mind was infectious

I pulled my phone out of my pocket. I was tempted to call Cassidy, but there were other things I needed to do first. I had to open my contacts list to find her number. I guess in retrospect, I wasn't really a good emissary. The number I was looking for was the Consul–General's number. She was supposed to be my second in command. I couldn't recall when last I had spoken to her. She answered on the first ring.

"My Lord–Emissary," She spoke in a formal, clipped manner. "How can I be of assistance?"

"Hello, Erzebet." I tried to send my smile through the phone. I'm not the most charming guy around, but it never hurts to try. "How are you?"

"Busy, my lord," She replied. "What can I do for you?"

"You've heard about recent events, I assume?"

"I have been briefed." The woman made ice seem positively tropical.

"Right. I'm gonna need a car and place to stay."

"Just as a reminder, my lord, you still have your quarters on the Upper East side. Will that suffice, or do you require additional space?" She tapped a pen against her desk as she talked. I was beginning to remember why I never spoke to her.

"That's fine, for now. I'll still need a car." I'd forgotten about the city apartment, to be fair. I hated living in the city. Too much going on, and too little time to deal with it all.

"I'll have a car come get you now and have your new car delivered to your home this afternoon. Will that suffice?"

"Yes, Erzebet, that will be fine." I paused a second. "Please send someone to the apartment to take measurements for myself and one other; I need new clothes as well."

"Very well, my lord," she really seemed pissed.

"Erzebet?" I was grinning fiercely.

"Yes, my lord?" Her exasperation was growing more and more apparent.

"By the five points and the fires of Perdition, may your soul rest in his hands this day." Someone found himself some religion. That would fuck her up a bit.

"...May his gaze rest ever upon you, as well, my lord." She hung up the phone slowly. I laughed.

Erzebet Balescu was a devout woman. She wasn't the greatest diplomat, but she could organize like no one's business. It must have severely chapped her ass to know that I was chosen as Satan's emissary without a day of service in the church. She hated me, not because I was her boss, but because I was flippant and so flagrantly impious. Perhaps now she and I might see a bit more eye to eye.

'Who was that?" Annessa jerked her head at the phone.

"The Consul–General," I shrugged. "My second–in–command, theoretically."

"I didn't know that Satan had a diplomatic corps. That's kind of weird," she chuckled.

"Wait till you meet her; trust me, it gets weirder."

A black limousine pulled up to the curb. I pointed and grabbed Annessa's hand.

"Our ride."

"That was fast. Did they use magic to find us?"

"Nope, GPS." I held up my phone.

"Magic would have been so much cooler."

"I suppose." I dialed Cassidy as we walked to the car. It rang three times and went to his voicemail. I hung up.

"Cassidy?" she asked.

"Yeah." I ran my hand over the back of my neck.

"Can you use magic to track him?" She grabbed my hand and threaded her fingers through mine.

"It's like trying to catch the wind, he's like a shadow at night when he's hunting." I kissed her head.

"It'll be ok."

"I hope so."

CHAPTER 2

      I stood at the window and looked down at the city. There were so many people. So damned many people, innocent and unaware of how much danger they were in. Few in the city knew what went on three months ago. Even fewer understood the implications and what could have gone wrong. I walked over to the cellaret, which I had mistakenly called a sideboard until Annessa mocked me for it. Actually, I think I called it a table first. Apparently rich girls get better etiquette training than I did.

      I'd showered and finally shaved. I felt a great deal more like myself than I had in a long time. I felt like I needed to be doing something, like I had wasted three months. I grabbed a decanter of whisky and poured myself a drink. I needed to calm my nerves. I hated the interminable waiting. Nothing seemed to be moving fast enough. I was still waiting for my car and my clothes. In case you haven't figured it out by now, I'm not a patient man. I dialed Cassidy again, nothing. I was beginning to hate his voicemail.

      "Master?" Annessa called from the bedroom.

      "Yeah?" I yelled back as I slid my phone back into my pocket.

      "What are you doing out there?" she asked.

"Drinking and looking at the city, why?"

"I'm lonely."

I laughed and put my drink on the windowsill. "I'll be right there."

Annessa was in the tub, her lush body hidden beneath what appeared to be a ton of bubbles. She looked up at me and smiled. "Hi."

"Hello there." I grinned as I sat on the edge of the tub and began trying to pop some of the bubbles that hid her from me.

She grabbed my hand and yanked me forward. I didn't have a chance; you know how strong she is. She stared into my eyes; those remarkable eyes of hers flickered from blue to green to a sort of violet color as her desire raged within. Her lips parted and she gently bit my lower lip. I pulled her closer to me and kissed her deeply. Her hands clawed at my clothes. I frantically tried to help, my pulse pounding in my ears. The room seemed to close in on us. All I could see was her eyes. I wanted her terribly. It was as if our desires were feeding on each other. I pulled her out of the tub, intending to take her on the floor. It was right about then that my luck decided to return. The intercom intoned a loud chime, alerting me that the doorman was calling. Fuck.

"Of course they'd get here now, why the fuck not?"

Annessa looked up at me and laughed. "You better get the door, Master. I'm not decent."

"Oh, you're going to pay for that, my mouthy little haemunculus." I mock glared at her. "You're going to pay dearly!"

She rolled to her side and lifted her hips. "Are you going to spank me, Master?"

I slapped her ass hard as I headed for the door. "This is not over!" I yelled over my shoulder. She just writhed around on the floor teasing me.

"Hurry back!" she moaned at me.

I incanted a minor spell to dry myself off and hit the button on the intercom.

"Yes?"

"Sir, there's a man here to see you." The doorman

sounded nervous. I can't really blame him. He had no idea who I was, but the attitudes of the people who own this building changed drastically when they found out I was coming here. When the only Lifeside vessel of your god moves in next door, I imagine it does something to you.

"Does he look dangerous?" I asked sarcastically.

"Uh, no, sir." That perplexed him a little.

"Send him up." So much for finishing up with Annessa.

"Get something on, Annessa," I yelled as I walked toward the door to let the tailor in.

Annessa came into the living room in a bathrobe; her hair bundled onto her head in that mysterious way that women seemingly just push their hair into a disorganized mess, which stays perfectly perched atop their head. In short, she looked adorable. I shook my head as I opened the door for the tailor. She was going to be the death of me.

The tailor wasn't a Normal. I knew that as soon as I opened the door. I could almost smell the Aether on him. He was short and slender. He carried only a small leather valise in his effeminate hands. He bowed low before me.

"My Lord Emissary," he spoke in a deep, airy voice. "I am pleased to be of service."

I gestured for him to stand and our eyes met. His irises were so pale blue that they were nearly white. His deep, black hair reminded me of someone, but I couldn't place it. I allowed my eyes to relax; the Aether flowed and eddied around him as if disturbed. It took a second, but without warning, it was like his soul suddenly darted out of his body and ducked back in just as quickly. Nephilim. He was the son of a mortal and an angel, likely a Fallen.

"Come on in." I stepped aside so he could enter. "Not every day you see a Nephilim."

"It is for me, sir." He nodded curtly and entered.

It took me a second to register his joke. I laughed. "Well played." He seemed like a normal sort. That is, until he laid eyes on Annessa, then that shit went right out the window.

"Who's this, Master?" she asked as she walked into

the room, her arms wrapped around her waist as she shivered in the air–conditioned room.

"By the five points, it can't be!" The little man dropped to both knees and placed his head against the hard wood floor. He began praying so rapidly, even I couldn't catch the prayers.

"Master?" Annessa looked at me questioningly.

I help up a hand. It isn't every day that you get worshipped; I figured there was no harm in letting him get it out of his system. After five minutes of it, however, I waved Annessa to his side. "Say something, Annessa, or he'll keep going all day."

'What do I say?" She threw her hands in the air.

"Try, 'get up; I've got shit to do'?" I shrugged.

She gently rested her hand on his head. "Rise."

The little man quieted and stood immediately.

"Now that that's out of your system, perhaps we get on with it," I said.

"Indeed, sir. I was unaware the Sacred Mother would be here." He bowed to Annessa again. "I was taken aback a bit."

"Right, I'd hate to see you really out of sorts then." I'm Irish, sarcasm is our second language. Our first is lying.

"I was told to bring you these." He handed me an envelope and a set of keys. "Your vehicle is waiting for you downstairs, my lord."

I took the envelope, nodded and stepped back to open the envelope. "You can start with Annessa, I'll be with you in a moment." As I turned away, I heard Annessa's robe quietly fall to the floor and the little man's harsh gasp. I grinned, for a religious figure, Annessa was like nothing anyone would ever expect.

The envelope contained a letter written in Erzebet's firm, flowing script. She would have made a penmanship teacher die of pure bliss.

My Lord Emissary,

Greetings. I have taken the liberty of sending Mr. Admah to assist you. He is quite capable and should serve you well as chamberlain. Should you need anything further

*from the consulate, please contact me directly and I will
ensure that your needs are met promptly.*
Very Respectfully,
E

Chamberlain? Well, that explained the gasp at least.
I turned and walked back into the living room, where Mr.
Admah was dutifully measuring Annessa's hips while trying
to maintain his composure.

"So, I'm gonna guess that you're not the tailor?" I
asked jokingly.

"No, but I am trained in basic tailoring, sir." He
continued his work without looking up at me.

"I guess she wasn't joking about the capable part." I
folded the note and sat on the arm of the chair and watched
him work. Well, I suppose I was more looking at Annessa's
body than watching. Ogling, really, not so much looking.

Annessa caught my eyes and grinned at me.
"Whatever clothes you find for me, please make them tight."
Her grinned turned wicked. "I have to look the part, you
know."

"As you wish, Sacred Mother," he replied as he
gingerly measured her inseam.

"Do you have to call me that?" Annessa asked. "It
makes me sound old!"

"What shall I call you, then?" He wrote her
measurements in a small notebook and stood.

"Just call me Annessa." She smiled brightly.

"Very well." He bowed at the waist.

I shook my head and stood up straight so he could
measure me. "And what's your name, Mr. Admah?" I
asked.

"Adrian, sir." He met my eyes as he said his name.

"Is it possible that I know your father?" I asked.

"Unlikely sir, he died a great many years ago." He
measured my waist as he spoke.

"Ah, I see."

"You are, however, acquainted with my mother."
He knelt to measure my inseam. "Which is why I am here."

"Really?" That was odd; Nephilim rarely

maintained contact with their human parent. "Who's your mother?"

"She is the Marchioness of Malebolge, sir."

I had to stabilize myself for a minute. See, that meant that his mother was a Fallen. What you don't comprehend is that meant that his mother had to possess a host body from the moment of conception to the moment of birth. The only reason that Fallen would do that was to intentionally give birth to a Nephilim. And the only reason that a Fallen would go through all of that trouble was the same reason humans do so many stupid things: love. For the Fallen, just as for humans, things were just so much fucking easier as a male.

And Adrian Admah was certainly right about one thing, I did know his mother. I knew her very well. Her name was Abbadonna.

"Abbadonna never told me about you," I said questioningly.

"My mother intends for me to make my own way in this world," he smiled. "I nearly studied with you in Nagg'Vathrymar."

"That would have made things easier; I was the only mortal there when I studied," I grinned. "That made life interesting, to say the least."

"What the hell are you guys talking about?" Annessa asked.

"Adrian is Abbadonna's son," I began. "And we studied sorcery in the same place."

"Well, sir, you studied. I pretty much bumbled my way through it." Adrian finished his writing.

"What do you mean?" Annessa leaned forward, interested.

"Well, Sacr–my lady," he stuttered over the title he was forbidden to use. "My Lord Emissary was the greatest mortal student the Ghūls ever had."

"So, you learned magic from Zombies?" Annessa looked horribly confused.

"Not quite, Annessa." I shifted my position. This was going to take some explanation.

"I'll just excuse myself, to get this taken care of,"
Adrian held up his notebook. He bowed low.
I nodded and walked over to get a drink; we were
going to be here awhile.

CHAPTER 3

I stood in front of the windows. I couldn't decide where to begin. After all, I'd never told anyone about my time in Nagg'Vathrymar. I idly played with my phone debating if I should just try Cassidy again and leave it that way.

"Well, are you going to tell me?" Annessa asked impatiently. "I mean, you can't have that much build–up and not tell a story!"

"I'm trying to collect my thoughts, trying to figure out where to start," I replied testily.

"Just start at the beginning." She rolled over on the couch, resting her chin on the armrest and lazily bouncing her feet from the opposite armrest to inches from her ass and back. The effect was distracting, to say the least.

"Ok, I'd just left Perdition. I was sent to Nagg'Varythmar to learn sorcery. I thought that it would be like any other school, any other time that I had been required to learn. I couldn't have been farther from the truth."

I took a drink and continued, "See, Ghūls aren't really human, they really never were."

"So what are they?" Annessa asked. "They're not zombies?"

"No." I shook my head and sat heavily on the other

couch. "Before they were called Ghūls, they were angels, of a sort."

"Angels?"

"Well, not like Satan or Satariel or any of the Angelics. They were servants of the Umbrals. Unlike the angels that you and I know, they had much greater authority and power."

"Like gods?"

"Not really, they had much too specific roles to be thought of as gods; they served specific desires of the Umbrals. And when the gods rebelled, some of their servants picked the winning side, mostly those that served Ninnaka."

"So they're friendly to humans?" she asked.

"You'd think so, but not really. See, humans create nearly constantly. Our imaginations are constantly active, and we reproduce like horny rabbits."

"So they don't like sex, then?"

"No, no, they love sex. They hate creation. They hate *being*."

"So how come they let you learn from them?"

"Well, I'm still at the beginning here. If you let me finish, you'll understand!" I looked pointedly at her.

"Right, Umbral angels, fell and stuff, go ahead..."

"Ok, so the Umbrals and gods commence to fighting. The servants of the Umbrals took sides, some with the gods, others with the Umbrals. When the Umbrals were killed, their angels lost their purpose; they lost their focus and basically lost their minds. They became insane, ravenous killers. They tore through creation, murdering anything in their path. But, creation took vengeance on them and as time wore on, the miasma of life itself began to kill them."

"Do they have a name?" Annessa rested her chin on her hands like a child as she listened.

"They called them 'The Unbound' back then." I took a drink. "But then something happened that changed everything."

"What happened?"

"Ninnaka was murdered by the Beggar Lord."

"Ok, how'd that change anything? You're confusing the shit out of me, Master," she sighed.

"All of these creature were hardwired to serve their masters forever. When Ninnaka was murdered, her soul, I guess, was unable to escape this reality and return to the Nothing from whence she came. So her angels could still sense her and were still bound to her. Yet, they couldn't receive orders or sustenance from her. Her angels were scattered and broken without her. They slowly started to die."

"Did anyone ever tell you that you tell the most heartwarming stories?" She rolled over onto her back.

"Quit interrupting, you wanted me to tell you." I tossed one of the ice cubes from my drink onto her flat stomach.

"Hey!" she giggled and threw it back at me.

"Well, do you want me to finish the story or not?" I caught the ice cube and dropped it back into my drink.

"You might as well, but I already know it's gonna be sad." She stuck her tongue out at me.

"Anyway, back to the dying angels. They searched the earth for signs of their mistress. One of them came upon an ancient Arabian tribe of shapeshifters. It saw the way that these tribesmen survived by luring travelers to their deaths and devouring them. The angel was spellbound by the aura of corruption that surrounded them, and it had an epiphany. The corruption inherent in the way these people lived could provide sustenance to the angels. So it hatched a plan. It entered the dreams of the tribal elders and convinced them to allow the angels to possess them and the elders agreed."

"Why would they agree to that?" Annessa shook her head. "I mean, how do they benefit, the tribesman, I mean?"

"Power. The angels possessed near limitless power, at least in the minds of the elders. A symbiotic life was nothing when compared to the power they expected to gain," I shrugged. After all, I took not too different a bargain. I gave up my own afterlife in return for power and the ability to strike back at those I hated.

"So what happened after they made their deal?"

"The angels taught them basic sorcery. Just enough to craft wards that would lock the angels inside their flesh forever."

"What kind of wards? Like the ones you use?"

I was flattered that she noticed. No, seriously, you have no idea what it took for me to cultivate my knowledge of sorcery. It's nice to be appreciated.

"No, their wards were both more crude and much more powerful than mine. They were blood wards etched into the skin of the tribesmen, from the inside," I cringed as I said that last part. That had to hurt bad.

"How do you do that? I mean, wouldn't that kill you?"

"No. The angels possessed the tribesmen as they did it, lending them energy and dulling their pain all at once. Were a normal person to try it without Umbral assistance, it would likely kill them. I'm sure it didn't tickle, but with a creature of that kind of power possessing you, you can do just about anything," I answered.

"I don't get how the angels would survive inside their new hosts. Didn't you say human life kills the angels?" She looked genuinely confused.

"Well, yeah, the act of creation does, but the new, symbiotic creature lacked the same level of imagination that its former host once had. As a side effect of the joining of the two entities, the human lost all but the most basic creativity." I stood up to refill my drink.

"Something still doesn't make sense to me, though." Annessa rolled off the couch to her feet and followed me.

"What?"

"How did the tribesman learn to shapeshift? And why the hell were they willing to teach you sorcery?" She took an ice cube out the bucket and popped it into her mouth.

"Well, take a guess where the tribesmen came from?" I leaned against the sideboar– cellaret, fucking table thing.

"I dunno, leftovers from the first earth?" She put her arms around my waist. "Just tell me, you know I suck at this."

"Satan and Lilith conceived them in the wastelands of

Nod." I grabbed another ice cube and ran it down her back.

"Hey!" She crushed herself against me to avoid the cold. "Quit it!" she giggled.

"And to answer your second question, they needed the same thing from me that you do." I bit her perfect lower lip.

"What, exactly, do I need from you, Master?" she asked, her voice husky with desire.

"Sex," I whispered as I bit her neck.

"Master is wise." She rolled her neck allowing me to kiss and bite my way down to her collarbone.

And right about then, the door opened.

"I have returned, My Lord Emissary." There was a rustle of bags and a short pause. "And I see that I am interrupting. I'll just leave these here." Another rustle of bags and the sound of retreating footsteps. He was capable indeed.

Annessa looked at the bags. "We have to go, don't we?"

I sighed. "Yeah, I suppose we do." I needed to know what was keeping Cassidy from answering my calls.

"I'm getting very impatient, Master." She stomped her foot in a mock tantrum.

"You're not the only one, trust me," I replied as I walked over to check the bags.

I was becoming increasingly impressed with Mr. Admah. There were three suits for me and an assortment of clothes for Annessa. The suits were perfect, and more importantly, they were black. Appearances have to be kept up and all. Annessa giggled as she tore into the clothes. I shook my head. Living, dead or somewhere in between, women are still women.

"We need to hurry, Annessa," I reminded her. I shook my head as she glared at me. I threw up my hands. "Just hurry, ok?"

She mumbled something about rushing her and not wanting to look stupid. I walked toward the door.

"I'm going down to check out the car." I jingled the keys. "Meet me downstairs when you're ready."

CHAPTER 4

I stepped out of the elevator and headed for the revolving door. The doorman looked up at me and smiled in that dear–god–please–don't–kill–me way as I passed him.

"I was told someone dropped off a car for me?" I held up the keys.

"It's over there sir, the black Range Rover." He pointed.

"What's your name?" I asked.

"Roger, sir."

"You have a nice day, Roger." I patted him on the shoulder and walked over to check out my new ride.

I expected another BMW, but as I looked over the frame of the Range Rover, I began to see possibilities. It was bigger, which meant it could hold more weapons. As an added benefit, it had a more powerful engine and more weight, which made it a more effective weapon with Abbadonna controlling it. I could definitely see the possibilities. I hit the unlock button on the key–fob. There was a hiss as the driver door popped open under hydraulic power. I grinned. The body was armored and I guessed the windows were bulletproof. Erzebet was getting a raise; this pretty much settled it.

Before I could drool over the new truck any more, I

caught sight of Annessa stepping out of the building. She
was wearing a plaid schoolgirl skirt with a black, lacy corset
and knee high black and red platform boots. She had her
hair in pigtails again, but she hadn't found time to do her
make–up. She caught me looking and gave me a self–
satisfied smile. Women always know when they've got you.
I'm not sure they can help that smile; they just have to set
the hook, I guess.

"What do you think?" she asked as she spun a slow
circle in front of me.

"I think you're going to give Roger a fucking heart
attack." I pressed the key–fob open again and her door
popped open with a hiss.

"Whoa." She poked her head in the truck. "This is
yours?"

"Yeah, I guess they thought I'd break another BMW."
I helped her into the passenger seat. Which is just another
way of saying I got a cheap feel as she sat down. Hey, being
the Devil's Emissary doesn't make me any less of a man.
Face it; if it were you, you'd have done the same thing.
Don't you fucking judge me.

"Abbadonna's gonna be pissed." Annessa ran her
hands over the leather as I climbed into the driver's seat.

"What, why?" I pulled the door gently and let the
hydraulics do the rest. "This thing is awesome."

"Yeah, but it ain't sexy." She pulled down the visor to
check for a mirror.

"Oh, yes the hell it is!" I protested. "It has hydraulic
doors, and room for stuff and it's armored and bulletproof.
This thing is fucking hot!" I felt like a kid with a Tonka
truck.

"She's going to feel like she has a fat ass," Annessa
shook her head knowingly as if she spoke the wisdom of the
ages. She pushed the visor up.

"There's nothing wrong with a big ass," I grinned.
"Nothing at all."

Annessa turned in her seat. "It does have a nice back
seat," she grinned. "You thinking what I'm thinking,
Master?"

I was, I really was, but my phone started playing "Psychopathy Red" and all else seemed less important.

"Little Brother." Cassidy seemed out of breath.

"Cassidy! Where are you?" I asked.

"I'm on my way back to the city." He coughed harshly. "Meet me at Harker's. We've got a huge problem." He hung up.

I stared at my phone for a second. I was unsure how to feel. I mean, Cassidy was alive and mostly well, I hoped. But when Cassidy says a problem is huge, it's time to grab the wife, forget about the livestock and get the fuck off the farm.

"Master?"

"Yeah."

"That was Cassidy, right?"

"Yeah."

"Well, what did he say?"

"We're fucked."

"Not likely if we keep getting interrupted."

I couldn't help but laugh.

CHAPTER 5

I drove through the crowded streets silently wishing that I could summon Abbadonna. New York drivers piss me off. I gotta give them credit for their ingenuity, they have this magical gift for creating lanes and this truly amazing ability to gauge exactly how much space it will take for them to cut you off just enough to make you want to pistol whip a baby. They must begin teaching offensive driving at the pre–school level to engender this level of expertise.

By the time we got to Harker's, the sun had nearly set and Annessa had found the world's harshest aggro–tech music to play at close to full volume. Between the music and the way she was contorting her body in time to it, I'm shocked we made it one piece.

The parking garage at Harker's was empty. I hopped out of the car and dug through my pockets. I swore when I realized that I left my cigarettes in my other suit, or what was left of it.

"What's wrong, Master?" Annessa turned the radio down.

"I forgot my cigarettes at the apartment." I leaned against the fender. She opened the glove box and smiled.

"I think whoever got this car knows you pretty well." She held up a silver lighter and pack of clove cigarettes. She climbed out of the car and tossed them to me.

I tore open the pack and lit one. I stuck it between her perfect lips and grabbed her around the waist. I lifted her up and set her on the hood of the car.

"What are you doing, Master?" She leaned back on her elbows.

I took the cigarette from her and took a deep drag, pulling the smoke to the bottom of my lungs. I handed the cigarette back. I closed my eyes and slowly spoke a Word. Reality shuddered for a second, like a ripple across a pond with me at its center.

"Whoa," Annessa looked around. "That was cool."

I reached up and pulled her toward me. As I kissed her deeply, I silently spoke another Word. She shivered as it ran over the surface of her skin, sanctifying her flesh to the Lord of the Fallen. I ran my nails along her inner thighs as I spoke another Word aloud, my lips following the trail left by my nails. She gasped, and then moaned as I kissed her in the most intimate of ways. Within moments, she came and I spoke the final Word, my hands clutching the hood of the truck. Smoke poured from my mouth and the garage hummed with the force of my sorcery.

"Abbadonna," I breathed, smoke coiling around my head like a crown. "To me, my beautiful one."

The truck jerked forward with the force of her arrival, launching Annessa into my arms and leaving a foot long trail of rubber on the ground. I put my hand on the hood, and I felt her presence arcing through the metal.

"Hello, Beautiful." I caressed the car gently as if it were flesh.

"Emissary," her rich voice rolled through my mind.
"Yes?"

"It will take me some time to adjust to this vehicle," she sounded disapproving.

"Really?"

"Yes." Her clipped tone carried the weight of her displeasure. "The rear end is a bit heavy, is it not?"

"I toldja, "Annessa chimed in dazedly from her perch in my arms. "I toldja she'd think it made her ass look fat."

I sighed. One evil woman was bad enough; how the hell was I supposed to deal with two?

"Shut up, Annessa." I dropped Annessa's legs. "Don't make shit worse."

"What'd I do?" Annessa sulked as her legs wobbled under her.

I stroked the hood again. "There is nothing wrong with the vehicle, Abbadonna. Let's face it; you could make a station wagon sexy."

"I am unconvinced." She sounded more petulant than upset now. Which made me think along another vein. Maybe it wasn't the vehicle as much as what I was doing on it when I called her. I'd never known her to be jealous before, but then, I'd never gone down on a lover on her hood during a summoning before.

"There has never been a sunrise or sunset that could rival your beauty. There is no vehicle that could ever be sexy enough to be worthy of you; this one is no exception." I stroked her hood.

"As you say, Emissary." She sounded mollified. "Be thankful that I favor you."

"And you know how glad I am of that. If I can't have you, Abbadonna, I don't want any Fallen." It was true; she's my favorite. The fact that she can get jealous only reinforced that. It meant, well, it meant that I meant something to her as well.

I kissed my fingers and touched them to the hood to the truck. "Glad to have you back," I thought. I felt her pleasure ripple through me as I turned to guide Annessa into Harker's.

"What was that all about, Master?" Annessa asked me as we got into the elevator.

"You didn't need to make it worse!" I said.

"No, I mean, yeah, I didn't mean to make it worse. I wasn't thinking right at the moment, but that's your fault!" she protested. "I mean I was minding my own business, then suddenly you're, you know?" She gestured between her legs.

"I'm just saying, you didn't have to make it worse!" I

shook my head.

"What was that all about, anyway?" she asked. "I mean, anytime you feel like that again, by all means, but why right then?"

"The truck was new, it was clean." I pulled another cigarette out. "I needed a channel to connect Abbadonna to the vehicle. I'm not recovered enough to use blood, so I used something else."

"What?" she asked as she reached for my cigarette.

"Desire." I kissed her, hard. "I can't get you out of my head."

"Does she usually get jealous?" Annessa took a drag of the cigarette and handed it back.

"Not usually, no," I shrugged. "But then, this is the first time I've done that."

I led her out into the club. My eyes were already scanning for Cassidy. Even though Harker hadn't awakened yet, the club was filling up. The younger, hungrier vampires in Harker's murder were already in the alcoves with their first victims of the night. I didn't see Cassidy anywhere. I took Annessa's hand and headed for an empty table near the back door.

"How come you never see any big, strong, football player type vampires, Master?" she asked as she leaned back in her chair and scanned the room.

"Potassium." I answered absentmindedly as I checked my phone for the third time since we entered the club.

"What?" She leaned forward and put her hand over the face of my phone. "He'll be here, Master. Try to calm down."

"Cassidy is rarely late, I'm getting worried." I took her hand and kissed it.

"I know, but he'll be here." She leaned over the table and kissed me. "He'll be here."

I just nodded and put my phone away.

"So what does potassium have to do with vampires?" she asked as she leaned her chair back again and looked back at the dance floor.

"It a makes your blood sour, so sour that they can't

bear to drink it," I explained. "Most bodybuilders, football players, etcetera, take massive doses of potassium to deal with muscle soreness. That's why your run–of–the–mill vampire is a pasty faced, nerdy type—no potassium."

"What about garlic? That always works in the movies."

I nodded. "Well, do you like garlic?"

"I'm Italian, or I was anyway," she shrugged. "I fucking love garlic, I think they put it in our bottles as babies."

"Vampires are the same way; they might go after an Indian or Pakistani if they feel like curry, or an Italian if they want more of a garlic flavor," I grinned.

"You're fucking with me, Master." She kicked me under the table. "That isn't nice."

"Ow, ok, ok!" I rubbed my shin.

"Well, what about the Irish?" Her head darted in that what–the–fuck–do–you–have–say–about–that kind of way that women use when we've painted ourselves into a corner.

"We're usually safe," I smiled.

"Yeah, why is that?" she asked.

"It's the smell, you see," Harker spoke from behind me. "Whiskey and cabbage, generally puts you right off your meal."

"Fuck you, Harker," I laughed. "I was going to say it's due to our abnormally high blood alcohol content, but I think I like your answer better."

Harker spun the last chair at the table around and sat on it. "What brings you two here tonight?"

"Cassidy." I checked my phone again. "He's supposed to meet us here. He sounded rough."

"Hasn't arrived yet." Harker looked around. He paused a second and one of his subs stepped out of the shadows, Bethany, I think.

"Take Annessa to the back, love, and find her someone suitable to eat." He took Annessa's hand and helped her from her seat.

Annessa looked at me questioningly. I nodded toward Bethany. I had no idea what was on Harker's mind, but I was certain it wasn't treachery.

"We'll be along in a tick," Harker assured her.

As soon as they were out of earshot, I turned to Harker. "What's going on Miles?"

"Very little, I'm afraid. It's been a bit boring since you took your little holiday."

"Okay, so what's on your mind?" I must have sounded as perplexed as I felt.

"Come along." He walked to the bar, stepped behind it and opened a concealed door. He motioned for me to follow.

"What's with the secrecy?" I asked as soon as I cleared the door.

"Must be a thing of wonder," he said.

"What are you taking about, man?"

"The guiltless life you lead." He turned to me, his eyes glowing in the dim light. He shoved the door shut with a heavy thump.

I froze. It took me a second to recognize what was going on. Harker wasn't pissed; he was mourning. Vampires don't do death very well.

"I don't know where you've been, man. But from here, let me tell you, it's been anything but fucking guiltless." I said, my hands raised in supplication.

"You kill a woman I loved and then suddenly you're happily tongue–fucking your slave in my fucking car park like we're best mates?" He held up his hands, faint scars covered them from the burns he'd gotten trying to save Sarah. "Forgive me for missing the regret."

"What am I supposed to do, Miles? Spend the rest of my life mourning a woman in paradise?" I stepped forward. "I don't have forever, Harker. I'm not you."

He made a choked sound and leaned against the wall. "I loved her, Jason." His hand splintered the oak paneling as he gripped it. "I waited to turn her because I loved her; I couldn't bear to see her like me."

"It was my fault, Miles." I shook my head. "If I hadn't barged in here that night, you would have—"

"Cursed her forever." He shook with emotion.

"She saw her end, Miles." I put my hands on his shoulders. "She saw what was coming and she chose her fate."

"How could you do it?" He turned from me. "How could you…kill her, when even I couldn't bear to?"

"Because sparing her would have condemned us all, and she couldn't bear that," I clenched my teeth. "And because I couldn't bring myself to make a monster of her any more than you could."

"I don't know that I can go on this way." He stood and slowly turned to face me. The blood from his tears had stained his eyes and left crimson trails down his pale face. "We didn't deserve her, none of us…"

"She's in a far better place than us, Miles." I shook him. "We should be celebrating, not mourning."

He closed his eyes, took deep breath and let it out slowly. Some gestures persist, even after death, apparently. He nodded curtly and opened his eyes. Nothing of his emotion remained. "Right, stiff upper lip and all that. An Irish wake, then?" He wiped his eyes.

"She'd like that. She'd rather see us happy than like this," I gestured around the small office in which we stood.

"Yes, I imagine she would."

I stood there a second thinking about her. She'd seen this; she'd known what was to come. She wouldn't have gone to her fate willingly unless she knew that something better awaited not just her, but all of us. Harker was wrong, it wasn't that we hadn't deserved her; it was the entire world that hadn't.

"Shall we lift a glass to Sarah, then? Give her a proper send off?" he asked.

"Definitely," I smiled.

He reached for the door. I reached out and gently grabbed his arm.

"What?" he asked.

I incanted a short spell and waved my hand past his face. The blood fell away from his face as a mist. "Can't let your public see you looking like hell, can we?"

He chuckled as he opened the door. I shut the door

behind me as I followed him toward the back of the bar. I
caught a whiff of lilies and jasmine. Strange, I hadn't seen
Sheena here tonight.

CHAPTER 6

Cassidy was lying on the couch when we walked in. Annessa stood between him and Mara, the youngest of Harker's subs. Annessa's fangs were bared and her eyes were glowing like balefire on Beltaine. Cassidy was dripping blood in the same manner that Hoover Dam drips water. It was oozing out of him in thumb thick streams. I ran past Annessa.

"What the fuck happened to you?" I asked Cassidy as I raced to his side.

"Cold Iron," he spoke in a hoarse whisper, "And silver, of all things."

I nodded. "Annessa, help me," I spoke forcefully.

Now that Harker was here, he'd be able to restrain his girls. I needed Annessa to help me maneuver Cassidy around. Annessa quickly moved alongside me.

"Help me get his clothes off," I said as I tried to firmly, but gently get his ever–present duster off of him.

"Stand back, Master." Annessa pushed me away from Cassidy. With two vicious slashes, her claws shredded his clothes and the remains of his duster. With a swift pull, she yanked them away from him and tossed them into a pile on the floor.

There were ragged holes all along the left side of his body, through his arms and legs and several large holes in his chest and stomach. I gasped when I saw the amount of damage he'd taken.

"What did this, Cassidy?" I asked, my voice a shocked whisper.

"Your Heavenly counterpart," he winced as I prodded at one of the holes in his bicep.

"What? We killed her!" I was going to be exceptionally pissed off if Rachel had somehow survived.

"No," he growled as I tried to pull a wickedly serrated piece of Iron from the wound. "There's a new one, and he's a twisted bastard."

"Cassidy, I'm sorry, man." I leaned back and looked him in the eye. "I'm going to have to pull these all out at once, and it's gonna hurt like hell."

He nodded. "Do it."

"Annessa."

"Yes, Master?" She appeared at my side again.

"You're going to have to hold him down." I stepped back and took off my jacket. "And he's probably going to try to kill us all."

"What?" She looked at Cassidy incredulously. "You wouldn't!"

"You just hold me, Annessa girl." He patted her hand. "You hold me like your master's life depends on it."

"Why?" She clamped down on his biceps and nearly forced him through the couch.

"Because he won't be in control." I rolled my sleeves back. "And the beast that will be, really wants to kill me."

"Why?" Annessa looked so strange, a tiny, yet viciously fanged girl holding down a naked man nearly twice her size.

"Because Satan stuck the monster inside of him to start with." I raised my hands and took a deep breath. I looked at Cassidy. "You ready?"

"Do it." He clenched his teeth.

I spoke several Words in rapid succession. I jerked my left hand toward the far wall and Cassidy howled as his wounds tore further open as the silver and cold iron ripped free. Annessa's strength held as Cassidy transformed. As I watched her struggle against him, my eyes were drawn to her body. I was stunned momentarily as I imagined her flesh against mine. She looked up at me with fear in her eyes and I was shocked back to reality. What the hell was that about?

I held up my Marked hand and spoke a Word of command. It wasn't my voice that issued forth from my lips but Satan's. For a moment, the room was still, as Cassidy, Annessa and the vampires froze in the grip of my command. I quickly spoke a prayer of healing over Cassidy, my Word would only hold him back for so long. As his wounds knit back together, he broke free from Annessa. He launched himself to his feet; he bared his fangs and hurled himself at me.

A thousand things raced through my mind at that moment. But the one thread that tied them all together was that I couldn't attack him. He was like my brother, and if he was meant to kill me, then so be it. Yeah, I'd be back, but resurrection isn't really as much fun as it's cracked up to be. After the first time, you begin to understand why Jesus waited three days. He wasn't playing a game; he knew that shit was gonna hurt. Just before he reached me, Cassidy got himself under control again.

"That was a bit too close, Little Brother." He dropped to a knee, gasping for air.

"You think?"

He grinned sheepishly at me and shrugged.

"What the hell happened to you?" I asked.

"Some of your friends decided that I was a liability, Little Brother." He looked at Harker. "Do you think you can find me something to wear, my friend?"

Harker nodded and motioned to Mara. She bowed her head and slid out of the room.

"I don't think I've ever seen you this hurt before, man." I remarked as I sat down in one of the overstuffed chairs.

"They were well armed and they were certainly organized." He winced as he stretched his newly healed muscles. "They were lying in wait for me at the mansion."

"You went back there to catch a scent, I take it?" I asked.

"Yes, in a sense." He pulled the remains of his clothes over his lap. "I thought that there might be something of the ritual left that I had missed the first time, the night that Sarah died. Some clue as to what the creature's intentions might be, in a more direct sense, if you follow."

I nodded. "I figured that, but how did you not see the ambush? I've never known you to be anything other than cautious."

"They were smart, Little Brother." He leaned forward. "They had no Gifted with them, no Host–Bound, not even a reliquary."

That made sense, in a twisted sort of way. With no Aetheric signature, they wouldn't stand out. There would have been no indication of danger. "So they just used conventional weapons with homemade ammo?"

Cassidy nodded. "If there is anything comical about the whole scenario, it's that they shot a werewolf with silver," he chuckled. "Why they actually thought that would work is beyond me."

"You don't go to the movies much, I take it?" I asked sarcastically. Cassidy is a Luddite of the first order. I had to force him to use a cellphone.

"I don't see why that is relevant, Little Brother."

"Nevermind that. The fact that they used Cold Iron is relevant, however." I stood up and began to pace. "It shows that they aren't stupid, just poorly informed."

"Maybe they just wanted to cover their bases?" Annessa asked. "You know, just in case the Cold Iron didn't work?"

"That is likely," Cassidy nodded.

"What's odd is that they knew to use Cold Iron," Harker began. "Unless there're Inquisitors about."

"Right, but the fact that they didn't have any Gifted with them says they don't trust Gifted or that they lack the resources to employ them," I shook my head. "The Church has tons of Gifted, why alienate them by calling in the Inquisition? This doesn't make any sense."

"What if the new guy doesn't like Gifted?" Annessa sat cross–legged in my chair. Somehow, she'd found time to do her make–up since we got to the club. Just looking at her made my head swim with desire. I couldn't keep my thoughts focused when I looked at her.

"There are many prohibitions on dealing with Gifted in the Old Testament. If this man is a fanatic, that could be the root of this," Cassidy shrugged. "It seems farfetched, but often the simplest solution in the right one."

"That's true," I was forced to concede. "But, why? Not having Gifted around makes it too easy for his enemies. Who would do that?"

"A fanatic. Look to your own past, Little Brother." Cassidy stood as Mara returned with clothing. "The men that fought and nearly killed you, they lacked the fancy tools upon which you depended, and it was that fact which made them so difficult to predict."

He was right. Insurgents could strike anywhere at nearly anything. Their plans were often daring and overly bold, but they lacked the fear that would make a more sensible man pause and rethink his strategy. They were entirely unafraid of death and that was the crux of their strength. If this new emissary was so bold, so unafraid, we had problems.

"But how did he know Cassidy would be coming back to the mansion? How did he know it wouldn't be us or anyone else?" Annessa grabbed my hand as I paced by her.

"I don't know." I shook my head, that was perplexing. I looked at Cassidy. "Did all of the men shoot at you?"

"Nearly all, yes." He pulled a t–shirt over his head. "There were several that seemed to hold back and didn't raise their weapons."

"Were any of them using basic lead, Liam?" Harker asked.

"Silver and lead?" Cassidy asked as he looked at me, following Harker's logic. "You might be right, Miles."

"Oh, come on," I said. "You're over thinking this! There's no way he was ready for all of us."

"Don't be thick, Jason," Harker interjected. "Obvious—"

"Hold on," Annessa stood up, waving her hands. "What they hell are you even talking about?"

"Silver and lead in equal measures would interrupt my Gift. Not for very long, but long enough for them to potentially exploit my weakness." I shuddered as I conceded that Harker was right. "This motherfucker is smart." I punched my hand in frustration.

"He can't be that smart," Annessa grinned. "He shot Cassidy, and that's pretty goddamned stupid."

I snorted. "Good point."

"Nevertheless," Cassidy shrugged. "He very nearly killed me. This man is dangerous, Little Brother. Don't underestimate him."

"Shit," I started pacing. "I wish I could a read on this guy. Rachel was easy…sometimes." I ran my hands through my hair and stretched my back. "At least I knew her."

"You ever hunted coyotes, cowboy?" Mara asked from the back of the room.

"Did we suddenly start playing the random question game?" I asked.

"Hear me out, dick." She stepped out of the shadow and wrapped her arms around Harker's chest from behind. "You start by shooting a rabbit, but you don't kill it."

"Sounds pleasant," I grimaced. "Go on."

"Once it's wounded, you stake it out in the middle of a field and let its screams bring in the coyotes."

"Screams?" Annessa asked.

"They sound like you're torturing a baby," Mara said, then licked her lips. "They can scream for hours."

"As heartwarming as this is, Mara," I shuddered. "Maybe you can, I don't know, get to the damned point?"

"The coyotes are so focused on the rabbit, they completely miss the hunter. BAM! Dead coyote."

"Wow," I said. "That's twisted, even for you."

Mara winked. "A girl's gotta eat."

"It might work," Cassidy said thoughtfully.

"Says the guy who doesn't have to play rabbit," I shook my head. "There's got to be a better way."

"The problem is that I still need to get to that house, and I need to do it before anyone distorts the Aether flows in the area." Cassidy walked over to the small bar and poured himself a drink.

"Do you really think they'll just stay there and wait for you?" Annessa asked.

"No," he threw back his drink. "Likely, they will leave a scout or a lookout, but I would prefer to work unrestricted by paranoia."

"Fine," I walked over to make myself a drink, no need to let Cassidy drink alone. "It'll be worth it, if I get a chance to see this bastard face to face."

"And how will you bait him, Little Brother?"

"I'll just call for a meeting in a neutral territory."

"You really think he's gonna show, Master?" Annessa asked.

"Of course he will." I looked at her over the rim of my drink. "He's going to try to kill me." I pointed at myself. "Rabbit."

"What?" She nearly leapt out of the chair. "I thought you said it would be in neutral territory?"

"Well, the territory will be neutral, but he won't." I smiled and drank.

"Then why go?" She looked around for support.

""Because dear Jason is having a go at being unpredictable," Harker answered.

"By doing what?" she asked, her hope evident on her face.

"Giving him a chance to try to kill me," I replied.

CHAPTER 7

I parked across the street. Feeling Abbadonna's displeasure, I stroked the steering wheel and sent calmness at her. Annessa fidgeted in her seat.

"Where's this neutral territory, Master?" Annessa looked around at the crowded streets.

I just pointed.

"Starbucks? Starbucks is the neutral territory? Are you fucking kidding me?" She turned toward me incredulously.

"Why not," I laughed. "Everyone loves coffee. If you blow up a Starbucks, then both sides are liable to suffer."

"Yeah, but Starbucks? That just seems...sacrilegious!"

"That's exactly why it's neutral territory." I grabbed her wrist and pulled her close. I inhaled her scent and kissed her passionately. I forced myself to break away before I lost control and dragged her into the backseat. "Now, get in the driver's seat and go." I opened my door.

"No way I'm leaving you here by yourself, Master!" she protested as she slid across into the driver's seat. "What if you need help?"

"I'm fine, I'm fine." I pushed her back as I hopped out of the SUV. "I've made arrangements, it'll be fine." I shut the door behind me.

"What arrangements?" she asked as she rolled down the window.

"The kind that are supposed to be a secret," I grinned. "Just go, you'll know if I'm in danger. Trust me, you'll know."

"Please don't get yourself killed, Master," she spoke softly.

"Would you just go?" I shook my head. "I'll be fine!"

The truth was, I was looking forward to this. It had been a long time since I'd had a new adversary. Rachel had been my first. I was actually eager to meet this bastard. He'd impressed me thus far. I doubted he would have Rachel's radical evangelical background or her drive to save everything that moved. I often wondered if she or those that lived like her had any idea how offensive the concept is to those that they're trying to save.

My pocket vibrated. I slid my phone out and casually peeked at the screen. It said, "dinner will be promptly at seven" in a several hundred-year-old Slavic dialect. What it meant was something altogether different. I smiled as I entered the coffeehouse, the tinkling of the bell made me wonder if at this precise moment an angel was getting her wings torn off. I truly hoped so.

I ordered at the counter, got my coffee and sat at a table facing the window. My eyes scanned all of the nearby buildings seeking sniper hides. I counted at least three. They were sloppy; I raised my coffee in a mock salute.

"I'm surprised that you asked to meet." He spoke from behind me. His voice was warm and calm.

"Please sit." I gestured to the chair across from me. I didn't turn around.

"I didn't expect to find that you had manners." He slid into the chair and set a glass teacup before him.

He wasn't what I expected either. He was thirty-ish, his head was shaved bald and he wore jeans and a grey hooded sweatshirt.

"I'd be lying if I said you were entirely what I

expected, so I guess we're even." I smiled.

"Well, let's get to the business at hand," he gestured expansively. "As we are both busy men and have far better things we could be doing than watching others indulge their addictions."

"Oh, I don't know," I winked. "I'm a rather big fan of indulgence."

"What did you hope to accomplish by this meeting?" he asked as he reached for his cup.

"First, I wanted to see what kind of man you are," I began. I held up my thumb.

"As you can see, I am rather unimposing." He smiled.

"Or you carefully cultivate that image." I smiled back. I held up my index finger. "Next, I wanted to see how you acted."

"Again, not much to see, I'm afraid." He leaned back in his chair.

"Third, I wanted to see just how bold you are." I lifted my coffee as I held up my middle finger.

"Well, there," he clucked his tongue and shook a finger at me. "There you've got me."

The first bullet shattered the window and punched a neat hole in my coffee cup. The second bullet slammed into my forehead. Before I could even fall, a thick silver chain with razor sharp lead and diamond barbs bit into my throat. I kept my thoughts serene and stopped my heart. Above all else, I kept myself calm. The last thing I needed was to let Annessa feel my distress. I laid my left hand on the table, all around me the patrons were panicking. As they raced from the coffeehouse, I spoke my Word. The man with chain hopped around like a toad on hot asphalt. I smiled and collapsed dead on the table. My last sight was the man with chain falling to the ground, his face a rictus of agony, eyes frozen in death.

I felt the water pooling around my ankles. It was as warm as bathwater. I was in complete darkness, which was odd. Usually, I came back to the same place when I died like clockwork. To be fair, I liked the predictability of it. Slowly, as I looked around the darkness, I began to feel a sense of déjà vu. I held up my hand and spoke a short incantation. My right hand burst into flame, I swept it before me like a torch. I was in a cavern as vast as my eye could see. I took a step and heard a voice that resounded throughout the entirety of my being, "No. This is not yet for you!"

The ground shook beneath me and the darkness swept in around me smothering my flame. There was sensation of falling and without warning I plunged into frigid waters. I was tossed and thrown about in the churning water and cast onto the rocks that framed the Eye of Eurydice. I coughed and spat out the awful water. I shivered in the cold and climbed out of the water.

"Perhaps, my son, I should build you a home here," he laughed at me. The bastard was actually laughing at me.

"Oh, yeah, I bet the fishing is great here." I dragged myself upright. "And the water's bracing, it keeps the blood moving." I couldn't help it, I grinned. "Fuck, that's cold," I managed to shiver out as I sat at his feet.

"I'm beginning to think that you enjoy Perdition far too much, my child." He waved his hand and the chill left me immediately.

"No," I shook my head and held up a hand. "This time, I win," I said.

"You wished to be killed?" He raised an eyebrow questioningly.

"Actually, I'd hoped his snipers weren't such great shots, but in a nutshell, this was in my plan," I shrugged. "I wanted to see how far he would go."

"Apparently, my son, this emissary is unafraid to violate even the most sacred of laws."

"Well, to be fair, his people shot up a Starbucks, not a preschool." I stood and stretched. "But, more importantly, he showed me something I can exploit."

"What would that be, my son?"

"My Father's sin." I knelt before him. "Pride."

"Indeed."

"My time is short, Father." I looked around, trying to gauge the passage of time on the Lifeside.

"Why is that, my child?" He looked both pleased and amused at the same time.

"I've made arrangements to revive myself." I turned a slow circle as if expecting my resurrection to occur any second.

"Is that so?"

"Well, I've arranged for, what I hope is, a competent sorcerer to do the work for me," I shrugged sheepishly. "I'm guessing he isn't as good as I am."

"What was that about your Father's sin, my son?"

"It isn't a sin for me, Father." I gave him a winning smile as I felt the tug of life upon my soul.

"No?"

"It's emulation." My soul was ripped across the Veil and hurled back into my body.

The Veilshock hit me first. I curled up in the fetal position and retched. Next, of course came the pain of my body knitting itself back together. Apparently, when I killed the goon that tried to garrote me, he'd torn off several of the barbs in my flesh. The lead and diamond barbs made healing magic difficult.

Diamonds are unique in one respect; you won't see any Gifted wearing them, ever. They aren't the pretty baubles that you Normals seem to think they are. See, they don't just reflect sunlight in pretty little rainbows; they act as a reflecting glass for magic. The magic strikes the reflecting facets and enters the gem, eternally bouncing from facet to facet. Have you ever wondered why people talk about bad juju from secondhand wedding rings? When a person dies wearing a diamond, the burst of thanatonic energy that kills them enters the stone. So, essentially, you're carrying a torch that attracts Spooks, ghosts and all manner of twisted Aetheric creatures. Yeah, that's gonna bring you some bad luck.

When I finally opened my eyes, I was lying in the back of an ambulance. Adrian Admah leaned over me.

"Welcome back, my lord," he said with a curt not.

"What took so long?" I asked with a voice hardly my own. I rubbed my throat; a ragged scar circled my neck.

"There were a few complications, my lord." He pulled me into a sitting position.

"Like what?" I rasped.

"They blew up the coffee shop, my lord." He produced a pile of fresh, folded clothes. "Your body sustained substantially more injuries than we planned for."

I looked over my body; there were a few new scars, but nothing I couldn't take care of myself when I was back on my feet. "I suppose some things can't be avoided, Adrian. No harm, no foul." I stretched. "We have people working damage control with the press?"

"Yes, my lord. It's being called a tragic fire, started by pranksters with a pipe bomb."

"Good," I said. "No need to kick up church attendance unnecessarily."

"I was instructed to take you to the Consulate when you were well, my lord," he spoke hesitantly.

"Erzebet's orders, I assume?"

"Yes, my lord," he nodded. "Though, should you wish to countermand that order, I am yours to command."

"No," I shrugged my way into my shirt. "I'll play along." I sent a mental summons to Abbadonna.

"Shall I call for your car, my lord?" he asked as he helped me into my jacket.

"Already taken care of," I frowned.

"My lord?" He paled. "Is there something wrong?"

"Are you up to a second resurrection?" I asked entirely serious.

"Why?"

"I'm pretty sure Annessa is going to kill me."

"Ah, yes, my lord," he agreed. "There is that."

The screech of tires outside the ambulance announced their arrival. The door of the ambulance was hurled open with such force that it tore the top hinge free. Annessa appeared, her eyes glowing an uncomfortable shade of green. My heart sank. She was really pissed.

"You said," she growled, "I'd know if you were in danger."

"Well, I wasn't really in any danger," I began.

"You fucking died!" she screamed. Before I could react she was on me. She hit me like a freight train and bowled me over.

"Annessa, I—" I stammered as I forced my way back to a leaning position.

"You. Fucking. Died." She leaned in close to me. Her fangs extended. "You lied to me."

"My lady," Adrian began.

"Get out, Adrian," she growled as she pointed at the broken ambulance door. "Go wait in the truck."

"But, my lady," he tried again.

"It wasn't a suggestion." Her voice dripped malice.

He looked at me and gave me a look that said *I tried, buddy, but you're pretty much fucked* and hopped out of the ambulance.

"We've decided that you're incapable of intelligent action, Master." Annessa shoved me back to the floor.

"We?" I asked.

"Abbadonna and me," she grinned. It wasn't a happy grin either.

"Abbadonna?" I leaned my head forward to look into her eyes.

"She's in here with me." Her claws bit into my chest. "Be thankful you aren't."

"Oh, trust me," I said with no trace of humor. "I am."

"Explain yourself," she demanded in Abbadonna's voice.

"Well, you just said that I should be thankful that I'm not in there with you two and I just agreed because—" She lifted my torso and slammed me back to the floor. I'm pretty certain there was a 'pung' sound as my skull bounced off one of the metal gurney stops. Fuck, that hurt.

"If dying isn't a big deal to you, then maybe we can arrange for a second death today." Her jaw distended. This was going too far.

"You've made your point, Annessa," I spoke firmly. "Get off of me."

"What if we don't want to?" She started to salivate. Abbadonna was pushing her too far. She didn't mean to, I'm sure, but it's hard for Fallen to control their anger. Well, hence the Fallen part of the equation. With her riding Annessa, who was hurt, angry and not exactly prone to exemplary emotional control, things were bound to get out of hand.

"I'll be forced to remind you exactly who's in charge here." I clenched my left hand and began to channel as much energy as I could without alerting her to what I was doing.

"I think that's apparent, Master." She released me and retracted her fangs. "We're not stupid. Don't treat us like we are." She turned and dropped out of the back of the ambulance. As she passed the front of the truck she traced her hand over the hood. There was a slight Aetheric ripple as Abbadonna reentered the truck.

I collapsed and took a long, shuddering breath. I released the energy I was holding. Of course she was right. I should have told her, I was just afraid of her reaction. Perhaps I should have considered that I might not be as expendable to others as I was to myself. Death doesn't really affect me anymore. I mean, it isn't final, for me anyway. I wouldn't recommend you try any of what I do; I'm a bit less fragile. I relaxed my mind. I bent my thought on Abbadonna. She tried to ignore my mindseeking, but I'm pretty persistent.

"Beautiful." I let my contrition flow through the mindlink.

"You really are an ass, Emissary." Her anger, though somewhat abated, was still quite apparent.

"I can't help it, I'm still a guy." I mentally shrugged. "I don't like getting you two upset."

"Upset?" The truck's engine revved suddenly. "Upset? I've been fighting battles for countless millennia before your kind was conceived! I'm not worried that you died; it was a sound tactical decision. I am infuriated that you chose not trust me. That you treated me as if I were a mewling child to be kept in the dark."

I had no words to explain what I felt or even why I felt as I did. I simply opened myself up and let the entirety of

my being pour out into her mind. She saw my worry about
Annessa, my concern that the two of them, together or
separate, might lose control in the face of my death and
attack the Angelics resulting in a higher civilian death toll,
which was likely to be worse for us than better. Mostly, I let
her see that I was a stupid, stupid man.

"I was unaware of your desires, Emissary." There was
something of a grin in her voice. To be honest, I hadn't
thought that I'd hidden my feelings for Abbadonna. In my
mind they were always right there on the surface. I also was
completely unashamed of them. To say that I desired her
was like standing on a street corner and yelling, "Hey,
everybody! I enjoy breathing!" It should have been
completely unsurprising to all concerned.

"I tell you that you're beautiful at least fifty times a
day, Abbadonna."

"Yes, but I was unaware of just how inventive you are,
Emissary."

"Well, I've had a lot of free time." If a man could
blush mentally, trust me, I was.

"I guess having a big ass might not be so bad after
all," she laughed.

"Do you forgive me?" I asked. This was getting
ridiculous.

"No." I could feel the mental shake of her head. "It
isn't that easy, Emissary."

"What more can I do?"

"Trust me," she responded firmly.

"I do," I assured her. "How many years was it just
us?"

"Six. I would have thought it enough time for you to
trust me as I do you."

"So you don't forgive me?"

"No, but I concede that the possibility exists."

I sighed and broke contact. I sat up and hauled myself
out of the ambulance. I'd almost rather that she killed me
than made me face her like this. How the hell does the
emissary of the Devil still wind up with women problems? I
ran my hand over the lines of the truck as I passed the hood.

Angry or not, she was still my Abbadonna and I loved her. I was also afraid that of the two, Abbadonna was going to be the easier one to deal with. I pulled the door handle and let it open itself.

"So you knew about this the whole time?" Annessa was grilling Adrian.

"Yes, my lady," he nodded.

"And you didn't tell me?"

"No, my lady." He shook his head and our eyes met for a moment. I felt sorry for him, I wasn't going to help, but I still felt sorry for him.

"Why didn't you tell me?" She leaned over the seat.

"I didn't have your cell number, my lady." He answered without missing a beat. Capable? The man was a fucking genius.

"Well, I don't have a cell phone." She sounded deflated.

"I will get you one as soon as possible, my lady."

I let my admiration for Adrian glide over my link with Abbadonna. To say I felt pride from her would be a bit like saying that Pompeii had suffered a small fire. "He's good."

"He's my son," she replied as if that were the only possible response.

"Adrian?" I looked in the rearview mirror.

"Yes, my lord?"

"Where the hell am I going?" I was genuinely at a loss. I couldn't remember where the hell the Consulate was.

"Brooklyn, my lord." He leaned over the seat to touch the GPS screen. "Red Hook."

"My father made me read a story about Red Hook once," Annessa mused.

"Lovecraft," I said. "I wonder what he knew."

"Too much," Adrian whispered. "Just a bit too much."

CHAPTER 8

The building was an unassuming structure. It was a simple red brick building in the middle of an industrial area. There was a small ramp that led to an underground parking area. As soon as you got below ground level, the simple facade disappeared. At the bottom of the ramp was a steel barricade; a small call–box with a keypad on a stand allowed you to request entry. Adrian explained that the wrong entry code triggered a second barricade behind the vehicle. After that happened armed guards would ensure that no one got out alive.

"That's a bit harsh," Annessa commented. "What if someone made a wrong turn?"

"What if they were Angelics with a car full of explosives?" he asked her.

"I didn't say it was wrong, Adrian, just that it's harsh." She turned around to look at him. "Don't you think so?"

"My lady, I've spent my entire life in this war," he answered. "You've only just arrived. Our enemies are without mercy. We need to be the same way."

"Yeah, but why can't we be better than they are?"

"In war, your enemy dictates the terms, Annessa." I spoke to her directly for the first time since entering the vehicle. "Anything noble in you will be used as a weapon by the enemy."

"So we should let the enemy bring us to their level?" She threw her hands into the air. "Doesn't that mean that they win anyway?"

"I'm not sure that I have the best answer for that." I put my hand on her knee. "After a while, fighting becomes reflexive and the reasons no longer matter; only winning."

"Winning a war and losing yourself doesn't really seem much like winning," she said as she shoved my hand off of her knee.

I punched in the code that Adrian gave me. The barricade lowered and I drove into the parking garage. I sent Adrian ahead and dismissed Abbadonna after I parked the car. I sat in silence with Annessa. After what seemed an interminable time, she spoke.

"I am so fucking pissed at you," she said in a furious whisper. "It isn't even funny."

"I know," I said quietly. "And for what it's worth, I'm sorry."

"It ain't worth much." She ran her hand over her eyes. "I thought that things would change after you set me free."

"What do you mean?" I turned in the seat to face her.

"I thought I would stop feeling this way." She looked away from me, out the window.

"What way?"

"I don't know, servile," she sighed. "Like pleasing you is the only thing that matters in the world."

"You still feel that way?" I wouldn't have been surprised if she shot me, to be fair. To hear that she still felt bound to me was kind of surprising.

"Well, yeah." She shook her hands in frustration. "And no. You infuriate me. Why can't I ever seem to stay angry with you?"

"That might not be any kind of magic, Annessa," I said solemnly.

"Yeah?" She finally looked at me.

"Let's face it," I shrugged, "I'm Irish."

"And that means what, exactly?" She fought a smile

that threatened the corners of her mouth.

"You just can't help but love me." I smiled at her.

"You really hurt me." She looked at her feet. "I mean it."

"I know, Annessa." I reached for her hand. "I was wrong, I was callous and I'm honestly sorry."

"I really want to be mad at you right now." She looked up at me, her eyes welling with black tears.

"I really wish you wouldn't be." I reached up and held her face in my hands. "I wanted to spare you the pain of seeing me die."

"Do you really think that lying to me was any less painful?"

"Not now, no," I shook my head. "I won't do it again."

"Lie to me or die?" she asked.

"Either, if I can help it." I leaned forward and kissed her. I swear I smelled lilies and jasmine again.

"You better not," She punched me lightly in the chest and sniffed. "I mean it; next time I'll fucking kill you."

"I believe you." I headbutted her.

I got out and walked around to let her out. As I took her hand, a wave of rampant desire hit me. It was a like an electric shock of pure animal lust. I nearly climbed on top of her right then. It took all of my self–control to pull myself away.

"Something's wrong." I turned away from her and clenched my fists hard enough to dig my nails into my palms.

"What is it, Master?" She reached out to touch me.

"Don't Annessa!" I jerked away from her. "Don't touch me!'

She recoiled as if slapped. "What is it? What the fuck did I do?"

"Something's wrong with me; I can't control myself right now." I trembled with want of her. You have to understand, it isn't that there was anything necessarily stopping me from taking her right then. We all know that I really did want to, but the problem was that this desire wasn't mine. Someone was fucking with my emotions, with my mind.

"There's a quick way to fix that, Master," she laughed throatily. "There's always the backseat."

I smelled it again, lillies and jasmine. I whipped around and pulled her to me. I inhaled her scent, starting at her neck and as I ran my face along hers, I found it. Her lips, I could smell Sheena's scent on her lips. Motherfucker. I raised my hand and spoke a short incantation that stripped away all of Annessa's makeup.

"Where'd you get this makeup, Annessa?" I asked as calmly as I could.

"One of Harker's girls, why?" she answered as she brushed her lips against mine.

"Do you know where they got it?" I pressed my lips against her neck and breathed in the true scent of her skin, which was only slightly less narcotic.

"No," she pressed herself against me. "You sure like garages, Master."

I laughed and the spell was broken. "Give me your makeup, Annessa. All of it."

"What?" She looked appalled.

"It reeks of faerie wine." I held out my hand.

"What the hell is faerie wine?" she asked as she reached for her purse.

"It's what the fae use to knock people out before they devour their souls and what Leanan Sidhe use as perfume to fuel the desires of their 'clients.'" I took her purse and began pulling out make–up. "Someone went through a lot of trouble to make sure I found you irresistible."

"So what're you saying?" She looked hurt.

I spoke a Word of destruction and watched as the makeup dissolved in my hand. "I'm saying someone wasted their time." I reached for her. "Magic or no, I know what I want." I kissed her gently.

"That's good," she smiled and headbutted me. "I'd hate to have to take you by force."

"That might be interesting," I grinned.

"Lets go before you decide to burn my clothes too,"

she laughed and pulled me toward the door.

"So, we're good, you and me?" I asked.

"We always were," she said over her shoulder. "You just needed a reminder that you aren't alone anymore."

The Consulate's interior couldn't have been more different than its humble facade. It was easily the most opulent place in which I had ever set foot. Not that it was gaudy; no, it was all very tasteful, but it just screamed wealth. Adrian led us into the elevator.

"When we get to the Consular–General's office, my lord, it might be prudent to give Annessa a moment alone with the Consul–General," Adrian advised me.

I thought of his reaction to Annessa and nodded. "That sounds wise to me, Adrian."

"I don't see what the big deal is," Annessa shrugged. "It's just me."

"You are a treasure of the faithful, Annessa." I pulled her to me. "And you're a pillar of their faith. Try to remember that."

"Well, right now, I'm a treasure with no fucking make–up." She touched her face. "I feel like a dollar–store Mona Lisa."

I laughed. "You look beautiful, Annessa. Don't be ridiculous."

Adrian was already on his phone. "It is taken care of, my lady."

"Don't enable her, Adrian," I shook my head. "You're only going to make it worse."

"I can't bear to see her pout, sir." He bowed in mock contrition. "It breaks my heart."

"I like him," Annessa giggled and clapped her hands like an excited cheerleader.

I threw my hands into the air. "And you people wonder why I worked alone for so long?"

The elevator doors opened sparing me any more idiocy. Adrian escorted us down a long hallway to Erzebet's office. There was a large waiting area with leather backed mahogany chairs just outside the office. I wondered just how many visitors Erzebet actually received. He knocked once, announced Annessa's presence and shut the door as soon as Annessa entered. He nodded at me.

"This might take a minute or ten, sir," he smiled.

"Good, there are some things I want to talk to you about." I motioned toward the chairs in the waiting area.

"Yes, my lord?" he asked as he sat down.

"Did our people track the snipers?" I touched my forehead reflexively.

"Yes, my lord. We accounted for all three." He pulled his phone out and tapped the screen showing a map of midtown Manhattan, three pulsing dots flared in the area of St Patrick's Cathedral.

"What the hell are they doing there?" I asked.

"I'd guess sitting in the pews, praying," Adrian answered. "You aren't known for your restraint, my lord."

"Well, we're going to need to get them out of there soon." I grimaced. "What about the others that were at the meeting, his lookouts and such?" An operation like this probably took close to thirty people.

"We have them as well, my lord," he nodded.

"Show me on the map," I gestured to his phone.

"You misunderstand, my lord," he chuckled. "We have them here."

I clapped him on the shoulder. "That's the best news I've had in a while."

My phone vibrated in my pocket. I slid it out and saw Cassidy's frowning portrait on the face of my phone. I held up a hand to Adrian and answered it.

"What's going on, Cassidy?" I hoped that the news was good, with Cassidy that was unlikely.

"The house is a mess," he said with a sigh. "The local magistrates got here, between them and the fools from last night, there is next to nothing here."

"So you have no leads?" This wasn't good.

"I have uncovered a few very tenuous leads, Little Brother, but I doubt they will amount to much," he sounded defeated.

"I'll see what I can glean from the men we captured, maybe between the two of us, we can come up with something." I tried to sound hopeful even though I was anything but.

"I appreciate your assistance, Little Brother."

"It's not like I don't owe you." I hung up.

"Nothing?" Adrian asked.

"Nothing worth mentioning," I replied. "Hopefully, the morons you collected have something worthwhile."

The door to Erzebet's office opened; her slight frame a silhouette against the windows behind her. "My Lord Emissary," she curtsied, the woman actually *curtsied*. "I bid you welcome and I humbly apologize for keeping you waiting."

"I understand, Erzebet," I smiled as I entered the office. "How are things?"

"Mostly just business as usual, my Lord." She gestured toward chairs in front of her massive oak desk. Annessa grinned at me from one of the chairs, her legs folded beneath her. Enchantment or not, it was still cute as hell. The walls of the office were covered in bookshelves.

I smiled as I looked around. "A man could spend eternity in here," I whistled as I looked at all of the books.

"I fear you would find yourself terribly bored, my Lord Emissary," she laughed lightly. "Most of these books are on subjects that you probably know better than the authors."

"Maybe, but it never hurts to read another perspective." I leaned forward in my chair, facing her. "So what's so pressing?"

"Nothing, my lord." She folded her hands before her. "I just wished to get a bit better acquainted now that you seem to have realized the usefulness of our organization."

"Was that an insult?" I smiled and held up a hand. "No, don't bother apologizing. I understand and I accept your criticism." I stood. I can't help pacing. "I've ignored the Consulate for the last six years. For your part, you've done exceptionally well, and I appreciate your recent assistance."

"We were truly honored to assist you, my lord." She sat back in her chair, relaxed. "We hope to be of greater assistance in the future."

"There are some things that we could use some help with now," I began. "We need to find out as much as possible about the new Heavenly emissary. We need to gather as much intelligence as we can on the changes to the structure of the Higher Church. This emissary seems to dislike Gifted. How are they adapting to the change, and more importantly, can we exploit this?"

"I will see what I can do, my lord," she replied as wrote furiously in a tablet on her desk. She set down her pen. "We've been seeing some interesting requests for asylum of late, my lord."

"Really?" That was interesting. "Like what?"

She picked up a pair of reading glasses as she flipped through her tablet. "Several unaligned sorcerers, a few witches and three werewolves." She set her glasses back down.

"Werewolves?" I made a face. "They were ours to begin with, how's that news?"

"No, my lord, you misunderstand." She sat back with a satisfied smile. "They were Hounds of God."

"What're Hounds of God?" Annessa asked as I paced by her.

"Morons," I answered. "Morons who thought that they could escape their curse by running to the Angelics."

"What my Lord Emissary means, Sacred Mother," Erzebet interjected in a school–marmish tone. "Is that these creatures sold their services to the Church, in the hopes that their souls would find their way to Heaven when they died."

"How does that make them morons?" Annessa made a face at me.

"Because werewolves aren't men that turn into killers." I reached out and touched her face. "They're killers that turn into wolves. They're barred from Heaven just like you and me."

"What about forgiveness?"

"It's largely a myth," I explained as I knelt beside her. "You can't just yell 'save me, Lord!' then keep murdering to your heart's content. It's kind of understood that you'll bring yourself under control and live the way Yahweh intends his followers to live."

"Living the will of Yahweh isn't exactly possible when your hands are perpetually soaked in innocent blood," Adrian spoke from the doorway. "Werewolves lack control, they're pretty much walking collateral damage, my lady."

"What about Cassidy?" Annessa protested. "He wouldn't kill like that."

"Ah, yes," Erzebet intoned condescendingly. "The Apostate. He's a unique case."

"Why'd you call him that?" Annessa sat up, offended.

"Cassidy served Satan about a thousand years ago. Shit happened; he left. End of story." I spoke harshly; this was a conversation that I wasn't going to have. Apostate or not, Satan had released him, and I wasn't going to hear him disparaged.

"So now these werewolves have turned traitor twice?" Annessa asked. "How's anyone supposed to trust them?"

"They have agreed to take the Traitor's Oath," Erzebet explained. "They are expected to die in the service of Satan, only an honorable death will expunge their transgression and grant them rest."

"They might be useful soon." I rubbed a hand across the scar on my neck. "Any other news?"

"Rumors, my lord." She reached for her tablet again. "Unsubstantiated at the moment, but nevertheless relevant. Apparently, a new murder of vampires has been seen in the city."

"Where?" This was unsettling; the last thing we needed now was a vampire turf war.

"Midtown, my lord." She set her glasses down. "However, as I said, this is entirely unsubstantiated."

"Try to find out more." I took Annessa's hand and helped her to her feet. "And let's hope it's unfounded." I guided Annessa toward the door.

Erzebet walked over to escort us out. She curtsied, took Annessa's hand and kissed it. "Your presence here today has honored me greatly, Sacred Mother."

Annessa pulled the older lady to her feet and kissed

her hand. "By the five points and fires of Perdition, may the Firstborn hold you in his hand."

I smiled; Annessa was learning.

"And you as well, Mother." Erzebet bowed her head as Annessa exited.

Erzebet placed her hand on my bicep. "A word in private, my lord?"

I waved Annessa and Adrian away, "I'll be right there." I turned back to Erzebet. "What's on your mind?"

She wrung her hands in uncertainty. "I'm unsure how to say this, my lord."

"I've found when you have something unpleasant to say, it's best to just spit it the fuck out and deal with it," I laughed. "Just say what's on your mind."

"She's not meant for you, my lord." Erzebet deflated a bit after speaking.

"Who?"

"The Sacred Mother, my lord." She paced jerkily. "I see the way that you two look at each other, and I fear for you both."

"When the time comes, what needs to happen will happen, Erzebet. Until that time, I think she and I are safe to make our own choices." I didn't like where she was going, not because it wasn't her place, but because she might be right. In my heart, she felt right. While Satan had, in essence, given her to me, she remained the Sacred Mother. At some point she would have to give birth to the Chosen Son, and I couldn't seem to find any way that I fit into that particular picture.

"My lord, look to the world around us," she sighed and took my hands. "I have walked this earth for two hundred years and I am young by all accounting, but never before have the signs seemed so clear; the End is coming."

I kissed her hands and softly spoke a Word and made the sign of the five points on her brow. "Thank you, Erzebet."

"For what, my lord?" she asked nervously.

"Your honesty." I patted her hand and walked out much more worried than I'd entered.

CHAPTER 9

I shut the door behind me as I left Erzebet's office. I caught up to Annessa and Adrian at the elevator.

"What was that about, Master?" Annessa leaned against me and put her arm around my waist.

"Just some friendly advice." I brushed a wayward strand of hair away from Annessa's face. "No big deal."

"Where are we headed now?" she asked.

"To get some answers." I stretched and flexed my back. "And more than likely, to feed you."

"You keep feeding me like this I'm gonna have hips like a cow," she laughed.

"You may need them sooner than we thought." I kissed the top of her head.

"What?" She looked up at me. "What's that supposed to mean?"

"Nothing," I pinched her ass. "I'm just in a mood, I guess."

"Well, get out of it." She pinched the back of my thigh, hard.

"Ow, shit, ok!" I jerked away from her. "Adrian, take us to where ever you stashed these bastards before she does that again."

"As you wish, my lord." He hit the elevator button.

"Though to be fair, it did get you out of your mood, sir."

Annessa did it again.

"Adrian," I started as I rubbed the back of my leg and swore profusely.

"Yes, my lord?" he asked, smiling innocently.

"Remind me to kill you."

"It will be on the very top of my list, sir."

I cleared my throat and rolled my neck as I got in the elevator. I couldn't help the nervous energy that flooded me. It was always like this. It was part of why I loved the job so much. It was like skydiving or bungie–jumping or whatever you people do as a safe alternative to real danger. I stretched my shoulders and chest. Annessa's eyes had begun to glow in expectation; she flexed her hands and her jaw. The elevator came to a halt and Adrian walked calmly out with Annessa and I following, huffing and puffing like prizefighters preparing to charge into the ring. The hallways were no longer richly appointed affairs, but brutal gulag–like concrete and steel. He stopped in front of a steel door with a massive security padlock on it.

"They're in here, my lord." He moved to unlock the door.

"Annessa, as soon as that door opens," I said. "Move in and kill all of them but one. We're going for brutal here. The last one alive has to have an idea of just how serious we are."

"My lord, there are eighteen prisoners in there," Adrian sounded incredulous.

"Oh, is that all?" Annessa asked, sweetness dripping off of her tongue. She flexed her jaw and growled as her fangs extended. "We shouldn't be but a minute, Adrian, dear."

He opened the door. I admit I cheated a bit; I pushed as soon as I saw the door open a slight gap, and flitted through the Veil as I had when I tried to fight Vincenze. It only gave me a quarter second lead on Annessa. I appeared in the room like a flash of lightning. I roared a Word and annihilated the first two men. It was as if I hurled buckets of blood through the room. The remaining men began screaming, praying, and begging—some of them all three at once. Annessa hurled through the door behind me, her claws and fangs reflected the horrifying glow of her eyes. She roared, deafeningly loud in the steel room. I hurled Words, fists and spells, but I couldn't keep up with her. She was like a whirlwind, dashing from body to body, her claws and fangs rending flesh in horrific ways. I'm pretty certain we set a record, which for us is saying something. Granted it was just a bunch of Normals, but hey, practice never hurts.

The last man sat crying in the corner of the room. The dead and rapidly dying lay scattered about him, in some cases literally. I knelt in front of him.

"Do you know who I am?" I asked calmly.

He nodded.

"Will you answer my questions?" I didn't bother to offer any incentive; he knew I was going to kill him. I didn't see any point in lying.

He shook his head and opened his mouth. His tongue was missing. I looked around the room; in every case where I could see an open mouth, there was no tongue. I hadn't noticed the strange intonation on the prayers, nor the lack of enunciation in the pleading during the fight.

"Adrian?" I called in a conversational tone.

"Yes, my lord?" he answered from outside the room.

"Were you aware the prisoners had no tongues?" I asked pleasantly.

"Why, yes, my lord," he called back. "I was."

I looked at Annessa and shook my head in disbelief. "Were you planning to tell us this at any point?"

"Well, my lord, I didn't think their lack of tongues would much affect your killing them."

I snorted. It was kind of funny; I'll give him that. "Would you come in here, please?"

He stepped into the room, gingerly avoiding the piles of entrails and pools of blood. He bowed crisply. "Yes, my lord?"

"How did you propose that we should extract information from a captive who can't speak well enough to make us understand anything," I asked him as I stood up.

"Well, my lord," he swept his hand over the piles of bodies. "You could always use Nagg'resh Vök."

My eyes widened. "On eighteen people?" I gagged reflexively. "I'd be sick for a month."

"What are you two talking about, Master?" Annessa wiped blood from her mouth with the back of her hand.

"Nagg'resh Vök," I explained, "is Necrophagic Sight."

"Necro—whatsit?" she cocked her head at me.

"If I eat their eyes, I can see what they saw for the last few days," I sighed. "It's fucking disgusting."

"You can do that?" Annessa's eyes widened. "You've done that before?"

"Yes and yes," I shuddered. "It's how I learned sorcery."

"So I'm not the only one here that's eaten somebody?" She seemed almost childlike in her pleasure.

"No, my lady," Adrian answered happily. "We've all eaten someone."

"Yeah, well you can fucking eat me, Adrian, if you think for one second that I'm the only one chowing down on eyeballs here." I snapped.

"Can't you guys get sick from eating dead people?" Annessa seemed concerned.

"No," I answered. "When we studied with the Ghūls, we had to drink some of their blood. Unlike normal blood, which gets recycled, their blood remains in our veins feeding on the innate corruption of our bodies."

"So?" Annessa asked. "How does that keep you from getting sick?"

"For a short time, I can use that blood to make myself more Ghūllish." I gagged again. "I really, really don't like doing it."

"It's not so bad, Master." She playfully bumped up against me. "I'll finish whatever you can't eat."

"See, my lord," Adrian smiled. "There's a silver lining to every cloud."

"Remind me to kill you," I growled.

"Top of my list, my lord." He knelt next to a body.

"Shall we begin?"

I sighed and punched the last living captive in the throat. I knelt and began chanting in Ghūllish, *"Kelæm Sûat Veym Nethrëk."* I held my hands in front of my face, my palms facing my eyes. My blood began to boil and I could feel the veins standing out all over my body as my skin went grey. My incisors lengthened and my jaw distended.

"Whoa," Annessa leaned close to my face. "Your eyes are doing that jet black thing again, Master."

I mock snapped at her with my fangs. "Careful not to get too close, little girl."

"I think we both know who'd win a biting contest, Master," she grinned wickedly at me. "And it ain't you."

I grumbled and snatched an eye out of the captive I'd just punched to death. I shook my head in disgust and tossed it back. Imagine for a second, your balance going haywire— like vertigo only about a thousand times worse, then, on top of that, your vision doubles. You can see what the original owner of the eyeball saw on top of seeing what your eyes are seeing now. For whatever reason, I always forget to close my eyes first, and it makes the nausea that much more fun. I slammed my eyes shut and fell forward onto my hands. I relaxed my mind and dove into his vision full–bore.

Unfortunately, you can't hear anything. That is, of course, unless you eat their ears too. As you can imagine, the disorientation is even more profound when you do. I watched as my victim walked around midtown, meeting seemingly random people and exchanging a variety of hand signals and chatting, though without tongues, I imagine it was more lip reading. I was pretty certain that this new guy was copying Iraqi insurgent strategy to a fault. My victim was meeting members of other cells; he didn't know them, so he was forced to use verification techniques like hand signals and though I couldn't hear them (or read lips), I bet he was using established passphrases. I dove through his ocular imprints as fast as I could, trying only to sort out relevant details. I watched myself getting out of the Range Rover and kissing Annessa goodbye. This bastard was so busy trying to get a cheap upskirt view of Annessa he didn't even manage to get my full plate number, idiot. I watched his memories right up until he was captured. Then I jumped out.

I shook off the effect of the magic and retched. I looked over at Adrian who was doing the same. "Only eight more to go, Adrian," I remarked, with mock enthusiasm.

"Only eight?" he grinned. "That isn't so bad, my lord. I had a light lunch anyway."

"Go fuck yourself, Adrian." I threw back another eye.

All in all, it took us about four hours. I really wish I could say that we learned a great deal, but we didn't. The cell structure that this new Emissary had developed was so decentralized that none of the team members that we captured even knew each other. Yeah, so in essence, I ate nine dead, gross human eyes for nothing. I was so going to kill this bastard slowly. I already hated him more than Rachel.

Annessa hauled me to my feet after the last vision was done. "Let's get you home, Master."

I nodded. I really didn't have much to say. I just kept praying I wouldn't burp. And this, right here, this is why you'll never learn sorcery. I really can't say I blame you.

CHAPTER 10

I fell heavily into the bed. I was exhausted. Between dying, resurrection, Veilshock, killing a bunch of people and eating their eyes, I was pretty well spent. Annessa came into the bedroom, with her hair down and wearing simple silk pajamas. She looked completely human. It was odd, really. I'd stopped seeing her that way a long time ago, it seemed. It was as if she had always been a sex–crazed, goth haemunculus. I could have been watching someone's wife come to bed anywhere in the U.S.

She saw me looking at her and stopped. "What?"

"You look normal," I smiled sadly.

She climbed into the bed and straddled me. She pulled her hair behind her ears as she leaned down to look me in the eye. "Is that bad?" she asked.

"I shot you right here." I touched her just above her nose, slight left of center. "I took your life away from you."

She sat back and laughed. "You took away my life?" She shook her head. "You gave me life, Master."

"You're not making sense, Annessa." I grabbed her hands. "I shot you in the face and killed you."

"Yeah," she nodded. "You did. And then you took your magic hand here," she grabbed my left hand and shook it, "and you brought me back. Why are we talking about this again?"

"You look almost like you did when you were alive," I shrugged. "It just brought it back, I guess."

"You have any idea what it's like being the daughter of a mob boss, Master?" She cocked her head to the side.

"No." I really didn't.

"Did you know I was a virgin until you took me in the Sacred Grove?"

"What?" That shocked me. "You've got a filthy mouth for a virgin."

"What's the point of being coy if you're already dead?" she laughed. "I only answered to one person: you. And if you didn't tell me to stop, why the hell would I?"

"Wow." I sat up. "I really had no idea."

"No, you didn't." She shoved me back to my pillows. "You know why I was still a virgin?"

"You were saving yourself for undeath?"

"Funny," she frowned at me. "My daddy was a mob boss. You know who wants to fuck a mob boss's daughter? No one."

"Yeah, I can see how that might be a bit of a problem."

"Do you know why I went to school for economics?" She ran a finger along my lips.

"I'm guessing your father made you?"

"No." She leaned forward and kissed me slowly. "I studied the science of choice because I envied people who got to make them.."

"I see."

"And then you showed up." She smiled. "I remember my last breath, you know."

"Yeah?"

"You were talking to Cassidy and swearing up a storm that someone had already killed me."

"Then you coughed blood all over me."

"And then you said 'Nevermind, we're good' after you shot me."

"Yeah, I guess I did."

"I remember a black tunnel and the sound of rushing water. It was so cold." She shivered.

"That's the Styx, the river of Hate. She and I go way back."

"There was a girl there, too. She had the prettiest eyes; I've never seen purple eyes before."

"Really?"

"Well, you ever seen anyone with purple eyes?"

"No, I mean you saw a girl with purple eyes in Perdition?"

"Yeah, I started to panic and she put her finger on my lips and she said 'Never look back.'" Annessa rested her finger on the bow of her upper lip. "I never have. She was right. There's no reason to ever look back."

"Purple eyes?" I asked again.

"Yeah, you know her?" She raised an eyebrow. "You fuck her too?"

"No, Death did." This didn't make any sense.

"What?" Annessa sat back up. "What do you mean, Death fucked her?"

"Her name was Eurydice; she was the wife of Orpheus."

"Yeah, I know the story."

"No, you don't." I shook my head. "The storybooks ruin everything." I sat up, pushing her off of me.

Annessa rolled onto her side and looked up at me.

"See, Death likes to play games with mortals. I've told you about Coinbound right?"

"Yeah, they're like Death's emissaries, like Ṣafira, right?"

"Right." I grabbed my glass of water from the nightstand. "Well, before he made the first Coinbound, he was forced to harvest the souls of the dead himself. That meant he was away from the Underworld for long periods of time. Well, his wife got bored. She began to entertain herself with several dead heroes, and, of course, word got around that the queen was getting around. Death decided he'd get even. Lo and behold, Eurydice dies suddenly and without warning on the day her wedding. So, brave, beautiful, golden–tongued Orpheus journeys to the Underworld. He begs an audience with Death and sings a song so beautiful that he entrances the Queen of the Dead, right?"

"Right," Annessa nodded.

"Wrong," I corrected her and paused to take a drink. "He gave the Death a means to strike back at Persephone, his queen. See, Persephone was so enamored of the idea of love that she couldn't bear to hold the soul of Eurydice any longer. She begged, pleaded and essentially threw herself at her husband until he relented. He made a deal with Orpheus that he would allow Eurydice to leave the Underworld if Orpheus would leave and not look back. To seal the deal, he gave Eurydice a dusk lily, a purple flower that bloomed on the banks of the Mnemosyne River, the river of Memory— the sister river to the Lethe. The lily was his pledge, the same pledge that he gives the Coinbound. A promise to withhold his touch for a specified time, after which the bound one must serve him, usually for all eternity."

"So, she was forced to serve him because Orpheus was a total fucking moron?" Annessa looked appalled.

"Well, in essence, yes," I conceded.

"That's bullshit, Master."

"That's dealing with gods, Annessa," I shrugged. "They screw you coming and going."

"So what was she forced to do?"

"You sure you want to know?" I asked.

"Well, now I gotta know. You can't just say something like that and expect me not to ask."

"He chained her to base of his throne and made Persephone watch as he took her time and time again."

"Why was he punishing her? Persephone was the whore!" Annessa yelled.

"Calm down, Annessa!" I put my hand on her shoulder. "He had Persephone 'filled' with the thorns from a blood–rose bush and mortared her into the base of the throne room floor, so that the tears of Eurydice fell on her face as she was repeatedly raped by her master."

"Why would he do that?"

"To prove his point. What's love in the face of Death? Nothing; a thing to be used and discarded." I sighed. "Maybe tomorrow we can read *Goodnight Moon* instead?"

"Yeah, I think I'd like that," she laughed. "But what was the point of all of this?"

"Oh, right. Anyway, when Mnemosyne saw what had become of Eurydice, she fell into a horrible depression. After a time, she withered and disappeared. Legend holds that she was so distraught that she killed herself that the dead might never drink of her, but instead of the waters of her sister, Lethe, and lose all memory. This loss of identity would allow the dead to better endure the torments of the Underworld. Yet, when Satan came into the Underworld and remade it in his image, forcing Death to flee into the wastes beyond the Plains of Acheron, neither the goddess, nor the river that is her body ever returned."

"What are the Plains of Acheron, Master?"

"The river of Pain, the Acheron, is the boundary between Perdition and the rest of the Underworld. It's the river from which the Styx, the Phlegethon and the Lethe originate. The plains are the open land between Perdition and the Acheron. Satan dammed the last river, the Cocytus, and formed it into a lake to contain those who betray him, frozen eternally in agony," I explained.

"So how does Eurydice figure into this; you still haven't told me why the girl with purple eyes is a big deal."

"Coinbound get the color of their eyes from the metal of the coin that the Ferryman gives them. Eurydice wasn't given a coin; she was given a purple flower. When her term of service began, her eyes became purple. But what makes this whole damned story relevant is that when the original House of Hades was destroyed and his minions were scattered by the coming of the Fallen Host, Eurydice was freed. No one's seen her since."

"Until me," she whispered.

"Right," I kissed her forehead. "And of all people, she knew the one that would follow her wishes."

"I wish I knew why everyone thinks I'm so special." She seemed genuinely confused.

"I know why I do." I pulled her close to me. "I can't think of anyone else I'd rather have with me."

"Except when you decide to get yourself killed." She gave me that look.

"Let's just forget that happened, ok?" I kissed her softly. "So what happened after Eurydice spoke to you?"

"I don't really remember, it felt warm and it was dark..." She scrunched up her face in concentration. "I can't really remember anything until I woke up on the altar." She looked at me pointedly. "I remember you calling me 'Dead Girl' and being a dick."

"You know what I remember?" I said quickly, trying to change the subject.

"What do you remember?"

"I suddenly remember that I'm exhausted and I need to sleep."

"Funny how that works," she shook her head and laughed.

"Yeah," I pulled her close. "It is."

She kissed me softly and lay next to me until I drifted off.

CHAPTER 11

I awoke the next day to the smell of coffee. I sat up slowly, rubbing my eyes. I'd actually slept through an entire night. I'm not sure you appreciate the gravity of that; I can't remember the last time that happened.

Unfortunately, this would be the last full night I'd get for a while. A small table near the bedroom door had a carafe of coffee and a plate full of pastries. I rolled out of bed, stretched and stumbled toward the coffee. There was a note from Annessa tucked under the coffee mug.

> *Master,*
> *Adrian and I went shopping. Back before you know it.*
> *—Annessa*

Well, that meant two things. First, I had some time. When a woman says the word 'shopping,' the phrase '*for fucking ever*' is implied. Second, I had a chance to take care of some things that needed taking care of. I took a quick shower, threw on a suit and raced out the door. As I stepped out of the elevator, I saw Roger, the doorman, hastily put away a cell phone. I grinned. I like rule–breakers.

"Roger," I asked. "Was that a cell phone?"

"Yes, sir," he responded.

"Are you supposed to have one on duty?"

"No, sir."

"Would you do me a favor?"

'Yes, of course, sir," he nodded.

"Can you text me with your non–existent cell phone, the minute my lady and Mr. Admah return?"

"No problem, sir," he nodded vigorously. "No problem at all."

"Good man." I shook his hand and gave him my number.

The last thing I needed was to give Annessa time to think about where I'd been. I had Roger hail me a cab. As the driver headed to Washington Square Park, I tried to recall every bit of information I knew about the Tuath'an. They were tricky bastards, the fae. The stories that they tell kids these days are nothing at all like the reality.

The Sidhe were a remnant from the last earth; they were creatures of the firmament that moved seamlessly between worlds. They had tricked the world into believing them gods, and thusly, they became gods. They were the greatest liars in all the worlds and they knew it.

Fae survive on humans in the manner of vampires, but they aren't nearly as nice. Fae like to make their prey suffer. But unlike vampires, they don't necessarily kill you outright. For example, you might trade your soul to have a Leanan Sidhe for a year and a day to live as your fae wife. But no matter how long you look, nor how hard you try, you'll never again find a lover that can quell your passion again and it eats at you like cancer. You might drown your sorrows but once with faerie wine and find that nothing in the world can ever bring you joy again. The gifts of the fae are tragedy in a bottle.

What made fae truly dangerous, however, was that even knowing the penalty, knowing the cost, you still hungered for their gifts. Something inside you screamed out in desire, begging, pleading for the one fix, that one little taste of heaven. Someone had paid dearly for Sheena's little trick with Annessa's makeup, and I wanted to know who and why.

Sheena wasn't one to work for promises or favors; she wanted her share of suffering. Don't get me, wrong, I liked her; hell if you saw her, you'd like her. She's a fae courtesan, a whore; her whole job is predicated on making you want her. And trust me, she's good. Oh, like you're shocked. We've already established that I'm Irish; why do you think we have so many kids?

I hopped out of the cab as we hit the park and headed north, my mind on bargaining strategies. The fae put a price on everything, especially information. I stopped for a moment, considering my options as I watched the students milling about near the Arch. They had no idea how close to death they really were. I really wished that I could have Abbadonna or Annessa with me.

Unfortunately, my emissarial authority only extended to me—according to the Tuath'an. I took a breath and threaded my way through the students. I gathered my will and stepped through the Arch. There was a shudder as I passed the Veil.

I stood in a stone hallway lit by torches that flickered and gave off a thick oily smoke. Two impossibly slender, tall, pale guards wearing chainmail and carrying slender swords flanked the doorway at the end of the hall. I nodded at them and stepped forward.

"Good afternoon, gentleman," I began. "Can you direct me to the lord's hall?"

They walked slowly toward me and moved to circle around me. This wasn't good. I looked over my shoulder; the doorway had faded leaving only a blank stone wall. Without the lord's permission, I wasn't leaving the Mound. That's what faerie dwellings are called, incidentally, I'm not sure why. I let the guards circle in behind me. What else was I going to do?

"Guys?" I asked. "Why so hostile?"

"Walk," one of them ordered, gesturing toward the far end of the hallway. I complied silently, my mind racing. What the fuck had these bastards so hostile? I'd never had bad relations with any fae, much less this particular Mound.

All I wanted was to talk to Sheena. This was not all how I had planned my afternoon.

By the time we had reached the huge steel–reinforced oak doors to the lord's hall, I was thoroughly confused, which was the idea, of course. If you managed to stumble into the Mound by accident, or by design, I suppose, the fae wanted you good and terrified before they had their way with you.

"So, one of you two want to tell me why I'm being detained?" I asked.

"Lord's orders," the one with the directions said. "Be silent."

And so I was. I stared at the doors wondering what the hell had gone wrong. I didn't have a long wait to find out. The doors slowly creaked open revealing a massive hall. The rear of the hall, which was closest to me, was full of rows of long tables, each covered with just about any kind of food or drink you could imagine. And crowded around those tables were the lord's nobles, warriors and vassals.

There was a wide walkway down the center of the tables, dividing them, which led to the front of the hall where the lord held court. Standing, grinning in the center of that walkway, directly between the Fae Lord and me was the Heavenly Emissary. Fuck. Me. Twice.

Apparently, his dislike of Gifted was just another layer of deception. I wanted to respect this guy; I really did. Instead, I hated him. He was outsmarting me at every turn and hitting me where it counted without fail. To top it all off, I was no closer to finding out where the hell the last two Umbrals were hiding. None of that mattered right at this moment, of course. What did matter was that I was trapped here, in what had become unfriendly territory with a man who very much wanted to kill me and, with all of the backup he had present, it was very likely that he might.

"Hello, Beckett," he smiled. "You've recovered nicely."

"I never did catch your name," I smiled brightly.

"Alfred St. George." He stepped forward as if he were simply crossing the street. "I wish I could say it was a pleasure to make your acquaintance."

I guess I should have seen it coming. Everything else this prick did was unexpected. But this, no, this was entirely fucking out of the blue. Before I had even realized he was close enough, he hit me in the throat with a vicious hammer fist. I think my Adam's apple hit my spine. The next hit was even faster; a low kick to my right knee sent me stumbling to the ground. He rained hits all over me, as I struggled to stand. I couldn't speak; I could barely breathe. I tried to silently use a Word, a spell, anything, but his fists and feet were striking me so rapidly I couldn't form a coherent thought. Finally, he grabbed my hair and pulled my head up to face him.

"You disgust me," he spat in my face. "Without your witchcraft, you're nothing." With a swift jerk of his wrist he tore my scalp free from my head. The motherfucker scalped me! I dropped to the dirt floor of the hall, my rapidly failing consciousness chased by the laughter of the gathered fae. Without meaning to, without even trying, I'd really fucked up this time. To make matters worse, when and if I finally got out of here, I was going to have to deal with Annessa. Man, was she gonna be pissed.

I awoke face down in the dirt. I struggled to my knees and looked around. My heart sank. I was in a cell; I didn't even need to look to know. The silence was my first clue; fae mounds are always chaotic, and they're never still. To find myself in such stillness meant that I was either outside the mound, or I was trapped. I couldn't imagine a scenario where they'd just let me go; that wouldn't be any fun.

"I am pleased to see that you yet live, Emissary," came a delicate voice behind me. "Though soon, you'll wish you hadn't survived."

I turned and sighed. Sheena Samhradh hung from the wall by her wrists. She was naked. I stood slowly, trying to keep my legs beneath me. I felt like a truck had hit me.

"You look ridiculous," she laughed.

"What?" I looked down at my body. And then the cool sensation on my head reminded me. I slowly reached up and touched my head. Fresh scar tissue covered my scalp. The rest of my head still had long hair. The bastard had given me a bald man's mullet. I think that hurt worse than the beating. I closed my eyes and tried to concentrate over the pain and humiliation. I incanted a spell and burned away the rest of my hair. I spoke a Word to heal myself and felt the scar tissue fade. I ran my hand over my now completely bald head. I resolved myself at that moment to invent a new torment for Mr. Alfred St. George. Something that took a long time to kill you and made burning alive seem fun by comparison.

"Interesting, Emissary," she smiled at me. "Very tough."

"Thanks." I wasn't in the mood.

I walked over to inspect her wrists. They were fused to the stone. That had to hurt a bit; she was supporting all of her weight with just her delicate wrists.

"What'd you do, Sheena?" I asked as I looked over her wrists.

"I sided with the wrong Emissary apparently," she frowned at me. "I had higher hopes for you."

"What happened, anyway?" I stepped back so I could see her face.

"The Angelic emissary made an attractive offer to Lord Eoric," she shrugged then winced as the pain rolled through her shoulders. "Your side failed to produce a counter–offer."

"I was unaware we were bidding for anything, Sheena." I reached out and grabbed her hips and lifted her gently to relieve the pressure in her wrists and shoulders. I swear that's only reason I touched her. It's got nothing to do with her body at all. Nothing.

"The souls of New York," she wrapped her legs around my waist and pulled me closer to her, "will be up for grabs in the near future; we want them."

"What?" I was too shocked by what she said to realize the dangerous position in which I found myself.

"The souls of the unaligned in New York," she strained her neck forward and ran her tongue over my lips. "I want them." The smell of lilies and jasmine slid across my brain. She could have whatever the hell she wanted.

I leaned forward to kiss her when my phone vibrated in my pocket. I shook my head, realized what she was doing and I slapped her. I mean I fucking slapped her; the kind of slap they'd teach in pimp school if such a thing existed. I pulled away from her, dug my phone out of my pocket and saw a text from Roger. That man was getting a raise.

"What the hell is wrong with you?" I yelled at Sheena. "Come on!"

"It was worth a try," she laughed throatily. "You're so damned easy, Beckett.

"This isn't funny, woman!" I grabbed her throat. "I need to get the fuck out of here."

"Good luck with that," she chuckled. "You let me know how that works out for you."

I tried not to lose my temper, but she had to think I was desperate. I turned back to her.

"How do I get out, Sheena?" I asked as calmly as I could.

"Lord Eoric has to decide to release you."

"You realize I could have the entire mound razed for this," I asked.

"You could try," she smirked. "But we all know it won't happen."

"What?"

"Oh come on, Beckett," she laughed. "Of all the men, in all of the worlds, you are by far the most false, faithless human being that's ever lived. Your petty god won't back you and you know it."

"You think so?"

"You've never held to an oath as long as you've lived," she snorted. "Why do you think I like you so much?"

"Well, why don't you just climb down off of that wall and come with me?"

"First, you aren't leaving and second, I can't," she sighed. "I'm geased." A geas is a sort of faerie curse, in a very simple manner of speaking.

"Really?" I turned back to her. "So you can't leave?"

"I'm stuck to a fucking wall, Beckett."

"That's too bad."

"You think?" She rolled her eyes at me.

"While we're here, maybe you can shed some light on a situation for me," I slowly ran my hand across the surface of the walls. They were all uniform with each having a sconce with a burning torch mounted at the top–center of the wall.

"What might that be?" she asked.

"How is that my haemunculus wound up with faerie wine laced make–up?" I pushed firmly against the wall across from Sheena.

"That's going to cost you, Emissary," she chuckled quietly.

"Really?"

"Nothing worthwhile is ever free."

"What do you want in trade?" I slid my hands along the next wall.

"A kiss." She smiled serenely at me.

"No." I shook my head as I pushed on the wall. "Try again."

"It's just a kiss, Beckett," she pouted. "Surely you won't deny me that?"

"I can and I did." I put my arms to either side of her and pushed on the wall; my face was dangerously close to her breasts. She needed to think I was going to fall for her glamour. "How about I get you down from this wall?"

"I wish you could." She thrust her chest out toward me.

I grinned as I slid my arm behind her and invoked the blessing of Leviathan. No wall, no barrier, no force in the universe would impede me. I yanked her off of the wall, my sorcery shattering the geas. I dove forward, crushing her to the ground.

"Tell me," I growled, my face inches from hers. "Now."

"Not fair, Beckett," she whimpered.

"Fuck fair, tell me."

"Sarah," she whispered.

"What?"

"Six weeks ago, Sarah Halverson came to me and we struck a bargain." She squirmed beneath me trying to get away.

"What were the terms?" I pulled her back to me.

"Whichever of Harker's girls that left his office first on the night you entered the club after Sarah's death, I was supposed to give her make–up dosed with faerie wine."

"What did you get in return?" My hand tightened on her throat.

"A memory!" She pushed at me. "Nothing more!"

"What memory?"

"The memory of her brother."

"Her brother?" I froze.

"Yeah, nice looking guy, too," she grinned. "Wouldn't mind trading him something."

"You sold it, didn't you?" I pushed her away. "You sold the fucking memory."

She nodded.

"To Eoric?"

She nodded again.

"You stupid, stupid bitch." I leapt to my feet. "Do you have any idea what you've done?"

"No," she shook her head. "Beckett, it was just a memory! What's the harm?" She staggered back to her feet.

"You've might have just damned us all." I knelt and closed my eyes.

'Beckett?" she asked quietly. "What are you doing?"

"Praying." I held up my hand to cut off any further words.

I focused all of my thought on my Lord. I stilled my heart and pushed all other thoughts to the side. I didn't need to contact him; I already knew what he would have me do. I guess I just wanted a moment to gather myself before committing myself to localized genocide.

I stood. I spoke a Word of darkness and extinguished three of the torches. I faced the corner, which was now deeply shadowed.

"Uthiel!" I roared. There was a familiar bass thump as he coalesced.

"My Lord Emissary." He looked down at me. "What is your bidding?"

"Tear the mound apart, kill everything that moves, except for Lord Eoric," I ordered.

"And this sack of meat?" he nodded at Sheena.

"Leave her with me."

"As you wish," he nodded. He turned toward the shadow and his pack flooded the small cell. With the slightest wave of his hand, he shattered the wall of the cell. He inclined his head at me quickly and with that he was gone. It only took a second before the screams began. It would take a long time before they ended.

"Beckett," Sheena whispered. "You can't leave me here."

"Can't I?" I grinned evilly. "I'm the most faithless, false human being that's ever lived, or hadn't you heard?"

"You don't know why she did it!" she nearly screamed at me.

"You owe me that for not letting Uthiel kill you." I stroked her hair with feigned kindness.

"What will it take, Beckett?" Her eyes were wild. Granted she was listening to the murder of her entire extended family, so it's fairly understandable. Before you judge, remember that they earned it.

"Your oath, binding eternal allegiance." I lifted her chin so she could see my eyes and just how serious I was.

"Fine, I'll swear loyalty to you!" Of course she would; she knew just how to manipulate me.

"Not to me," I lifted my left hand. "To Him."

She froze. I turned and walked toward the hole in the wall.

"It's too much, Beckett," she whimpered. "It's too much."

"Nothing worthwhile is ever free."

I made it about ten steps before she ran screaming after me.

"Please, Beckett! Wait!"

I turned.

"I'll do it," she nodded frantically.

"This is of your own free will?" I asked.

"Yes!" She grabbed my left hand and kissed it. "Please!"

I placed my hand on the right side of her face. "Swear, if you so choose."

"I swear to serve the Lord of Perdition for the entirety of my existence." She placed her hand over mine.

"So be it." I made the sign of the five points on her forehead and kissed the mark gently. "Welcome, sister."

She nodded mutely then gasped as she felt the magic take hold. She ran her hand over her heart and looked up at me.

"Take me to the Lord's Hall," I ordered. I didn't have time for her to adjust to her new place in the world.

"This way," she said and took off down the hall.

I chased her through the blood–soaked labyrinthine tunnels. It's funny when you consider the fae were used to being the hunters, not the prey in these very same tunnels. As we entered the Lord's Hall, Uthiel was tearing one of the tall, skinny guards in half. I can't say I felt any remorse. Three of the Daephym had Lord Eoric pinned against his throne, their spears at his neck. I walked to the throne and stood before him.

"Hail to you, Lord Eoric." I bowed low.

"H–Hail to you Emissary," he stammered. "I bid you welcome."

"See?" I smiled. "This is how such things are meant to be done. But you," I waggled a finger at him. "You decided on a different route today."

"I was misled, Emissary!" he cried.

"No," I said. "You were mistaken."

"I was!" he nodded, as much as the encroaching spears would allow. "But now, now I see the truth."

"I can't tell you how that gladdens my heart." I clapped my hands together. "And now, you're going to tell me what you bargained for all those souls promised you by the inimitable Mr. St. George."

"A memory!" he yelled almost before I finished speaking. "Just a memory, nothing more!"

I stepped forward onto the dais. "Didn't it strike you as strange that so much could be purchased for a memory?"

He yelled something in Faery to Sheena. I turned and faced her.

"What'd he say?" I demanded.

"He commanded me to kill you since your back was turned." She glared at him. "Normally, I'd have had no choice."

"Bad form, my Lord," I said as I turned back to him.

"She's the one who took the memory!" he screamed. "Kill her, not me!"

"Oh, I'm not going to kill you, Lord Eoric," I smiled brightly at him.

"You're not?" he asked cautiously.

"No." I stepped closer to him. "You allowed an Emissary to be attacked and illegally imprisoned within the confines of your domain. In keeping with the Accords, you will be brought before the Lord whose emissary you imprisoned. So you see, killing you would have been a mercy." I sneered at him, "I'm not feeling very merciful today." I gestured to the Daephym holding him.

He screamed as they ripped him from his throne. It's a shame, really. He should have held the scream; it's all he'll be hearing for the rest of eternity. I sat heavily on the dais. I pulled out my phone and called Adrian.

"Is Annessa with you?" I asked.

"Yes, my lord," he answered.

"You know you just sold me out, right?" I asked. Now Annessa knew it was me on the phone for sure.

"Yes, my lord."

"Where are you?" I asked.

"Home, sir," he replied.

"Tell him we got him presents!" I heard Annessa yell.

"We've got presents for you, my lord."

"Thanks."

"It's the least we could do, sir," he replied flippantly.

"I'm going to kill you, Adrian."

"Yes, sir, I'm to remind you," he commented. "It's on the top of my list."

"Just come get me," I said.

"Where are you, sir?"

"Washington Square Park, the Arch." Shit, Sheena. "I'm going to need you to bring me women's clothing, Adrian."

"Trying something new, my lord?"

"What?" Oh for fuck's sake. "They're not for me, you asshole."

"I'm not judging, sir. Brave new world and all that."

I put my head in my hands. "I hate you so much."

"What size should they be, sir?"

"About your mother's size," I said.

"That's not funny, sir. I love my mother very much."

"ADRIAN!" I screamed at the phone.

"With or without wings, sir?"

"Without." I looked down at my blood soaked clothes. "Bring me something to wear too."

"We should be there in ten minutes."

"She's going to kill me," I moaned.

"Chin up, sir."

"Just call me when you get here." I hung up and put my phone away.

Sheena sat down next to me. "What now?"

"Now, you tell me why," I began. "Why Sarah wanted me clouded with desire for Annessa."

"I don't think it's quite that simple, Beckett." she sighed and leaned toward me. "She knew something."

"What do you mean?" I asked.

"Well, she knew that something momentous was happening; I could tell that from her body language," she grinned like a satisfied cat. "I've been trading secrets long enough to know when someone has one, and she had a big secret. She reeked of it."

"Can you maybe not talk in circles?" I tapped my wrist. "We're short on time."

"More than you know." She stood and walked down the dais steps. "She knew she was going to die, that much I know for sure."

"Go on."

"I'm not really sure how to say this, Beckett." She put her hands behind her back and looked up at me.

"Just fucking say it, then," I growled. "I'm sick of waiting."

"I'm guessing she knew that something big was happening, and she wanted you focused on something other than her death." She gave me a sly wink. "She picked the one thing that was sure to distract you."

"Sex?" I asked derisively.

"No," she laughed lightly. "A woman to protect."

"What?" I snorted and shook my head. "Annessa hardly needs protecting."

"Spoken like a fool," she sneered. "When battle is joined does no one worry for your safety, oh great and terrible Emissary?"

"It isn't the same."

"No?" she laughed again. "Even the bravest man, the strongest soldier, is held to be fragile by someone, not by virtue of their skill at arms, but of their value to the heart of the party principally concerned."

"That doesn't sound like Sarah." I stood violently. "Our friendship meant more to her."

"That's why she sought to protect you." Sheena spoke as if she were talking to a child. "If you were busy trying to protect someone, you would be on top of your game."

"So she paid you to dope Annessa's make-up?" I shook my head, something wasn't adding up. "Sarah would've seen that I'd come to care for her regardless."

"Maybe she wanted to make sure?"

"Sarah was the most Gifted seer in a hundred years," I protested angrily. "She didn't need to 'make sure.' She knew she was right."

"So what did she hope to accomplish, then?" Sheena threw up her hands. "Because obviously I'm completely fucking stupid." Why do women always equate being wrong once with being stupid? It's just, well, it's just stupid.

"Don't be so dramatic." I started pacing. "What if it had nothing to do with Annessa and everything to do with you?"

"You mean she set me up so you would come looking for me?"

"No," I paused as the gravity of the situation hit me. "She wanted to give you her memory."

"Why?"

"So she wouldn't have it when the Umbrals took her." I paced rapidly.

"Ok, why does that matter?"

"Her brother is the last son of Solomon."

"Sweet Danu," she whispered. "What have I done?"

"Did Eoric sell that memory to anyone other than St. George?" I wasn't so much pacing now as jogging back and forth.

"I don't think so." She ran her hands through her hair as she turned a slow circle.

"You don't think, or you don't know?"

"Not that I know of," she spat. "How's that, you self–righteous prick?"

My phone rang. I answered it without looking. "Just come through the Arch, and hurry." I hung up. As I lowered my hand it dawned on me that I didn't know the number on the face of my phone. I felt the sick, sinking sensation that always accompanied the return of my luck.

"What is it?" Sheena stepped toward me as she saw my face go pale.

I held out my hand to push her back. As I registered the yielding flesh of her breast on my palm, I heard the heralding cry of my luck's arrival.

"Master," her voice was icy. "Care to explain yourself?"

I hate being Irish.

CHAPTER 12

I turned as I tore my hand away from Sheena's breast. Annessa walked into the Lord's Hall with Adrian in tow, and her eyes were glowing like lanterns in the dark. Adrian had his hands full of shopping bags.

"I was just trying to push her away," I started. I realized immediately that that was the wrong choice of words.

Annessa launched herself forward, reaching Sheena before I could even correct myself. She grabbed Sheena by the throat, jerked her off of her feet and slammed her to the floor. Her fangs were extended as she pulled Sheena's stunned and startled face within inches of her own.

"Annessa!" I screamed. "Let her go now!" I reached down and grabbed Annessa's arm.

"Give me one good reason why I shouldn't tear off this whore's tits, Master," she growled.

"Nothing happened, Annessa!" I, somewhat carefully, took her chin in my hands and made her look at me. "Nothing happened or was going to happen. This is all a misunderstanding," I spoke calmly and quietly.

Before Annessa could release her hold, Sheena shifted. Fae can shapeshift like few other creatures and Leanan Sidhe moreso than most. Sheena became smoke and slowly coalesced into a hazy silhouette of herself in front of Annessa. As Annessa turned to face her, Sheena threw a punch and in the microseconds before impact, she shifted to stone. The punch hurled Annessa half of the length of the hall.

"I don't know who the fuck you think you—" Sheena began. She stopped short as the barrel of Adrian's .45 came to rest just below her left ear.

"She's the Sacred Mother," he growled. "And these bullets are cold iron." He cocked the hammer.

I'd had enough. I raised my Mark and roared a Word of command. Everyone froze, their eyes locked on me.

"That's enough!" I yelled. "Everyone needs to calm the fuck down!"

I walked over to Annessa and picked her up like an injured child. I turned to face Adrian.

"Lower your weapon." I nodded at Sheena. "She's one of ours."

As Adrian complied, I looked down at Annessa in my arms. "Why can't you ever come in when I'm talking about how amazing you are?"

"What happened to your hair?" she asked dazedly.

"I thought I'd try something different." I set her down. "I'll tell you about it on the way."

"Where are we going?" she asked.

"Harker's, we're going to need all of the help we can get." I looked at Adrian. "Did you bring the clothes I requested?"

He nodded back to the pile of bags he'd left behind in order to subdue Sheena.

"See if any of that fits, Sheena," I ordered.

I don't think Adrian's eyes left her the entire time. I also don't think his interest was entirely protective. I can't say I blame him. Annessa ran her hand over the back of my head. I turned to face her.

"Why didn't you wait for me?" she asked.

"To be honest, I really thought this was going to be a friendly visit." I put my arms around her. "Had I known what was going to happen here today," I breathed in the scent of her, "I wouldn't have gotten out of bed."

"I really hate it when you do things like this." She

rested her head against my chest.

"No you don't," I chuckled. "You just hate it when I do it without you."

"So?" I felt her grin.

"I prefer it when you're with me, you know." I kissed her head.

"Yeah?"

"I get my ass kicked a lot less when you're around," I sighed.

"I got you presents," she said.

"Yeah?"

"Yeah, but I don't think you get them today." She shook her head.

"Why not?"

"You had your hands all over that whore's tits." I could feel her smile against my chest.

"It was only one tit," I grinned. "And I was thinking of you the whole time."

"That's not funny," she protested as she kicked my shin.

"I never figured you for the jealous type," I said as I gritted my teeth against the pain.

"No?" She frowned at me. "Why not?"

"You can feel my emotions," I said as I leaned down to rub my shin. "Can't you?"

"Yeah."

"What was I feeling when you came in here?" I asked.

"Her breast," Annessa answered quickly.

"Smart ass." I took her hand. "Let's get the hell out of here."

"It wasn't you I was worried about, Master." she explained. "That woman needs to know her place."

"Well, she's aware of it now," I chuckled. "She's very aware of it now."

I lead her over to Adrian, who was still watching Sheena.

"Where are my clothes?" I asked him.

He looked at Annessa and raised an eyebrow questioningly. He opened his mouth, shut it and pointed at the only bag that Sheena hadn't emptied.

I opened the bag. I looked over at Sheena who was now dressed in a business suit with a skirt. It was bit tight in the right places, but professional nonetheless. I looked back in the bag.

"You got her a suit," I tried to remain calm, "and you got me this?" I lifted a Behemoth concert t–shirt, a pair of black jeans and black Doc Martens out of the bag.

Adrian's mouth worked like a fish out of water for a second. "It was entirely her idea, sir," he pointed at Annessa.

"Presents!" She smiled brightly at me. "We can match." She did a slow turn so I could see her matching t–shirt and jeans. I was thankful my jeans weren't so tight.

I threw off my shredded suit and put on the new clothes. It wasn't so much that I disliked the clothes, as it was that I had a standard to maintain. At least I liked the band; all in all, it could have been worse.

"Let's go." I was already dialing my phone as we headed for the exit.

"What are you going to do with the Mound, Beckett?" Sheena asked as she passed through the Arch.

"Sever the gate, and leave it abandoned as a warning to those who would doubt my faith." I rested my hand on the Arch and spoke a Word of destruction, severing the gate and making the Arch just a landmark once more.

"For what it's worth, Beckett," she looked at the Arch sadly, "I'll never doubt you again."

CHAPTER 13

Cassidy picked up his phone as I was climbing into the truck. I took a deep breath and told him what had transpired at the Mound.

"Do you have any idea where this St. George is at the moment, Little Brother?" he asked.

"None."

"Then I shall make inquiries." He was so goddamned calm.

"Harker's in an hour?" I asked.

"Very well."

I hung up and started the truck. I had no idea where to even begin solving this problem. Annessa climbed into the Range Rover and looked at me.

"You ok, Master?"

"No," I answered honestly. "We have a serious problem."

"We always have serious problems." She took my hand. "And we always get through them the same way."

"I'm not sure rolling in with guns blazing will make anything better this time," I said. "I can't get my mind around this guy. What does he need with Solomon's heir?"

"You remember Cassidy saying how the simplest solution is usually the right one?"

"Yeah."

"Maybe we're looking at this wrong. What's the problem we're dealing with?"

"Why does St. George need the identity of Solomon's heir, I guess."

She shrugged. "Ok, so why does he?"

"I have no idea."

"What if wasn't a memory he bought."

"What do you mean?" I asked, confused as hell.

"Just go with me, my dad used to do this."

"Do what?"

"Talk it out. He used to say the dumbest mook in the room had all the answers; it was a matter of knowing the right questions." She grinned.

"Great, so now we've resorted to Mafia self–help tactics?" I shook my head and rested it on the steering wheel.

"My dad owned this fucking city," she said heatedly as she threw her finger in my face. "Joke all you want, he wasn't fucking stupid!"

"Whoa," I sat up and put a hand on her thigh. "Easy, I didn't mean it like that," I sighed. "I'm just at a goddamned loss here."

"Fine." She sat back in her seat.

"Okay," I stared out the window into the park. Twenty feet from my window, a kid in an NYU hoodie palmed a tiny plastic bag to another kid who handed him a fifty-dollar bill. "Heroin."

"What?" She looked over at me, her anger and consternation plain on her face.

"Hypothetically, St. George bought heroin," I said, still staring at the dealer. "From that little prick right there." I pointed.

"Okay," she sat forward to look past me. "So what's he gonna do with it now?"

"Shit, I don't know." I shook my head. "Cut it with baby laxative and sell it to hipsters in Brooklyn?"

"So, he's gonna sell it?" she asked.

"Right," I nodded.

"Who needs information about Solomon's heir cut with baby laxative?"

"The Umbrals."

"Makes sense," she shrugged.

"Why would he want to help the Umbrals? If they kill Solomon's heir, we're all dead."

"Why's that kid selling heroin?" She waved her hand vaguely at the park.

"Extra money," I thought about it for a second. "Pay off a debt, maybe?"

She cocked her head to the side. "What happens if you don't pay off a debt?"

"Your dad's goons show up and kneecap me." I made a shooting motion with my thumb and forefinger.

"So you pay to stay safe and keep Mikey and Jimmy away?"

"Yeah, but," I shook my head. "The Umbrals are already locked away; he's already safe from them."

"Who else is he afraid of, then?"

"Satan, but that's not really an issue until…" I waved off the rest of the sentence.

"Until what?"

"Until the Man Upstairs kicks off the War."

"That doesn't make any sense," she looked out her window, lost in thought. "My uncle, Giovanni!" she sat bolt upright and punched my shoulder hard.

"Ow, shit!" I rubbed my arm. "What the fuck are you talking about?" Subconsciously, I looked for Volkswagens.

"My uncle, Giovanni," she gestured furiously with her hands. "You know, he got killed last year."

"Right," I nodded slowly, backing away from her. "It was in the news; he started a gang war or something?"

"Yeah, he pissed off a bunch of Cubans and some Mexican gang." She waved her through the air as if conducting the world's most spastic orchestra. "Get it?"

I nodded. "No," I said after a dramatic pause. "Did you sneak out and buy something from that little shit," I jerked a thumb at the drug dealer, "when I wasn't looking?"

"He started the war so he could grab territory from both of them." She grabbed my hands. "My dad told him not to, but he did it anyway."

"Ok, lesson learned," I said. "I promise not to fuck with Latino gangsters."

"Gah," she threw herself backwards and collapsed against her door. "Think about it, Master."

"What, St. George is starting a war between us and the Umbrals? So our Upstairs Neighbor can get some real estate?" I shook my head. "No way, once the Umbrals get released, it's over for this reality."

"Yeah, but what if," she pointed up, "isn't trying to get territory? What if he's just trying to kill 'our gang' for good?"

"You really think that he would—" I trailed off. The possibility was terrifying. If she was right, and the other side was cooperating with the Umbrals, they were trying to end us all. Unless the tricky bastard upstairs was planning to kick off his little war early. Then it made perfect sense, the Fallen would be fighting a two–front war to his one. He could snatch his faithful and leave this reality before the war was even decided. I looked at Annessa, my eyes wide.

"What are you?" I asked in a half–whisper.

"I already told you once, Master." She smiled beatifically. "I'm whatever you need me to be."

I reached out to Abbadonna.

"Emissary." Her mind felt agitated.

"What do you think? Would he do that?" I asked.

"He slew the Midianites and Amorites to a man. He rained death upon Sodom and Gomorrah. He instructed his faithful first to hold him above all other gods." She laughed derisively. "He chains his worshippers and wonders why they chafe. Yes, Emissary, should he find that he is not favored by his creation, he would not hesitate to destroy this reality."

"But to betray mankind to the Umbrals?" I shuddered.

"What better way to destroy his rivals exists, Emissary?" She laughed again. "He knows that Satan is vested in this sphere, and Satariel would not readily abandon Ninnaka's tomb. No, this may be his intended masterstroke."

"This isn't going to get any easier, is it?" I asked.

"No, Emissary," she replied. "It will only get worse. An end rapidly approaches; what that end may be is yet to be decided."

"Will the Chosen Son be summoned soon, do you think?" Worry began to creep into my brain.

"Only Satan knows, Emissary," she mentally shrugged. "If you don't know, no one else will."

"Yeah."

"Why so worried?" she asked.

I just looked at Annessa. "No reason." My heart sank.

"I see."

"Yeah." I broke contact and hit the horn startling Adrian who had been casually leaning on the hood talking to Sheena. I jerked my thumb toward the truck. The bastard held the door for Sheena. How do you go from putting a gun to someone's head to trying to get in their pants? I looked at Annessa. How indeed?

The ride to Harker's was oddly subdued. It wasn't altogether surprising. I mean, let's face it, I'd just destroyed Sheena's home, the theory that Annessa'd laid out was pretty much terrifying and we had no idea where to find either the Umbrals or St. George. We pretty much had nothing but a loaded gun against our collective temples. We all jumped when Annessa turned on the radio, which was exactly how she left it—at full volume.

"Sorry!" she yelped as I swerved into oncoming traffic and Sheena screamed.

I started laughing uncontrollably. It was the stress, I guess. Well, that or Sheena's exceptionally high–pitched scream. It took me the better part of five minutes to get myself under control.

"What's so damned funny, Beckett?" Sheena

demanded.

I snorted as I tried to answer, which only served to make me laugh harder and caused Annessa to join in with me.

"It wasn't that funny," she muttered.

"Not at all," Adrian nodded sagely. "Motor vehicle accidents are no laughing matter."

I pulled up to Harker's garage still laughing. I stopped laughing when the club exploded. I stopped cold.

Abbadonna took control of the vehicle, the tires squealing as she reversed out of the garage at full speed.

"Abbadonna, stop!" I screamed through our mindlink. "We need to go back, Harker's in there!"

She didn't slow. She broke off contact with me and if anything, she went faster.

"Annessa," I pointed toward the burning club. "Go, get Harker!"

She rolled out of her open window in one smooth motion and dashed toward the club with speed born of desperation.

Abbadonna locked the doors and the windows shut in a single guillotine thrust. She wasn't making this easy.

"Adrian," I started as I unbuckled my seatbelt and turned to crawl into the back seat. He was already holding a shotgun for me; the weapons locker in the rear of the vehicle was open wide. "Thank you."

Abbadonna braked hard and spun the vehicle around in a vicious one hundred-eighty degree skid. Three men stood in the middle of the street. They leapt toward the vehicle hopping through the Veil as they did so. Vampires.

"Emissary," Abbadonna's mindseeking was full of dread. "You must escape."

"I'm not leaving Annessa," I spoke to her with cold certainty. "Unlock the doors or I'll dismiss you immediately."

The doors unlocked. "As you wish," came her angry reply.

The vampires hit the car like a tornado, slamming into the driver's side and sending us into another spin. I heard

Sheena's door open as I struggled to get my bearings.

I looked down at the shotgun shells in the carrier on the stock. They were all Cold Iron. I looked hopefully at Adrian.

"You wouldn't happen to have any gold back there, would you?" I asked.

"None at all, my lord," he replied sadly.

"You aren't a quick study in transmutation, are you?"

"No." He shook his head.

I dropped the useless shotgun onto the passenger seat. "Me neither." I threw open my door as he dove out of Sheena's open door. By the time I shook myself free of the truck's mangled door, he was already halfway to Sheena.

Watching Sheena was like watching the primordial chaos; her form was fluid and ever–changing. The three bloodsuckers surrounded her, their claws and fangs couldn't keep up with her. She was chanting something in a voice far too deep for her feminine form, something Old. She flitted from smoke to stone to fire and back again, never staying tangible long enough to be vulnerable.

Adrian walked toward her, rolling his shoulders and shaking out his hands as he did. Behind me I could hear the truck shut off. He threw his arms wide and spoke a single word, "Mother."

He threw his head back as Abbadonna launched herself from the truck into him. There was a shudder in reality, and I saw Adrian's soul dart out of his body as Abbadonna hit his flesh like a train. There was a brilliant flash as his flesh gave way to her will and it reshaped itself to mirror the Fallen that now controlled it. It's called Fleshbinding; I'd never seen it before. Nephilim are the only ones that can do it; by detaching their mortal essence, they allow a Fallen to take full control of their body. The Fallen's essence reshapes the vessel to suit its needs for the duration of the exchange.

Adrian's soul floated, a ghostly blue silhouette. His voice shook the air as he incanted. Around him the air began to shimmer as a heat mirage. His voice grew stronger with each phrase of the incantation. It took me a second to recognize it, and I grinned when I did. I opened my eyes to the flows of aether and joined my voice to his chant creating a sympathetic bridge between us. I poured my strength into his spell, overloading him with power. He swayed in the air, his aetherous form began to glow an angry red as the spell took hold of him.

Abbadonna leapt into the air and hurled herself at the vampires. Her wings glinted like black diamonds in the dim streetlights as she hit the closest vampire and ripped him off of his feet. She spun in the air like an arrow in flight, tossing the vampire into a lamppost as she flew by it. It didn't hurt him much, but it got his attention and he raced after her, launching himself into the air to give chase.

Sheena's strength began to wane. Hers was an impossible battle, fighting against tireless creatures for which speed came as naturally as breathing to a human. She began to slow; her shifts became less frequent and the vampires' attacks came faster in the face of her weakness. One of the leeches threw a lucky haymaker that dropped her to her knees. They closed in for the kill.

Adrian released his magic. The darkness fled as the sun rose in the center of the street. Daylight burst through the night and the vampires threw their arms up and screamed in terror. It was only an illusion, a Ghūllish battle illusion used against other creatures of the dark to be precise, but it was effective as hell. Before the illusion could fade, I hurled Words of flame and agony. One of the vampires dropped to the asphalt in paroxysms of pain as the flames tore his immortal flesh to shreds and the Word of agony mangled any thoughts of escape.

The remaining vampire was on me before I could blink. He grabbed me by the throat and hurled me into the side of the Range Rover. It wouldn't have been so bad if I'd been closer than sixty feet away and the fucking truck wasn't armored. He skittered through the Veil at me. I dodged through the Veil as he landed in front of where I'd just been sitting. Tricky, remember? I screamed a Word of abjuration and slammed my Mark against his back. My hand burned through his cheap leather jacket and seared the Mark of the

Adversarial Beast into his lily white, neck–sucking, ass–kissing, pretty–boy back. I shoved him against the truck and invoked the blessing of Leviathan, then I headbutted him. The gore sprayed everywhere as his head exploded and his body thrashed itself into a pool of foul smelling ichor.

I staggered backwards, both from the shock of the hit and the stench of the vampire's leavings. Sheena was kneeling across the throat of the vampire I'd hit with my Words. Her stone fist glinted gold in the flickering illumination of the remaining streetlights. Adrian hung in midair, slowly chanting binding curses on the vampire that Sheena held down. There was a sickening ripping sound as Abbadonna tore the final bloodsucker apart over our heads. She landed gracefully in front of Adrian. She inclined her head at me and surrendered Adrian his body. I turned and looked toward the club. Where was Annessa? I walked to the truck to retrieve my shotgun. I don't remember leaving the truck, I don't remember running and I damn sure don't recall Veil–jumping my way up the elevator shaft. I didn't even know I could do that. I do, however, remember coming out of the elevator shaft and into the mouth of hell itself.

I jumped free of the elevator cables and landed in the entryway of the club. Annessa was standing over Harker's body in the center of the club, flames surrounding her. Her fangs and claws were extended and her eyes competed with the fire for brightness. She turned a slow circle, her body low, legs wide. I froze. Something was hunting her; she was waiting for it and guarding Harker as she did. I shoved my mind toward her. I felt myself enter her mind and meld with her completely. I gasped. I'd never experienced this level of mindlink with anything other than a Fallen and even then only with Abbadonna.

"Master," she spoke out loud. "You really shouldn't be here."

"I couldn't leave you, Annessa."

"I have this under control, Master." She sounded so grim and stoic.

"What is it?" I asked.

"I don't know." She turned slowly toward me, her eyes peering into the rapidly fluctuating shadows created by the flames. "But it's fast, and it's angry."

It tore free from the shadows and darted toward me. I cocked my head. It couldn't be. Nope, shit—it was. I dropped the shotgun and spoke a Word—in Ghūllish. The creature froze. It hovered and whirled around itself in the air. It looked like a man with the lower body of a snake, made entirely of darkness and smoke. It was Unbound, but of the lowest order. It was a spirit of war; the Ghūls called them Varg'Thūl, Souls of Rage. My Word confused it. The Varg'Thūl were allies of the Ghūls and, while I was clearly not a Ghūl, I bore their blood and their sorcery. The Varg'Thūl's eyes flared flame as it spoke to me.

"Who art thou to bear the black flame of the Umbral Host and the tongue of the forsaken sons?" it shrieked at me in Ghūllish. To be fair, they always shriek; it's that whole Soul of Rage thing.

"I am the Will of the Lord of the Fallen, Emissary to this reality and the Regent Consort of the Eldest of Nagg'Varythmar." I held up my Mark.

"Why am I set against thee, Son of the Dark Halls?" it asked, its tail chittering as the scales scraped together.

"I do not know, Honored Spirit of War," I spoke carefully. "But I have no wish to test myself against you."

"We do as we are bound," He roiled in the air, a mass of hateful energy. "Until all endings are manifest."

Fuck. I didn't bother reaching for the shotgun; there was no way that I could reach it in time. I incanted a Ghūllish blessing: the cloak of Ninnaka'Varylethkinaya. It was one of the most difficult incantations I knew. It would render me mostly safe from the claws and fangs of the creature, but only for a short time; I didn't have the energy to maintain the spell for very long. Thankfully, it didn't keep me waiting.

I'd like to tell you what happened then, I really would. I have no idea, though. The damned thing was all over me, striking and biting so fast I couldn't follow it. After about three seconds, I heard a horrific crunch, one that I

desperately prayed hadn't come from anywhere on my body.
With a rather comical look of surprise, it flew backwards as
Annessa pulled it off of me and hurled it against the wall.
She roared at it, sounding almost as impressive as
Abbadonna. It rebounded from the wall and charged her.
They rolled around each other, savagely slashing and biting.
Annessa kicked away from it with a scream. I waited for it
to counterattack as I raced toward her, terrified that she was
mortally injured.

The spirit shuddered in the air. It roared once, as if it
were challenging the universe itself. It lowered its gaze to
Annessa. "Thus, thou art worthy," it spoke quietly and
collapsed into ash.

Annessa stood over Harker's body and in her hand she
held a glowing shard of black adamant. She'd torn out the
creature's heart. I stared at her. I'd never seen anything like
her. I shook off my reverie; Harker hadn't moved since we
arrived. I ran over to him and looked him over with my
Sight. He was hemorrhaging thanatonic energy. I rolled
him on to his stomach and hissed through my teeth as I saw
his back. His back was punctured in at least a dozen places
with serrated chunks of gold. If I didn't do something
quickly, he'd die.

"Master," Annessa spoke urgently as she gently
pushed me away from Harker and lifted him easily. "We
need to get out of here before this place collapses."

"Yeah," I nodded. "We do."

She led the way to the elevator shaft. She leaped
down, bouncing from side to side in the shaft to slow her
descent. I followed her, though with a bit less grace. I
found myself uttering a short prayer as we left the club; it
collapsed only seconds after our exit.

Annessa laid Harker down gently on the pavement.
It's hard to tell the relative health of an unconscious
vampire, let me tell you. I couldn't just yank the gold out of
Harker the way I had pulled the Cold Iron out of Cassidy.
The gold was poisoning Harker, but yanking it out would
allow him to bleed out, which as more good blood left him,

increased the concentration of poisoned blood in him; you get the picture. I held my right arm out to Annessa.

"Bite me." I grit my teeth, I knew from last time just how much this would hurt.

She bit down quickly, though with a bit more control this time. My forearm was bleeding like mad. I held it over Harker's mouth. I consciously held back the Ghūl blood in my system, since I had no idea what that would do to Harker and now was not the time to find out. Slowly, his mouth started working until without any warning, he latched onto my arm and his fangs tore into me. I'm not sure what you've read in books or seen in the movies, some of them describe the sensation as ultimate pleasure and others as horrible pain. It hurts. It's a bit like a hickey, but with razor blades. But that isn't even what really matters. It's the magic inherent in vampires that makes their bite unique; their minds drive into your own, not really like mindseeking, because they aren't looking for anything. It's more like a constant droning buzz that drives rational thought from you and replaces it with a desire to please the creature that's feeding on you.

I'm not real big on mind control. I put my Marked hand on Harker's brow and pushed. Not with my hand, mind you, but with the Mark. My Lord's will can trump a vampire's any day. Harker's eyes fluttered open and he looked at me in horror. I pulled away from him, carefully, I didn't want to hurt him, only keep him from killing me by accident.

"Relax, Miles," I said gently. "There's been something of a setback."

He nodded. He was too weak for words.

"I'm going to roll you on your side and try to get the gold out of your back now." I patted his shoulder. "I need you to hold on, bro. Hold on like there's no tomorrow, because if we fuck this up, there won't be one."

He nodded again and reached up to squeeze my good forearm.

I rolled him on to his side. I held up my forearm to Annessa. "See if you can fix this."

She slashed her palm with a claw and let her blood drip into the wound. As before, it closed without even a slight scar. It took what seemed like hours to pull the gold out of Harker. I set it aside in a pile. It might come in handy later. After I pulled the last piece out of him, I had Adrian and Sheena drag their captive vampire over to us. Here's something else the movies get wrong: if Harker drank the other vampire, all he'd get is a stomach ache. Vampires use blood. Their bodies burn it at a ridiculous rate. If blood were gas and humans were cars, they'd be hybrids. Vampires, however, would be Hummers. They don't drink blood because it's stylish; they drink it because they need it to survive. Horror writers are morons. You know what, I take that back, I'm beginning to wonder if they aren't traitors paid off by the worst of the worst on the Veilside.

"Do you know this bastard, Harker?" I asked as Harker slowly sat up.

Harker shook his head, "No."

"I do." Cassidy stepped out of the shadows.

I thought Adrian was going to jump out of his skin. At least I wasn't the only one that bastard startled.

"Where the hell have you been, man?" I asked.

"I got ambushed on the Shadow Road." He threw a severed head on the pavement.

"Just one?" I asked. "That wouldn't hold you up long."

"I couldn't fit the angel wings in my pocket, Little Brother." He knelt beside Harker. "How are you, Miles?"

"Been better, Liam," Harker slurred. "I have been better."

CHAPTER 14

Cassidy stood and walked over to the prone, bound and thoroughly roasted vampire. He knelt beside the creature and shook his head.

"Little Brother, you have all the subtlety of a sledgehammer." he said as he looked up at me.

"Only when I'm pissed off," I replied testily.

"You're always pissed off, Master," Annessa added.

"You're not helping, Annessa," I said as Cassidy smiled and nodded at Annessa.

"No, but she is right," Cassidy remarked.

"Yeah, yeah," I waved him off and gestured to the vampire. "Who is this bastard?"

"His name is Reginald Ross," Cassidy explained. He reached down and tore away the vampire's shirt.

I gasped and I wasn't alone. The creature's back was covered in scarred over lash marks and there were crucifix–shaped brands all over him. His body looked like a torturer's handbook come to life.

"He's a member of the Itinerant Brotherhood of St. Lazarus." Cassidy looked up at me. "He's an assassin, and you were his target."

"So the Church has vampires now too?" Annessa asked. "This is bullshit; they keep stealing our monsters!"

"What do you mean, Annessa?" Cassidy looked up at

her curiously.

I sighed. "We just gave a pack of God Hounds the Traitor's Oath," I said.

"Who?" Cassidy asked.

"Victus, Riley and Ouillete," Adrian answered. "Your pack, Lord Apostate."

Cassidy's pack. That was a shock. I didn't know that any of them were still alive. We didn't offer sanctuary to any old werewolves; no, we just gave sanctuary to the oldest known pack of wolves anywhere.

"I see," he said quietly. "Little Brother, did you know?"

"No," I shook my head. "I knew that some traitor wolves requested sanctuary. I didn't know who."

He looked at me and spoke very quietly. "I should very much like to speak with them."

"I'll arrange it," I quickly agreed. From what little I'd ever been able to glean from Cassidy about his past, there was some serious bad blood between him and his pack.

"My Lord Emissary, we have offered sanctuary," Adrian began cautiously. "We have extended them our protection."

"Yes," I agreed. "And they have agreed to die for Satan. Right now, the Lord's domain is under assault by both Umbrals and Angelics. Whatever aid these rabid wolves can render pales greatly in comparison to the Damascene and his Emissary." I turned to face Adrian. "The next time you have information of this magnitude and you withhold it from me..." I met his gaze and held it until he looked away.

"Jason." Harker stood slowly. "Where are my girls?"

"I don't know," I said as I turned around. "There was nothing alive in the club when Annessa pulled you out."

"I can't sense them." He wobbled slightly as he turned a slow circle. "I can't sense them at all."

"I'm sorry, man." I didn't know what else to say. "I'm really fucking sorry."

"I need to feed." He leaned on Annessa. "No offense, Jason, but you're not my type."

"You're going to go batshit after you feed, aren't you?" He was taking this too well.

"I am," he nodded.

I turned back to Cassidy. "We need to get out of here, man." I looked around, the explosion and fire had already attracted too much attention. "Come to my place, we can figure this all out."

He nodded. "Very well."

I gave him my address and helped Annessa load Harker into the truck. Adrian and Sheena dragged the semi-conscious Ross to the back of the truck and tied him to the weapons locker with tow straps and binding spells. Though, in his condition, they probably could have just asked him nicely to stay put. That bastard was *hurt*. Yeah, I sound a little proud. Next time your sorcery burns downs a vampire, I'll let you brag a bit, I promise.

I paused a moment before I climbed into the truck. I looked at the burning wreckage of Harker's Place. I let the image sear into my brain. This had to end, and it had to end soon. I had to find some way to de-escalate the conflict back to the cold stalemate that existed before the Umbrals showed up. I wasn't sure if it was possible anymore, but I had to try. I climbed into the truck and headed back to my apartment.

"Adrian," I looked at him in the rearview mirror.

"Yes, my lord?"

"Let Erzebet know what's happened," I ordered. "Have her send a car to pick up our new friend in the back and have her send a girl for Harker."

"As you wish, my lord," he nodded and pulled out his cell phone.

"Master?" Annessa leaned against me.

"Yeah?"

"What did you mean when you called yourself the Regent Consort of the Eldest of blah blah blah?" She waved her hand at the end.

"Remember when I told you that the Ghūls wanted me for the same thing you wanted?" I asked trying to be as obtuse as possible.

"Ye–es," she replied slowly.

"Well, the one that I was chosen to..." I looked around the vehicle and everyone was staring at me. Even Adrian looked up at me from his phone call. He threw me an impish wink. "What? Don't you people have anything more interesting to do than eavesdrop?" I barked.

"Not where this is concerned, Beckett," Sheena grinned lasciviously.

"I haven't the faintest what we're discussing, Jason." Harker's head bobbed with each bump in the road.

"What?" Annessa asked. "Why's this a big deal; what's it mean?" She looked around.

Adrian put his hand over the mouthpiece of the phone. "It means he paid his breed–price to the Ghūl Queen, my lady."

"You did what now?" Annessa looked at me.

"I had to," I searched for the most mundane words possible for the act, "Impregnate the Ghūl Queen."

"You had sex with a Ghūl?" Her mouth fell open.

"It usually takes more than once, my lady," Adrian added helpfully.

"Only you, Beckett," Sheena laughed. "You sick bastard."

I looked at Annessa. "I did what I had to," I shrugged. "I didn't have much choice."

"But the Queen?" She shook her head.

"It's not that big a deal," I said.

"It's a pretty big deal," Adrian said at the exact same moment.

I sighed. I glared at Adrian in the rearview mirror. "Adrian had to do the same thing, Annessa."

"Except not with the Queen," he added.

"Why did you have to do it?" Annessa asked.

"Ghūls can't reproduce as a species," I explained. "They need human assistance, and it's the price they demand to teach sorcery."

"I thought that they didn't like creation." she said.

"They don't," I nodded. "Except that if they don't reproduce, they die, as a species, I mean."

"But how can they, if creation hurts them?"

"The act of creation is usually corrupt in and of itself, where Ghūls are concerned," I shrugged. "The actual pregnancy isn't detrimental to them."

"Why not?"

"Ghūls are mortal; they're terribly long–lived, but mortal nonetheless. From the moment of conception, they begin dying. As the flesh begins its decline toward putrefaction, it feeds the hunger of the angel within."

"Wait," Annessa tapped her nail against her teeth. "If the Ghūls are shapeshifters and Umbral angels, how can they reproduce at all? Wouldn't that require a new angel for each baby?"

I looked at Adrian and we both shuddered. "No."

"Why not?"

"Their young are born without souls." I pulled the truck over in front of the apartment. "They get their souls from their old bodies."

"How?"

"Nagg'resh Vök," I answered. "They devour their old corpse."

"How can a baby eat an entire body?" She made a face.

"Slowly." Somehow, that made me think of Sarah.

"Funny, Beckett," Sheena chuckled. "Sick, but funny."

I flashed her a quick grin in the rearview and shut off the truck. "In a nutshell, that's the deal with that title, Annessa." I looked at her. "I didn't have much choice in the matter."

"Was it terrible?" She looked concerned.

"The sex or the experience?" I asked as we all got out of the truck.

"The experience," she glared at me. "No woman wants to hear about your past lovers, Master."

"Amen," Sheena echoed with a meaningful glance at me.

"Yeah," Adrian agreed. He looked at me as I glared at him and stammered, "I mean, who knew? Right, my lord?"

"You fucking traitor," I laughed and shook my head at him.

"Well, Master?" Annessa stood at the curb and shut the door.

I walked around the truck and checked my watch. Where was Erzebet's car? I wasn't about to unload a mostly dead vampire and just wait curbside.

"It wasn't terrible, Annessa," I said. "Verhghana was a brutal teacher, but she's a friend now. It was worth it."

"Yeah?" she asked.

"Without it, I'd never have been able to raise you and then where would I be?" I smiled.

She smiled back and took my hand.

Adrian whistled quietly as a black sedan doubled parked alongside us. "It's ours, my lord. I recognize the driver."

We conducted the world's fastest mostly dead vampire car swap. I incanted a quick binding on the trunk that even a half–decent sorcerer would be able to dispel. I banged on the trunk and the car slid seamlessly back into traffic and disappeared into the city. As we entered the building, I handed the night doorman, or Not–Roger as I thought of him, five hundred dollars to conveniently forget what he'd just not seen.

We stood in the elevator. Annessa rested against me and poor Harker rested against her. He looked like a drunk *Twilight* convention kid. The elevator opened and we all staggered out. It'd been a long night and it looked to be just beginning. After we got into the apartment Adrian began making drinks for everyone.

"Adrian, where is Harker's girl?" I was getting agitated.

The intercom rang. "I'd guess the lobby, my lord." He talked quietly into the handset and returned to the cellaret. "In the elevator, my lord."

Harker nodded at me and staggered toward the entryway. The door opened, and he was on her. I shook my head. What would the horror writers think of that? No preamble, no vague sexual innuendos or gods help us all—

sparkling. He just hit her like an express train and drank her into unconsciousness. I hoped it was unconsciousness. I sighed and got up to check.

"Harker?" I called as I approached the entryway.

"Beckett," he answered tersely. He sat on the floor with her draped across his lap.

"Is, uh, she sleeping, bro?" I asked nervously.

"Yeah," he grinned sheepishly. "She's still alive. Barely."

"Did you," I cocked my head, "do that on purpose?"

"I need to replenish my ranks, Jason." He looked meaningfully at me. "My girls are gone."

"She's Satan's," I spoke quietly but firmly. "She's not for slavery, Miles."

"You would deny me," his voice raised. "After all I've done for you?"

"Yes." I very much would. "She's not meant for slavery. I can't let you do that to her."

"You owe me." His eyes were like steel.

"Yes," I replied as I entered the elevator. "I do." I picked her up. "I'll make it right, Miles. Trust me."

"How?"

"We're at war." I looked him in the eye. "I'll lay my enemies at your feet, and you can do with them what you like. Let's not lose our principles before battle is even joined." I walked out of the elevator, into my bedroom and laid the girl gently on my bed. She'd be ok with some rest. I intoned a quick blessing over her and kissed her forehead. She'd done well.

Harker took a moment and walked into the living room. He looked at me strangely for a moment as I re–entered the living room. "You've changed, Jason."

"Have I?" I asked.

"The man I met six years ago would have let me have her without blinking if it served his interest to do so." He leaned against the cellaret.

"I probably would have," I agreed.

"That's what I liked least about you," he said.

"Yeah?" I grinned back and prayed that he wasn't about to go completely apeshit.

I heard the elevator doors close as it returned to the lobby.

"Cassidy?" I wondered aloud.

"If it isn't," Sheena laughed, "whatever it is, it's going to have a very bad night."

We all tensed as the door opened. Cassidy walked into the apartment slowly.

"Welcome to my home, Cassidy," I greeted him.

"I wish I came with better news, Little Brother."

"So do I." I had no idea what he was going to say, but I already knew I wasn't going to like it.

CHAPTER 15

Cassidy leaned against the arm of the couch. He was too agitated to sit. The ache in the pit of my stomach had butterflies and those butterflies had bowel obstructions. If Cassidy was this bad, I was going to need therapy.

"It seems the Church has called in every favor it has amassed in the last two thousand years," Cassidy began. "And they all seem focused on one thing: destroying you." He nodded at me.

"Why?" I asked. "What's changed?"

"There's one less Umbral in the world, for one," he said.

"Two less," I corrected.

"What?"

"Annessa, show him your little trophy," I said.

She threw Cassidy the adamantine heart. He whistled when he caught it.

"Not bad, Annessa girl." He tossed it back. "Not bad at all."

"So that probably won't make things any better, huh?" I sat down with my drink.

"No." He took the drink that Adrian offered him. "But, we do have one advantage."

"What's that?"

"They think," he pointed at Harker, "he's dead and all of his murder with him."

"They're not?" I stood up, spilling my drink. Harker was already on his feet, granted he cheats.

"Lila and Katya have passed on, my friend," Cassidy put his hand on Harker's shoulder. "The rest of your murder has gone to ground."

"Thank you, Liam." Harker's eyes ran with blood. "Thank you for that."

"Don't thank me yet." Cassidy shook his head. "You might wish to sit, Miles."

"This is why I've come to loathe you bringing me news, Cassidy," I told him.

"I care for bearing such news even less than you enjoy receiving it, Little Brother."

"Fair enough," I conceded.

"Master, let him talk!" Annessa scolded me.

"The Itinerant Order of St. Lazarus has marked you, Little Brother." He took a drink, facing Harker as he did so. "The Prioress has come to New York with the rest of the order, but she wasn't hunting Beckett. She was hunting you." He pointed at Harker.

"Me?" Harker asked incredulously. "Why was she looking for me? I don't even know her."

"I'm afraid you know her quite well, Miles. Her name is Wilhelmina."

I didn't think Harker could get much paler, but he did. He wilted back into the couch.

"Why does that sound familiar?" I asked aloud. Then it hit me. "Really, Harker? Really? And here I though that you leeches didn't get that fucking melodramatic."

"What?" Sheena asked. "What the hell are you going on about, Beckett."

"Wilhelmina Murray–Harker." I raised an eyebrow at her. "Ring any bells?"

I got blank stares all around the room. "Not even you, Adrian?"

He just shrugged, "I've no idea what you're talking about, my lord."

Harker sighed, "It's from *Dracula*. You know, the book? Bram Stoker; Irishman?"

"I'm beginning to see where your *Twilight* fixation comes from," I laughed. "Is this a big deal? With your Mina?"

"She's the one who turned me." He put his head in his hands. "She's..." He paused, grimaced and looked at me. "Nothing about which I would joke, Jason."

"Ouch," I said. "No silly British phrasing."

"Is she powerful?" Annessa asked.

"Very," Cassidy answered. "She's fairly young, but she is very powerful."

"What makes her so dangerous?" I asked.

"She's off her rocker." Harker stood and walked to the window. "And her Gifts aren't like mine."

"What do you mean, 'like yours?'" I asked. As far as I knew, Harker was pretty much standard as far as vampires go.

"Limited," he shrugged. "I didn't take to immortality like she did. She views this as the ultimate gift. Her reality is shaped by her madness."

"So, she's faster and stronger than you?" Sheena asked.

"I'm like a child at her feet." He turned to face us. "She has every one of our Gifts, and she can use them like no other vampire I've seen."

"So what you're saying is that we're in deep shit," I summarized.

"She's after me, Jason." He sounded so defeated. "I don't think she'd even notice you."

"I'm rather hard to miss, Miles." I stood up. "And I don't think that she's your problem alone."

"No?"

"No." I started pacing. "The problem is that we keep giving everyone far too much credit."

"Explain yourself, Little Brother." Cassidy sat in my vacant spot.

"What if we're piecing this together wrong?" I asked. "What if it isn't St. George masterminding this mess?"

"Who, then?" Adrian leaned forward. "Who else could do this?"

"This bastard's only been in command for a few months now and he's made this much progress?" I shook my head. "There's no way; coordination of this magnitude requires a centralized command structure, which he doesn't have."

"So you think that someone else is calling the shots, Beckett?" Sheena set her drink down and began tying her hair back.

"It makes sense. If St. George is a just a cog, as much as that hurts my ego, then our focus was on the wrong person the whole time. How much have we missed by looking the wrong way?" What had gone on behind our backs?

"Who could do this?" Annessa asked. "I mean, who on the other side has that kind of authority, Master?"

I shrugged, "I have no idea. My involvement only went as far as dealing with Rachel first and now this St. George prick."

"All of the attacks have been focused on one thing," Adrian noted. "Destroying your support system, my lord." He looked at me.

"Why, though?" I paced faster. "What sense does that make; I'm not that much of a threat."

"You might be misjudging what you know and so might they," Sheena observed. "You knew about Sarah's brother. Even if you know nothing else, they might believe that you do."

"Add to that the fact that you've killed two Umbrals," Cassidy chimed in. "And you've a potent reason to be marked for death."

"I'd like to point out here that I've killed exactly zero Umbrals; Sarah killed one and Annessa the other." I waved my finger in the air as if correcting a class full of children.

"It's good you surround yourself with such strong women, my lord." Adrian's eyes were glued on Sheena even as he spoke to me.

"Well, if they're focused on me, then let's do what they don't expect," I looked at Annessa.

"Let's roll through the front doors and kill everything that moves," she said as she crossed the room and put her arms around my neck. "No need to fuck around."

"Well said," I grinned.

"I'd like to know a bit more about what we're likely to face before committing to such a plan, Annessa." Cassidy looked thoughtful.

"Mina's not someone you trifle with," Harker whispered harshly.

"Why are you so damned afraid, Harker?" I disengaged myself from Annessa and sat on the coffee table in front of him.

"She is terror incarnate." He flickered and was in front of the window, his hands clasped behind his back. "She's a ghost in the darkness, all claws, fangs and hate."

"What's she doing working for the other side," I asked gently.

"I've no idea." He looked over his shoulder at me. "But I can't imagine it's improved her temperament."

"What can she do that you cannot, Miles?" Cassidy asked. "We need to know if we are to plan for her...end."

"She's a master shapeshifter and a telepath the likes of which I've never seen." He stared through his own reflection. "Flesh is an instrument for her, a finely tuned weapon."

"No sorcery?" I asked.

"No," he shook his head. "No need, she can break your thoughts and shatter your will. Words won't save you from her."

"That's refreshing." I threw back the rest of my drink. Adrian took my glass and headed for the cellaret.

"What else do we know?" Annessa asked.

"The Umbrals and the Angelics are working together for their mutual benefit; I think that's plain at this point." Everyone nodded as I looked around. As nice as it was to be believed, this is one time where I'd much rather have been convinced that I was crazy.

"Here's a fun thought," Adrian called over his shoulder as he poured more whiskey into my glass. "What if the Angelics are just along for the ride?"

"Thank you for making my already fucked up night

that much more disturbing, Adrian." I looked at Cassidy. The fear in his eyes mirrored my own. Shit.

"Little Brother," Cassidy spoke quietly. "This is getting more dangerous with each passing moment."

"I've noticed." I stared into my drink. "I need to find St. George."

"Why?" Sheena made a face. "What good is he if he isn't in charge."

"One," I held up a finger, "I owe him pain." I held up another finger, "Two, I'll make him tell me everything he knows."

"Revenge may not be the best course of action at this point, Little Brother," Cassidy advised.

"I didn't say it was about revenge." I looked at around the room, meeting everyone's gaze. "It's a trap."

"A trap for whom, Beckett?" Sheena furrowed her brow. "And how do you plan on trapping them?"

"Well, if everything has been leading up to killing me, as you've all agreed, then let's do the sensible thing," I grinned. "Let's give me to them."

"Has anyone ever told you you're a moron?" Sheena snorted at me. "So then what, you're surrounded, captured and most likely killed, and none of us are any better off."

"No, I'm not going for predictability here." I stood. "I'm waiting on some intelligence from the Consulate. Once I have that, we are going to give the Angelics back everything they gave us in spades."

"How, Little Brother?" Cassidy asked.

"I'm still working that out." I started pacing in earnest.

CHAPTER 16

St. Patrick's Cathedral at dawn is beautiful to behold.
I know I shouldn't, but I love Gothic churches. The lines,
the decorations, they entrance me. I'm not an architecture
buff, so I can't really offer any decent commentary on them,
except to say that they are some of the most beautiful,
majestic structures ever built. And today, well today, I was
going to blow one up. Erzebet had come through much
more effectively than I could have ever hoped. Not only had
she identified St. George and decoded the complex
relationship between the various cells that comprised the
Church's structure, but she'd identified their drop sites, safe
houses and much of their membership.

St. Patty's wasn't any of those things. It was a
magnificent structure that exemplified the ties between
Heaven and Earth. It was a locus of attention that injected
the possibility of salvation into the minds of the populace. It
gave people hope. By taking that hope away, I was hurting
my cause in the short run, as the sheep raced into the arms of
a forgotten faith that they nursed only in their wallets and in
the cheap, gaudy crucifixes they wore to showcase a false
devotion they failed to understand. But I needed to make a
statement, one that would be understood by the Angelics and
their horrible allies.

The church was empty. It isn't so much that I was

unwilling to hurt anyone, but anyone in the church ran the risk of being a True Believer. I wasn't going to give the other side a single soul in the course of my work today. Besides, I needed as many people as possible to flood the remaining churches in the city. I was counting on record numbers. Bear with me here; it'll all make sense soon. Annessa and I sat in the Range Rover just down the block from the church.

"It's pretty, isn't it?" Annessa asked as she rested her head on my shoulder.

"Yeah," I turned and kissed her lightly.

"I feel almost bad about this," she said quietly.

"I don't."

"No?"

"They've brought this on themselves." I gripped the steering wheel tightly. "I've completely run out of sympathy."

"You really think this'll work, Master?" She looked me in the eye.

"Yeah," I nodded. "It only needs to work for a second or two."

"You're putting Harker and his girls in a lot of danger, Master." Her irises fluctuated between green, red and blue as her emotions warred with one another.

"We're all at risk, Annessa." I looked at the church. I shut my eyes. I focused on the ground beneath the sidewalk in front of the church. Twenty feet below the church, in the steam tunnels, two men wearing utility uniforms were setting a few rather complex explosives around a rather sizable gas main. The gas main had been shut off nearly three-quarters of a century earlier as the church and surrounding businesses had moved from gas to electric power, but a couple of welders and a few well–placed faithful at the utility company ensured that the gas was flowing again. The explosives they were setting were completely untraceable. They were made from sections of the gas main that had been cut away. No investigation would find them to be more than cast off detritus from the main itself. The explosives were alchemical in nature, and no forensic tests existed to identify them. For all intents and purposes, the explosion would be an accident.

My cell phone buzzed in my pocket. The screen read, "Five minutes." I started the truck.

"We're just about ready," I lifted Annessa's chin and kissed her deeply.

"What is it?" She caught my face as I tried to turn away. "What's been bothering you? Every time you look at me I feel pain."

"I don't want to lose you, Annessa," I said as I set the timer on my phone for four and a half minutes.

"I'd like to remind you, Master," she said in that tone. "You're the only one here who's died recently. I'm not going anywhere."

"I'm not worried about you dying, Annessa," I sighed and turned to face her. "I'm worried about losing you."

"How?"

"You're the Sacred Mother," I reminded her. "And I'm just his fist."

"Why are you worried?" she chuckled.

"You're going to give birth to his Chosen Son and keep him safe, that's your job."

"And you think that He's going to swoop in here and fly me away to push out rug–monkeys, Master?" she giggled.

"Why's that so fucking funny?"

"Why the hell would he do that?" She leaned back against her door and smiled at me mockingly.

"How else are you going to get pregnant?"

"I take it you never read the Bible," she snorted. "He doesn't even need to touch me, Master. I'm his creature; all he needs to do is will it."

"I hadn't considered that." I admitted somewhat sheepishly. I felt pretty dumb.

"You really think he'd take me away from you?" She leaned across the seat to look me in the eye. She kissed me softly and bit my lower lip.

"No," I breathed. "I'm beginning to think he keeps you here to torment me." I reached to grab her and my phone vibrated in my lap as the cathedral erupted. The explosion was phenomenal. A massive pillar of fire roared up through the church. I summoned my will; I screamed a Word and made the fire my own. It ravaged the church, melting steel, stone and vaporizing wood. I shaped the pillar with my magic. Anyone looking toward the explosion would remember a clawed, demonic hand reaching up from the ruins, reaching up toward Heaven. I poured all of my malice and hate into my sorcery and it showed. I threw myself into the spell, burning all of my energy at once. The spell flared only for a second, but every Gifted in the city knew what had happened, and they knew exactly who had done it. Against the flames, etched in midnight black smoke and brilliant blue flames, my Mark was emblazoned on the palm of that clawed hand advertising my involvement to all who bore witness.

I collapsed, spent and weak in the driver's seat. Annessa pulled me into her lap and shimmied underneath me to get in the driver's seat.

"Just give me a minute, Annessa," I protested. "I'll be fine."

"Shut up, Master," she grinned at me. "You need rest." She threw the vehicle into drive and put her foot to the floor. I put my seatbelt on as quickly as I could. With her reflexes, she's a hell of a driver, but that doesn't really make it any less frightening.

All over town, the faithful children of both of the Fallen Lords were quietly dosing holy water fonts, sacramental wine and baked goods with faerie wine. Three hundred churches were poisoned, but only about thirty were hit really hard. See, faerie wine acts as a very strong emotion enhancer. As a secondary effect it reduces inhibitions to negligible levels. So many people crammed into a small space, heavily drugged and scared is bad enough. But I wasn't done yet. The initial news reports would be of terrorist plots and threats against New York, and the faithful servants of Satan would deliver them. We had people at every major news network. They would only remain on the air for a few hours, but that's really all it takes.

I just needed to push these people ever so slightly. One sexual act, one violent assault in those thirty churches, and I would have my desired end. Any act of desecration, no matter how minor and the sanctity of the sanctuary was violated. Now, I'm not one to play anything entirely fair. I had men and women in as many churches as possible with the sole purpose of seduction or provocation. Yeah, I cheat, get over it.

As the day progressed, reports flooded news stations and police departments describing suspicious people. Riots broke out in Times Square as the police tried to shut down traffic. There were impromptu demonstrations all over campuses throughout the city. It was chaos, and it was beautiful. To know that I was entirely responsible was a pretty immense ego boost. I'm sure you're misunderstanding me here. I'm not proud of scaring people; I really don't care about that. What I am proud of is that all over the city, people were standing up against the system; they were defying the fear that confounded the sheep and rebelling against the herd. All over the city, humanity was rising up and coming into its own, and it was beautiful.

When dusk finally settled across the city, the first reports from the remains of the church were hitting the airwaves. They tried to calm the populace, but it was already too late. Churches were packed as the fools tried in vain to advertise their faith to the higher world in hopes they might be spared. They were like lambs to the slaughter, pun intended. It took a matter of minutes for the faerie wine to weave its spell over them. It was over in less than an hour. No one noticed, they were too busy fighting and fucking to see the flickering shadows that moved among them like wolves among sheep.

From among the roiling masses of the faithful, in their now defiled chapels, death had arrived. Victus, Riley, Ouillette, Harker, Bethany, Sophia, Tanya and Mara— predators all, like lightning they grabbed their prey and fled through the Veil. In the time it took for the average reality television show to render its viewing audience less intelligent, the entire structure of St. George's organization had been abducted.

Annessa stopped the truck in front of a rundown warehouse in Red Hook. It wasn't exactly the most prestigious place for the Angelics to die, but we weren't looking to make friends tonight. I lit a cigarette and leaned against the truck.

"What's up, Master?" Annessa gestured at the warehouse. "They're waiting for us."

"I just a need a minute," I shrugged.

"What's wrong?"

"Nothing," I drew deeply on the cigarette. "It's just going to get a bit crazy after this."

"I thought you liked it crazy?"

"I like living," I snorted. "And I like having my friends survive my stupidity."

"It's a good plan, Master," she reassured me.

"That's the problem," I flicked the cigarette away. "Plans go to shit the moment the first punch is thrown." I headed toward the door.

"Stop worrying," she slapped my ass as she ran up alongside me. "I'm here."

"I think that's the problem."

Inside the warehouse, the captives were lined up in three rows of thirty. The two outside rows faced out, none of the men could see each other. They were bound to rings driven into the floor. They'd been gagged and blindfolded before they arrived and Adrian had cast a basic masking spell over each of them. The enemy couldn't track them; they were alone and helpless. Before you get too comfortable on that high moral horse of yours, understand that this was war. They struck first and they'd made a bargain with an evil that made Satan appear tame. They had earned this death. Harker and his girls were on the far side of the warehouse. Victus, Riley and Ouillete were waiting for us when we entered.

"My lord," a short, muscular brute of a man greeted me. "I am Victus." He bowed low.

"Riley," a blonde giant of a man, nearly seven feet tall, bowed alongside Victus.

"Ouillette," another short, dark man, he actually knelt.

"Get up, Traitors," I said tersely. "Good work tonight."

"Thank you, milord," Victus nodded.

"Go, get ready," I said. "We're going to have some very pissed off guests soon."

I stepped past him and entered the warehouse. Harker sat on a cargo container, his feet dangling over the side. Bethany was draped across his lap. Sophia, Tanya and Mara prowled the rows of captives, ready to strike if one somehow managed to escape his bonds.

"You guys did really well tonight," I noted as I walked up to him.

"These bastards owe us," Harker stroked Bethany's face as he spoke to me. "This is only the beginning."

"You'll have a chance to kill as many as you want, Miles."

"They owe me three new girls." He cocked his head. "Unless you have a problem with that?"

"No," I shook my head. "They're slaves already, take what you want."

"Good," he smiled at me; his fangs gleamed in the low light. "I'd hate to have to go behind your back."

"What now, Master?" Annessa hopped up next to Harker and Bethany.

"Now we wait for Adrian, Sheena and Cassidy." I began to pace.

Adrian was fetching weapons. I wasn't about to face what could potentially the largest number of dangerous Gifted I'd ever dealt with empty handed. Fighting a vampire without gold was a fool's errand to say the least. If Mina was half as dangerous as Harker had predicted, we were already in deep shit. Add to that the potential for any Umbral minions, and it was going to take a ton of firepower.

Cassidy was trying to drum up the rest of the support we needed. He'd made his case to Satariel that this was an Umbral problem and not a Yahweh/Satan problem and the Damascene was sending help. I didn't know what that help was, but I hoped it was enough.

I was waiting to call for Abbadonna. She'd really extended herself during our last little dance with the vampires, and I didn't want to waste her strength before what promised to be a trying battle. I'd had an idea that I wanted to try; it would leave me exposed but the added strength we would gain might offset any possible issues from my vulnerability.

My phone rang bringing me out of my reverie. It was Sheena; I quickly answered it.

"Beckett," she sounded disgusted. "To say that you owe me doesn't even begin to describe this situation."

"You got it?" I asked.

"Yes," she groaned. "But I'm not sure it's worth what I paid."

"It was worth it," I reassured her with great confidence. In reality, I had no idea if the plan would work, but I wasn't going to tell her that.

"Yeah, it better be," she lamented. "Or you get to have the dirtiest sex of your life with a Coinbound just so I'm not the only one."

"Just get back here, there isn't much time," I urged her.

"I'm almost there, keep your fucking pants on!" she snapped.

"What'd she get, Master?" Annessa hopped off the container and paced with me.

"A Mnemosyne Phial," I answered. "For you."

"For me?" she clapped giddily. "You shouldn't have!"

"You don't even know what it is!" I laughed.

"It doesn't matter," she grinned. "I like gifts."

"Oh, I think you'll like this one," I smiled.

'What does it do?"

"It's what the Coinbound use to bring souls to Pandaemonium for judgment," I explained.

"Why do I need one, Master?"

"Well, if I'm right, it will allow Abbadonna to stay on the Lifeside longer," I shrugged. "I think I'm right, but I don't know that anyone's ever tried."

"Why not?"

"No Coinbound's ever given up their phial before."

"That's what you sent Sheena to get?"

I nodded.

"And she had to…" she made an obscene gesture with her mouth and hand.

"Among other things, I'm sure."

"She's not real pleased right now, is she?" Annessa grinned.

"Nope."

"Good."

"You really don't like her, do you?" I chuckled.

"Do I have to?" she asked poutily.

"What's wrong with her?" I asked.

"Would you be inclined to be friendly with a man who'd had his dick in my hand, Master?"

"Point taken."

Adrian arrived with a rather upset Sheena in tow. He nodded to me.

"I've got the weapons in the car, my lord."

"Good, we better get everything ready. Cassidy will probably be late." I turned to Sheena. "Do you have it?"

"Here," she handed me an inch long, black dipyramidal crystal with a radiant, glowing center. "I never want to see this or the Coinbound that I got it from again." She shuddered. "She was a fucking freak."

"Coming from you that's saying something," I grinned as I held the phial up to the light.

"Go fuck yourself, Beckett." She stormed off toward Harker and his girls.

I turned the phial around in my hand. It was darker than Ṣafira's and it felt…older. I couldn't really get a read on it with my Sight, but it seemed somehow *heavier*. I took the adamant Umbral heart out of my pocket and rolled it around in my hand. I looked at the two crystals with my Sight, they were both aetheric sinks; the ambient aether roiled around them as it was slowly consumed. I spoke a silent prayer; what I was about to do had never been done before. I had only the most basic conjecture and fragments of Ghūllish legend to work with.

Each rock had its own particular resonance. The phial absorbed the ambient thanatonic energy given off by the death of the cells in my body; the Umbral heart devoured the energy of the Universe's slow decay. Each one had a specific kind of pull, almost magnetic. I spoke a Word of transmutation and rendered the phial insubstantial. Another Word changed the aetheric "polarity," for lack of a better term, of the phial. Instead of channeling the thanatonic energy that it absorbed back to the Coinbound from which it was made, it now slowly channeled it directly into the Umbral heart.

The heart shook in my hand. A crack appeared in its center. I wedged the phial against the edge of the crack and pushed with my Mark. I spoke a Word of binding and a blessing over it as I pushed against it with all of my will. It resisted at first, what I was forcing it to become was contrary to its nature, but my Mark and the sheer force of my desire shattered what defense it could mount. The phial slammed home into the heart with a crack.

Fine dust rained out of my hand as I opened it. In the center of my palm rested the center of heart pierced through by the phial. It was the size of an egg, black as obsidian and shot through with pulsing crimson veins. It throbbed with an angry purple light, and it felt as if it were beating in my hand. In my Sight, the aether now roiled around it in a slow, graceful figure eight. At either end of its arc, it had a black corona as it released a halo of pure thanatonic energy.

I turned to Annessa. "For you," I smiled. If this thing could do half of what I hoped, Annessa would become a force to be reckoned with.

"Ooh, it's pretty. What do I do with it?"

I wrapped my hands around hers and spoke a Word of binding. I released her hands.

"Swallow it," I instructed her.

"If I had a nickel for every time you said that to me..." she grinned.

I shook my head. "Just do it, please."

"Seriously, you want me to swallow this thing?"

"Yeah," I nodded.

She threw her head back and dropped it down her throat. She didn't even choke. I placed my left hand between her breasts. As soon as I felt the stone's energy, I spoke another binding, this time just simple sorcery and fused it behind her sternum. It faded as it passed through her esophagus and re–solidified as it bonded to her bone. Her chest glowed a brilliant purplish–red for a moment.

"Whoa." She put her hand over her chest. "That was weird."

"I bet."

"How does this keep Abbadonna here longer?"

"Because rather than fighting your body, she can bond with the Phial, and it won't try to dislodge her like your body would."

"Wait," she looked concerned. "Then how's she supposed to bond with you?"

"She isn't," I shook my head. "She's of more use with you, Annessa." I shrugged, "She can only do so much for me."

"Yeah, but she's saved you a bunch of times before."

"And I've seen what she can do inside of you," I put my hand on her face. "And of the two of us, you are by far the most important."

"According to who, exactly?" Annessa's eyes flared.

"Satan. The faithful," I kissed her cheek. "And most of all, me."

"I don't like this, Master." She leaned in close to me and looked in my eyes. "It's my job to keep you safe."

"Think of it this way, Annessa," I held her face. "Now you can do that even better than before."

I kissed her and turned to go help Adrian with the weapons. As I walked away, I could see her standing with her hand over her heart, rubbing her chest. She didn't look pleased.

CHAPTER 17

Adrian and I stood in the center of the prisoners. Chalk lines ran from prisoner to prisoner in geomantic shapes. Each one was surrounded by glyphs of binding and of pain. This wasn't meant to be pleasant. I'd like to take credit for this idea, but it was actually Adrian's.

The energy released by the prisoners at the moment of their death would be used to fuel the rebirth of another prisoner in a long, elegant chain. Taking a page from the Umbrals' playbook, we were going to make the enemy into our own soldiers. Granted, they would be mostly mindless and of limited use, but they only had to get us through the night. More than being functional killing machines, they were meant to be terrifying to the enemy, to demoralize them before they even got close enough to inflict any damage on us. We were expecting the full Angelic war machine, and we were ready for it.

I nodded to Adrian, "Go for it."

He spoke the first word of the binding spell. The chalk constructs on the floor lit with flowing blue fire. It spread from pattern to pattern, circling over every glyph, jumping from prisoner to prisoner. It only took a second before the screaming began. I waited until the first prisoner dropped to his knees and I joined in with Adrian's chant, punctuating it with Words of binding, command and fire.

The prisoners began to burn from within as ice blue flames erupted from their eyes. It didn't take all that long. For as much as we hated these soldiers, neither of us was a sadist. We barred them from their afterlife, which was the true punishment, but oblivion is better than eternal torment, which is what they offered us.

The prisoners hovered between life and death, every second pure agony. I stopped chanting, lifted my right hand and spoke the incantation to animate dead flesh. I nodded curtly to Adrian before I intoned the final syllable. He dropped the binding spells and removed the masking spell that had hidden them from St. George and the Umbrals. I screamed the final word of the incantation. Fire leapt from my hand and raged through the ranks of the prisoners. They threw their heads back in soundless howls of agony. Maybe in those final moments they prayed, maybe they asked for forgiveness and maybe they thought of their families. I thought of Sarah, bound to an altar and repeatedly raped. I thought of killing her. Suddenly, I no longer cared what they thought about.

I felt them die. I watched them fall to their knees. I felt them rise again, mindless and full of rage.

"I have them," I called to Adrian.

He nodded and threw off his sport coat and adjusted his .45s in their holsters. "I imagine your guests will arrive shortly, my lord."

Annessa slid up behind me and wrapped her arms around my chest. "I'm going to the roof." She kissed my neck. "You better be alive when I get back."

"I will be," I grinned. "What could possibly go wrong?"

She snorted and hurled herself into the rafters. I summoned Abbadonna and felt her presence fill me.

"No, Beautiful." I looked up at Annessa as she climbed through a skylight. "Up there."

"Emissary," she hissed at me. "This isn't wise."

"Why, because I'm likely to do something stupid?"

"Don't you always?"

I shook my head. "Go, Abbadonna. Keep Annessa

safe."

I felt her rage as she left me. Good, that would keep Annessa on her toes. The newly raised haemunculae crowded around me, mewling like sick kittens. I looked at them in disgust. How could I have ever thought Annessa was like them? They were hungry, but thankfully they wouldn't have long to wait. I felt the portal before I saw it. I yanked my Beretta free of my holster.

The Angelics can't use the Shadow Roads like we can; they can't pass the Veil easily and more than that, sorcery and many other aetheric arts are forbidden to them. They rely on Angels to transport them. The Angels use hidden doorways leftover from creation. Think of them like seams of a massive tapestry. The Angels know how to tug the seams apart far enough to pass through without rending the tapestry. It was a neat trick, but not really worth the price of admission in my mind.

I sent out a mental warning to Abbadonna that the door was opening. I whistled and cocked my head toward where it was going to open. As Adrian, Harker and the wolves hid themselves, I moved toward the center of the room. The haemunculae surrounded me, they growled and snapped at each other as my adrenaline fueled their rage. The door burst wide and black uniformed soldiers flooded the room. I released the haemunculae as I turned, gun at the ready. It all moved in slow motion, the rush of wind as the haemunculae hurled themselves at the soldiers, the vapor trails of the bullets as they whipped by my face and the sound of the inquisitors chanting battle prayers. I smiled as I fired at the inquisitors. St. George wasn't playing; he'd brought his A–game.

The air in front of me vibrated; it wasn't much of a warning, but it was enough. I stepped through the Veil and rolled to the side. A vampire landed where I'd been standing. He was dressed as a priest, but the look on his face was anything but peaceful. He turned to look at me, his fangs dripping blood. I raised my pistol, but it was already too late. The air behind me rippled and I heard a feminine voice.

"Hello, Handsome," Mara laughed maniacally as her claws rent him from navel to neck. A second strike from Sophia severed his head.

Mara yanked me back to my feet. Her face was splattered with blood, but her smile was euphoric. "Don't just sit there, Jason," she grinned. "Kill something!"

"I'll see what I can do," I grinned and fired at an inquisitor. The bullet ricocheted off of his forehead; he made the sign of the cross and began hurling curses at me. The bastard had a reliquary on him; no bullet of mine was going to strike him. I smiled at him and sent my haemunculae after him, en masse. I turned my attention to the soldiers. I emptied my pistol, reloaded and emptied it again. There were just so damned many of them.

Adrian stepped out from behind a cargo container and leveled an M-4 with an under–slung M-203 at the mob of soldiers. As I called my haemunculae back to me, the grenade sailed over their heads and landed in a cluster of soldiers. I spoke a warding incantation and threw a shield between the blast and me channeling and compounding the force of the grenade blast back at the soldiers. Adrian immediately began to lay down suppressive fire, and I sent my haemunculae back into the fray. It was odd; St. George had sent his inquisitors and a metric ton of manpower, but no Host–Bound, and so far, only one vampire. He was holding his really heavy hitters in reserve. I mean, I was too, but I really wanted to know what he had. This was simply taking too long. If I'd been smart, I'd have realized that he'd been using my impatience against me from the beginning, but we've been over this a time or two—I'm not too bright.

I saw him a second too late. In reality, I saw the sole of his foot, but it'd hit me enough times in the past for me to have an intimate knowledge of its shape. The kick hurled me off of my feet. I rolled through the Veil. I came up, pistol at the ready. He was gone. The motherfucker was wearing the same black uniform as the soldiers. He'd been here all along. What else was hiding in plain sight? What else was clothed as a human?

"He's here," I screamed through my mindlink with

Abbadonna and Annessa. "Be ready."

"We await your command," I could hear the rage in their collective voice, "Master."

I rolled out of the line of fire as the soldiers shifted their attention to me. I stepped behind a cargo container and came face to face with Victus.

"Milord," he bobbed his head. "We are ready whenever you are."

"Not yet," I shook my head in response. "He's up to something."

"As you wish," he replied. I could see his disappointment. He was probably hoping to get himself killed before Cassidy arrived.

I slipped back around the cargo container and fired a shot point blank into the face of a soldier. I caught him and held him up as a shield. I could hear that fucking inquisitor still chanting. I'd had just about enough of that. You can only hear so many "Our Father's" and "Though I walk's" before you become a bit unstable. Looking back, I think that was the point. It might not have been damaging to me, but it was damned annoying. I hurled the dead soldier at the inquisitor.

As the corpse flew, I raced behind it. I incanted the blessing of Leviathan and charged through the ranks of the soldiers. I almost had him; my hand was just about to grip his collar when it happened. St. George appeared in my peripheral vision, and he was grinning like an old man in the middle of a sorority pillow fight. He kicked my trailing leg as I raced by him. He fucking tripped me. Damn, I hated him and admired him all at once. He did nothing to impede my forward progress, thus the blessing didn't harm him at all. It just knocked me ever so slightly off course. I slammed through the wall of the warehouse and rolled to a stop in the dirt outside.

I leapt to my feet, my hands at the ready. He kicked the Beretta out of my hand and without even slowing, hurled that same foot into my throat. I threw my elbow up and shoved the next kick aside as I backpedalled to give myself some room.

You have to understand, the Air Force had taught me to defend myself, to take down basic violent offenders and very simple ground fighting. But St. George, he was a martial artist. You know, martial artist, as in he made killing the most beautiful thing you'd ever seen. He made a brawl into a fucking Rembrandt. I had nothing on him.

I couldn't breathe, and he'd kicked my weapon out of my hand. I threw up the hand that wasn't clasped around my throat. I waved it like a retard chasing a balloon. When I saw his eyes focus on my hand for a second; I did what I was best at, I cheated.

See, I'm not really stupid. No, I'm a kid with ADD in a room full of video games and candy. I'm usually too busy running around like an over-caffeinated chimpanzee to pay attention to any one thing. But, you'll only get a chimp on a roller coaster once. And St. George had put me on one already. Just below the collar of my shirt carefully clipped to my shoulder holster was a second pistol. As soon as my hand closed on it, I rolled away from him and dove through the Veil.

He whirled to face his rear, expecting me to attack where he was most vulnerable. I stepped through the Veil exactly where I'd left it. I fired all five shots from the little .357 into his pelvis. Neat little thing about the pelvis, if you weaken it, it doesn't crack or break—it disintegrates. He pivoted and as he did, he collapsed in a heap, his body no longer able to support him.

I carefully cleared my throat before speaking. The last thing I wanted was to begin my victory speech and have my voice crack like a twelve-year old. Not that it would have mattered much, he was screaming so loud, he probably couldn't hear me. His screams were like a symphony to me. He'd beaten me like a rented mule, scalped me and left me to die at the hands of the fae. More than that, he'd sold out all of humanity—he'd made Sarah's sacrifice meaningless and for that alone, I had no sympathy for him.

"What you're feeling now," I growled. "Is only the smallest taste of the fate to which you've condemned all of mankind." I walked around him mindful of what little striking distance remained to him.

"Your stinking master," he spat, "condemned you all."

"My Father," I smiled beatifically as I reloaded my revolver. "Is guilty of nothing more than the sin that you, yourself, just exhibited." I bent and picked up my beloved Beretta and holstered it. "My Father has freed us all," I shook my head. "You're just too damned servile to see it."

"Your words are meaningless," he laughed. "You've accomplished nothing, Beckett."

That's where you're wrong, you arrogant son of a bitch." I shot him in the balls. "I've managed to take some measure of satisfaction." I leveled my little revolver at the back of his head as he flopped and screamed in agony. "If you're lucky, your god is more merciful than me." My finger closed on the trigger and that's when the bitch shot me.

I saw her move an instant before the bullet hit me. She hadn't even aimed. She was standing in plain sight on a roof adjacent to the warehouse. She casually held the double rifle in her left hand. The bullet struck me in the ribs just below my heart. It pretty much vaporized my left lung and left a fist–sized hole in my back. Based on the fact that the entry wound in my chest was about the size of my thumb, I guessed the rifle was at least a .375. I staggered back. I stopped my heart and quit breathing. I quickly fired twice into St. George, the first shot into his right knee, and the second into his face. Likely, he'd survive, but it wouldn't be pleasant. I turned and fled toward the warehouse. I didn't make it.

She landed gracefully before me. I saw that Harker was right, about everything. She was dressed like a nun and wore a flowing black tunic with a hooded cloak in place of the traditional scapular. She backhanded me, and I flew into the side of an immense shipping container. The impact jarred me back into breathing, which was not a good thing. Before I could do anything more than gasp and aspirate blood, she gripped my throat and lifted me.

"Strange," she spoke without an accent, I'd expected her to sound like Harker. "I was expecting more fight out of you." Her fangs flashed in the low light.

"Me too," I coughed blood as I spoke. It spattered her pale features. It seemed to suit her.

"Call for help," she smiled. "Now."

"Blow me," I spat blood in her face. "Sister."

"I can smell him on you," she pulled me close and inhaled my scent. "My Jonathan."

I rolled in her grasp and slapped her with my Mark. "Get back!" I yelled weakly.

She dropped me and staggered back. My Mark had left an angry burn on her pale white cheek. She growled at me.

I pulled my Beretta and fired.

She dissolved into smoke and reformed before me. She charged forward and slapped me like a petulant child. It nearly knocked me out.

"Call for help," she demanded again.

"No," I shook my head woozily. I held my hands in front of me palms facing in. It looked a lot less threatening than it really was.

"I can make you," she flashed her fangs. "I can take away your choice."

"No," I said. "You can't."

She buried her fangs in my neck.

Kelæm Sûat Veym Nethrëk. I felt my veins pulse with Ghūllish blood and energy, my fangs ripped through my gums.

She gasped and pulled away from me as the Ghūl blood burned her. I buried my fangs in her face and bit down with all the force of a ravenous Ghūl. I felt her cheekbone shatter and I tore out her eye. She shrieked and dove through the Veil to get away from me. I kept my eyes locked on hers as I swallowed her flesh. I felt a surge of power ripple through me as I took her Gift for my own. I shook with the force of it. She clapped a hand over her mangled face and backpedalled away from me.

"You bastard!" she screamed. "I'll have your heart!"

"You...Fuck," I shook my head to try to clear it. I could feel the grip of Nagg'resh Vök beginning to take hold of my brain. I saw double. I staggered and dropped to a knee as her vision overtook my brain. The strength of Mina's flesh was too much for me to bear and I collapsed.

It hit me like an uppercut, stunning me with its clarity and pure tactile sensation. Because I had torn away nearly half of her face, I could feel as well as see. I saw her praying in a small room somewhere before a shrine to the Virgin Mary. I felt the red–hot blessed gold brands that the inquisitors rammed against her naked flesh. It was excruciating, but her eyes never left the statue of the Virgin. I couldn't hear her prayers, but I could feel her lips moving in time to familiar prayers. I lost her for a minute as my brain shut down until the vision of her torment passed. She was a vampire and she knew how to handle pain; Gifts aside, I was still human and there was only so much that I could take. As the vision overtook me again, I saw that she was in a van with St. George and Father Jacob and the three vampire goons that we'd fought outside of Harker's. My heart surged with hate as I laid eyes on Father Jacob. I couldn't hear what they were talking about, but I saw her take a sacrificial dagger from Jacob. She tucked it into one of her boots. The van stopped down the block from Harker's; Mina and her goons jumped out.

She entered Harker's Place like a vengeful god of death. She hit the bouncer so hard he was dead before he landed on the floor. She grabbed one of the fragile little humans that frequented the bar. She spoke two or three words and buried the dagger in the poor bastard's chest. The Varg'Thūl tore itself free from the shadows in the corner of the room and bowed low before her. She didn't wait around to watch it work.

Lila and Katya tried to stop her at the door; even with her eyes, I couldn't see what she did to them. She didn't even wait to see them hit the floor. A second before the elevator door closed she casually tossed a bag into the back of the bar. If I had to guess, I'd bet it was about fifteen to twenty pounds of C4.

She hit the garage moments before we arrived. She raced out of the garage and caught up to the van about ten blocks away. Time faded as the van drove and there was another black spell, which I assumed to be dawn when she would have had to sleep. When she awakened, she met with St. George again. He was showing her a cage. I'd seen another just like this one before. The two morons in the cemetery had one like it bolted to the floor of their van. They were after Annessa, again. Why?

St. George pounded on the cage as he explained something to her. He grew more agitated and he hit her, hard. She dropped to her knees before him and started praying again as he beat the unliving shit out of her. The beating went on for what seemed like hours. When it was done, he dragged her to a sand table where there were rough models of the Red Hook warehouses outside of which we were currently standing. They'd known what we were planning. How the fuck could they have known? My mind raced. Before they gave away their source, her vision faded from me and left me gasping as I was thrown back into my own senses.

Mina slowly circled me. The strength of her blood had shoved her memories through my brain at lightning speed. I woozily pushed myself up to a kneeling position and tried to assess my surroundings. St. George was gone. Fuck, I knew that was going to come back to haunt me. I staggered to my feet and squared my shoulders.

"How'd you know?" I snarled. "Who told you where we'd be?"

She shook her head and hissed at me. "I'm going to kill you, Emissary." She touched her face gently. She seemed surprised that the ragged wound wasn't healing.

"It'll never heal, Mina," I said. "You'll be hideous forever."

"You son of a bitch!" She flew at me with her claws outstretched and her face contorted into a mask of horror.

"Father," I whispered. "Walk with me." I stepped through the Veil as she reached me.

Every time she slashed at me, I dodged through the Veil. It was if I could sense her attacks, as if I knew her every thought. Normally, I'd have been grinning like a fool and talking as much shit as possible. Right now, I was scared. The thing is, she was faster than even Vincenze had been. I couldn't keep up with her for long. It wasn't a matter of if she were able to get through me, but rather, when she got through me. When she did, my friends were in deep shit.

Where the hell was Cassidy? It's sad how much I relied on him for the heavy lifting, but let's face it, I'm not exactly a monster in hand to hand combat and werewolves are.

"You can't run forever, Beckett!" she spat. "What are you going to do when you tire?"

She was right. I couldn't keep this up for much longer. The blessing of foresight from Nagg'resh Vök was going to fail eventually and this Veil jumping was going to wear me out. I had no choice; I called for help. I whistled through my teeth. She immediately looked over her shoulder and in that half second, I leveled my Beretta and fired. The gold–tipped bullets tore through her right knee. It wouldn't stop her, but it might give us a fighting chance.

She whirled back to face me as Victus, Riley and Ouillette hit her like fur covered bullet trains. She might have been strong, but no one can dismiss three, thousand-year old wolves out of hand. She dissolved into smoke before she hit the ground. The smoke eddied for a minute and solidified into the shape of the biggest wolf I'd ever seen. Harker hadn't lied; this bitch was truly something else. I should have remembered Stoker's story, but at that point, I really wasn't thinking of literature.

Mina darted forward; her fangs bit deep into Riley's foreleg. As soon as she'd locked her jaws, she rolled hard, snapping the limb like a twig. The other two wolves wasted no time, they tore at her flanks. As soon as the wounds opened, they began to seal as she drained Riley's blood to heal herself. In essence, we weren't getting anywhere. I summoned Abbadonna; as much as I didn't want to involve Annessa in this fight, I didn't have any other choice.

I'd held Annessa in reserve, not because she was weak, but because she was the most powerful weapon I had, my Queen, if you will. The cage in my vision made me terrified to involve her in anything. Let's face it; I have shit for a track record when it comes to protecting women.

Annessa threw herself off the roof and landed lightly just outside the pile of wolves. She grinned at me and charged in. With a vicious swipe of her claws, she hurled Mina out of the pile.

"You!" Mina whispered as she stared at Annessa. She threw her head back and screamed something in Angelic. I didn't quite catch it; the volume of her scream nearly ruptured my eardrums and forced me to my knees. "Now you will see His glory!"

It was like the stars rained down from the heavens. I felt so many Angelic doorways opening that I couldn't keep track. Fuck me. I ran back toward Annessa.

"We need to get back inside, Annessa!" I grabbed her hand and was stopped short when she didn't move.

"No." She shook her head. "These motherfuckers want to take me? Let them try." She dug her heels in and faced the inbound Angelics. She'd seen my vision, or at least seen enough of it to know that they were after her. Stupid, stupid fucking mindlink.

"Annessa, this isn't a game." I yanked her arm and did exactly nothing.

"We know." she replied, her voice frighteningly low. Abbadonna wasn't helping anything. Shit.

"I guess I brought this on myself," I muttered.

"Yes, you did." She smiled at me, her fangs glinting coldly.

The first doors opened and Host–Bound poured out like ants from a hive. I really should have saved those haemunculae. They were all dead now, wasted on the Angelic's cannon fodder. Abbadonna must have called for Adrian. He came out of the warehouse, loaded down with weapons. Sheena, Harker and his girls raced out behind him.

"Only you, Beckett," Sheena said as she shook her head. "Only you could piss this many people off."

Harker's eyes locked on Mina. "Mina," he breathed. His girls spread out behind him.

Where the hell was Cassidy? At this point it wasn't even the threat of imminent death that had me concerned. He was always fashionably late, but I knew something was wrong now. Things were getting serious.

It was like a comic book standoff. The good guys all lined up behind their vampire–nun leader and the bad guys were lined up behind their angry haemunculus–Fallen Sacred Mother.

Harker moved first. He launched himself past Adrian, snatching a pistol from Adrian's belt as he went by. He aimed and fired all ten gold–tipped rounds at Mina as he charged. He must have been a pretty good shot; he actually landed a single hit on her leg. The girls flew behind him like an angry shadow; they hit her in a wave.

The Host–Bound took that as their signal to attack; they charged en masse, chanting battle hymns. With each step, the ground trembled. My stomach fell, these weren't run of the mill soldiers; they were dedicated soldiers who were used to being possessed. I dodged and shot my way to Adrian's side. He was like a machine; he turned and fired round after round from both of his pistols. It was a sight to behold; his head was in line with his right arm, but his angelic soul would duck out and aim down his left arm. Both guns fired simultaneously and with each shot another target hit the ground.

I grabbed the M-4 he'd slung over his back. He ducked out of the sling and nodded at me. I yanked the charging handle back and leveled the weapon at the Host–Bound. I whispered a blessing over the rifle. I found Annessa and started dropping targets around her, not that she needed it, but it made me feel safer.

Adrian and I guarded each other, which was probably for the best as we were easily the two physically weakest combatants on the field. As more and more Host–Bound flooded the area, it became apparent that this was a losing proposition.

"Reinforcements are en route, my lord," Adrian yelled over the gunfire and screams.

I nodded. "Good, I don't think we can hold out for

much longer," I replied. I contemplated calling Uthiel, but that risked a cascade of full–blown Angels. I decided against it and focused on the charging Host–Bound.

I fired my way through another magazine and reloaded. These things were never ending; it was as if they were coming off some sort of angelic assembly line and diving right into battle. Annessa was literally standing on a pile of corpses; she was like death in motion. She leapt from combatant to combatant, her claws shearing through both flesh and angel alike as Abbadonna lent her essence to each hit. They couldn't keep this up forever. I had to do something. Unfortunately, I had no idea what that something was.

Harker and his girls were containing Mina, but that's really all they were able to do. She was like lightning, striking rapidly and shifting between forms so fast that they couldn't attack fast enough to hit her. I saw Sheena stalking her way across the field like a vengeful god, striking down her enemies with righteous anger. She was making her way to Harker's side. If I could have placed money on that fight, I'd have been on the phone with a bookie already.

A solid kick to my midsection ended any speculation on my part. My ribs broke and punctured my lung, for the second time tonight. The Host–Bound who'd kicked me grinned like a retard that'd just farted. I charged him and slapped him across the face with my Mark as I shouted a Word of abjuration. The force of my Word drove the angel right out of him, and he collapsed to the ground gasping. He looked up at me fearfully.

"No!" he shouted as I leveled my rifle.

Without a word, I shot him in the throat. After watching him thrash for a second, I made my way back to Adrian.

"Any luck with those reinforcements?" I coughed out.

"Yeah, they're on their way." He grimaced as he reloaded and burned himself on the hot slide of his pistol.

"Any idea when they'll get here?" I asked between shots.

There was a roar as a mass of possessed soldiers

poured out of the shadows behind us.

"I'd say about now–ish." He grinned and began firing with renewed vigor.

"About time." I looked for Annessa. She was starting to slow; the Host–Bound were wearing her down. I spoke a Word of healing as I raced to keep up with our soldiers.

"To the Sacred Mother!" I commanded.

They obeyed without question, driving through the Host–Bound in a tight phalanx. As we reached Annessa, the soldiers formed a circle around her. She darted in and out of the ranks with abandon, her claws ending lives with each slash. I looked to find Harker and Sheena. Sheena stood toe to toe with Mina, flitting from shape to shape giving the vampire no rest. As they tore at each other, Harker and his murder struck at Mina with every opportunity. Slowly, they wore her down. I ran to Sheena's side.

"Don't kill her!" I yelled as I ran.

"What?" Harker turned to look at me for a fraction of a second. "Are you off your chump?"

"I need to know what they're planning," I huffed out. Even partially healed, this one lung business was bullshit.

Sheena punched through Mina's chest as Mina shifted into smoke. Sheena shifted with her, her intangible hand gripped Mina's heart. As they shifted back to flesh, Sheena didn't release her grip. Mina froze in mid transformation. Sheena grinned.

"You're mine," Sheena laughed in Mina's face. She looked Mina in the eye. "Start talking, Leech," she demanded.

Mina grinned slyly and my heart sank. I felt a pulse, like mindseeking, only much more focused. I ducked as Sheena's fist sailed over my head. Mina's telepathy was amazing! No one should have been able to do that, not to a fucking Sidhe anyway. Miles had warned us. Sheena was strong, but I knew that even a creature as powerful as Mina couldn't hold a Leanan Sidhe for very long. I backpedalled and tried to avoid Sheena's stone fists. I turned my face at the last minute, dodging her deadly fist. As her fist whipped by my face, I gripped her forearm with my left hand and pushed with my Mark. I saw Annessa racing toward us; I had to snap Sheena out of it, or bad things were going to happen.

"Sheena Samhradh," I thundered. "Be free!"

She hit me with a pretty wicked jab as she returned to her senses. I rolled away from her as I hit the ground and came up holding my left cheekbone.

"You're going to pay for that, bitch," she spat at Mina.

Mina dodged away from Sheena right into Harker's arms.

"Hello, Mina," he growled as his hand closed over her neck.

"Jonathan," she croaked. "My love."

"My name is Miles," he shook her violently. "You crazy bint! My fucking name is Miles!"

She tried to shift into smoke. Annessa's claws ripped through the night, and Abbadonna's clove the Veil, both, as one, ripped into Mina's rib cage.

"You aren't going anywhere, bitch," Annessa roared.

Mina smiled. Something in me screamed at that moment and I knew Annessa had made a terrible mistake. Mina grabbed Annessa's wrist. A small, gold reliquary dangled from Mina's wrist and glittered brightly for a second. As it spun in the poor light, I saw the letters C–S–P–B flare for a moment and I dove to grab Annessa.

The air pulsed with pain and panic as the light of the reliquary tore through the night. It was like a nuclear explosion; waves of heat and light blasted my face, and I was blown off of my feet and hurled to the ground. As quickly as it had appeared, the light faded.

I sat up holding my head. My vision swam, and my lungs felt scorched. I could hear screams intermittently over the sound of the ringing in my ears. As my eyes cleared, I could see corpses of Host–Bound and Possessed Soldiers scattered over the smoking ground. Their flesh was seared to ashes and their souls destroyed in the light of Mina's attack.

Adrian lay on his side next to me, gasping and clutching at his chest. The light had seared him terribly, but he still lived. I put my hand on his blistered face and spoke a Word of healing over him. My eyes darted around the remains of the battlefield seeking any other survivors. Sheena, Harker and his murder stood staring at the desolation around them. Mina was gone and with her Annessa.

"Harker," I said, trying to keep my voice calm. "Help me with Adrian." Harker was at my side in a flash, helping me lift Adrian back to his feet. He looked at me over Adrian's head.

"Was that...a Benedictine Flask?" he asked me, nodding at the dead all around us.

"Yeah," I said. A Benedictine flask is one of the holiest relics of Yahweh's forces. They contain dust from St. Benedict's bones and fragments of his fabled poisoned cup. There wasn't much holier other than a fragment of the True Cross itself. Invoking one was like dropping an atomic bomb as far as Angels and Fallen were concerned, exorcism on a massive scale.

"She's in for a pound isn't she?" He raised an eyebrow.

"No." I shook my head. "She's got Annessa. This was their master stroke."

"What do you mean?" he asked.

"If they kill her, then no Chosen Son," Adrian gasped.

I thought of the cage. "They're not going to kill her," I said. "They're going to breed her." I let go of Adrian as he got his legs back under him. My eyes were already searching for any remnant of the door Mina used to escape.

"Breed her?" Sheena asked. It hit her as the last word left her lips. "If she's tainted, then..."

"We're all dead," I said.

CHAPTER 18

It took about twenty minutes to dig the wolves out. They were buried beneath a mound of Host–Bound corpses. It was all taking too long. I needed to find out where Mina had taken Annessa. I took a deep breath. I had to remain calm. If I charged into where ever they were holding her alone, I was going to die. I stilled my heart and tried to mindseek Annessa again. I'd been trying about every five minutes; it was long shot, but it was better than anything else I had at the moment.

Adrian looked up from his cell phone and gave me a half smile. "Finally, some good news, my lord," he said.

"What?"

"Mr. Reginald Ross has regained consciousness, my lord," he smiled evilly. "I believe we may have a lead."

"That bloodsucking fuck better talk," I said. "I'm in no mood for bullshit."

Adrian drove us to the embassy. Harker and his girls fled for the coming dawn, and I sent the wolves to track down any remaining Angelics in the area.

"What would you like to do first, my lord?" Adrian asked as we pulled into the embassy garage.

"I'm going to see Erzebet," I replied.

"As you wish, my lord."

"Go find the prisoner," I said. "Make sure that he's been prepped for interrogation."

I stood outside Erzebet's office. I took a breath to compose myself. I didn't want to charge in there like an emotional wreck. Irrational anger, while the natural choice for someone in my shoes, was counterproductive. I knocked once and entered.

The old woman jumped up from her desk to greet me. "My Lord Emissary," she curtsied.

"Call me Jason, it's faster. We don't have much time."

"I understand," she said. "If you'll follow me, my Lor—Jason, I have something to show you."

She led me down the corridor to a large conference room. A huge LED screen occupied the better part of the largest wall of the room. She motioned for me to sit in one of the chairs as she picked up a remote and pointed it at the monitor.

"This is a map of the United States, as I am sure you can see." She motioned at the screen, which blazed to life. She hit another button on the remote and the slide advanced. "And these are the major population centers in the US, with their populations." Numbers popped up all over the map.

"Erzebet, I know you're trying to help," I said, my exasperation bleeding through. "But death by PowerPoint isn't the way to do it."

"Bear with me, Jason." She waved at the screen. "This is relevant."

New York, Los Angeles, Dallas, Fort Worth, Seattle, Atlanta, all of them lit up like Christmas trees with pulsing numbers on the screen. She advanced the slide again.

"These are the populations as of last month," she said. She advanced the slide again. Each population fell by a few thousand. "As you can see there was a significant change."

"Yeah, but given the immense population of New York alone, this is statistically insignificant," I said.

"Perhaps for New York alone, my lord," She said. "But in aggregate, this represents roughly one percent of the population of the United States as a whole. One in every hundred people in the United States gone in a single month and no one blinks an eye?"

"That can't be right," I said. I leaned closer to peer at the screen.

"Let me make it clearer for you, my lord." She advanced the slide and thousands of cities across the US lit up. "These are the American cities whose population decreased by more than nine-tenths of a percent between January and February."

"What the fuck?" I said.

She advanced the slide again. The globe swirled, lit up like New York on New Year's Eve. "This is the global picture."

"This can't be," I said. No one could have missed so much death, on either side of the Veil. "Someone had to notice this," I said. "This many people can't die and not alert anyone."

"I never said anyone died, my lord." She set the remote down. "These people just vanished."

"Have you been able to track the number of Angelic incursions in December and February against this information?"

"We have, my lord," she said. "In the time that you were...away, there was an eighty percent reduction in Angelic incursions."

I swallowed. "And what about Umbral activity in the same time frame?"

"Increased by over five hundred percent."

"And our people within the Church?"

"There has been no news," she said as she wrung her hands. "As I said when last we met, my lord, the End approaches, if it hasn't arrived already."

I blessed her as I left the room. I walked to the elevator in silence. I pulled my phone out of my pocket. Still no word from Cassidy; I was no longer worried. I was certain that something had happened to him. He'd never gone this long without contacting me, at least not when I was desperate to hear from him.

I hit the elevator button and stepped silently in. I wanted to scream and thrash and beat my fists against the walls of the elevator. I fought to control my rage. I knew that it was only my fear trying to reconcile itself with my helplessness. I paced, which was more like rocking back in forth in the elevator. There was something going on that defied the obvious, something deeper. I wanted very much to talk to Mr. Reginald Ross, to pick his fucking leech brain and find out what he knew.

As the door opened I thought of the last time I'd been here, with Annessa. I had to get her back; she was the key to the whole thing. I reached the door to the interrogation room and took a deep breath. I closed my eyes and said a silent prayer and opened the door.

I smelled the blood first. It was thick in the confines of the small room. Reginald Ross was bound in gold chains to a thick wooden pillar in the center of the room. His wrists were staked to the pillar by cold iron spikes plated with pure gold. Around him, six naked girls danced. Small incisions had been made at their wrists, throats and thighs. As they danced blood flowed in small rivulets down their lush bodies. Ross was also covered in hundreds of tiny incisions. He strained against his bonds like a madman. His body vibrated with restrained force as the gold pinned him against the pillar.

I shut the door hard behind myself. The girls stepped back from the ravenous vampire and dropped to one knee before me. Adrian stepped away from the far wall and moved to stand at my side.

"Mr. Ross," I said. "Welcome to Perdition's Embassy." I stepped closed to him and stood directly in front of him. "I trust everything is to your liking?" I gestured to the girls.

"Give 'em to me!" he yelled, hoarse with dehydration and desire. "I need 'em!"

"No." I shook my head. "That's not how this works."

"Please!" He thrashed against his bonds, his eyes never leaving the girls. "I gotta feed."

"I thought you holy leeches only fed on animals or choir boys?"

"I don't care 'bout any of that." He flickered as he tried to dart across the Veil. The chains kept him from going anywhere.

"And here I thought that you were devoted to your god and your Prioress." I turned my back on him.

"We din' want no part of that!" he said. "She made us! She made us kneel and let 'em burn us!"

"Well, that explains why you're still here, but I need more if I'm going to let you feed."

"I'll tell ya whatever you want!" He nodded furiously. "You just ask me, and I'll tell you! You just say, 'Reggie, tell me why kumquats are round and boxes are square' and I'll tell ya! You just ask!"

I nodded to Adrian. He rolled up one of his sleeves and grabbed a sponge from the floor. The girls made a tight circle around Adrian and he ran the sponge slowly over their naked flesh. It didn't take long until the sponge was red and full. Ross moaned and flexed his jaw making sick sucking sounds as he tried in vain to pull the blood across the room into his waiting mouth. After filling the sponge, Adrian squeezed it slightly dripping blood onto the nipple of one of the girls. He leaned over as if he were going to lick it off.

"For fuck's sake!" Ross screamed. "You're wastin' it! Bring it here! Bring it here and I'll squawk. I'll sing like a horny fuckin' parakeet!"

I held out my hand. Adrian tossed me the sponge. I held it out in front of Ross. "Where's the cage meant to hold the Sacred Mother?"

"It was at Saint Paddy's," he said. He paused to stick his tongue out, desperately trying to reach the sponge in my hand. "But they moved it, on account of His orders."

"St. George?" I asked him.

"What?" He looked at me and half grinned. "The pretender? Psh, no."

"Who?" I held up the sponge.

"The Voice." he said.

'Whose voice?"

"His Voice," he looked toward the ceiling as he spoke and I heard the capitalization as if he'd written it.

I tried to run through the Angelic rolls in my head to remember who'd been designated as The Voice. Finally I looked at Adrian.

"Enoch, my lord." he said. "The Metatron."

"Right," I turned back to Ross. I squeezed the sponge lightly as I flicked it toward him, showering his face with blood.

"Oh god." Ross licked his lips and contorted his face in an attempt to force the blood into his mouth. "Oh sweet buttered Jesus," he moaned. "I need more!"

"Then you need to tell me what I want to know." I said. "How did the Voice know that we were going to blow up St. Patrick's?"

"I don't know that he did," he moaned as a small trickle of blood managed to drip into his mouth.

"What do you mean?" I asked.

"Well, them's that call the shots, they was more concerned with where the altar was for the ritual and such." He shook his head. "Mina and the rest, they was all bowin' and scrapin' and makin' a fuss. They din't seem much worried about explosions."

"Where'd they move it, Ross?" I leaned close with the sponge. It was like teasing a junkie with a full needle.

"Across the park." He stuck his tongue out as far as it would go. "They took it to St. John's."

I looked back at Adrian. "The Line?"

His eyes widened. "I'll check."

"Warn Corrigan, just in case," I said. I frowned. "The Line" or "The Maiden's Girdle" is the name of the ley line that crosses Central Park connecting two major confluences, one in the Pine Barrens over in Jersey and the other upstate in Newburgh. St. Patrick's and St. John's were built to hedge in the influence of the Grove on the surrounding city. If the Umbrals or the Angelics were going to try anything involving sorcery of any kind, they might try to harness the energy of the line. The sigils and signs etched into the cage might also need a power source as potent as the Line to keep Annessa contained.

"Tell me more about the Voice," I said.

"Never seen 'im," he said absently as stretched his tongue toward the sponge.

I pulled the sponge back away from him.

"Alrigh',' alrigh'!" he yelled. "I ain't ever seen 'im, but I heard 'im once. Scared the shit outta me."

"Why?"

"'Cause I know what a killer sounds like, and I know what color crazy is and this bastard sounded like he needed a dye job and a straightjacket. He was crazy as a cat–fucking dog and the rest of them fools just nodded right along with 'im." He shook his head. "He sounded *hungry*." Ross seemed to deflate. "Look, man, you can do this all day. I get it." He hung his head. "Or you can just fuckin' feed me and let me tell ya what I know, civilized like."

I thought about it for a second. I motioned to one of the girls. She swallowed hard and stepped forward. "I won't let him kill you," I said.

"Yer a saint," Ross said. "Come to Reggie," he said to the girl.

CHAPTER 19

Any other day, in any other place, Reginald Ross and I might have been friends. I sat across from him in the small room and listened to him lick his lips. The girl, his meal, had been escorted someplace where she could recover in peace.

"Oh, man," he slurped the blood from his lips and licked the corners of his mouth. "That. Was. Delicious."

"I'm thrilled."

"Well, fair's fair. Ask your questions."

"That's it? You'll roll over that quick?"

"Ain't no rollin' over, friend. This here's more my speed anyway. I din't want no part of that other nonsense. Mina dragged me and the others with her."

"Why'd you stay?"

"'Cause tryin' to fight Mina is like tryin' to stop the sun from rising. All it gets you is burned."

"You don't like St. George?"

"Fuck that mouthy, howdy doody, dandy prick!" His fangs extended and his eyes blazed with feral menace. "Gimme half a chance, and no Mina, and I'd tear him apart."

"You called him a 'pretender,' why?"

"He ain't got no indigestion. He ain't nothing special. Thinks he's special, he's just a fucking bleeder, no offense."

"Indigestion?"

"You know, 'And the Lord said, YOU THERE, BE SPECIAL!'" He wiggled his shoulders as if he were waving his arms.

"Investiture?"

"What'd I say?" He cocked his head.

"It doesn't matter."

"But, no, he ain't got one them things you said neither."

"If he's not invested, why did you, fuck—why did Mina listen to him? Why'd she let him torture her?"

"The Voice. It told us that ol' Georgie–Boy was chosen."

"So you did what he said?"

"No," he shook his head violently. "No, sir, I did what Mina said."

"So you were afraid of Mina?"

"Yeah."

"Is there anything else you'd care to tell me?"

"If it ain't too much to ask, I'd really rather not die."

"Other than that?"

"Watch out for the Voice. It ain't right. It does things to you, to your head."

"I'll keep that in mind."

I stepped out of the room and shut the door behind me. Two guards waited outside with M-4s loaded with gold–tipped rounds.

"Orders, my Lord Emissary?" The ranking guard asked.

"Keep him here, and keep him fed until I return." I thought I might need more information from him at some point. And if he'd lied to me, I wanted to be sure that he could pay for it. But if he'd told the truth, at the very least, I could offer him the Traitor's Oath. Adrian stepped out of the elevator as I approached.

"I spoke to Corrigan Alefarn, sir."

"And?"

"He said that there was interference within the Line."

"It can't be that easy. They had to know that we could track them this way."

"Maybe they weren't counting on having two sorcerers and a priest in the mix. Magic can be a Achilles Heel for all of us at times, sir."

"But magic's so much cooler," I said as I pulled my cell phone out of my pocket. "Fucking genius."

"Sir?"

"You reminded me of something Annessa said once. I know how we can find her."

"How?"

"You gave her one of our phones, right?"

"My god!"

"No, I'm just his Emissary. Get the Embassy operator to track the GPS on her phone."

"Don't you think they'd have searched her?"

"Would you search Annessa?"

"No," he chuckled and shook his head. "No sir, I would not."

"Find her phone, Adrian."

CHAPTER 20

Annessa was being held in a small warehouse outside of Tarrytown or at least her phone was. Satellite imagery showed a limited presence there. St. John's, however, was full to bursting with Angelics. I looked at the screen as Adrian pointed out the various entrances and exits of the warehouse. I held up my hand to stop him.

"Don't waste your time telling me; brief your team, Adrian."

"My team, sir?"

"Yeah, you're taking Sheena, the wolves and whoever else you can scrape together to go and get Annessa. I'll call Harker and see if he wants to play, and if so, you've got him too."

"What about you, my lord?"

"I'm going here," I pointed to St. John's.

"Why?"

"Because they expect me to."

"But…that doesn't make any sense." Adrian cocked his head and squinted at me.

"If they don't see me at St. John's, they'll assume I know where Annessa is. That means she'll be better defended."

"My lord, I know it's not my place, but don't you think that's, oh I don't know, fucking stupid?"

"They expect a serpent, Adrian; I'm going to give them a dragon."

"Yeah, but—" he started.

"You just worry about getting Annessa and bringing her back here," I said. "Let me worry about getting myself killed."

After sundown, I called Harker and arranged for him to meet with Adrian. I made one other call.

"Hello, Jason. I'd wondered when we'd hear from you again."

"I told you it might be a mistake to offer your help, Corrigan."

"You are ever in the eyes of the Goddess, Jason Beckett. Where she is concerned, there are no mistakes, my friend."

I explained my plan to Corrigan and headed for the armory. If there's one thing the Devil lacks, it ain't guns. I turned a slow circle and whistled as I looked over the sheer variety of firearms at my disposal. I grabbed a shotgun, a silencer and more ammo for my Beretta. I needed to keep my load light, but as versatile as possible. For the kind of close up work that I was planning, a silenced pistol would work best. I suppose a knife would have been more efficient, but that takes skill I simply don't have. Normal silencers make noise; they kind of sound like someone dropped a phone book on tile. This one was enhanced with the sort of guile only the Devil can provide. I checked my watch; I had less than an hour to make it to St. Johns. I function checked my weapons, loaded them and headed for the garage and my waiting ride.

I slid out of the shadows in the West 111th Street Garden and crouched in the shadow of the Peace Fountain. The Cathedral of St. John the Divine sprawled before me. Its massive gothic architecture dominated the street and projected an aura of angelic strength like a blanket over the area. Seeing no motion, I silently slipped over the fence and pressed back against it as I surveyed the south side of the cathedral. There were soldiers everywhere. I counted thirty on the south side alone. I shook my head. None of them were Host–Bound. Apparently, St. George was running out of angels. I slid my pistol out and whispered a short blessing over it. I lowered myself into a crouch and waited for Corrigan's signal that he was in position.

A massive explosion rocked the entrance of the cathedral. I snorted and darted forward, Corrigan had all of the subtlety of a tactical nuke. I slipped from shadow to shadow as I approached the Cathedral. I hopped through the Veil to land in the shadow of a tree near the street and hopped twice more through the shadows of the trees until I was within sprinting distance of the south side of the church. My last hop brought me next to a guard. I fired a near silent shot into the base of his skull as I ran by. Before he hit the ground I spoke a Word of strength and hurled myself upwards and forwards through the massive stained glass windows.

I rolled as I hit the solid stone floor and came up with my gun at the ready. It was absolute chaos inside. Apparently, Corrigan had decided that a diversion wasn't enough and had launched a full–blown assault on the cathedral entrance. Flames and smoke billowed from the direction of the doors. I could hear him chanting hymns of darkness and death as he stalked through the halls toward me.

"I guess I didn't fully explain my definition of the word 'diversion,'" I yelled.

"The Dark Maiden has grown tired of these," he gestured around the room, "insects."

"Would've been good to know before we started."

"With all of the killing, there simply wasn't time," he grinned at me.

A burst of machine gun fire cut the air, and we both dove to either side of the main aisle. The pews in the center of the sanctuary had been piled into a massive barricade blocking off the altar. I looked over at Corrigan and winked as I rolled back to my feet and fired a hammered pair at the gunner. My mind raced as I charged the barricade. The

Angelics had piled in behind the barricade and were making their stand. If we didn't end this quickly, the bastards from outside would hedge us in and mow us down with crossfire.

"Corrigan," I yelled as I fired. "The barricade!"

He tapped his cane twice on the ground and released it. It stood perfectly straight, but its shadow raced forward like an arrow and sliced through the barricade like a razor. He chanted Words in a guttural voice and the shadow opened like a set of razor tipped wings, hurling huge chunks of pews and unfortunate soldiers in every direction. With a silent flick of his wrist, he called the cane back to his hand and nodded at me.

I raced down the center of the divide Corrigan had made. When I reached the space where the barricade had been, I launched myself into the air and slid through the Veil. I spun in mid-transition as I slid back onto the Lifeside. As I fell, I faced the back of the barricade. All of the defenders were still focused on where I'd been. I fired as rapidly as I could; my cursed rounds ripped fiery holes in their targets. I dropped six before the remainder turned on me. I swallowed hard. I threw my Marked hand forward and screamed a Word of light. Blinding brilliance filled the sanctuary. I released the spell and dove through the Veil again. I landed on the right side of the divided barricade and fired two shots, dropping two of the blinded soldiers. Before the others could clear their vision and fire at me, I hurled Words of flame and torment across the gap in the barricade and six more dropped.

I dropped into a crouch and rolled off the side of the barricade. I had to keep moving; there were still at least twenty of the bastards left, and I couldn't keep this kind of pace up indefinitely. A roar erupted from the base of the far side of the barricade and three massive dogs made entirely of shadow hurtled over the side. The soldiers broke and ran before the monstrous dogs. I said a silent prayer of thanksgiving to Hekate; these were her hunting hounds and she'd loaned them to Corrigan. Remember what I said about not fucking with Corrigan Alefarn? Yeah, this would be why.

The soldiers raced toward the shattered entryway of the cathedral, with the hounds of Hekate in full chase. Corrigan nodded toward the doors.

"You go on. I'll finish up out here."

"Thanks." I turned toward the altar.

"Goddess be with you, Jason."

"Satan walk beside you, man."

I walked up the steps toward the high altar. The air was disturbed and what candles remained lit flickered madly. I slid the half spent magazine out of my Beretta and replaced it with a full one. Reaching back to make sure my shotgun didn't bang against the floor; I crouched and ducked around the altar. A jagged hole had been ripped in the floor of the chancel, just before the east wall. I could see flickering lights below.

I leaned forward and tried to gauge the depth of the hole. I couldn't see a damned thing. I tried to be sensible and think through what I was going to do, I really did. As I moved back toward the altar, my foot slid on loose gravel and I staggered, slid and generally flailed my way to the edge of the hole. As I fell, I saw the circle of cold iron spears unevenly reflecting the torchlight below. I hurled myself through the Veil and landed just outside the deadly trap. Before I could take a breath of relief, I felt a familiar foot slam into my lumbar spine with bone shattering force.

My legs went rigid and pain shot through my body like wildfire. My Beretta flew from my hand, and I fell forward onto my face. I saw his hands grab my shotgun sling and I tried to snatch it away, but he was way too fast. He twisted the sling around my throat and drove his knee into my shattered back and bent me double, the wrong way. I would have screamed, if I could feel my vocal cords or had any air with which to make a sound.

"It's fitting that death should find you below ground, in the dirt like an animal," he growled into my ear, his face pressed up against the side of my head.

My vision began to fade into a rapidly dwindling pinhole of light and my mouth worked like a fish out of water. I couldn't shake him off, couldn't do anything to stop him. In my mind I was raging, thrashing against the walls of my consciousness to stay awake. A second before my lights went out, St. George released the sling. I gasped in air and fought for more. He drove his knee into my kidney and I screamed.

He laughed as he stood. He stepped in front of me so I could see him. His simple, but previously impeccable, clothes were covered in dried blood and filth. His eyes were wild and unfocused. A dirty bandage had been wrapped around his face, lending an air of madness to him.

"And lo,' the mighty have fallen." He laughed that wild laugh again. His eyes darted from me to something in the shadows. "I thought you might come to rescue your pet."

My stomach fell like an express elevator. I'd been fooled again. The motherfucker had found the cell phone. St. George held up his bloodstained hands.

"It wasn't quick, I promise you. I have no mercy for those like you, those who flagrantly violate the laws of the Almighty." He threw his head back and laughed madly. He grabbed my head and twisted it toward the shadows. I shut my eyes. I couldn't bear to look. Annessa. I'd failed again.

"Look!" He slammed his thumb behind my lower jaw and thrust it into the pressure point with fury.

My eyes opened and through the tears of pain I saw the impossible. My heart shattered like crystal, and I knew that something of beauty had been torn from the world forever.

'After all," St. George laughed madly. "Every boy needs his dog!"

There, in the shadows of the ruin of St. John the Divine, lay Cassidy. His body had been driven through with spears of cold iron and his face torn to shreds. There, in the shadows, my best friend, my brother, my shield, lay desecrated and dead.

A fire lit within me, an all–consuming inferno that beat in time to the screaming of my shattered heart. My lips pulled away from my teeth in feral snarl and I roared. I let loose the pain in my soul in a single resounding cry. I threw myself to my feet, my rage pouring through the shattered bone and severed veins, healing as it went. I whirled to face St. George.

He staggered backwards. I threw a vicious punch to his gut and doubled him over. My knees hammered against his head, driving him back toward the wall. He tried to defend himself; he punched me in the throat with enough force to rip the skin. I caught his forearm and bent it back so rapidly it snapped the bone in two. I twisted it until I heard the pop of his elbow dislocating, and I pulled him to me.

"You should've killed me," I growled at him, my torn vocal cords rendering my voice bestial. "The pain you're feeling now, this horrible, gut–wrenching pain," I twisted his shattered arm. "This is nothing compared to the pain that's coming." I yanked his arm. There was a sickening sound as it ripped free, just below the elbow. I tossed it aside like a broken toy.

He screamed, and I shoved him. As he staggered backwards, I stomped on his shin, shattering it. I jerked him up off of the floor, my adrenaline and hate pushing my body beyond even its invested limits. "You should have killed me instead, and you should have been sure to make it stick this time." I roared the blessing of Leviathan and hurled him down toward the floor. I wasn't aiming at the floor, but the Veil.

There was a flash of heat, then mind numbing cold, as we burst through the clouds over Lake Cocytus. I clutched his throat in my hand as we fell. I screamed inarticulate litanies of pain and hate as my other fist pounded against his face over and over.

CHAPTER 21

We hurtled through sky over Perdition, the ground whirling to meet us. I saw my Lord atop the Tower of Grief, and for the first time ever, I saw him astonished. I didn't care; my mind was fixated only on St. George. The icy surface of the lake filled my view. I pulled St. George close to me and I rolled with him, allowing my body to take the brunt of the impact with the ice. The last thing I wanted to do was kill him.

We hit the frozen surface with a thunderous crash. It shattered beneath us; massive chunks of foot thick ice hurled twenty feet into the air, thrown by the force of our impact and the blessing over my flesh. I shoved his head under the water. He tried to fight his way to the surface. I forced him under again, my hand clenched at the back of his jaw forcing his teeth open and letting the vile, freezing, briny water of Cocytus fill his mouth as I pulled him to the surface. Before he could spit it out, I threw an elbow into his jaw. The shock forced him to swallow it He screamed, blood and icy water spraying my face. The power of the river of Lamentation filled his soul. His eyes widened in terror and he shrieked. I forced him under the water again, holding him under until he swallowed again. I forced him under again and again. Each dose of the foul water increased its hold on him. He was going mad with pain and loss. I didn't care; I couldn't make him suffer enough.

I remembered when Cassidy told me that he'd given up his immortality. I'd been confused when we spoke about it. Cassidy was adamant, though.

"I've no need for sorcery such as that, Little Brother." He'd said.

"What, resurrection? I'd be terrified if I only got one shot to get this right."

"Give it a millennium, and see how your theory holds. Peace isn't something that frightens me."

"How do you know Satariel won't just jerk you out of the grave by your strings and make you dance to his tune all over again?"

He gave me that look. The kind of withering look that only a thousand years of being the most dangerous motherfucker in the room can teach. "That's not his way, he keeps his covenants."

"All I know is that if I die before the end of my term, the Old Man will drag me back to the Lifeside every damn time until I do what he wants."

"You're still raw from dying the first time and things seem much bleaker than they truly are." He lifted his whisky and drank. "That'll pass in time."

"So, how's it feel to be the only vulnerable emissary on the block?"

He grinned wolfishly. "Call me an emissary again, Little Brother and we'll see just who's vulnerable here."

I'd made a smartass remark, and we drank to youth and foolishness. And now I'd never lift a drink with him again. I shook the memory out of my head and dragged St. George under the freezing water again.

There was a scrape, like wood across jagged ice. Ṣafira stood over me, her barge sliding across the surface of the ice. She raised her spear and thrust it at St. George. I caught it just above the phial and held it in place, hovering an inch over St. George's heart.

"No." My breath came raggedly as I strained to hold her back. I didn't look up at her. St. George shoved against me screaming, trying desperately to drive the spear into his chest. I pushed him back.

She leaned against her spear, and I held firm. "You can't stop death, Jason."

"No, he cannot. *I* can, little Coinbound," Satan spoke from behind me. I hadn't heard him land in the scuffle.

"My Lord sent me to claim this soul for the Angelic assessor, Lord Satan. You have no right to stop me," she said. She continued to lean on her spear.

"Wrong. According to the Accords any person who dies in my domain is mine to claim. Clearly, child, you stand in my domain." He smiled at her.

Şafira's eyes rolled back in her head and twitched for a second as she communed with The Ferryman. "I guess this bastard's yours, Jason." She shuddered for a second and flew away as a stark white raven. Her barge faded through the ice and disappeared.

I looked to St. George as the last light of hope faded from his eyes. In that moment, in the death of his hope, I felt the smallest spark of vindication flare to life. Satan gripped my shoulder and pulled me out of the water like a toy. He looked down at St. George.

"Now, Alfred St. George, you will tell me all that I wish to know." He gestured toward the hole in the ice. The waters surrounding St. George froze solid, crushing him slowly. St. George screamed.

"Who commands the forces of Heaven?"

"Almighty God!" St. George shouted defiantly.

Satan clenched his fist and the ice surged against St. George, I heard bones snap. "Do not trifle with me!"

St. George's eyes bulged in their sockets. He made gasping noises as his lungs were crushed under the weight of the ice.

"Someone called 'The Voice' was giving them— him," I kicked St. George's face, "instructions."

"Enoch?" Satan shook his head. "No, the son of Cain was ever devout. He would not for a moment entertain the notion of betrayal. Ere the moment he was brought before the Throne and transfigured, he has served faithfully."

"It might not be betrayal, my Lord." I told him about the information that Erzebet had uncovered.

"Long have I been aware of the movements in Heaven. I thought it but the massing of the Host for a push in another Sphere." He gestured and a massive black spear appeared in his hand. I recognized it, *Morningstar's Folly*. It was the spear that Michael had driven into Satan's chest during the Battle at the Gates, the spear which nearly killed him. He bore it now, as a reminder of his hubris and a goad to push him beyond fear in battle.

He placed the long, leaf shaped blade of the spear under St. George's chin. "Who now commands the forces of Heaven on Earth?"

"I am a loyal servant of God." St. George stared at Satan, with firm resolve.

Satan said nothing. He thrust *Morningstar's Folly* through the ice and into St. George's side. St. George screamed, a thin, shrill scream as the ice crushed against him. Satan left the spear in his side and turned back to me.

"Return to Earth, my son. Find out who, or what leads this Angelic...remnant. If YHWH means to move against our interests elsewhere, we have little time to waste on a war that we've already won."

I nodded. My throat clenched as I thought of what I was returning to. "Please, Father, make him suffer. Make him suffer like no one has ever suffered before."

"Go, my child. There will be time for mourning later, but we must end this conflict before another begins; we can ill afford to fight a war spanning multiple spheres."

I closed my eyes and fought to control my emotions. I focused on the Veil and pushed against it. As I slipped through the Veil, I heard Satan speaking to St. George. Though his voice rose scarcely above a whisper, it carried unmistakable menace.

"You killed my former emissary, little slave. Apostate or no, Cassidy was loyal and he was ever in my sight. Your suffering shall be spoken of only in fearful whispers. You will beg for mercy, for peace and finally for oblivion. To this, I tell you now; abandon hope."

CHAPTER 22

I slid through the Veil and threw up, hard. I spit to clear my mouth. The cathedral was silent, save for the popping of the burning barricade above me in the sanctuary. I stood for a long moment and looked at the floor, unwilling to lift my eyes. I knew he was there, but I didn't want to say a word.

"I'm so sorry, Jason," Corrigan said.

I looked up at him. He stood in front of Cassidy's broken body. I nodded mutely.

"I'll give you a moment, my friend."

"Thanks."

"Be quick, the police will soon be here." He levitated out of the hole above us and stepped out of my view.

"I knew you were gone when you didn't call me back," I said in a hoarse whisper. I knew, logically, that Cassidy was gone and wouldn't hear my words. But somehow, in some way, not speaking to him was worse. It wasn't that I had any hope of bringing him back, just that I couldn't bear to let him go.

"Why didn't you call me? I would have come running, man. I don't care what it was, where I was…oh fuck me." I collapsed to my knees. The tears poured out of me. I held my face in my hands and sobbed like a child.

"*Get up, Little Brother. You've no time for this,*" I felt him say. I shook my head and wiped my face.

I half stood and stumbled over to him. I wiped my eyes. Hallucination or no, he was right. I had no time. I forced myself to look down at him. They'd nearly torn his face off. Both of his eyes were missing and one of his ears; it looked like Ghūls had been at him. They usually devoured the eyes and ears of their enemies. His right hand had been torn off and was impaled on one of the spears. His left hand was under him.

"You didn't," I whispered. "You said I'd never…"

I touched him, tentatively. It seemed almost sacrilegious. I grabbed his duster and pulled him toward me. His left hand slid out from under him and I slowly lowered him back to the floor. I knelt beside him. His hand was closed around something bloody. I gently pried his fingers apart and in his hand were both of his eyes and his right ear. He'd torn them out when he realized he was going to die. He'd torn them out so that I'd find them. I took them out of his hand reverently.

"You crazy Irish bastard," I laughed, then sobbed. Leaning forward, I kissed his forehead. "I don't know what I'm going to do without you, brother."

I heard the wail of approaching sirens. I heard Corrigan shout something from above. I stood and stepped back.

"Go, Corrigan," I yelled. "I'm right behind you."

I lifted my Marked hand and spoke a Word of purification. My Mark flared, and Cassidy's flesh ignited. His body collapsed into ash, but strangely, his duster remained. I stepped forward and lifted it. It was heavy. I pulled it open and the hilt of a sword slid out. I'd seen it before, on the night that Sarah died; Dominus had brought it to Cassidy. Boots sounded on the floor above. The cops were here. I threw Cassidy's duster over my shoulder and Veil–jumped out of the hole.

I landed in front of a very well–armed SWAT team. Their weapons immediately swiveled toward me.

"Your hands, motherfucker! Show me your hands!" the point man yelled.

"Ok." I lifted my hands, my left hand closed.

"Open your hand!"

I spoke a Word of panic as I opened my hand. My Mark flared and the SWAT team scattered, screaming as their resolve broke. They raced to get as far away from me as possible. I walked toward the door and the sea of flashing lights outside. I spoke a Word of conflagration as I approached the hole that was once an entryway. Flames and smoke burst from the front of the cathedral. A quick jump though the Veil as I reached the flames and I came out behind the cops, who were too busy ducking and screaming for the fire department to notice me. Staring back at the burning cathedral, I dialed the embassy and requested a ride.

* * *

The driver was pulling up in front of my apartment when I got Adrian's call. I prayed fervently that it was Annessa calling me from his phone.

"My lord," he said.

"Tell me you have her, Adrian."

"I'm sorry, my lord."

"Tell me you got a lead, at least."

"No, my lord. They just disposed of her belongings here, including her clothes."

"Get back here, now."

I poured myself a double shot of whiskey, tossed Cassidy's duster over the back of the couch and sat in the center of the living room floor. I lifted the shot.

"Wherever you are now, Cassidy, here's to peace and large-breasted redheads." I threw the shot back and tossed the glass behind me. His eyes and ear were in my Marked hand.

"Kelæm Sûat Veym Nethrëk." I felt the blood boil in my veins as the transformation took hold. I breathed in slowly, steeling myself for what was to come. I threw back the first eye, then the second and finally the ear. I tried not to gag on the cartilage and consciously avoided thinking of what I was doing. Instead, I imagined something I had never seen before, Cassidy happy.

It took less than a second for the vision to hit me. My senses reeled. This made Mina look weak in comparison; the strength of Cassidy's flesh was profound. Everything around me seemed to thrum with hidden power and the world moved as if it were in slow motion. After a millennium of trials and combat, there was nothing about Cassidy that wasn't dangerous. The vision jerked me out of reality with hurricane force.

I moved through the grass, my nose lifted to the wind every few seconds. Something reeked of decay. A low growl escaped my throat. I kept low as I approached the house; my ears swiveled from side to side, and I could hear voices. I raised my head above the grass for a second and looked at the huge mansion as I approached. I recognized it, though it took me a minute; I hadn't seen the Francione house in the better part of a year. Between the damage incurred in the fight with the Cathdronai and abandonment, the place was a wreck.

Two people were moving something heavy; it looked like a cage. It smelled wrong, like Umbral wrong. I slid forward, crawling on my belly, to get closer. Another man came out of the house, I smelled him. I recognized the scent right away; Cassidy didn't. It was St. George.

"Yes, my lord," he said to someone over his shoulder. I couldn't see or sense them yet.

"We don't know where they are yet; I've sent Mina ahead to scout. She will be starting at the club; they overcame her assassins there. She thinks they must have left a trail of some kind."

"You must find her soon. The timing of the rite must be perfect." Another voice. This one made Cassidy's fur stand on end. His paws quivered and I felt his muscles tense, as if he were enraged.

The other man moved into view. It was a shriveled, ancient figure of a man. He had razor sharp features, a nose like a hawk and eyes that were black all the way through.

*He moved with an easy grace, his withered flesh belying
unnatural strength. I didn't need Cassidy's agitation to tell
me the creature wasn't human.*

*I felt myself charge forward. The ecstasy of
transfiguration was upon me. Cassidy shifted into his hybrid
form and roared a challenge.*

"God preserve us," St. George whispered.

*Two men stepped from the shadows with machine
guns. Cassidy changed direction in midstride. He hit the
closer of the two at full stride; his clawed hand ripped a
massive furrow in the man, splitting him from crotch to
clavicle. As he turned for the other man, he twisted his
claws and jerked his hand away, surgically spilling the
man's guts onto the cold ground. The second man threw
down his gun and ran, screaming.*

*Cassidy turned his attention to the old man. He
ignored St. George. I immediately thought it was a horrible
idea to turn your back on that wily fuck, but then this was
Cassidy. Who the fuck's going to punch a werewolf? The
old man answered that question for me. As Cassidy closed
in, the old man ripped through the Veil and grabbed Cassidy
by the throat, lifting him easily. His clawed fingers dug into
Cassidy's flesh.*

*"Hello, Dog." The old man laughed a horrible laugh.
"I wondered when next I'd see you."*

*Cassidy's claw slashed across the old man's face.
"This will be the last time!" he growled.*

*The old man spoke a Word. I couldn't hear it. That
was strange. Why couldn't I hear it? It affected Cassidy,
though. He thrashed and his vision went black for a
moment. Suddenly, I was in agony. My world spun, and I
wondered if the men that killed Cassidy had trapped me. My
vision began to fade in the face of the madness and I lost
consciousness.*

"Hello, Little Brother."

I jerked awake to the sound of his voice.

He sat in front of me in the lotus position, his hands
resting on his knees.

"Cassidy?"

"Good to see I am not forgotten," he smirked.

"How? You're dead."

"Am I then?"

"Yeah."

"It is a strange thing to hear."

"How are you still alive?"

"I'm just an echo, really."

"How?"

"It's a Old Talent, passed from emissary to emissary."

"Why can't I do it then?"

He raised an eyebrow.

"Oh, right." Because I'd never consumed my predecessor. Until now, that is.

"We would have had this conversation years ago, Little Brother, had things turned out differently."

"That's all fine and good, Cassidy. Who did this to you? Who was that old man?"

He paused for a second as the image of the Old Man flashed across my mind. "The Beggar Lord."

"He's the goddamned Beggar Lord? I though you said he was in hiding?"

"His hand is played, Little Brother. He has not yet found the last scion of Solomon, but he has begun his preparations to bring the full force of his might upon this reality."

"How?"

"The Angelics have retreated. Only a small portion of their forces remain here. The War of the gods is over. The Umbral War is about to begin anew. The Beggar Lord has corrupted the Commander of the Angelic Army and placed within him an Umbral seed."

"What the hell's an Umbral seed anyway? Vincenze was going on about them before Sarah killed him."

"The source of the Cathdronai infection. A nascent Umbral feeds on the soul of its host until it has complete control, then it consumes the soul and replicates itself to infect another."

"Yeah, but if Yahweh snatched all of his favorite toys and got the fuck out of dodge, who's left? I mean, why is this remnant fighting anyway? If they had real faith, they'd have been on the party bus with the big guy, right?"

"Perhaps, Little Brother, they had so much faith that they agreed to stay knowing that they were sacrificing themselves for the good of others."

"That doesn't make me feel any better, Cassidy."

"Nor should it; let that guide your thinking. This remnant, as you call them, is composed of highly motivated people with no fear and nothing to lose."

"I think we already killed most of them, man. At the warehouse when you were supposed to meet us, we killed hundreds of them, and Corrigan and I killed another forty or fifty when we stormed St. John's to get you."

"You killed the humans, Little Brother. How many Cathdronai have you fought?"

"None."

"Then you have not yet begun to diminish their numbers. Annessa's mother is still at large and she is by far the greater danger now."

"Where is she?"

"I don't know; I thought she might be at the mansion."

"What happened after you charged the Beggar Lord?"

"He nearly beat me to death. I surmise that your Angelic counterpart finished the job at the cathedral."

"Why did you attack him like that? I've never known you to be so reckless."

"You've known me for a heartbeat, Little Brother. My history with the Beggar Lord goes far beyond my service with Satariel."

"You aren't going to tell me, are you?"

"No. I died and I failed; the matter is decided."

"How much longer do we have?"

"Not long, your body is still too young to have fully mastered Nagg'resh Vök."

"I'm going to miss you, man. I don't know what I'm going to do without you." My eyes filled with tears.

"You will survive. You have faith that I never did; the Old Man will keep you safe."

"He's pretty torn up that you're gone. I've never seen him angry like that. He stabbed St. George with *Morningstar's Folly*, after he imprisoned him in the Cocytus."

"He will calm with time, Little Brother. His temper is legendary, but his logic will bear him through the storm of his passion. It gladdens my heart that he has forgiven me, though."

"Will I ever see you again?"

"There are infinite possibilities, Little Brother. Only time will tell."

CHAPTER 23

I woke on the floor. Adrian was shaking me and Sheena knelt beside me, holding one of my hands. The room around me was devastated. The Beggar Lord's Word must have made me thrash like mad. The couch had been knocked over and the coffee table's legs were snapped and broken. My whole body ached.

"My lord?"

"I'm ok, Adrian." I sat up.

Adrian stood and got me a drink from the cellaret.

"We found nothing, my lord."

"Cassidy's dead."

"What?" Sheena and Adrian gasped as one.

"The Beggar Lord and St. George killed him." I shook my head to clear the tears that were forming.

Adrian handed me a drink; my hands shook as I took it. "Are you ok, my lord?"

"I'll cope." I threw back the drink and handed him the empty glass. "I have the rest of my life to grieve. Now, we need to find Annessa, fast."

"They've disappeared, Beckett." Sheena pulled the couch upright and flopped onto it. "I couldn't make the bastards at the warehouse talk. They didn't know anything."

"Where's Harker?" I asked.

"Sun's up, my lord." He refilled my drink.

"Shit." He was going to lose his mind when he found out about Cassidy. No one handles the loss of a friend well, even less well when you've been friends for over a hundred and seventy-five years. I'd only known the man for six years and it tore me up so bad it was difficult to think.

"Where do you want to start, Beckett?"

"I want you to cripple them." I grabbed Sheena's hand and pulled myself upright before I took the drink from Adrian.

"How?" Sheena asked.

"Adrian, I want you to have our contacts in the D.A.'s office file charges on every known associate of St. George for child abuse, push their pictures through every major news outlet. We want the world to think he's heading a major child slavery ring."

Sheena grinned, "You have such a beautifully fucked up mind, Beckett."

"Manufacture pictures of him or his pals with senators, CEOs, prominent clergymen, whatever. Generate so much fucking scandal that housewives from here to Los Angeles know what they all look like. I need them to go to ground. They can't make a fucking move if everyone's looking for them."

"It shall be done, my lord." Adrian pulled his phone and walked toward the kitchen speaking quietly.

"Beckett, if they've got Umbral support, they don't need to move on the Lifeside."

"I know, Sheena. That's where you come in." I put my hand on her shoulder. "I need you to take a trip for me."

"I think I know where this is headed." She smiled wryly.

"You need to go to Tír na nÓg. I need you to mobilize the Tuatha'an."

"I'll go, Beckett, but I don't know how much help they'll be. They view this as an Angelic matter, not one that affects the People."

"Do it; the Fae are the only ones with enough strength to hold the inner Veil against the Umbrals. We need this. If we fail, this reality is going to fall."

"How is it every time you ask Adrian to do something it involves a phone call," she shook her head. "But I wind up on my knees?"

"Because juggling doesn't get us allies," I said. "Go," I pointed at the door.

Adrian and Sheena left, each on their respective tasks. I sat in the middle of the living room floor in the lotus position. There was someone else I had to tell about Cassidy. I spoke a Word of summoning. Reality flexed around me like a plucked guitar string. I closed my eyes and waited for her response. The room went dark a second later. I felt her arrival as she pulled me across the Veil.

"Blessings upon you, my consort," Verghana's airy voice carried with it an overt sense of power and sexuality.

"Verghana." I bowed my head.

She put her delicate clawed hand under my chin and lifted. I looked into her eyes. Ghūl eyes have pupils like a goat's, and they change color in response to the emotion. Her eyes were a luminous blue, with hints of scarlet. The brightness of her eyes stood in stark contrast to her pale flesh. She wore her true shape for me. Her long black hair cascaded over her naked flesh and hung to her waist. Her delicate horns curved back from the crown of her head, spiraling ivory against the raven black of her hair. Her skin had been painted with sigils of war and sorrow that stretched from the hollow of her neck, over her small breasts and down her shapely legs to end in silver paint on her black cloven hooves.

She ran her eyes over me. "You have conducted the rite of succession. I can see it in your soul. Liam Cassidy has become one with the line of the Dark Father?"

I nodded.

"Your pain is unnecessary, Dear One. You mourn the passing of the fallen, though you carry within you the strength of his heart. He lives through you."

"I expected you to mourn, Verghana. You and Cassidy were close."

She stepped close and held my face in her hands. She kissed me softly on the lips. "You mourn for us both, Consort."

"I need your help."

"You always did."

"The Beggar Lord killed Cassidy."

"Are you certain?" Her fangs extended at the mention of his name.

"I am; I have seen it."

"Join with me," she commanded.

I presented her my right arm. "Kelæm Sûat Veym Nethrëk"

I took her right arm, our fangs pierced each other's flesh and the magic took hold. I couldn't do this with any other Ghūl, except my son, who I'd never met. Of course, he wasn't really my son anyway, but you catch my drift. Joining required blood, and Verghana's blood ran in my veins. For a split second, the entirety of my being was open to her. A lifetime of experience and knowledge flowed between us. It took her less than a second to sort through all of it and see The Beggar Lord through Cassidy's eyes.

She broke contact. "I must return, Consort. The council must be notified, and Holy Ninnaka made aware."

"Will you help me?"

"I will do what I can, Dear One."

The world went black for a second. I slid back through the Veil and ran for the kitchen. I threw up in the sink. As I stared at into the sink, spitting to clear my mouth, it struck me that there was no blood. I'd drank a sizeable amount of Verghana's blood. Strange.

My phone rang, just a simple ring. I'd only ever set a special ringer for Cassidy. In the beginning, he was really the only one I called. I sighed and pulled it out of my pocket.

"Yeah?"

"You should turn on the TV, sir."

"Adrian, I'll take your word that you got the job done."

"No sir, you need to turn your fucking TV on now!"

"Shit, OK, OK."

I darted back to the living room and turned on the television. I sat down immediately. There in bold color, on CNN, was a man screaming in Ghūllish. He was outside a museum in Corpus Christi, Texas and he was killing people. Killing them by the dozens. The camera crew was dead, but the camera was still recording. The man was tall, about six feet, bald and in remarkable shape. He had a sledgehammer whose handle had been broken off about halfway down its length and he was using it to devastating effect on the cops that were futilely trying to tase, shoot or otherwise incapacitate him.

It wasn't the killing or even the screaming in Ghūllish that had taken Adrian and I aback. It was what he was saying. He kept repeating the same phrase over and over.

"I am Gar'Varaakh, the Judge of Rage and I find you wanting!"

"Did he say what I think he just said, Adrian?"

"The declaration of Judgment?"

"Yeah, that."

"Yes, my lord, he did."

"Verghana didn't tell me the Seven had been summoned."

"It's safe to say that she really didn't need to, sir."

"It's just professional goddamned courtesy, Adrian."

"Agreed."

"You got your message out?"

"I did, but somehow, I think it might not be as popular as we had hoped."

"Start getting your people together; we're going to move tonight."

"The Francione place?"

"Yeah." Back to the beginning, back to where this all began.

I hung up the phone and walked over to the window. It was nearly sundown. I looked at my phone. I didn't know where Harker and his murder were hiding from the sun right now. But I knew that in a few short minutes, I was going to make a close friend lose his mind. I sent him a text.

"Feed, then meet me at my place. Deathly important."

I sent one more text, this time to Corrigan. After that I paced back and forth thorough the apartment. As I paced through the bedroom, I saw Annessa's pajamas folded neatly at the end of the bed. I picked them up and held them to my face. I could smell her; if I closed my eyes, I could almost feel her next to me. I drifted off for a moment.

I could see her eyes staring at me. They glowed a faint green as if their light were dimming.

"Hey, you," she whispered hoarsely.

"Annessa?"

"How many other dead girls do you dream about?"

"I'm not dreaming. I don't dream, love."

"I've missed you. We've missed you."

"Where are you?"

"I don't know. They kept the fucking cage covered."

"What are they doing to you?"

"The cage is killing us. It drains my energy and it keeps Abbadonna from leaving. She's not doing so well, Master. They keep trying to feed me corpses full of Umbral maggots. I'm so hungry…"

"I'm coming for you, Annessa."

"I'm waiting, Master."

"I love you, Annessa."

"Wake up," she said in a strange voice.

"Wake up, Jason." Her lips were right next to my ear. "Wake up."

I shuddered as her breath tickled my ear. My eyes opened. Mara crouched next to my bed. Her eyes glowed red in the dim light. I recoiled, a Word on my lips.

"Easy, killer," she grinned, showing her fangs. "Don't knock it till you've tried it."

"Where's Harker?"

She nodded her head towards the living room. I set Annessa's pajamas back on the bed reverently. I walked out of the room slowly, knowing what was coming.

Harker stood behind the couch, holding Cassidy's jacket in one hand.

"Miles."

"Jason." He turned to face me. "Where's Liam?" He asked it slowly, as if he already knew. He held up the bloodstained duster.

"He's gone, Miles." My eyes teared up. I cleared my throat and spoke again, hoarsely. "The Beggar Lord killed him."

Harker turned away from me. His shoulders shook. "That's it? A thousand years, and it ends like this?"

"I don't have any answers, man."

He whipped around and crossed the room in a instant. His face stopped just shy of mine, his eyes flared with crimson light and his fangs were bared. "I want blood, Jason. I want to wade through fucking RIVERS OF BLOOD for this!"

"I understand."

"No, you fucking don't! I'm about to go spare. I've known Cassidy for five generations; you've known him for a heartbeat. He was the only constant in this shit life of mine. You can't possibly understand."

I held up my hands. "I misspoke, man. I'm sorry." The last thing I needed was an angry vampire ripping my fucking arms off.

"When are you leaving?"

"Tonight, Miles. I have one thing left to do."

"See that you do it in a tick." He turned away from me. His shoulders shook and for a second, the way he stood, with the duster held out before him, reminded me of a child clutching a blanket.

I reached for my phone as I turned away. Without warning, her scream cut the air like a blade. I whipped around to see Harker holding Sophia, her hands digging furrows in her perfect face, her eyes locked on the bloody duster. Sophia's eyes were wild and the grief etched on her face was painful to behold. She collapsed against Harker. He held her tightly, one hands smoothing the hair away from her face, the other cradling her against him as he whispered soothing words into her ear.

I picked the duster up off the floor as Harker stood with Sophia cradled in his arms like a child. He looked at me, the trails of bloody tears wending their way down his face and staining his white shirt.

"Be quick about whatever business you have," he said quietly. "This will not go unanswered." Without another word, he and his murder stepped through the door, leaving me alone with my pain.

I stood for a long moment staring at the duster in y hands, swallowing back my own grief. Harker and I were both on our own now. Two children lost in the world, bereft of the only solace and protection which it had ever seen fit to give. Yet, even we were better off than Sophia. What is eternity, when the world is nothing but cold loneliness?

CHAPTER 24

I stood in the center of Grand Central. People milled about me, a vast sea of ignorant humanity. I wove through them, my eyes searching the periphery of the halls, looking for him. The Damascene was nowhere to be seen. I headed toward the corner where Annessa and I had entered his lair when we first met him.

I slid through the Veil into his sanctuary. All around me were discarded remnants of his obsessive quest to destroy the Beggar Lord. Sitting, head in hands, in the midst of this angelic detritus was Satariel.

"My Lord Satariel."

"I see you, Jason Nathaniel Beckett."

"My lord, Cassidy is dead."

"I am aware." He fell silent again. I waited a second for him to speak again.

"That's it? He served you for close to a thousand years, and that's all he gets?" I asked, disbelieving.

He raised his head and looked at me. Tears streaked his angelic face. "What more can be spared at this late hour, child?"

"Rage, anger, vengeance, fucking anything but apathy, my lord!"

"I have committed what small forces I possess to the defense of Nagg'Varythmar. I have nothing left to send against him who has slain my most favored son."

"Then give me your blessing, my lord. I'll find those responsible and make them suffer."

He stood slowly and walked toward me, his form shifting with each step. When he finally stood before me, his angelic face looked like it had been chiseled out of black marble, his wings crafted of diamond and his eyes made of luminous garnets. This was his true face, the face no one ever saw. He placed his hand upon my forehead.

"Go with my blessing, Emissary of my brother. Carry with you the strength of the Watcher and wield the sharp sword of my vengeance." He smiled wanly at me. "When at last you strike, invoke my name and I shall be with you, Jason Beckett."

I slipped out of the Damascene's sanctuary as quietly as I had arrived, and still the droning mass of humanity moved along, none the wiser. As I headed toward the 42nd Street exit, I felt them. It was like a slight thrum along the periphery of my consciousness. I turned to my left, and I saw them moving to intercept me. Victus, Riley and Ouilette moved through the crowd, pushing past people, shoving them out of the way. I waited for them near the doors.

Victus spoke first, "He's dead, my lord?"

I nodded; I didn't need to ask who.

Victus turned his back to me for a second. "I never thought it possible," he said hoarsely.

"The Beggar Lord killed him with help from the Angelics."

"What will you do about it, my lord?"

"Kill everyone even remotely involved."

"We are yours to command, my lord." Victus spoke eagerly.

I explained my plan to them and sent them to prepare.

I lit a cigarette as I stepped out of the station. I inhaled deeply, the winter air and the smoke biting my lungs.

Adrian pulled the truck up curbside, and Sheena waved to me from the passenger seat. I flicked my cigarette butt and walked over to the truck. Sheena climbed into the backseat, and I pulled Cassidy's duster off of the back of the seat and put it on.

"Is everything prepared?" I asked.

"I've asked, Beckett. The People are mercurial, and you can never tell what they'll do." she replied.

"It didn't help that you work for me now, did it?"

"No. They heard about the scouring of the Mound, and they weren't pleased."

"Fuck." I pulled another cigarette out of my pack. This was not a good start.

"But, after an hour or so with Lord Lugh, I think I might have brought him around."

"I should've stolen you sooner, Sheena." I lit my cigarette. If anyone could convince an Earthbound God to send his forces, it was Sheena. And after an hour with her, hell, he might just show up himself. I turned to Adrian. "What about the rest of our people?"

"We're as ready as we can get, my lord."

"And Corrigan, he knows his part?"

"Yes, sir. He'll cut off access to the Line when we need him to."

"Good." I looked out the window as the city gave way to the suburbs, which gave way to countryside. My heart was pumping hard. I had no idea what to expect when we got to Little Haven, but I assumed that it wasn't going to be good. I pulled a second Beretta out of the glove box and slid into my waistband. I nervously checked and rechecked my guns as we drove.

"Beckett, the guns haven't moved. You're starting to freak me out."

"I get nervous, Sheena. I'm human."

"You're about as human as I am, my lord," Adrian scoffed.

"We can't fuck this up. Not even a little." I lit another cigarette. "Too much depends on this."

"Everyone knows their role in this; there are no amateurs. Everything will work out fine," Sheena said. There was a hint of glamour on her words, which meant that there was a metric fuck–ton of glamour hitting my brain. She was sneaky. If there was a time to let someone instill you with confidence, though, this was it.

"We're twenty miles out, my lord," Adrian warned.

"Time to call in the wolves," I pulled out my phone. "Time to start killing."

CHAPTER 25

We parked in the woods about a half-mile from the house. The silent trip through the woods was like déjà vu. Sheena moved soundlessly beside me. Adrian followed behind, his silenced M-4 held at a low ready. I thought of Cassidy walking back through here with me on the night I killed Annessa. If I hadn't been so fucking weak, he'd still be alive. If I'd been strong enough to kill Father Jacob the first time around, this would have ended before it began. I bit my cheek and focused on the task at hand.

We slid into the final copse of trees that flanked the once manicured lawn. The huge overgrowth of bushes and weeds would give us a little more cover for the final assault. There were multiple sentry teams on the roof and moving around the perimeter of the property. I felt the push of the wolves against my mind, just like in the train station. I looked across the lawn and saw them on the far side of the property. I motioned with my hand. Victus nodded from the brush. The wolves shifted and slipped silently into the grass.

I pulled my phone out of my pocket. I dialed Harker.

"Time?" he answered on the first ring.

"Go."

There was a sound like pheasants bursting from cover as he and his murder launched into the air over the house. They landed on the roof silently. Harker was a nightmare in action; he flitted from peak to peak on the roof, and he snatched a sentry by the head. He closed his hands and pulled them apart with a vicious jerk, tearing the man cleanly in two. He turned on the man's partner and backhanded him across the throat snapping his neck and sending his head lolling back between his shoulder blades. His fangs tore into the man's neck and he savagely splayed his throat wide open. In the seconds it took the rest of the murder to act, Sophia dove across the roof and tore the throat from one sentry with a backhanded slash. The final man tried to move, but Sophia brutal left-handed hammer fist shattered his sternum and crushed his heart, killing him instantly. Before his body hit the ground, she tore him to pieces. Blood rained in a fine mist over the house; Sophia stood in the center of it, a terrible widow whose world had become a vast, empty web.

The sentries on the ground fared no better. The wolves hit the first group from behind. Victus launched himself into the air, his fangs closing on the sentry's neck from behind. He twisted in the air snapping the man's neck. Before the second sentry could react, Riley snapped upward from between his legs, severing everything that made him a man, as Ouillette hit him from the front, shifting into hybrid form to tear the man's head from his shoulders.

The last sentry crossed in front of us. I pulled my silenced pistol and rolled out from behind a tree, firing point blank into the back of his head. He crumpled into a heap in front of me. I knelt. I closed my eyes and pushed, mindseeking Annessa. This close to her, there was no way that they could interfere.

"Annessa."

"Master." She sounded so weak.

"Get small, beloved. Get as small as you can."

"Hurry."

I reluctantly broke contact. I nodded at Sheena. She grabbed the body at my feet, drew back at hurled it at the front of the house. I nodded and Adrian spoke into his phone.

"Now, Corrigan."

I spoke a Word of conflagration, my focus on the body in the microseconds before it hit the entryway of the house. The impact was like a mortar shell. Flames erupted out of the body and spread across the entire front of the house. Adrian leveled his M-4 and slipped a grenade into the grenade launcher mounted underneath. The first soldiers charged out of the house, disregarding the fire. Adrian grinned and fired. The grenade spiraled slowly over the intervening distance. My eyes tracked it and I tensed, waiting for my signal.

The stairs exploded; the soldiers were thrown into the air like twisted rag dolls. I launched myself forward, incanting the blessing of Leviathan over myself. My feet pounded into the soft soil, propelling me forward, a juggernaut in motion. I pulled my Beretta as I charged the house. I bypassed the stairs and jumped, my feet clearing the sill of the bay window. I whirled in the air as I hit the glass, skipping through the Veil. Cassidy's duster floated around me like a shield. I fired at the soldiers stacking up on the wall inside the house, preparing to charge out. I emptied my magazine and reloaded. They dropped as the sorcerous ammo burned, corrupted and exploded their flesh.

I turned for the center of the house. It was full of goons. They ran at me from the kitchen, the living room and the far wing. I pulled my second pistol, screamed a challenge and leaped over the couch in front of me to meet them. As my back foot hit the couch, I launched myself into a flip and hurtled through the Veil. I skipped across the Veil, firing with abandon as I did so. I hit the ground and rolled back to my feet. I let my mindseeking loose in a pulse around me. I felt Annessa's answer from above. The attic.

I ran toward the center of the house, the mark over the confluence. The bastards were counting on the confluence to increase the chance of breeding with her. I didn't pause, I didn't engage any of the other soldiers, I just ran. I threw myself into the air with a scream when I hit the trapdoor, my weapons clutched close to my chest as I burst through the floor of the attic. My feet snapped out as soon as they passed the hole, slamming to a halt on either side of the hole. The cage holding Annessa was the size of a large dog kennel. She was crammed into it, bent double. She looked like she'd been beaten badly. The guards in the attic were shocked into inaction by my sudden appearance.

I shoved out with my mindseeking, finding Annessa's mind and melding with her. If it moved in that attic, I shot it. My hands worked independently, targeting and firing with an efficiency even Adrian would have envied. As my hands moved from target to target, I saw them through Annessa's eyes as well as my own. It all took only a matter of seconds.

I looked to one of the bodies at my feet.

"Is he clean, Annessa?"

"Yes, Master." She pushed against the bars of the cage. With no magic from the Line, it wasn't able to hold her back.

I leveled my pistol and fired at the lock on the door. The sorcerous ammo shattered the binding magic. Annessa hurled the door off of the cage and crawled out. I dragged the body to her.

"Feed, Annessa." My heart surged at the sight of her. I hadn't failed. I'd gotten here in time.

Her fangs were out before I finished my thought and she tore into the guard. I didn't look away. I was no longer horrified, only worried. I knelt beside her, my weapons at the ready. No one would touch her again.

She came up gasping for air, her face covered in blood. I grabbed her; my hand knotted in her hair and pulled her to me. I kissed her deeply. Her hands slid over the back of my head and our tongues met. The taste of blood filled my mouth. I felt my fangs extend and my jaw distend. Two monsters making love at a murder scene. I could taste the memories of the soldier lying half–devoured beside me, Verghana's blood worked like mad within me. I caught glimpses of what had occurred here; Annessa felt them through our mindlink.

I jerked back as a strong memory hit me. The soldier had seen 'The Voice.' It was an angel. Father Jacob walked beside The Voice, and they talked in conspiratorial whispers. The soldier had lowered his eyes as they passed. I wasn't able to make out anything that was said. More importantly, though, I knew that it was an angel working with the Umbrals.

"Annessa, we need to go." I kissed her softly and rested my forehead against hers.

"I know."

"Is Abbadonna still in there with you?"

"She's in here, but she's not talking to me anymore. She's in bad shape, Master."

"Some bloodshed should help her. We need to get out of here; I'm sure we'll have plenty of chances to feed her too. Where's Mina?"

"She's been gone for days."

"Let's hope she stays that way."

I dropped down through the hole in the floor. Annessa followed behind me. I grabbed her hand, and we ran for the window I busted on the way in. The floor of the house shook suddenly. It rippled beneath our feet and shook itself off of the foundation. Annessa and I slid across the now slanted floor toward the window.

"Get outside, Annessa!" I pointed at the window. "Run!"

She leapt through the window and rolled across the grass. Adrian and Sheena darted from their cover in the forest to pull her to safety. I threw myself out the window a second behind her. Something exploded from the floor of the house and launched into the air. It burst through the roof of the house. Bright, sickly green light trailed in its wake. After reaching nearly thirty feet over the roof of the house, it spread its wings. The Voice.

"Kill that fucking thing!" I screamed.

Adrian lifted his rifle and began firing rapid pairs of shots at it. I leveled my Beretta and carefully fired several double taps. The Voice threw his hands out to his sides and shrieked, the white mane of his hair floated around him like wildfire in motion. The sound was so loud that it rippled the air around him and bent the nearby pine trees. I instinctively covered my ears. Everyone hit the ground around me, except Annessa. She stood, a tiny girl against a hurricane of violence. Her little fists were clenched at her sides.

"Is that all you've got?" I heard her whisper.

The Voice whirled in the air and dove at her. It mouth opened in a horrible snarl. I fired shot after shot in the second it took him to reach the ground. Annessa relaxed her hands and her claws slid slowly out. She was enjoying this. I could feel her desire for revenge pump through my mind like hot blood through my veins. I raced to her side, reloading as I ran. There was a blur and Sheena was beside me.

"Protect her at all costs!" I yelled.

"Done."

Adrian was already on his phone. I assumed he was calling Corrigan. The Voice shouldn't have been on this plane. In order for him to remain for so long, he had to be feeding on the raw energy from the confluence. If we could choke off the energy completely, we could break him reasonably fast. I spoke a Word of abjuration and hurled it at him.

My sorcery broke over his skin as he hit Annessa like a bolt of lightning. She rolled with his hit and kicked out a leg to sweep his. He darted back into the air. Sheena was there waiting, like smoke over a fire. She turned to stone and fell on him, driving him down. Her fists pounded against him. She did little damage, but caused him to hesitate, giving Annessa enough time to bury her claws in his gut. She jerked him to the ground. He screamed again, but before his volume could raise, Annessa reversed her claws and stabbed them deep into his lungs.

Sheena rolled over him and hung from his neck, her hands clasped at the base of his neck, pulling him face first toward the ground. Annessa rolled between his legs and came up swinging. Her claws ripped through the tendons at the base of his left wing. He threw his head back and screamed.

"Try to fly now, motherfucker!" she spat on him. She grabbed the base of the wing and tore it free.

He threw his head back and roared, "Enough!"

An immense shockwave exploded outward from his deafening shout. Annessa and Sheena were thrown back twenty feet. I was knocked to the ground. I staggered back to my feet, my ears ringing from the concussive force.

"I will not be trifled with!" the Voice screamed. "I am The Voice, the Face and the Power before the Throne!"

I looked at Adrian. He'd just described three separate angels, Enoch, Uriel and Phanuel. Uriel was the Keeper of the Keys, the one angel with the keys to the Seal of Solomon. Adrian was counting on one hand. Shit, he came to the same conclusion. My heart took the express elevator down. If this creature had somehow murdered Uriel, or it was Uriel corrupted, I needed to know. With Abbadonna out of reach at the moment, I had only one other option.

"Uthiel," I whispered. "To my side."

I heard him coalesce behind me.

"Emissary."

"Which angel is that," I pointed, which was unnecessary, based on the fact that only one angel was present.

"Phanuel." He looked closer. "With an Umbral seed in his gut."

"Kill it, please."

"It will be my honor, Emissary."

I fired a shot at Phanuel. He turned to face me and saw Uthiel, and Uthiel's pack who had begun to manifest.

"Uthiel, my brother! Have you come to pledge yourself?"

"To you, Phanuel? Never." He pulled his massive spear from empty air and moved to face Phanuel.

"I am the Voice, the Face and the Power before the Throne, Uthiel. Submit to me and know peace."

"YHWH has departed this sphere, Phanuel."

"I speak not of YHWH, brother! Come to my side and see the glory of the God–That–Waits!" He let out a horrifying shriek. It drove me to my knees. Everything human in me screamed for me to flee.

Uthiel hurled his spear. Phanuel batted it aside with a flick of his wrist. "I will show you the glory of the God–That–Waits!" He threw his head back and shrieked again.

I felt reality shiver; it stunned me for a second, so much so that I nearly missed a sound even more terrifying, angelic doors opening.

"Incoming!" I screamed at the top of my lungs. Everyone threw themselves to the ground. As each door opened, machine gun fire preceded the onslaught of human soldiers. Adrian fired a grenade into the midst of one of the groups. It hurled their bodies aside with vicious force. It was only after they landed that I realized how much trouble we were in. Mental static flooded my brain as the corpses jerked themselves back to their feet, their movements awkward but powerful and fast.

Cathdronai. Cassidy had been right. I raced toward Annessa, firing shots at Phanuel as I passed. I could hear Adrian and Sheena at my heels. The doors kept opening, more and more of the horrible creatures poured through. How many had they created?

"Sheena, where the fuck are your people?" I yelled.

"I told you they might not show, Beckett!"

"Shit!" This wasn't good. With no Fae to guard the inner Veil, we were completely exposed.

I pulled my phone out of my pocket. I dialed *616 and hit send. Every Satanic soldier, diplomat and partisan was about to know that I was in very deep shit. It was one of Adrian's tricks. I just thought the bastard had a lot of friends. I stuffed my phone back into my pocket.

"Harker!" I yelled.

There was a flicker and he was at my side.

"What?"

"Tell your girls not to drink from these bastards; they're Umbrals."

Phanuel and Uthiel circled each other. The Cathdronai closed in around us. I put my hand on the small of Annessa's back.

"Be ready," I whispered.

"For what?"

"Chaos."

I screamed Words of conflagration, storm and decay. I threw my hand skyward, my Mark burning like an inferno. The clouds above us roiled and spun. Red cinders flickered in the substance of the clouds and fire rained from the heavens around us. I shoved the flames forward, my will forcing the magic. The first rank of Cathdronai burst into flame but didn't break stride. Adrian opened fire with his grenade launcher. In the space between fire and explosions, Harker and his murder wreaked havoc amongst the ranks, their claws and fists hurling bodies in every direction.

I sent a mental call to the wolves who burst from the shadows to harry the rear of the Cathdronai force. They moved toward us like an unwavering force of destruction. Their very touch was dangerous, carrying with it the promise of Umbral taint. We weren't going to make it. Not even with Uthiel and his pack holding off Phanuel. We needed more help. The fact that Umbrals were present gave me a slightly better chance, but if Fae were flighty, what I had in mind was even less certain.

"Verghana." I pushed my words through the aether across the Veil to Nagg'Varythmar. I felt her mind instantly. I opened my mind to her and let her see through my eyes. I closed the connection before getting a response; there was no time left to wait.

Annessa stepped in front of me as they grew closer.

"I love you, Master," she said quietly.

"Don't say it like that, Annessa. We aren't dead yet."

"My lord," Adrian pointed. A deep shadow roiled in the woods beyond the Cathdronai. A Shade–Well, a portal to the deepest recesses of the Veilside. A portal used exclusively by Ghūls.

The Ghūls burst forth from the well, hurling themselves into the fray. There had to be a hundred of them, sigils gleaming on their naked flesh, fangs bared, screaming battle–hymns as they dove into the Cathdronai. I wanted to shout for joy. Instead, I screamed Words of fire and pain, throwing all of my energy into weaving sorcery.

Annessa dove into the first rank, her claws shredding the walking corpses. A second later, Sheena was beside her, her skin shifting from fire, to stone, to air. The wolves and the vampires moved to circle Adrian and me as we alternated between sorcery and lead.

I shifted my attention to Phanuel. Every slash, every cut that Uthiel rent into Phanuel's flesh was bursting with Umbral filth. Mouths with jagged fangs had opened on the sides of his face, screaming litanies of madness. From the jagged hole where his wing had been, dozens of tentacles with vicious bone barbs had sprouted. The tentacles writhed and slashed at Uthiel who was now hard pressed to hold them back. He was in trouble.

"Annessa!" I pointed at Phanuel. She nodded.

I ran at her; when I got close enough, she grabbed me, spun and hurled me over the heads of the Cathdronai. I twisted in the air, firing as I fell toward Phanuel. I hit the ground and rolled out of the way of tentacles that slammed deep into the ground where my face had been. I ran, barely staying ahead of the plunging, razor sharp tentacles. I skipped through the Veil and landed on the far side of Uthiel's pack. Annessa landed beside me a second later.

"Sheena," she said when I looked at her questioningly. "Bitch has a great arm."

"Good to know." I turned back to Phanuel. As I raised my pistol, one of his tentacles smacked it out of my hand. I threw myself backwards to avoid the follow up slash and I tripped. I hit the ground hard, the hilt of Cassidy's sword dug into my kidney. I kicked my way out of range of Phanuel's attack and threw myself back to my feet.

Annessa and Uthiel were on the offensive now, forcing Phanuel back.

"It is no use! The God–That–Waits is nearly at hand! The might of the Umbral Host is without peer!" He screamed as he tore at his own flesh, each wound revealing new, more profane mouths, eyes, limbs, just beneath the surface of his flesh. Each new mouth gibbered madness–

inducing litanies. If we didn't kill him soon, the tainted magic of his Umbral seed was going to unhinge all of us.

I hurled a Word of purification at him. The flames of my Word splashed over his flesh like napalm burning away his remaining wing. He screamed and thrashed as the touch of my magic seared the obscene mutations on his flesh. He turned to face me, all of his many eyes wild.

"You would profane the flesh of the God–That–Waits?" He grabbed more fistfuls of his own flesh and tore them away. "Hail Arikael! Hail, the God–That–Waits!" He screamed as he charged me. His mouth opened wide and disgorged a huge flood of maggots.

Reflexively, I screamed a Word of flame. The force of my sorcery hurled me away from him. I slammed into a pack of Cathdronai. I bounced off the vile flesh of one of the creatures and hit the ground, hard. For a second, my mind froze in panic. The creatures turned and looked at me as one. Up close, they were a hundred times more hideous than I imagined. The way they moved, with that jerky, disjointed shambling, I'd guessed them more like zombies. I couldn't have been farther from the truth.

I'd expected Cathdronai to be idiot creatures animated by magic. That wasn't even remotely close. These were intelligent, vicious creatures motivated by hate. Their eyes throbbed with radiant darkness, a darkness that devoured all light and stilled the blood in my veins. I've been afraid of many things in my short time on Earth, but this was something different. They offered limitless pain and eternal suffering, the likes of which I'd never truly contemplated.

They turned to face me, surrounding me in a tight circle. I was trapped, and I was going to die. Of that, I was certain. As they closed in around me, the mental static got louder. It was much weaker than any other time I'd felt it, but it still jarred me like the jolt of foil on a metal filling. I tried to pull myself away from them, but there was nowhere to go.

I shook my head violently, partially to clear it, to get the static out, but mostly to deny this reality. To force the world to correct itself and reassert the fact that I *was not* going to fucking die like this. I pushed against the static with my mind and the Cathdronai jerked to a halt. They froze in midstride, their hands still outstretched. I lifted my Mark and pushed with all of my strength as I threw myself back to my feet and screamed the blessing of Leviathan. I nearly passed out. A shriek tore through my brain and I staggered. As one, the Cathdronai hurled themselves back into furious motion. The blessing hit my flesh and I raced forward, toward the creatures, towards freedom and likely death.

I hit the wall of their flesh and was thrown back. It was like hitting a sledgehammer with a sledgehammer. They exploded away from me and I staggered backwards, stumbling, desperately trying to both catch myself and figure out what the hell had just happened. A strong hand stopped me. I turned to look and was forced to avert my eyes. The brightness of his flesh was painful. He was like a sun in miniature, forged into the shape of a man. His armor gleamed and the long spear he carried exuded an aura of deathly menace. The Fae had arrived.

"Be at ease, Emissary. No harm shall come to you." His voice was soothing and frightening all at once.

"Lord Lugh," I managed to remember enough of my manners to bow my head.

He waved his hand and the air around us erupted with battle cries and a hail of luminous spears hurled over our heads driving into the Cathdronai and pinning them where they stood. His Fae soldiers flooded around us, throwing themselves against the Cathdronai. In seconds, they had destroyed the pack. It was a hard–fought victory; Lugh lost more than one of his soldiers. They were ancient, battle–hardened Sidhe and not even they were immune to the horrible talons and fangs of the Umbral host. What hope would I have had alone? I turned back to Lugh and bowed my head again.

"We shall keep safe all approaches to this reality." He clasped my shoulder once and stepped away from me, fading as he crossed over. His words echoed in the air as he and his host disappeared. "And for this, you shall owe us."

"I'm sure I will," I muttered. The last thing I needed was a debt to an Earthbound god. On the other hand, he'd saved my life, so there really wasn't much for me to bitch about. At least no more Cathdronai would be joining the party, which was worth its weight in gold.

Phanuel let out another shriek, and my world shuddered again. There was another huge pulse of that horrible feedback–like mental static, and I was driven to my knees by the sheer force of it. There was no meaning to it, at least none that I could figure out. It was like he was somehow broadcasting pain. My world went red as blood vessels burst in my eyes, and I screamed for all I was worth. It was a ragged, horrible scream that raged through my throat and shredded the tissues as it tore free from my mouth. I think I yelled 'Stop,' but I couldn't have told you then in what language. All I knew was that a silence as heavy as lead descended over the area.

"You dare?" Phanuel whispered. It carried across the field like a gunshot in a closed room. His whisper was echoed by the hundreds of horrific mouths across his twisted flesh. Looking at him was like staring at madness itself.

"Master!" Annessa's scream was the only warning I had. She leaped to interpose herself between Phanuel and me as he charged.

She didn't make it. He smacked her aside like an insect in his eagerness to get to me. I dodged through the Veil. He gave chase, unrelenting in his assault. He slashed at me with hands that had far too many fingers, claws and mouths. I dodged for all I was worth. One of his tentacles slashed at me and would have torn through my hip if it hadn't hit Cassidy's blade first. I grabbed the hilt of the blade and drew it as I spun back across the Veil. Holding it in a reverse grip, I planted my feet as I landed and drove the blade out behind me. My Marked hand pushed with all of the will I could muster against the pommel of the sword.

I was thrown forward as Phanuel dove through the Veil after me, driving himself onto the point of the blade as he landed on the Lifeside. I released my will, forcing a silent Word of purification through the strange shadow blade. I saw through Annessa's eyes as the blade pierced Phanuel's back, black fire roaring along its length. He backhanded me away. I staggered forward, my hands gripping the right side of my face, where his claws had torn away most of my skin. I spoke a Word of healing as I stumbled away from him. I heard the thump of Uthiel's arrival behind me and felt Annessa land next to me. She threw her arms around me protectively.

"Are you OK?" She tried to pull my hands away from my face.

"I'm fine," I pushed her away. "I'm fine!"

I traced her eyes as they crisscrossed my face trying to find a reason, any reason to send me away. As if I would just walk away now.

"You're sure?" The concern in her voice was sweet, but a little misplaced just then.

"Yes," I growled. "Let's finish this."

Uthiel and the remnants of his pack were forcing Phanuel back. He was trying to keep them at bay, but the sword in his chest was slowly destroying his flesh as my sorcery and whatever crazy enchantment Dominus had put on that blade discorporated his body an inch at a time. I nodded to Annessa and raced forward. I was going to repay that motherfucker in spades for what he'd done. I owed him for Annessa, for Cassidy and for Sarah.

As we closed on him, he looked at me and for a second our eyes locked. A shudder ran through his flesh and for a moment, his features changed. His eyes, the two normal ones, I mean, became almost human.

"I forgive you," he whispered. "You know not what you do." He held his arms out and even his tentacles fanned out behind him, like a peacock's feathers.

I leapt forward and gripped the hilt of the sword. Yanking it out of his chest, I whirled around. The blade bit just above his clavicle and sliced through his deformed neck, severing his head in a burst of black and green gore.

I tried to speak, to keep my promise to Satariel, but strangely, my lungs wouldn't work. I looked down at my chest, a foot-long bone barb stuck out just below my sternum, paralyzing my diaphragm.

Annessa saw it next. "Master!"

She leapt forward, her claws slashing through the tentacle just behind the barb. She yanked the remainder out of my back and caught me as I collapsed. Laying me gently on the ground, she bit her wrist and poured the blood into the wound. It burned like mad and the wound seemed to close slower than it had every other time. At that moment, I chalked it up to Annessa's exhaustion.

"I'm ok," I said as I saw the look of terrible concern on Annessa's face.

I looked back to see how the battle with the Cathdronai was going. They'd been forced back. The Ghūls were tearing them to shreds with claws, fangs and sorcery. Harker's murder and the wolves fell upon the stragglers, while Adrian and Sheena were burning all of the corpses to keep them from rising again. I let my head fall back. We'd won. Annessa touched my face gently as Uthiel reached down to help me up.

"You're a useful one to keep around, Emissary. You always throw the best parties."

I started to laugh and then thought better of it as it hurt like hell. "Glad I could help." I leaned on Annessa

"What the fuck was that thing?" Annessa asked.

"An angel infected with an Umbral seed," I said.

"Has that ever happened before?" Annessa asked.

"It has, Lady," Uthiel nodded. "When first we wrested this reality from their clutches, it was not uncommon."

"I'm more concerned with him calling himself the Keeper of the Keys," I said.

"If he killed his brother, Uriel, that news is dire indeed, Emissary."

"I'll have to try to talk Satariel into checking the Seal," I said.

A roar went up from the Ghūls as they killed the last of the Cathronai. I staggered out to meet their leader.

A younger looking Ghūl stepped out of their chaotic formation and held his hand out to me. I took it.

"Thank you for your aid," I said in Ghūllish.

"The Eldest sends her regards, Regent Consort."

"Please convey to her my sincerest thanks." I bowed as low as my injured chest would allow me.

I staggered back to Annessa as the Ghūls departed. Uthiel and his pack returned to Perdition to give their report to Satan. One by one, group by group, everyone left until it was just Adrian, Sheena, Annessa and me.

"Let's go home," I said. "I could use some rest."

CHAPTER 26

I slept fitfully. I didn't have much time to think before I passed out when we got back to the apartment. My dreams were of darkness and death, of Jessica and Sarah. I dreamed of Jessica's screams for me to save her. I dreamed of Sarah begging me to kill her. I dreamed of Sarah's rape and of Cassidy's death. I dreamed of the Umbral's Word that had nearly driven me insane. I couldn't wake myself.

It might not sound that strange to you that after a traumatic day, I might have nightmares, but the moment they began, I knew something was horribly wrong. See, I don't dream, ever. My Lord sends me orders while I sleep; he owns my dreams. To have something else intrude on his domain terrified me.

I woke bathed in sweat. Annessa was in the living room watching infomercials. I don't know why; it's just something she does. I don't judge. I slipped into the bathroom and ran the sink. I knelt and began to intone a Satanic prayer. Within seconds my mind was transported to the parapet of the Tower of Grief.

"My son, what so terrifies you?" Satan landed lightly behind me.

"Something's wrong, Father." I looked at him with fear in my eyes. "We have a serious problem."

"What is it, my child?"

"I think I've picked up an Umbral seed," I whispered.

"Such a thing is possible, my son." He leaned in close, as if he were inspecting me. "If that is case, there is much to be done."

"What should I do, Father?"

"Confer with the Titan–Goddess," he nodded as he considered his words. "She has great knowledge of such matters."

"Father, wouldn't it be wiser for me to speak to your brother?"

"No!" he shouted.

"But of all of us, he knows the most about the Umbrals."

"My son, our objective is preserving your life. What would my brother do should an infected creature stand before him?" he asked me.

"Point taken," I nodded. Satariel would cut me down the moment he realized I was tainted. "Couldn't I just kill myself, Father?"

"I fear that the taint would extend to your soul, my son." He shook his head sadly. "If that be the case, resurrection would become impossible."

"Shit." I sat heavily on the flagstones of the tower. "Today sucked."

"Enough." He looked at me fiercely. "Waste no more time on idle self–pity. Take yourself before the Titan–Goddess!" He waved his hand and hurled me back into my body. I threw up quietly, brushed my teeth and went to get dressed.

I was pulling my shirt over my head as she entered the room.

"Master?" She ran her nails across my stomach, giggling as I pulled away from her.

"Yeah?"

"Where are you going?" She kissed my neck as I popped my head through the shirt.

"The Grove."

"Why?"

"I can't say, Annessa." I kissed her quickly. "Orders are orders."

"So I can't come?" She pouted.

"No." I shook my head.

"That's bullshit," she swore.

"It is what it is." I pulled my shoes on. "I gotta go." I kissed her again and headed for the door.

I drove in silence. I couldn't stop thinking about what Satan said. If this thing had tainted my soul, that was it. There was nothing else. No afterlife, or life for that matter, just oblivion. Or worse yet, I faced an eternity as an Umbral slave.

I parked as close as I could to the Park and hiked in. I must have projected my mood because nothing living came near me. I knelt in the shadow of Cleopatra's Needle, spoke the prayers and waited for the Grove to welcome me.

The trees opened the shadow gate, and I entered. The Temple was silent, save the occasional popping of the thick, black candles on the altar. I looked to the Font. Standing nearly twenty feet tall, the Goddess, herself, stood in the waters. I froze.

I'm not sure how to describe it. Imagine that your guardian angel just suddenly popped in for tea. This was kind of like that. She'd saved me through both artifice and indirect action so many times. As a sorcerer, I was one of her faithful. Though my allegiance was to Satan, I would always be welcome in her temple.

"Lady Hekate," I knelt at the edge of the water.

"Rise," she spoke in a voice that was both powerful and comforting. "I know why you have come."

"I pray that you have kinder news for me than Lord Satan did, my lady."

"I fear that my news is at once more kind and more dire, child." She walked toward me, slowly shrinking with each step.

"I'll take what I can get, my lady." It was turning out to be one of those days.

"You are infected, Emissary." She gently touched my brow. "That is the truth of the matter."

"I figured," I sighed.

"Your soul remains safe, at the moment."

"What do you mean, at the moment?" I asked.

"Within a day it will become tainted." She anointed my brow with water from the font. "There is nothing anyone can do."

"I thought you said you had kinder news, my lady?"

"You can save yourself, little one." She smiled at me. "But that comes at a great cost."

"What do you mean?"

"In order to save yourself, you must allow your body to become infected; you must allow the Umbral Seed to take root within your flesh."

"Why?" I couldn't think of anything more disgusting than that.

"In order to discover the Umbral's designs and means on this plane, you must become one with them."

"How will that save my soul?" I was confused. "The Umbral taint destroys everything it touches."

"You must relinquish your soul."

Again, this might not sound so terrible to you. After all, I'd already sold my soul to the Devil, right? Wrong. Without my soul, I couldn't carry my Lord's investiture. Without my soul, I had access only to the most basic of my sorcery. It was like walking into a lion's den with only a book of matches and sign that read, "Please don't eat me."

"What do I have to do?" I asked quietly.

She told me. The first part was fine. It was the second part that made me cringe.

CHAPTER 27

I walked into the apartment. Before the door had shut behind me, Annessa ran to me from the living room and jumped into my arms. I pulled her to me and kissed her hard. Pressing her against the wall, I tore at her clothes. She ripped at mine, and I bit her neck savagely. I shoved her to the floor and took her with no reservations. I made love to her as if tomorrow no longer existed. I carried her into the bedroom and threw her onto the bed and drove myself into her again.

"Master," Annessa growled at me as she rolled me onto my back and climbed on top of me. "We weren't expecting this."

I grinned fiercely and gave them everything I had ever reserved from them both. At the moment of our climax, I rested my hand over her heart. I spoke a Word of sleep. She collapsed and I rolled her off of me. I went to the kitchen and cut my hand with a knife. Returning to the bedroom, I drew a sigil on her chest with my blood. I spoke a Word and tore my soul free from my body. As the strength of my investiture left me for good, I collapsed.

I dragged myself to my feet. I leaned on the couch, the end table and even the damned cellaret as I staggered out of the apartment, stopping only to grab Cassidy's duster.

When I hit the lobby, I walked out onto the sidewalk and pulled the stained and weather–beaten green duster on. The cold wind ravaged my face. My body felt weak and very mortal. I walked until the buildings were no longer maintained and the people were no longer polite. I ducked into an alley and knelt in the trash.

I whispered a quiet prayer to the Lord of Perdition, closed my eyes and focused on the skin on the inside of my eyelids first. I began to recite the Prayer of Incarceration. I watched as the whorls and glyphs etched themselves on the inside of my eyelids. It hurt so badly that I had to stop to vomit. I took a deep breath and continued until every inch of my skin was covered with the designs that would imprison the Umbral inside of me.

The entire process took four agonizing hours. I stood weakly and staggered from the alley. I needed to find a portal to the Shadow Road. There was a long walk ahead of me.

Author's Note:

This book began as a 100-page novel written for National Novel Writing Month. Without the first round of edits by my lovely wife and the second round by Dolly Vachon, it would have stayed that, and only that.

It took the criticisms and skilled editing of Mike Rizzuto, one of my best and dearest friends, to beat the stupid out of this book and make it something wonderful.

Byron Rader, whose scathing criticism of the Angelic faction forged them into weapons of which the Heavenly Host could be proud, burned my cardboard villains at the stake.

This book would be faceless, were it not for the skill of J. Jerkins. He took my vision for the cover and made it much better than I thought anyone could. Without the helpful words and editing of his lovely wife, I'm not sure I'd ever have gotten this damned book done!

Arlene Talbot, Bonnie Mallon (aka Mom), and Don Albee all provided insightful and infinitely helpful feedback and any thank you list would be empty without them.

Finally, a heartfelt thank you to Lucy, who kept me company through the long nights of writing. Yes, I just wrote a thank you to my cat. Shut up, she's awesome.

9344033R0028

Made in the USA
Charleston, SC
09 September 2011